VENGEANCE

THE VIGILANTES, BOOK TWO

STONI ALEXANDER

SILVERSTONE PUBLISHING

This book is a work of fiction. All names, characters, locations, brands, media and incidents are either products of the author's imagination, or have been used fictitiously. Any resemblance to actual persons living or dead, locales, or events is entirely coincidental. The author acknowledges the trademarked status and trademark owners of various products referenced in this work of fiction, which have been used without permission. The publication/use of these trademarks is not authorized, associated with, or sponsored by the trademark owners.

Copyright © 2022 by Stoni Alexander LLC

Developmental Edits by Johnny Alexander
Copy Edits by Proof Before You Publish
Cover Design by Better Together

All rights reserved.

In accordance with the U.S. Copyright Act of 1976, the scanning, uploading, and electronic sharing of any part of this book without the permission of the publisher is unlawful piracy and theft of the author's intellectual property. Without limiting the rights under copyright reserved above, no part of this publication may be reproduced, stored in or reproduced into a retrieval system, or transmitted, in any form, or by any means (electronic, mechanical, photocopying, recording or otherwise) without the prior written permission of the above copyright owner of this book.

Criminal copyright infringement, including infringement without monetary gain, is investigated by the FBI and is punishable by up to five years in federal prison and a fine of $250,000.

Published in the U.S. by SilverStone Publishing, 2022
ISBN 978-1-946534-20-0 (Print Paperback)
ISBN 978-1-946534-21-7 (Kindle eBook)

Respect the author's work. Don't steal it.

NOVELS BY STONI ALEXANDER

THE TOUCH SERIES

The Mitus Touch

The Wilde Touch

The Loving Touch

The Hott Touch

In Walked Sin

Dakota Luck

THE VIGILANTES SERIES

Damaged

Vengeance

Savage

Wrecked

Broken

Rebel

BEAUTIFUL MEN COLLECTION

Beautiful Stepbrother

Beautiful Disaster

Available on Amazon or Read FREE with Kindle Unlimited

For Professor Eustis
With love and gratitude

ABOUT VENGEANCE

Catch me... if you can

My sister's murder gutted me... then I got angry. *Real angry.*

If you're a sexual predator, I'm coming for you. I won't let you hurt another woman, ever again. The hatred in my eyes will be the last thing you see.

Each kill blackens my shattered soul. Still, I have no regrets. That's how messed up I am, how far I've fallen.

Evil would have sucked me into its dark, sinister vortex if it hadn't been for *him*. He's flat-out gorgeous, a total alpha, and so damn intriguing. I find him *impossible* to resist. Being with him gives me hope, something I haven't felt in a long, long time.

The only blemish on his beautiful, fearless soul is that he's spending every waking moment hunting me.

1

THE MISSION

COOPER

Adrenaline pulsed through Cooper Grant. From where he sat, he had a clear line of sight to the private night club. Peering through the binos, he'd be able to ID his target, no problem.

It was a little after nine and the liquor stores, pawn shops, and food marts in the seedy DC neighborhood were shuttered for the night. Foot traffic beelined into the club. Attentive valets rushed to park cars that pulled up out front, while members slipped discreetly inside.

Cooper didn't give a fuck about the traffic, the stores, or the neighborhood. All he cared about was whether or not his target would show up alone. If he did, the mission moved to phase two. If he didn't, Cooper and his team would abort.

He lowered the binos before glancing in the SUV's rearview mirror. Sitting alone in the back seat was Slash. Real name: Amanda Maynard.

"How you doin' back there?" Cooper asked.

"I'm here." Her gaze stayed trained on the club, the streetlamp bathing her purple hair in diffused light.

"He's on the move," Herrera said through the comm tucked in Cooper's ear.

Those words snapped Cooper to attention.

"Alone?" Cooper asked.

"Abso-fucking-lutely," Herrera replied, a smile in his voice.

"Wipe that grin," Cooper grumbled. "We're a long way from a win."

"We gotta celebrate the small victories along the way," Herrera said.

"I'm with Cooper on this one," Slash replied. "Target's slippery, like an eel."

Cooper flicked his attention to the club. Several people were waiting while the line manager checked his tablet.

Years ago, when Cooper worked for the Bureau, he'd brought Ivan Salimov in for questioning, but he had to let him go. Diplomatic immunity. Then, the high-powered Russian complained and the State Department made the FBI drop the investigation. Cooper was forced to stand down, but he would never walk from Salimov.

Never.

He hated every fucking thing about him.

Now, as an ALPHA Operative, Cooper was about to get some answers, the old-fashioned way. By beating them out of him. This mission wasn't on the books and it wasn't sanctioned. In fact, no one but Cooper and the two Operatives joining him knew what he was about to do. He'd played by the rules for as long as he could remember and he was so damn sick of it.

Salimov was never alone. *Ever.* His bodyguard went everywhere with him. His other companions varied. Wife, mistress, women on the side. The son of a bitch even used his children as shields. If Salimov was surrounded by people, he couldn't be taken without witnesses or collateral damage.

Tonight, was the perfect storm. Ivan Salimov was expected at his club... alone.

The diplomat's wife and children were en route to Russia, which meant he had the night to himself. His mistress was at the bedside of her dying father, and not even Salimov could pry her away. And that dutiful bodyguard? His wife had gone into labor and he was at the hospital.

For the first time in years, Cooper had a real shot at nabbing him.

"Two minutes out," Herrera said.

"Did you get on the list?" Cooper asked Slash, who sat like a mannequin.

"Nope."

"How do you plan on getting inside?"

"Charm," she replied.

Agitation swirled around him. Tonight was too damn important to wing it. "And if that doesn't work?"

"I got an undercover friend, who owes me. He's in there."

"So, you are on a list?"

She flicked a glare in his direction. "Not on a list. No way to trace me."

Cooper nodded. "Got it."

"The black sedan pulling up is him," Herrera said through the comm. "I'm circling the block to park."

As Cooper peered through the goggles, his heart rate kicked up. Salimov exited, handed his keys to the valet. His mid-section had filled out since Cooper had last seen him, but that was definitely Ivan Salimov. About six feet, crop of short, graying hair, and a thick mustache that covered a scar above his upper lip that trailed through his lips and stopped at his chin.

A growl erupted from Cooper. "I'd like to kill him."

"I can make that happen," Slash said.

"We stick to the plan," Cooper replied, his gaze cemented on Salimov.

The line manager offered a little bow before opening the door. Salimov vanished inside. The private Russian club was for the uber elite, but the neighborhood was not. If someone wasn't looking for the place, they'd walk right past it. The building blended in with heavy bars on the windows and graffiti blanketing the bricks.

Cooper flicked his attention to Slash. "You're up."

"Time to fuck with an asshole." Slash exited the SUV, crossed the street, and sauntered toward the building. Dressed in torn skintight jeans and a lowcut shirt, she was all muscle and total business. He'd seen her smile, maybe twice. But he didn't give a damn about her appearance or her personality. She got the job done and that was exactly what Cooper needed.

When she couldn't get past the doorman, he went inside, returning with a beefy dude. Seconds later, she disappeared into the building with him.

"Now, we wait," Cooper said to Herrera. "Where are you?"

"Parking," Herrera replied.

Cooper went for his phone, but he'd left it at ALPHA. Mission Dark was standard operating procedure. That meant, no identification and no personal phones. If something went sideways, there were measures in place to handle emergencies. Except tonight. No one at ALPHA knew what he was doing.

Risky, yes? But that risk would pay off if he could get his hands around Salimov's throat.

Cooper loved being an Operative. Being back on the street felt damn good. His ass had grown sore from the never-ending stream of meetings at the FBI. This was his dream job, but he was six months in and hadn't gotten the type of case that kept his blood pumping. So, to hell with the rules. He was going after the Russian, his way.

Herrera opened the passenger door. Before he slid in beside him, Cooper moved his ski mask and leather gloves out of the way, set his Glock on his thigh.

At the start of their careers, Cooper and Antonio Herrera—who went by Herrera—had trained together at Quantico. Cooper thought Herrera had gotten transferred out of the DC area. Turned out, he'd joined ALPHA. When Cooper came aboard six months ago, the two friends picked up right where they'd left off.

"Any word?" Herrera asked after pulling the door shut.

"She's gone dark. I was hoping she'd leave the comm on so we could hear her."

Herrera glanced over his shoulder, then reached back. He held Slash's comm in his palm. "She left us a present."

"Dammit," Cooper bit out. "How the hell are we gonna know if she's coming out with him?"

"Well, that is a problem."

"I get that she hates the rules more than I do, but I don't need her going rogue on me."

Herrera chuckled. "You're one to talk." After a pause, he said, "Ya know, I don't remember you ignoring protocol when we worked at the Bureau."

"I never did, but I got questions. Salimov's got answers."

"He's never gonna admit to raping and assaulting those women. You know that, don'tcha?"

Cooper shrugged.

"And if he finds out who's behind this little... er... business situation...he'll try to kill you."

A smile tugged at the corners of Cooper's mouth.

Herrera chuffed out a laugh. "You'd love that, wouldn't you?"

"He pulls a gun on me, he's dead. I've been in law enforcement for years. It's my word against a dead man's."

"You left the FBI, and ALPHA doesn't exist."

"It does to the people who matter. If Salimov's taken out, that's one less scumbag masquerading as a good guy that I can cross off my list."

The door to the club opened and Cooper lifted the binos. A couple strolled down the sidewalk to a parked car.

"How's Estrella feeling?" Cooper asked.

"She's good, man. First trimester, she had these crazy-ass cravings. Being pregnant is pretty cool. We read to our little guy every night, in Spanish and in English. I can't wait to be a dad."

The two men chatted for a few more minutes, then grew quiet. Cooper's attention didn't stray from the front door of the club. Since Slash had removed her earpiece, he had no idea what the hell to expect. But he was ready.

Twenty-seven minutes later, the front door to the club opened and Salimov exited, a woman on each arm, a small man close behind.

"What the fuck?" Cooper growled, the blood in his veins turning cold.

The valet hurried to bring Salimov's car while Cooper studied the other people. He'd never seen any of them before and handed the binos to Herrera.

"I recognize the blonde," Herrera said. "She's one of his regulars when his wife and mistress aren't around. I can't remember her name."

"*Fuck.*" Cooper wanted to pound his fist on the dashboard. Instead, he'd let the frustration fester, so, when he did get his chance at Salimov, he could unleash a tsunami of rage.

The tagalong jumped behind the wheel and Salimov slid into the back with the women. The car pulled onto the quiet DC street, but at the end of the block made a U-turn and headed in their direction.

"We've been made." Cooper picked up his Glock as the sedan glided to a stop alongside them.

Salimov unrolled the back window. Cooper did the same.

"Mr. Grant, you need new hobby, no?" Salimov said.

"Fuck you."

Salimov's lips split into a sinister grin. "Find one or I pay your lovely sister a visit. She remembers me, no? I see you watch me again, you will regret."

Cooper curled his finger over the trigger. "You go near my family and I *will* kill you."

"Next time girl with purple hair spy, I kill her. Many friends protect Ivan."

Cooper released a low growl. He could take Salimov out with a single bullet... and there was nothing he wanted more.

As fury raged through Cooper, Salimov barked, "Idti," to the driver and the vehicle sped away.

Heat flamed Cooper's chest. "That motherfucking son of a bitch. He must have someone tailing me."

"You gotta watch your six, bro," Herrera said. "He's crazy enough to take you out."

Cooper hated that he'd put his teammates at risk. "I'm sorry I brought you with me."

"I love working with you," Herrera replied. "I'm hard to trace, so no worries."

"You want me to put protection on Estrella? One call to Hawk—"

"When I became an Operative, I hired Hawk's company to beef up my home security system. That and keep my wife safe."

The front door of the club opened and Slash exited. Instead of crossing the street, she moseyed down the block, crossed over, and slipped into the back seat. "What a cluster. Where's my comm?"

Herrera handed it to her.

"We got made," Cooper said.

"What the hell?" Slash replied.

"He threatened my family." Cooper's guts churned.

"I would *love* to make him vanish," Slash continued.

"Me, too, but you can't." More than anything, Cooper couldn't stand that Salimov had the upper hand... again.

"I didn't see any surveillance cams," Slash said. "Inside or out."

"Of course not," Cooper bit out. "He leaves no trail."

After driving Herrera to his vehicle, Slash jumped to the

passenger seat. Cooper pulled onto the quiet DC street and headed over the bridge and into Northern Virginia. Rather than question her, he stayed quiet. He'd worked with Slash on another mission—one that did go according to plan—and she liked her space before she debriefed.

"What a time suck," she murmured after he took the ramp onto Route 66. "I chilled at the bar, but couldn't get near him. He was already seated at a table with the guy and those two women. They spoke in English and in Russian. I caught a few words and none of them were G-rated. The man likes sex and was excited the blonde had brought along a friend."

"Thanks for doing this with me." He paused. "You got made. I can hire protection for you."

Slash cracked her neck. "Nah, don't need any. I read Salimov's file. Man's a monster. Say the word and I'll slit his throat. I didn't get my nickname by playing nice."

"He's never alone," Cooper said. "That's why tonight was—" He stopped. *Let it go. Move on.* "I'll take the hit if Dakota or Providence ask."

"Only Dakota tracks assignments and he'll wish he'd been invited." She chuckled. "I went on a mission with him a while back and he's ruthless. It was fun to see."

Cooper glanced at her. One of those rare moments when her lips lifted in a subtle smile. Slash definitely had a dark side.

Cooper turned up the tunes and opened the sunroof. Ten minutes later, he pulled down a quiet street in Tysons. It dead ended at ALPHA MEAT PACKING, a large, warehouse-looking structure that served as HQ for the off-the-books, quasi-government group that worked under the radar. Most employees had been former military and law enforcement who liked coloring outside the lines.

He drove around back and tapped the remote on the visor. One of the oversized garage doors rolled open. He parked beside another black SUV, and they exited the vehicle.

"I'm gone," Slash said.

"Don't you need your phone?" Cooper asked as Herrera entered the hangar that housed a fleet of black SUVs.

"Left everything in my car." Slash ducked under the massive door just before it closed.

Herrera waited in front of the retina scanner. The light turned green, but the door didn't open. The sensors had detected another person. When Cooper moved into place, the scanner flashed green, and the doors slid open.

As they headed toward the locker room, Dakota Luck turned the corner.

Ah, fuck.

"Hey, guys, what's the word?" Dakota asked.

"Hey, boss," Herrera said, but he kept on walking past him.

Dakota stopped. "Cooper, I was gonna call you. Got a minute?"

Herrera shot Cooper a sly smile before vanishing around the corner.

"Sure." Cooper wasn't gonna lie, but he wasn't volunteering any information, either.

His blood pressure remained steady as they entered Dakota's office. No one working at ALPHA displayed family photos or even their kids' artwork. Nothing existed that could ID them if the building was compromised. ALPHA, as an organization, did *not* exist.

Dakota Luck co-ran ALPHA with his wife, Providence. His office had two desks facing each other, a small conference table in the corner and a framed piece of art on the wall. It was a picture of a tree.

Dakota set his computer bag on his desk. "Don't let me forget this or I'll be back in twenty minutes." He eased into his chair. "How you doin'?"

Cooper was pissed. Pissed he hadn't captured Salimov and even more pissed he wasn't beating the truth out of him.

"Good." Cooper would keep his answers short. "You working late?"

"I drove over to grab Providence's laptop. She's working from home tomorrow." He paused. "I didn't see a mission on the books tonight."

"Recon."

"Didn't go well, did it?"

"That obvious?"

"Been there. Anything I can do?"

"I'm good," Cooper replied.

"I need your help with something," Dakota said. "Hear me out before you reject my offer."

Cooper chuckled. "That bad?"

"You know my ALPHA cover is my real estate company, right?"

Cooper nodded.

"My business partner at Goode-Luck is taking a leave of absence and we can't operate without a full-time broker, so I've gotta step away from here until she returns. While I'm gone, Providence and I want you to head up Ops."

I wasn't expecting that.

Leaning back, Dakota crossed his legs. "I know you left the FBI because you were done managing, so if you don't want this gig, we understand."

That was only half the truth. Cooper *also* left because he'd pulled Salimov in for questioning *again*, and got slapped with a "promotion" to Nevada. That was Salimov flexing his muscles and showing Cooper who the *real* boss was.

"You're our first choice, hands down," Dakota added.

"Bribing me into doing more work by stroking my ego."

Dakota cracked a smile. "You've managed large teams, so getting up to speed won't be an issue. If it's any consolation, you don't answer to anyone. I mean you do, but—"

"I'll take it," Cooper said.

Now, nothing would stand in his way of taking down Salimov.

"You can keep your cases or reassign them," Dakota continued. "Up to you."

"Got it."

"There's just one condition."

Figures.

"You can't go after Salimov."

Fuck.

"If something happens to him, you're the one with a target on your back. So, you good with those terms?"

I'll find a damn loophole. "Never better."

Dakota stood. "Thanks for stepping up."

Cooper rose and shook Dakota's hand.

After shouldering his bag, Dakota said, "You can keep your office." Both men headed down the hallway. "So, who were you hunting, tonight?"

"Doesn't matter."

Dakota glanced over. "Tell me it wasn't Salimov."

Silence.

"Look, I get it, I do, but you gotta stand down on this one. He's never even been arrested." Dakota stopped at the employee exit. "ALPHA Ops go after convicted felons with long rap sheets."

"Everyone knows he's a monster."

"Taking Salimov out is personal for you, but you can't go after him. If you do, you'll be the one ALPHA arrests. You gotta let him go."

Never.

"Understood."

"I can't put you in charge if you go rogue."

Cooper stayed silent while the air grew charged between them. As massive as Dakota was, Cooper was just as big and, at the moment, a hundred times angrier.

After a few seconds, Dakota said, "If Salimov finds out you're an Operative, you put the entire organization at risk. Stand down, Cooper."

Cooper gritted his teeth. "No worries. Thanks for the opportunity."

"You'll do a great job. When I get home, I'll give you online access to everything. Familiarize yourself with the current missions."

"Will do."

"Let me know if you have questions." Dakota pushed open the door. "You heading out?"

"I gotta grab my things."

"Thanks for stepping up. I'll swing by in the morning and we'll tell the team, together." After Dakota left, Cooper slammed his fist against the wall and let out the growl he'd been holding in.

What a cluster.

He headed into the men's locker room for his cell phone and wallet. After pocketing those, he stopped in his office for his laptop.

I got a promotion I never wanted and a shit-ton more work than I have time for. And Salimov is a human wrecking ball.

Frustration slithered down his spine as he strode out of ALPHA and into the night.

I might not be able to go after Salimov, but that won't stop me from making his life a living fucking hell.

2

SECOND CHANCES

DANIELLE

Despite being at a job she loved, Danielle Fox was having hella trouble concentrating. The problem wasn't the work, the company, or anything else at Truman CyberSecurity.

The problem was Danielle. She was angry all the freakin' time.

"Thank you," Pete said with a grin.

The grateful employee snapped Danielle from her dark thoughts.

"Not gonna lie, I was peeved," he continued. "But after I reread your review, I decided, you were right. I wasn't taking my job seriously. Thanks for giving me a second chance."

"You've been killing it," Danielle said as she glanced from her laptop to her fledgling team member. Up until three months ago, Pete was headed for termination, but Danielle had offered her guidance and coaching. And Pete had accepted it.

He'd stopped strolling in late, started putting forth effort, and was showing his true potential as a hacker. Danielle was pleased that he'd turned things around for himself.

"This is a great company," he said. "You've been a strong mentor and I told all my friends what a great boss you are."

You wouldn't be so thrilled to be working for me if you knew the truth about me.

Danielle forced a smile. "Thank you. What questions do you have for me?"

"None. I'd like to be considered for Pod Lead when something opens up."

On a nod, Danielle typed that into her notes. "You're eligible for promotion after you've been in your current position a year." She closed her laptop. "You've worked hard to turn things around for yourself. Congratulations."

Pete showed himself out of her office.

Danielle had some personal business to take care of, so she hurried out. Rather than take an elevator, she trotted down the stairs to the lobby. Once outside, the sunny, October day had her popping on her sunglasses, which had been perched on her head all morning.

October in the DMV—the District, Maryland, and Virginia—meant less humidity and crisper days. In the parking lot, she unlocked her car door and slipped inside. She wasn't one to take off, but the urge to blow off work sent a surge of energy galloping through her. Instead of skipping out, she reached under the front seat, pulled out her burner phone and flipped it open. Excitement coursed through her. There was a text.

"Hi, Ursula," Stu had texted. "I had a change of plans and can meet you tonight. Still interested in discussing that job opp'y?"

The text had come in over an hour ago. She typed, "Absolutely." Rather than send it, she stared at it. If he agreed, there would be no going back. No rewind or deleting. She would set in motion a chain of events that would further mar her soul.

What soul?

She hit send.

Come on, asshole, take the bait.

Nothing. She waited. Still nothing. As she was about to hide the phone beneath the seat, dots appeared. A few seconds later, another text.

"Meet me at my condo at nine," Stu texted.

What a pig. He could have chosen a restaurant or his office during normal business hours. But Stu Sisson had a plan of his own, which he'd perfected over the decades.

As an advisor to the President, Sisson worked upwards of fourteen hours a day. But his career was of no interest to her. Neither was the fact that he was married. His wife lived in Pennsylvania and they got together on weekends, maybe twice a month. Danielle wasn't interested in his marriage, his job, or his hobbies. She was only interested in killing him.

She blinked away the dark fantasy and typed out, "Sure. Address?"

He sent it.

Tap-tap-tap.

Danielle startled as she glanced out the windshield. Her boss, Stryker Truman, shot her a smile. "You heading inside?"

Fuck.

"Sure," she replied, before typing, "See you tonight." Danielle sent it, snapped the burner shut, then dropped it under her seat.

Ignoring her accelerated pulse, she exited her car.

Stryker was Danielle's dream boss and her best friend's fiancé. Despite his handsome face, muscular physique and long, dark hair, he wasn't her type. Even if he had been, she wouldn't have started up a workplace romance. Those rarely ended well and she loved her job. She'd steered clear of dating a coworker and had every intention of keeping it that way.

"You're running as late as I am," Stryker said as they made their way toward the building that bore the initials TCS and housed some of the best hackers in the biz.

If Stryker had noticed her flip phone, he didn't comment. She appreciated that he never pried.

"I've been here since nine doing quarterly reviews," Danielle replied.

"How're they going?"

"Good."

Stryker opened the front door and waited for her to walk through. Sunlight streamed through the floor-to-ceiling windows and bounced off the shiny marble floor. The brightness had her squinting, even in her shades. As they passed the four-person reception desk in the two-story lobby, one of the receptionists flagged him over.

Rather than head over, he held up a finger. "One minute." Then, he shifted his attention back to Danielle. "Everything else going okay?"

"Of course," she lied. "See you upstairs."

She continued toward the elevator bank and into a waiting cab. On the ride up, her thoughts jumped to later that evening. She had a lot to do and not much time. But Danielle wasn't going to pass up an opportunity to spend the evening with Stu. He'd been on her radar for weeks.

The elevator doors slid open and Danielle made her way down the hall to her office. As the morning rolled into the afternoon, her mind kept wandering to that evening. In the end, it would all be worth it.

I'm coming for you, Sisson, and I'm coming for you with a vengeance.

COOPER

Earlier that day, Cooper had been handed the reins of ALPHA Ops when Dakota announced to the organization that, for the foreseeable future, Cooper was point man. The next few hours had been one interruption after another. After a working lunch with Providence, he returned to his office hoping to knock out some work.

Knock-knock.

So much for getting anything done. "Come in."

Herrera and Slash entered his office and shut the door. Herrera slid into one of the guest chairs, Slash stood behind the other one.

"You two look too damn serious," Cooper said.

"The two women with Salimov—" Herrera said.

"They're dead," Slash blurted.

Fuck, no.

"Their bodies were found behind the dumpster at that Russian club," Herrera said.

A growl shot out of Cooper. *Salimov.*

"A hacker friend confirmed Salimov had made a reservation the night he was there," Slash explained. "I just asked him to check for me, again, and Salimov's name is gone from that list. Poof, his trail goes cold."

"Slash, you gotta be careful about who you ask to hack for us," Cooper said.

"No shit," Slash snapped back, before pulling a pack of cigarettes from her pocket.

"We need a hacker," Herrera added.

"I'll talk to Providence," Cooper said.

"On behalf of all the Operatives, I'm begging you." Slash's lips twitched with what looked like her best attempt at a smile.

As they left his office, a pop-up reminder on Cooper's computer screen grabbed his attention. He dialed and pressed the phone to his ear.

"Hey, Coop," his dad answered. "I'm about to jump on a conference call."

"The parole board hearing is this afternoon. I'll pick you up in forty, or did you want to meet me there?"

"I'm not going, son."

Silence.

"That's my call. I've gotta run—"

"Wait," Cooper blurted. "Why the hell not?"

"Hold on a second." A few seconds later, his dad said, "It's time to let it go."

"Are you for real?" Cooper ground out.

"We'll talk about it later. I think you should move on, too." His dad hung up.

After all these years, his dad was done fighting for justice? Just like that? Cooper raked his hands through his hair. His dad might be moving on, but Cooper never would. He would fight this to his death.

He continued working, but he couldn't concentrate. Rather than risk getting stuck in traffic, he shut down, slid his laptop into his computer bag, and left. The forty-five-minute ride to the maximum-security prison in Jessup, Maryland took an hour. With his Glock locked in the glove box, he exited his Jeep.

After signing in, he was escorted back to a conference room, a déjà vu of what happened two years ago. This was Cooper's third appearance at a Renfrow hearing. He would do whatever it took to keep that monster behind bars.

There was a long table with three chairs at the head of the room, a handful of chairs on the left, and two chairs and a table on the right.

Too fired up to sit, Cooper stood in the back.

Just past four o'clock, two commissioners and the institutional case manager walked in. Then, William Renfrow entered the room, along with a prison guard. Cooper's blood turned to ice. He curled his fingers into tight fists. If he could breathe fire, he would burn Renfrow to a pile of fucking ashes. The destruction and devastation that man caused had ended too many lives, and irrevocably changed so many others.

To Cooper's surprise and disappointment, he was the only one speaking out against the prisoner. Renfrow had been sentenced to life in prison, with all but forty years suspended, eligible for parole after seventeen. At the first hearing, sixteen people had spoken out against Renfrow. Today, Cooper was there alone to speak on behalf of the dead and the injured.

A growl rumbled from the back of his throat as he eased into a chair on the left side of the room. *No problem. I'll do it alone.*

The clean-shaven prisoner dressed in an orange, short-sleeved jumpsuit wore his neat, brown hair parted on the side. A short man, William Renfrow hadn't gained a pound. Nothing about him stood out to Cooper. He looked like an average Joe. Only, he wasn't. He was a fucking monster.

"Good afternoon," said one of the commissioners from the front of the room.

Renfrow eyed Cooper. Cooper would have stared him down until the son of a bitch melted into a puddle of piss. That's how much he hated him.

The commissioner introduced the attendees before stating the reason for the meeting.

Cooper knew this part by heart. They were there to discuss whether William Renfrow should be granted or denied parole.

"I've reviewed Mr. Renfrow's case," said his case manager. "I believe he's rehabilitated, and here's why. He's held several jobs while serving, and he has performed satisfactorily at each of them. He's earned a bachelor's degree and mentors others on the benefits of education. He's communicated remorse for what he's done and is an example to the younger men of how someone can learn from their mistakes and want to do right going forward."

"Mr. Renfrow," said the commissioner, "do you have anything you'd like to say."

"Yes, sir," began Renfrow. "I want to begin by thanking the parole board for the chance to talk. I regret what I did and wish it never happened."

Cooper didn't give a fuck about any of the crap spewing from Renfrow's mouth. The words sounded hollow compared to the suffering that had followed in the wake of the shooting. That day was seared into his soul and he could relive the painful tragedy with very little effort. There were nights, when he couldn't sleep, that the vision of his dead brother and his unconscious father would shatter his heart into a thousand pieces. He suffered in silence, never wanting to burden his family, but he couldn't shake the memory and the magnitude of the loss that followed.

"I have a special person in my life," Renfrow continued. "And she says I can live with her. I'd like to make a home with her and be a productive member of society. If I get paroled, I'd like to continue working with inmates to help them realize their dreams through education. Thank you for hearing me out."

Cooper couldn't look at him. He wished his father had been there so the parole board could see his dad confined to a wheelchair. While his dad claimed he was living his best life, he faced challenges that most people never even thought about.

The facilitator turned to Cooper. "Mr. Grant, you'd indicated you wanted to speak. The floor is yours."

"I'd like to thank the commission for this opportunity. This is the third hearing I've attended for Mr. Renfrow. Based on the severity of the crime he committed, I do *not* think he should be paroled."

He paused for a split second and glanced over at Renfrow who sat stone faced, staring straight ahead.

"I don't doubt that Mr. Renfrow is a model prisoner. He's had two decades to perfect that role. I don't doubt that he's a mentor to others and a lover of education. Let me remind you that Mr. Renfrow is a cold-blooded killer who walked into a middle school twenty-one years ago and opened fire with a semi-automatic weapon. He unleashed so much terror on so many innocent people that the aftermath of his destruction lives on to this day. The three people he killed are gone. Long gone and forgotten, but not by me." Cooper recited their names.

"Eight additional victims were shot, but they survived.

Countless family members and friends were traumatized. Those are the stats. Can't change that."

Pausing, he gritted his teeth. Talking about that hellish day never got any easier.

"Mr. Renfrow murdered my younger brother, Alan, that day. He was only twelve. He loved playing soccer and football. He was a straight-A student. He was the funniest person I'd ever known. Everyone loved him. He's dead, gunned down by Mr. Renfrow because he was in the wrong place at the absolute worst time. My dad was signing Alan back in at the front office after an orthodontist appointment."

He glared at Renfrow.

"A normal Thursday turned into a blood bath when Mr. Renfrow charged into the front office. A twenty-one-year-old man with a semi-automatic and another slung over his back if that one jammed. He blasted everyone in that office. Even though my dad was hit, he charged Mr. Renfrow, who did not stop firing his weapon.

"My father was left for dead when Mr. Renfrow took off down the hall, shooting everyone in his path. When security caught up to him, the school looked like a war zone.

"As we were led out, I looked in the front office to see my father and my brother on the floor. I ran to them, but there was nothing I could do. I stood in shock next to my dead brother while the paramedics worked on my dad. My dad made it, but he's confined to a wheelchair. If you think I'm going to allow Renfrow to walk out of here without a fight, you don't know who you're dealing with. If my father never gets to walk again, then neither does he." He paused while a vortex of fury swirled around him. "Thank you for allowing me the opportunity to speak on behalf of the victims and their families."

The silence was deafening.

The representative from the commission cleared his throat.

"Thank you, Mr. Grant. We'll take your statement into consideration when we make our decision."

As Cooper slugged through traffic, he called his dad. "Why didn't you come with me to the hearing?"

"I'm done fighting," his dad said. "It's time to let it go, Cooper."

"I will never let it go, Dad. *Never.*"

3

THE NO-SHOW AND THE PREDATOR

COOPER

At eight thirty that evening, Cooper strode into Jericho Road. After the nonstop day at ALPHA, then the anger over seeing Renfrow, he couldn't wait to chill with a beautiful woman.

"Hey, Cooper," said the smiley hostess. "I'll take you to Jericho's booth."

As she led him through the popular western-themed bar and restaurant to the horseshoe booth nestled in the corner, she put an extra sway in her hips. While Cooper appreciated that she was putting on a show for him, he wasn't interested.

He'd been looking forward to getting to know Danielle from the moment he'd first laid eyes on her, six months ago. Not long after they met, she suffered a tragedy. He'd passed along a message that he wanted to talk to her, but she'd said no, so he backed off. Fast forward to now. When he hadn't been able to shake her from his thoughts, he asked her to meet him for drinks.

To his surprise, she agreed.

After the hostess left, Cooper glanced around. The place was packed to capacity.

A server breezed over, took his drink order and returned with a beer. This was the first time all day Cooper had had a chance to breathe. While waiting for Danielle, his thoughts turned to Salimov and Renfrow. He hated both men with a vengeance.

The minutes ticked by. It was five after nine and he was still sitting alone in the damn booth.

Cooper downed the remains of his beer before checking messages one more time.

Nothing from Danielle.

A low, deep growl rumbled from the back of his throat. He wanted to play tonight chill, but *not* this chill. Danielle had stood him up, and he was pissed—though it didn't take much to set him off.

A redhead moseyed over. "Hi, I couldn't help...um...I saw you back here in this big booth all alone." Her cheeks flushed. "Are you waiting for someone?"

"Yup. How 'bout you?"

Her lips split into a smile as she slid into the booth. "I'm celebrating a friend's birthday. We're line dancing and I saw you on my way to the bar."

"I'm Cooper."

"Suzette. What do you do, I mean, where do you work?"

"I own a gym in Tysons. You?"

"I'm a paralegal in DC. Are you on social media?"

"No." Cooper knew he wasn't encouraging conversation, but he was *not* in the mood to chat. He wanted to be angry and cursing the universe for not cooperating.

First, Salimov. Then, Renfrow. Now, Danielle.

"Who are you waiting for, I mean, if you don't mind my asking?" Suzette asked, plucking him from his thoughts.

"A woman I asked to have drinks with me."

She smiled. "That's romantic."

"You think?"

"Have you hooked up with her or been following her on social media?"

"No. She's someone I've wanted to get to know for a while, but the timing was off."

"She had a boyfriend, right?"

"Her sister was murdered and I bought the gym, then left my career to run it."

Suzette's eyes bulged. "Did you say her sister was murdered?"

"Yeah."

"That's awful. What was your job before you owned the gym?"

"FBI. You ask a lotta questions."

She smiled. "How else am I going to get to know you?"

"Good point, except I'm not someone you wanna get to know."

"Why not?"

"My life's too fuckin' complicated," he said, rubbing the knot in the back of his neck.

Suzette stood. "I hope your date shows up. She's an idiot if she doesn't. If a man who looked like you asked me out, I would show up. You know, eighty percent of life is just showing up."

That made Cooper smile. She was right about that. "Thanks for stopping by, Suzette. Have fun at your party."

"See ya 'round, Cooper." She leaned forward. "You've got a killer smile."

She left as Cooper's phone binged with an incoming text from his sister. He sent off a reply as the owner of Jericho Road eased down across from him.

"Did you scare her away?" Jericho asked.

"That woman who just crashed my party of one?"

"No, Danielle."

Jericho Savage was one of Cooper's closest friends. The man looked like he'd been living in the wild, surviving off the land. Large, loud, and cocky as hell, everything about Jericho screamed out of control. His hair was long and wild, his gaze intense. His clothing was well-worn and tattered. He appeared one second away from total fucking madness. That was part of the ruse. The truth couldn't be farther from the image Jericho had created. Jericho was in control every moment of every day.

"She stood me up," Cooper bit out.

Jericho chuffed out a laugh. "You ask out one woman on one date and she ghosts on you *before* you get together. How'd you fuck *this* up?"

Cooper shrugged. "No idea. Maybe it was too soon."

"Too soon?"

"Stryker said her sister's death really messed her up."

"Death messes everyone up. It's one of life's curve balls."

A server appeared. "Hey, Jericho." He regarded Cooper. "Can I bring you an appetizer while you wait? Our loaded potato skins are dope."

"You want the usual?" Jericho asked Cooper.

"I'll eat whatever," Cooper replied, shoving his phone in his pocket.

"Two cheeseburgers, fries, coleslaw," Jericho said.

"Cooper, you want another beer?" asked the server.

"Water," Cooper replied.

"Two waters," Jericho said before the server bolted.

The conversation flowed, the food was served, and the men dug in. If there was anyone Cooper could count on, it was Jericho. Their friendship ran blood deep.

After they'd eaten, he jumped into his Jeep and drove toward home, but he couldn't shake the disappointment that had settled into his bones. Salimov had slithered away *again* and the one woman he'd been looking forward to seeing blew him off.

Every time things didn't go according to Cooper's plan, the anger in his soul festered. In the past twenty-four hours, *nothing* had gone his way.

Absolutely nothing.

DANIELLE

At five minutes past nine, Danielle street parked half a block from Stu Sisson's Northwest DC condo building, dismounted her bike, and locked her helmet. Before setting off down the street, she grabbed a large envelope and a small leather bag from the side satchel.

As soon as she'd gotten home from work, she'd hacked into the traffic cams in a three-block radius of Sisson's building and turned them off. She'd also deactivated his home surveillance system and the cameras in his building. Her long blonde hair was hidden beneath a short dark wig with bangs and her blue eyes were made dark with brown contact lenses. Her Glock was in one pocket of her leather jacket and the silencer in the other.

No one had been able to stop this long-time predator, so she would. And she could not wait.

She strode to the front door and buzzed his place. No response. After several seconds, she buzzed him again.

"Hello," he answered.

"It's Ursula."

The door clicked and she sailed inside the quiet lobby. Despite her deactivating the building's surveillance system, she kept her head down as she made her way to the elevator.

She rode to the sixth floor, eyes down. When she stepped out, she glanced down the hall. Stu was waiting, wearing what looked like a lounging robe with black, silky pants.

Acid churned in her guts. He thought he was going to get laid.

Think again, asshole.

She'd originally met him at an upscale DC restaurant where powerful politicos, lobbyists and high-end government types hung out. She'd positioned herself at the bar and waited. Night after night, for five nights, until he showed. After he'd had a few drinks, she moseyed past his table and caught his eye. It didn't take long for him to find her, sitting alone at the bar. From there, it was rote. She was new to the area and really wanted to work as a White House intern or maybe land an entry-level position with a congressperson or senator. Whatever, it didn't matter. It was all a ruse. Stu told her he might be able to help and suggested they meet to talk more.

This was that meeting.

As she sauntered down the hallway in her skintight, black leather pants, he eye-fucked her, then licked his lips when she pulled to a stop in front of him. The stench from his overpowering cologne made her want to gag. She wanted to choke the life out of him on the spot. Instead, she offered a demure smile.

"Thanks for seeing me, Mr. Sisson."

The longtime power player was average height with a decent physique. His hair was thinning and it appeared like he was using plugs to shore up the front.

"Good to see you, Ursula." He gestured and she entered his home. While she could be anxious about stepping inside a strange man's home, she wasn't. Despite the fact that he could probably overpower her, her heart beat calmly in her chest. Her breathing didn't shift and her palms had stopped sweating inside her black leather gloves.

She followed him into his living space. The small kitchen was tidy. The living and dining rooms were filled with outdated, bulky furniture. But Danielle wasn't there to redecorate. She glanced around for the surveillance cameras she'd turned off earlier and found one perched on the refrigerator and another in the corner of the living room. If she'd done her job, they were off. If not, she'd be working into the wee hours of the morning ensuring the footage got erased.

After setting her items on the kitchen table, she removed her gloves, then slowly unzipped her jacket. Staying organized and efficient was critical. Zero room for error.

His gaze dropped to her chest. She'd worn a V-neck shirt that hinted at cleavage.

"Can I take your jacket?"

"I'm okay, thanks."

"Would you like wine?" he asked while pouring himself a glass of red.

"No." This was supposed to be an interview, so she eased onto a barstool appreciating the cold, granite counter that separated them.

But Sisson wasn't interested in interviewing her. He wanted to assault her.

"Let's sit in the living room." With glass in hand, he sauntered past her, taking that stinking cologne with him.

She slid her hand into her pocket and ran her fingers over the barrel of her Glock. Comforted by her weapon, she followed. He relaxed in an upholstered chair and she sat on the sofa.

"Tell me about yourself," Stu said before sipping the wine.

"Not much to say." She crossed her legs. His gaze followed. "I moved to DC a coupla months ago to pursue my dream. I'd love to work at the White House."

"Long hours," he said.

"Uh-huh."

"Not much money."

"I'd get a part-time job."

"Might be difficult, you know, with the long hours."

Her shoulders slumped. "It *is* super expensive around here. I'll have to save for a year, then try again." She pushed off the sofa. "Sorry I wasted your time."

She bit back a smile. She'd read enough about Sisson in the online chat room to know he'd proposition her.

"I might be able to help you, so you don't have to wait a year."

"Really?" she asked, raising her eyebrows in anticipation.

He sauntered right up to her and stared into her eyes. Then, he leaned forward to kiss her. She jumped back. "What are you doing?"

He grabbed her shoulders to hold her in place. "I'm going to get you a job, plus help you with rent, but you have to do something for me."

Glaring at him, she shrugged away. "What'd you have in mind?"

"Consensual sex between two willing adults."

"You know, Stu—you don't mind if I call you that, do you?— I wasn't expecting that."

"Why not?"

"No one's ever held a job opportunity ransom, you know, in exchange for sex."

"You want to work at the White House. That's not an easy job to get. Gotta have connections. I'm yours. You'll learn that in Washington it's always a give and take. Push and pull, back and forth." His creepy smile had her biting back a grimace.

"Well, I *was* on my way to my kink club…"

His pupils dilated and his breathing shifted. "Kink club, eh? We have a shared interest."

"What's your poison, Stu?"

He took her hands in his. "I'm at your mercy, Ursula."

Breaking away from him, again, she sashayed over to her bag. After opening it, she fished out a small, leather whip. Slowly, she turned back to him and slapped it against her thigh.

His wide grin sent a shiver streaking through her.

She extracted a blindfold and dangled it in front of him. "I like things wild and rough."

"Ohgod, yes," he bleated. "This is unexpected. Normally, I get more pushback. Most of the ladies I help *don't* want to be intimate with me."

"I'm full of surprises," she murmured as she sauntered close. His pupils were so dilated, they obscured his drab eye color. "Let's get started. You look like you're dying for this." That made her smile.

"I love hard fucking," he said, his voice tight with need. "Just love it."

She collected her bag and the envelope. "Where's your bed?" Without waiting for a response, she headed down the hallway, passing his home office and a hall bathroom. As soon as she entered his bedroom, she pulled the BDSM bed restraints out of her bag and slid them under the head and foot of the mattress, laying the attached cuffs on his made bed.

"Don't you want me to get under the sheets?" Sidling close, he tried to kiss her again.

"No kissing, yet." She led him to the bed.

He started to remove his robe, but she stopped him. "So impatient. Haven't you heard of the art of seduction?"

"Mmm, I like your style." As soon as he lay down, she secured his wrists and ankles.

"Can you escape?" she asked.

He tugged on the wrist cuffs. "No."

She pulled out what looked like duct tape, but it was designed specifically for skin. She tore off a piece, then stood at his bedside.

"What are you doing with that?" His tone had turned gruff.

"Making sure your neighbors can't hear you screaming when you come." She covered his mouth.

His boner tented his silk pants.

"Someone's excited. I like to start with a dirty bedtime story."

"Mmmm," he uttered.

"Once upon a time there was a man. We'll call him Stu. He worked hard, earned a coveted position inside the President's inner circle. Stu realized that with this position came power...so much power. And Stu liked women. But he didn't just want to admire them from afar—"

"Whaaaaa goin' on?" he muttered through the tape.

"I'm telling you a story, you know, to get you hot-n-horny.

Now, where was I? Ah, yes. Stu loved women and he loved his power. One day, he decided to use that power and he manipulated a woman into having sex with him. Maybe she was scared, or she felt like she couldn't speak up, or she was in denial that it was even happening. She could have been desperate and saw no other option. Stu got exactly what he wanted and he was very, very happy. So happy that he tried it again. And just like that first time, it worked. He dangled jobs and career opportunities. He promised these women all sorts of things. Some were willing to go along, others were not." She glared at him. "He didn't care, because he had *all* the power."

"Uuuuuunie me!"

"How do you feel now, Stu? How do you think all those women felt when you were taking advantage of them?" She got in his face. "They fucking hated it, just like you do now."

"Aaaaahieeeeeee!"

Backing away from him, she pulled photos from the envelope and showed them to him. "These are some of the women who filed lawsuits against you for sexual harassment and sexual assault." She read their names. "They each claimed you invited them here, for an interview. You assaulted most of them. Some agreed, but only because you used sex as a weapon. Just like you did with me."

"Ge meee ouuu ooooo heeere," he bellowed from behind the tape. "Uuuntie me!"

Danielle pulled her Glock from her pocket and pointed it at his face. "I'm looking for a little honesty, that's all. You tell me the truth and I'll be on my way." She stroked his hair. "Relax and take a nice, slow, deep breath."

When he did, she nodded. "Did you offer those women jobs in exchange for sex?"

He stared at her, hatred pouring from his eyes.

She flipped to a different page. "There are dozens of chat rooms for victims of sexual assault. Most use their first names, but a few brave souls use their full names. There are over a hundred women who mention you by name. You've even got a nickname, did you know that?"

His cheeks flamed tomato red. If he had a heart attack, that would make her job that much easier.

"They call you the White House Predator." She shook her head. "You should be ashamed of yourself." She read through more names. "Do you remember any of these women?"

He shrugged. She glared at him. "I need the truth, Stu. *The truth*. Most of these women were paid off for their silence and dropped their lawsuits."

This time, when she got closer, he tried to kick her, but the restraint held him in place.

"Ay dell you da truf," he grumbled.

"I'm going to remove the tape. If you scream, I'll cover your mouth again. Will you behave?"

He nodded, quickly. She removed the tape halfway and he sucked down a lungful of air.

"Why would all these women complain about you if it weren't true?"

"They wanted me to—" he cleared his throat—"help them, so I did, then they accused me of raping them."

"All of them?"

"There might've been a misunderstanding with a few of them," he murmured.

"How?"

"I don't remember."

Up went her eyebrows. "I find that hard to believe. Why don't you search your soul and tell me the damn truth? Be a man and own what you did."

The silence was deafening and comforting at the same time. Danielle believed these women. Why would all of them lie? What would they have to gain? Money, possibly, but these women were traumatized by what had happened. Some had committed suicide.

Not ten minutes ago, he'd propositioned her—dangling a job and help with rent—in exchange for sex.

"Time's up." She lifted the gun, pointed at his head.

"I did assault those women. All of them...and more." He sighed. "I've been getting away with it for my entire career. The more powerful I became, the easier it was to manipulate them. I forced them all to have sex with me."

"Thank you," she said. "Now, don't you feel better confessing your sins?"

"Untie me and get the hell out. I'm not gonna help you land a job at the White House, on the Hill, or any-fucking-where else."

She slid the papers and photos into the envelope, stepped into the hallway, attached the silencer to her Glock, and returned to the bedroom.

"Let me tell you how the story ends. You'll never stop preying on these women. Why would you when you've gotten away with it for decades?" She raised her weapon. His eyes widened. "Not anymore, asshole."

POP!

The bullet penetrated his forehead.

His eyes went flat. She removed the silencer and slid it, and the Glock, into her pockets. After collecting the cartridge casing, she removed the restraints, and the tape from his mouth. Though her heart was pounding out of her chest, she kept going. After placing the items back in her bag, she stared at his lifeless face.

"I hope the victims find some peace after they learn you can't hurt anyone, ever again."

Not wanting to risk leaving a fingerprint, she couldn't feel his carotid artery, so she watched his chest. There was no movement. He was gone.

She pulled out the half piece of paper from the envelope and read the words she'd typed.

I'm a dead man talking. I bribed and coerced women for sex, using my power and position as leverage. Some agreed to have sex with me because I told them I would help them. Some did not and I raped them. Either way, I abused them, over and over, and over again.

She included an abbreviated list of victims, along with the crimes Sisson denied committing. And she'd listed the website addresses for the chat rooms where the women had talked about Sisson.

She retrieved her leather gloves from the kitchen, pulled them on, and returned to the bedroom where she crumpled the piece of paper, pried open Sisson's mouth, and shoved it inside. With the envelope in hand, she collected her bag, and left.

Head down, she took the stairs. Once outside, the cool night air whisked away the perspiration on her brow. She hated herself for what she'd done. But she hated him even more.

One less monster to prey on the vulnerable.

She hurried to her Ninja, placed her items in the satchel, pulled on her helmet and swung her leg over the bike. The engine roared to life. After glancing over her shoulder, she rolled onto the quiet DC street. It was almost eleven.

As she rode home, she thought about the three other men she'd taken out. No one had been able to stop them, either. Lawsuits didn't slow them down, nor did the suicides of their victims. They didn't care about the women they assaulted, didn't give a fuck about the lives they ruined. They wanted what they wanted and they took it without fear of penalty or punishment.

Someone had to stop them, and that someone was her.

Once home, she confirmed that Sisson's surveillance system was still off. She turned the traffic cameras back on, along with the surveillance in Sisson's building. Next, she checked her cell phone.

There was a text from her mom, another from her bestie, Emerson Easton, and one from Cooper Grant.

"Hi honey," texted her mom. "How are you doing? I miss you. Dad and I want to video chat with you whenever you have time. Love you."

If her parents learned what she'd become, it would probably kill them. "Let's video chat this weekend. I love you, too." She sent the text.

Emerson's said, "Are you excited for tomorrow?"

What's tomorrow?

She tapped her phone's calendar. Tomorrow night was their fifteen-year high school reunion. She'd forgotten all about it.

"Can't wait!" she texted back.

Dots appeared, then another text. "Come over after work and we'll get ready together. Love you." Emerson had included heart emojis with her text.

Danielle replied with a thumbs-up emoji and several hearts, then read Cooper's text.

"I'm in the owner's booth. Look forward to seeing you."

Oh, no! I stood him up.

She'd forgotten to cancel with Cooper after Sisson had replied. His second text came in after ten. "Sorry it didn't work out."

"I'm so sorry Cooper," she texted back. "I had a last-minute work thing and I didn't have my phone with me."

No dots appeared, so she turned on her security system and headed upstairs.

Six months ago, Cooper Grant had crashed into her life during a girls' night out with Emerson and her sister, Claire-Marie. Her attraction to him had been immediate and intense.

Shortly after meeting him, her sister had been killed and the happy, easy-going Danielle was replaced with an angry one, hellbent on vengeance. Her thoughts had turned dark, so it hadn't mattered that Cooper was sick handsome with a killer body. She'd become obsessed with taking out the bad guys, not hanging out with one of the good ones.

When Emerson told her Cooper wanted her number, she'd

said no. He worked for the FBI. No way was she cozying up to a lawman.

But when she ran into him at her gym last month, they talked. A week later, she saw him there, again, and they exchanged phone numbers. When he asked her out, she agreed to meet him for drinks.

Despite her attraction to the uber-sexy blond with the translucent blue eyes, strapping broad shoulders, and nice tight ass, she wasn't getting close to someone who worked for the Bureau.

In her bathroom, she stripped down and stood in the shower, hoping the hot water would rinse away the sadness. But the loss never left and she choked back a sob. She'd cried so many tears for so long, there were none left. The emptiness left her wishing for things that could never be. She wanted her sister back. She wished she could stop the evil.

But she couldn't. There was too damn much of it.

She toweled off, then lifted the diamond, heart-shaped pendant necklace from the vanity and clasped it around her neck. A birthday gift from her sister that she wore as a reminder of why she was going after these men. The only time she *didn't* wear it was on nights like these.

After dressing in her comfiest jammies, she crawled into bed and turned out the light. Like most nights, sleep would not come.

Bing!

She read Cooper's text.

"Glad you're okay," he replied.

I'm not okay, Cooper. Not at all.

4

THE HIGH SCHOOL REUNION

DANIELLE

Danielle stared at herself in Emerson's bedroom mirror, then regarded her friend beside her.

"I don't know about this," Danielle said, eyeing the backless pantsuit. "What do you think?"

"My vote is on the black dress I bought you," Emerson replied.

"It is beautiful," Danielle said. "But, then, we'll both be wearing black dresses."

Emerson laughed. "We spent our *entire* senior year dressing exactly alike. Your black dress is short sleeved with a streak of red on both sides of the slit and the back is open. Mine is long sleeved and clingy."

"I'll wear it," Danielle said. "Thank you for the dress, Emmy."

"It's perfect for you, and you'll look great in it." Emerson ran a comforting hand over Danielle's back before heading into her bathroom.

As Danielle changed, she glanced around the bedroom Emerson shared with her fiancé, Stryker Truman. Everything from Emerson's townhouse had been replaced with new furniture and new bedding. All that remained from her old life was her cat, Pima, who was attacking a toy on the king bed.

A smiling Danielle joined Emerson in the expansive bathroom.

"You look happy," Emerson said while applying eyeshadow.

"It's Pima. He's nutso over some toy." Danielle fished out a smoky gray eyeshadow from Emerson's cosmetics drawer.

Both were blondes with fair complexions and blue eyes. Danielle was a little taller, otherwise, they were the same size and liked similar clothes. But their taste in men varied greatly. Stryker had long, dark hair and Danielle loved athletic blonds.

"I feel like we haven't talked in forever," Emerson said while brushing her hair.

"That's 'cause we haven't," Danielle replied. "Every time I'm at work, which is three days a week, I stop by to see you, but you're never there."

"Where are you the other two days?"

"At a client site with a team member and sometimes I work from home. Why aren't you *ever* at work?"

A brief shadow flitted across Emerson's face. It was subtle, but Danielle knew that whatever Emerson said next would be a lie. That's because they'd been best friends since first grade. Emerson was keeping something from Danielle and it was driving a wedge between them.

"I guess I'm just there when you're not." Emerson rummaged through her cosmetic bag. "Oh, I almost forgot." She disappeared into the bedroom, returning with two unopened mascaras. "I read that these are *the best*, so I bought them for us." She handed one to Danielle.

"That was sweet." Danielle tore open the package and lifted out the tube. "I miss you, Em, that's all."

Emerson wrapped her arm around Danielle and gave her a little hug. "Just because we don't hang out at work doesn't mean we aren't still besties. No one will ever replace you, Danny, not even Stryker."

Danielle forced a smile. "Thanks for saying that." No matter what Emerson may have been hiding, Danielle's secret was ten times bigger and a hundred times worse. She'd become a cold-blooded killer.

A shiver skirted through her.

As Emerson thickened her lashes with mascara, she said, "You aren't okay and I wish you would let me in."

Talking about her sister only made her sad, then angry. Plus, she'd already talked to Emerson so many times, she couldn't burden her friend anymore.

"Thanks for being there. I'm managing." Needing to change the subject, Danielle said, "I checked the social media page for the reunion and it looks like half the class will be there. I saw a bunch of people we were friends with."

"I can't believe it's been fifteen years," Emerson said. "It's gonna be fun seeing everyone." Emerson pulled out her crème blush and gently rubbed some over her cheekbones before offering the jar to Danielle.

While Danielle was applying it, Emerson got busy choosing a lipstick. "You haven't said anything about Cooper. I've been dying to know how your evening went."

"It never happened."

Emerson stopped rolling on the dark, red lipstick. "Did he cancel?"

"No, it was me."

"You changed your mind?"

"I had a work thing come up." Danielle pulled her long blonde hair into a ponytail, then pulled out strands to frame out her face.

"He's a great guy," Emerson said. "Are you going to try again?"

Danielle shrugged. "Now's not a good time."

They finished getting ready in a silence that cut like shards of glass. Danielle wasn't about to confess her sins. Not now, not ever. Emerson was no longer a police detective, but she sure as hell knew a lot of them. All Danielle had to say was, "Hey, Em, I killed four men to stop them from hurting innocent women. I couldn't help my own sister, so I'm going to help everyone else."

That would be the end of their friendship and the beginning of her life behind bars. Thanks, but no thanks.

"You ready to slay this reunion?" Emerson asked, plucking Danielle from her thoughts.

"Absolutely." She wished her heart was in this event, but she'd rather be at home, sleuthing in chat rooms and hunting her next target.

They left the bathroom, slipped into their stilettos, and headed downstairs.

"I'm going to say goodbye to Stryker," Emerson said when they reached the first floor.

"I'm in the front room, babe," Stryker called out.

As Danielle turned in that direction, two men rose. Stryker from the sofa and Cooper from the chair.

Ohmygod, he's here.

Her gaze locked with his and her heart flipped, then started galloping in her chest. The man was scorching hot. Dressed in a dark, flannel shirt, worn black jeans and scuffed cowboy boots, his well-defined muscles could not be contained. Every single time she laid eyes on him, she reacted the same damn way. Soaring pulse, warming cheeks, jolts of adrenaline powering through her.

It was impossible *not* to react. Those soul-piercing eyes, chiseled cheeks and sculptured jawline captured her complete attention. Tonight, however, he had no smile. And she couldn't blame him. She had stood him up, offered a lame excuse, then hadn't even suggested they get together again. But keeping him at a distance was for his own good.

And mine.

Her insides came alive and she bit back a moan. Cooper Grant was too easy on the eyes. Much, much too easy.

With his attention firmly set on her, he gave her the once-over.

It was slow, deliberate and sexy as hell. Then, it was over. Did he like what he saw? Did he think she looked pretty? She could not get a read on him. Despite how she needed to keep her distance from him, she *wanted* him to find her attractive. She was so hot for this man, it was insane.

And so not happening.

"Hey, Danielle." She couldn't miss the irritation in his deep, sexy voice. Strangely, she liked the angry vibes he was shooting her way. By pushing him away, she'd done herself a favor. If he wasn't interested, her dark secret was that much safer.

As she opened her mouth to reply, he shifted his attention to Emerson. "Hey, Emerson," he said. "How's it goin'?"

"You're gonna break some hearts tonight," Stryker interjected. "You sure you don't need a bodyguard? I can lurk in the shadows and—"

Emerson laughed. "Babe, we'll be fine. What are you guys doing tonight?"

"Chillin' at Jericho Road," Cooper answered. His smoldering gaze cemented on Danielle. "Swing by on your way home."

When Stryker kissed Emerson goodbye, Cooper sauntered close. Danielle's pulse kicked up while she soaked up all that alpha male hotness. His bright eyes drilled into her and she glanced at his mouth, then at what looked like day-old scruff. She'd never seen him this close and the view was simply spectacular.

Cooper Grant had to be six two. She wanted to run her fingers through his thick head of blond hair—long on the top and cropped short on the sides—pull him close, and kiss those full, luscious lips.

"Next time you *don't* want to go out with someone, just say 'No'." His low, rumbling growl hit her smack between her legs. The effect he was having on her was both intoxicating and annoying.

"I'm going to start the car," Emerson said before heading toward the garage.

Cooper hitched a brow. "See ya."

After saying goodbye to her boss, Danielle followed Emerson. They collected their clutch bags from the kitchen and left.

As soon as Danielle slid into Emerson's car, she sighed.

"Well, you pissed him off," Emerson said, buckling in.

Danielle clicked the seat belt. "He has got to be the most gorgeous man I have *ever* seen."

Emerson backed out of the garage, tapped the door remote, and waited for a car to drive by before she pulled onto the street.

"He's totally your type, Danny," Emerson said. "All you have to do is ask him out. I'm sure he'd say yes."

Danielle wasn't looking to get close to anyone, especially not now. She had much more important things to do, though she had to admit that hooking up with him would be a terrific distraction. Only, Danielle didn't do hookups, and she didn't need any distractions. She was on a mission, and not even that gorgeous hunk of a man would get in her way.

COOPER

The chip on Cooper's shoulder had morphed into a damn boulder after seeing Danielle. Despite her stunning beauty, the woman was a liar. *If you're gonna make up some bold-faced lie, come up with something that can't be fact checked.*

"From the heat rolling off you, I take it you two didn't hit it off," Stryker said as Cooper drove out of the neighborhood.

"She never showed."

"That doesn't sound like Danielle."

Cooper shrugged. "I didn't push it. She said she had a work thing. I've been interested in her for a while, but I'm gonna move on."

"I don't understand women, and I'm gonna marry one."

Cooper chuffed out a chuckle. "What am I missing with her?"

"Hell if I know. I don't want to get in the middle—"

"I don't want you to either."

"But..." Stryker paused. "There was no work thing last night, at least, not a formal thing. Maybe she took her team out or joined them for dinner."

"Doesn't matter," Cooper said as he turned onto the main road.

"Danielle hasn't been okay since her sister was killed. Could be that she doesn't want to get close to anyone."

Cooper was done talking about Danielle. Based on how hot she looked tonight, however, he wasn't done thinking about her. But that's all he was gonna do. Danielle Fox was a dead end. "I got promoted at work."

"That was fast," Stryker said.

Cooper pulled into Jericho Road's parking lot, found a spot, and cut the engine. "Dakota is stepping away for a few, so I'm helping out."

"You can't get away from management, can you?"

The men headed toward the entrance.

"Looks that way," Cooper replied.

They entered the noisy restaurant and stopped at the hostess stand. "Hi, guys. Jericho mentioned you'd be stopping by." She gazed up at Cooper. "I'm off at eleven if you wanna line dance."

"Sure," Cooper replied. "If I'm here, that dance is yours."

She grinned. "I'll come find you. You can head on back to his booth."

As the two men wove their way through the crowded restaurant, Stryker said, "She's not your type."

"Well, my *type* isn't interested, so I'm branching out."

DANIELLE

Danielle and Emerson entered Hotel X and followed the signs to the reunion. A table had been set up outside the ballroom entrance and they stood in the short line.

"I'm a little nervous," Emerson whispered.

"You've entered crime scenes with confidence. You took out a serial killer. You're the bravest person I know. And you're nervous about a class reunion?"

"Thanks for saying that, but my stomach is in knots."

Danielle squeezed Emerson's hand. "I'm right here, and we're gonna have a fun time. If it's a bust, we'll leave. This is no big—"

"Danielle! Emerson!" They turned around. A smiling man glanced from one to the other.

Danielle was drawing a blank.

"Dave Tilgrath," he said. "We had English together."

"Good to see you, Dave," Emerson replied.

Fortunately, he'd brought along his yearbook to help jog their memory. Dave had gained a lot of weight. He'd also grown a beard and mustache and had a terrible haircut.

"How've you been?" Danielle asked.

Dave chatted away as they moved up in line. He was still talking when the woman behind the table said, "I had a feeling you two would show up together."

The woman on the reunion committee had been on their field hockey team.

"Good talking to you," Emerson said to Dave before they got themselves checked in. They were each handed a lanyard with a picture of themselves from senior year.

After walking into the ballroom, they studied their photos.

"We don't look that much different," Emerson said.

"Our hair looks better, now," Danielle added. "We had those silly bobs back then."

They ran into several friends and split off to talk to different people. Conversations came easily and Danielle appreciated the light-hearted distraction. A lot of her friends had gotten married and had families. Some were divorced. At thirty-two, she was none of those.

Dave sidled back over. Slowly, the people Danielle had been talking to moved on, leaving her alone with Dave. "So, you're single. Me, too. I was seeing someone for a while, but it didn't work out. Want to get together for a drink sometime?"

As Danielle opened her mouth to answer him, a woman rushed over to join them. "Danielle! I recognized you right away!" She gave Danielle a warm hug.

"Lori, it's good to see you!"

Lori Shannon had been on their field hockey team up until her senior year, when she quit to spend more time with her boyfriend. In addition to cutting her hair short, she'd gone from brunette to auburn. Beyond that, she looked the same.

"Do you remember Dave—" Danielle glanced at his nametag—"Tilgrath?"

Lori shook his hand. "Good to meet you."

"What are you up to these days?" Danielle asked, grateful someone had interrupted her conversation with him.

As Lori chatted away, Cooper floated into her thoughts. Maybe she should apologize and ask him out. And what was so wrong about a late-night hookup, anyway? It had been a while since she'd been with anyone, so long, in fact, that she'd named her vibrator.

I'm pathetic.

"I love running the women's shelters," Lori said. "It makes me feel like I'm doing something good for someone else, and for our community."

"How many shelters do you have?" Danielle had missed a little of what Lori had said and hoped she hadn't noticed.

"Three. One in DC, one in Virginia, and one in Maryland. They're my babies. Enough about me, what about you?"

Someone came over to talk to Dave and he turned away from

them. This was Danielle's opportunity to break away from him. "I'm gonna grab a drink. Join me."

The two women headed to one of the bars. Once in line, Lori said, "What's your story? Are you married? Where do you work?"

"Not married and I'm a computer geek. Are you married?"

"I'm seeing someone. What kind of work do you do with computers?"

Danielle didn't tell people she was a hacker. Most didn't understand what true hackers did. "I manage several teams at a computer company."

Lori paused to order a glass of wine. Danielle was a lightweight when it came to alcohol and she wanted to stay sober. She'd homed in on her next target and she wanted to start researching him as soon as she got home.

"Sparkling water with a lime wedge," she said to the bartender.

After they collected their drinks, Lori fished a business card from her handbag and offered it to Danielle. "Would you be interested in teaching a computer workshop at my Alexandria shelter?"

"I'd love to," Danielle replied. "I've taught a class about online computer safety. You know, making sure hackers don't get access to your online accounts and how to stay clear of online scams. Would something like that work?"

"That would be awesome," Lori replied. "How long is it?"

"About an hour."

"That's perfect." Lori gave her a hug. "Thank you so much for being willing to do this. I can offer you a little money—"

"I'm happy to volunteer my time," Danielle said.

"Danielle, you were so sweet in high school and you haven't changed a bit."

I'm not as sweet as you think I am.

Dave popped over, two glasses of wine in his hands. "I got you a glass of wine."

"Good seeing you," Lori said. "We'll talk next week." Lori vanished into the crowd, leaving her alone with Dave, again.

"No, thanks." Danielle glanced around for Emerson and spotted her talking to a group nearby. "I haven't had a chance to catch up with everyone, so I'm gonna—"

"Can I get your number?" Dave asked. "Dave and Danielle. Sounds pretty cute, don'tcha think?"

No, I don't.

"I'm sorry, Dave. I'm gonna pass, but I appreciate you asking me."

She excused herself and headed over to Emerson. They spent the next hour catching up with so many old friends before Emerson fished out her phone. Laughing, she showed Danielle the pictures.

There was one of Stryker and another of Cooper riding the mechanical bull at Jericho Road.

"Those two are idiots," Emerson said with a smile. "You ready to head over there?"

Danielle could beg out and call for an Uber or she could go with Emerson and have some fun. *Isn't that better than going home, alone, and spending the next few hours digging up dirt on a scumbag?*

"I'm in," Danielle blurted before she could change her mind.

Emerson grinned. "That's my Danny."

The women hurried out and jumped in Emerson's car. They chatted the entire way about everyone they'd seen and caught each other up on the people the other one hadn't seen.

Twenty minutes later, they arrived at a super busy Jericho Road where they found Stryker and Jericho in Jericho's booth, but no Cooper.

Stryker pushed out and kissed Emerson hello. "How was it?"

"Great!" Emerson replied. "We had a blast!"

"I'm Jericho," he said to Danielle.

Danielle remembered him from the night she, her sister, and Emerson had gone to Raphael's for dinner. He was a beast of a man with long, wild hair, and a thick beard and mustache. Yet, he had the kindest eyes.

"Danielle," she replied.

"Whatcha drinking?" Jericho asked the women.

"Pinot Grigio," both women replied in unison.

Jericho raised his massive arm and two servers flew over. Danielle and Emerson exchanged glances. That man was definitely commander of the ship.

After their wine had been delivered, the women tapped each other's glasses before taking a sip. The chilled liquid rolled down Danielle's throat and she took another mouthful before setting down the glass.

"Let's line dance," Stryker said.

Danielle had never line danced and she flicked her gaze from Stryker to Emerson to Jericho.

Emerson set her glass on the table and clasped Danielle's hand. "I know that look and you are *not* staying here."

"I gotta help out at the bar and bust up the crazies," Jericho replied. "Table's yours all night." He tossed a nod at Danielle. "When you're done dancin', go tame the Beast."

"Is that the mechanical bull?"

"Sure is, darlin'."

She and Emerson followed Stryker toward the back of the massive restaurant that spanned an entire city block. They passed a few smaller dining rooms that were filled to capacity before Stryker turned into a room that housed the Beast. A group was watching while a guy rode the bull. Seconds later, he got tossed onto the mat and the small crowd cheered.

"Did you fall off?" Emerson asked Stryker.

"I got tossed. Cooper stayed on the entire time."

"Where is he?" Emerson asked.

"Line dancing."

They entered an oversized room with wood beams that ran the entire length of the ceiling, a large, scuffed hardwood dance floor and several tables crammed together on one side. The lively country music filled her ears, but Danielle wasn't interested in the ambiance. She was there for one reason, and one reason only.

Cooper Grant.

On first glance, she didn't see him. When she scanned a second time, she spotted him line dancing in the back row, surrounded by women.

Danielle's heart tightened while her body burned with desire. If she let this man get away, she'd be making a colossal mistake. *I need to fix this, and I need to fix it now.*

"Ready to do this?" Emerson asked, crashing into her thoughts.

"Yes, I am," Danielle replied.

The song ended. "Break time," said the DJ. "Back in ten." He turned on a country ballad before stepping away, and a bunch of people stayed on the dance floor.

"Let's find a table," Stryker said.

"Go dance," Danielle said to them. "I'll find us something."

Stryker flashed her a grateful smile and whisked his woman onto the dance floor. As Danielle went in search of an empty table, a cute guy sidled over. "Are you looking for a table?"

"Sure am."

"I'm here with my buddies, and we'll squeeze you in," he said.

"How many—"

Movement caught her eye and she flicked her gaze over the man's shoulder. Cooper loomed into view. He was surrounded by a gaggle of women. His fiery gaze turned her into a ball of pent-up need. She couldn't look away, didn't want to. All she saw was this strikingly beautiful man glaring in her direction.

The guy who'd offered to share his table had taken a few steps, then turned back. "Hello? Our table's right over here."

She couldn't drag her gaze from Cooper. But she wasn't going to him, either. Despite what *hadn't* happened last night, she needed to play this cool. So, she cocked a brow and hitched a hand on her hip.

One of the women wrapped her hand around Cooper's biceps, stood on her toes, and whispered in his ear. He said something to the women. All four of them whirled around and shot daggers at Danielle. A hint of a smile tugged on her lips. Watching the scene unfold was the most entertained she'd been in a long time.

He broke from the group, and a hit of adrenaline pounded through her.

One sexy step at a time, he made his way over to her, his cold glare slicing through her. "You owe me a dance, Danielle."

He hadn't said hello, he'd skipped the small talk, and he sure as hell wasn't smiling.

The cute guy hurried back over, as if protecting his turf. "She's sitting with me."

Cooper held out his hand. She regarded his large palm and thick digits before returning her attention to those hypnotic eyes. She felt the pull, his intensity, and his charisma enticing her forward.

All she'd have to do is take that step and slide her hand into his.

Do it.

Frozen in place, she could not budge.

He walked right up to her, peered into her eyes, and released a deep growl. "So damn difficult."

The energy surging between them stole her breath and her thoughts. All she could see was him, his beautiful face and powerful gaze. Every muscle, every cell was screaming out for him. It was a desperate, suffocating need that hijacked her entire being. Their connection was so immediate, it bordered on dangerous.

When he reached down and clasped her hand, every damn thing in her world shifted. Her heart skipped a beat, warmth soared up her arm. She loved the feel of their entwined fingers, his large palm dwarfing her smaller one. Despite his size, he clasped her hand with so much tenderness, she melted... just a little.

Danielle dragged her gaze to the other man. "Thanks for the offer to share your table, but I'm—"

"Unavailable," Cooper said with a commanding tone.

"Whatever," the guy said, before taking off in the other direction.

A slow song filled her ears as Cooper led her onto the dance floor. When he turned to face her, she went willingly into his arms. He enveloped her, like she belonged there... like she'd always belonged there.

She wrapped her arms around his muscular neck and sunk her fingers into his soft hair. His low, rumbling growl had her biting back a moan. Pressed against him, her body roared to life, like her Ninja motorcycle after a kick-start.

When she cast her gaze up at him, he was waiting. Cooper Grant up close was a jolt to her senses. Clear blue eyes peered into hers. His whiskey breath warmed her forehead, and his hard body pressed against hers made her feel like a woman.

The joyous feeling sent guilt plunging through her.

He must've felt her go tight because he slid his hand under her hair and gently rubbed her neck. "I got you."

Ohgod.

Never had anyone made her feel so safe and so utterly alive. Her head was spinning and her insides were a ball of coiled need.

And then, she was rewarded with a brief flash of his smile. Fast and bright, like when the sun peeks through the clouds and the warmth fills your soul. And then, the clouds close in, as if protecting their queen, and the sky goes gray and the day turns cold.

"You look beautiful, Danielle." The deep timbre of his voice made her knees weak.

"Thank you," she replied, her voice escaping in a whisper.

The love song came to an end, but he didn't let her go. She

didn't want to break away from him, but she couldn't stand there like a cling-on. If she did, she'd be no better than the adoring groupies following him around like puppies.

His lids were more hooded than she expected. "You ever line danced?" he murmured.

"No."

"Wanna learn?"

As she peered into his eyes, then flicked her gaze to his mouth, the ravenous urge to kiss him made her breath hitch. The rawness in his voice sent a quiver of excitement racing through her. She couldn't resist his invitation.

"Only if you're my teacher."

5

THE KISS AND THE CARDIO

COOPER

Cooper didn't care that Danielle had stood him up. He didn't care that his new job—and his cover job—would be monopolizing all of his time. In the moment, he didn't give a fuck about Salimov or Renfrow, either. All that mattered was the strikingly beautiful woman in his arms. Despite the upbeat tempo of the next song, he hadn't let her go. He couldn't stop staring at her, either. And, damn, she smelled good.

Danielle Fox up close was way better than all the times he'd checked her out at his gym.

Did she realize she was stroking his hair? Soft, gentle caresses. He'd turned hard and she hadn't moved away from him. Kinda hard not to notice his pocket stick.

The dance floor was too crowded for him to teach her a basic line dance and the music was too loud. "Come with me."

He led her off the dance floor and down the short hallway toward the restrooms. At the end of the hallway was an emergency exit. He stood in front of a scanner and the red light turned green. He pushed the door and gestured for her.

"Why are we going outside?"

"To dance."

She walked outside and he followed, the fire door closing behind them. The cool breeze felt great against his heated skin and he raked his fingers through his hair. The rear parking lot was well lit and quiet. Being alone with Danielle only turned up the heat, but he needed to keep his hands to himself and his body off hers. Frustration burned through him and his dick stood down.

"This is the cowboy hustle." With his backside facing her, he walked through the first basic steps, twice. Then, he glanced back at her. "Try it with me."

"Alright," she replied.

"Out in, out in," he said while moving his right foot, but this innocent dance step took on a whole new meaning around Danielle. Fighting the desire that was challenging his concentration, he spent the next few minutes teaching her the basics.

Once he'd done that, he pulled up a song on his phone and stood beside her. "Ready to line dance with me, cowgirl?"

A little smile lifted the corners of her mouth. "Yeah."

Together, they repeated the steps enough times so that they'd completed a full turn and were back to their original positions.

"You're a fast learner," he said, pausing the music.

"You're a good teacher," she murmured.

The energy swirled around them, the sultry sound of her voice tugging him closer. He took a step in her direction. Her breathing changed. Then, she turned to face him. That instant connection had him snaking his arms around her and pulling her tight against him.

On a soft moan, she kissed him, hard. With one hand cemented on the small of her back, he cupped her cheek in his hand and kissed her back. She opened her mouth and moaned into his, deepening their passionate embrace.

As their kiss continued, she ground against him, pressing her breasts into his chest. Normally in complete control, their kiss had rocketed him to the moon. One damn kiss and he was ready to bury himself inside her.

His phone rang in his pocket. *Fuck, fuck, fuck.* He wanted to ignore it, but as head of ALPHA, he could not.

He fished out his phone. It was Stryker. "Yeah," he answered.

"Where are you?"

"In the parking lot teaching Danielle how to line dance." The grittiness in Cooper's voice had him clearing his throat.

Stryker chuckled. "We thought you guys left. We're in Jericho's booth." The line went dead.

Cooper's hand was glued to Danielle's ass. She was staring into his eyes while caressing the back of his hair.

"That was Stryker." He leaned in to kiss her again.

She broke away. "I shouldn't have kissed you."

Agitation burned through him. "Why not?"

The passionate woman who'd been pressed close and stroking his hair had been replaced with an uptight Danielle, touting pinched brows and tight shoulders.

"I'm sorry." She tugged on the back door, but it was locked.

He stood in front of the scanner, the light blinked green, and he opened the door. Without so much as a backwards glance, she took off down the hall. In a few easy strides, he caught up with her, wrapped his hand around her arm, and gently pulled her to a stop.

"Danielle, dance with me."

"I gotta go."

The guy from earlier was headed toward the men's room. As he passed, he asked, "Hey, girl, is he giving you trouble?"

Danielle regarded Cooper. "No, he's fine."

"I've still got room for you at my table." This time, the guy offered Danielle his hand.

Cooper wanted to laugh. Dude was stealing his move, only, he didn't have a clue who he was dealing with. Though Cooper hardly knew her, as well, he could see that she was hurting. There was a time when he, too, pushed everyone away.

"No," Danielle said to the stranger.

On a shrug, he moseyed into the restroom.

Without another word, Danielle returned to Jericho's booth. The second Emerson saw her, she flicked her gaze from Danielle to Cooper. "Come sit with me," Emerson said.

"I'm heading home," Danielle replied.

Emerson pushed out of the booth. "I'll drive you."

"I'll take you home," Cooper said.

"Stay," Danielle said. "I'm fine, really."

She was anything but fine.

Emerson pushed out of the booth. "Danny—"

"I had fun with you, tonight." Danielle hugged Emerson, then regarded Stryker. "See you at work, boss."

Then, she slid her gaze to Cooper. "Thanks for the dance lesson." Without waiting for a reply, she left.

"I got this," Cooper said.

He made his way through the packed restaurant, catching Jericho's eye as he walked past the massive bar. Jericho tossed him a nod as Cooper pushed open the front door, leaving the noise, the heat, and the crowded club behind him.

Danielle was head down, tapping on her phone.

"C'mon," Cooper said. "My Jeep's right over here."

Sad eyes peered into his. Cooper didn't know the depths of Danielle's grief, but he did know his own. Despite that, he didn't want to push her, so he said nothing.

She closed the ride app on her phone. "Okay, thanks."

He purposefully didn't lay a hand on her as he led her to his vehicle. But he did open the door for her. As he walked around, his phone rang. This time it was an ALPHA operative.

"Cooper Grant," he answered.

"It's Slash."

"I'll call you back."

"When?"

"Fifteen." He hung up and got behind the wheel. Then, he glanced over at Danielle. "I need your address."

She took his phone, opened his nav app, and typed in her Alexandria address. When the driving directions started, she set his phone in the console tray.

On the short drive to her place, he stayed silent. If she had something to say, she would say it. He was hyperaware that she was inches away from him, yet emotionally unavailable.

Earlier, the hostess had told him she wanted to hook up with him. Not the first time he'd heard that. Years ago, he would have taken her up on her offer. Not anymore. Cooper Grant had become selective. His family told him the perfect woman didn't exist.

He wasn't looking for perfect. He wanted real and flawed. He wanted someone who took his breath away and left him craving more. He wanted smart, independent and interesting.

From where he was sitting, that woman was inches away.

He pulled up to her townhouse and parked behind her car in the driveway, with his Jeep jutting into the quiet neighborhood street. He pushed out, leaving his engine running, on purpose.

She headed up the walkway. After keying her lock and opening her front door, she turned back to him. "I had fun with you tonight. The most fun I've had in a long time." She rose up and kissed his cheek, letting her lips linger on his skin for an extra beat before pulling away.

Despite the anger and frustration that nipped at his heels every fucking moment of every single day, he breathed easier around her.

Rather than head inside, she hesitated for a few seconds.

Staring into her eyes cranked up the heat. He wanted her to invite him in. But fucking her was not the answer. He needed to leave. Now.

He stepped off her front stoop. "Take care of yourself."

On a nod, she walked inside, shut the door, and bolted it behind her.

His chest tightened as he hopped into his Jeep. Driving home, he returned Slash's call.

"I'm sooooo freakin' pissed," Slash said. "I spent the *entire* evening trying to make headway with a case, but I'm crap at hacking," she said. "Total crap. We need a cyber operative."

"When does Tom leave?"

"He left two weeks ago."

Right. "I'll talk to Providence Monday."

"Please, make it happen." She hung up.

He drove the rest of the way home thinking about Danielle. That kiss was the first of many. He was confident about that. She needed time, something he had very little of. But, for her, he would find some.

THE NEXT MORNING, Cooper swung through the drive-thru on his way to his mom and dad's. He street parked in front of their single-level home in Vienna, grabbed the food, and entered the house through the open garage door.

"Hey, guys, where is everyone?"

His dad came wheeling into the kitchen, his dad's close friend, Geoffrey Edelman, by his side.

"Hey, Coop." When his dad eyed the bags in Cooper's hand, he asked, "Extra hash browns?"

"Three," Cooper replied, setting the bags on the kitchen island. "Last time, I thought you and Chantal were never going to speak to me again."

"Hey, Geoffrey," Cooper said.

"How you doing?" Geoffrey replied.

Cooper looked like his dad, though Eric Grant's light hair had started graying. His dad's upper body was stronger than most men half his age and his abs rivaled Cooper's.

Also in his mid-sixties, Geoffrey Edelman was his dad's oldest and dearest friend, as well as Cooper's godfather. Geoffrey's short, silvery hair was never out of place. He sported a tan, a trim physique, and he always dressed in designer duds. Today, he wore a tweed sport jacket, dark blue shirt and black pants.

The two friends couldn't be more different. His dad had been an English Lit professor, then segued into running a successful home-based consulting business. Eric Grant put his family first—always had.

Geoffrey's great love? Money. He'd earned millions as a financial advisor, then millions more as a hedge fund manager. Nowadays, he was a philanthropist. He'd never married, and his romantic life was a never-ending revolving door. The women never stuck around for long, but Cooper never knew if it was their choice or Geoffrey's.

Geoffrey was like a second dad to Cooper. Back in high school, Geoffrey had taught Cooper the value of investing. Thanks to Geoffrey's financial tutelage, Cooper was a wealthy man.

Eric Grant rolled his wheelchair over to the kitchen counter, pulled on mitts, and opened the oven door, revealing a quiche, which he set on the island.

"Looks good," Cooper said. "Where's Mom and Chantal?"

"Mom convinced Chantal to go with her on her morning power walk. Mom's showering and I don't know where your sister is."

Chantal strolled into the kitchen. Her shoulder-length blonde hair was damp on the ends. She eyed the carry-out bags. "Dad, please don't hog the hash browns, this time."

"No worries," their dad replied. "Coop bought extra."

"Thank you, Cooper." His baby sister flashed him a sweet smile before pulling out the orange juice from the fridge and filling small glasses.

Cooper set mugs on the counter. "Dad, coffee?"

"Just a half, if we're headed to the gym."

"Yes, to the gym," Cooper replied as he poured coffee.

"Geoffrey?" He offered up a mug and Geoffrey took it.

Chantal set the table, but only after she set a box of hash browns on her plate, then smirked at their dad.

"My arms still work," he said, "and I can snatch that away from you."

Cooper's chest tightened. He appreciated that his dad had a sense of humor about being a paraplegic, but Cooper did not. Seeing his dad only reminded him of the worst day of their lives, and the years of pain, heartache and challenges that followed.

"You'd never do that because you're the best dad in the world," Chantal said. "Those hash browns are safe, I'm sure of it."

Chantal placed a box of hash browns on their dad's plate, then pulled out all the other food. "I love that we do this once a month."

Cooper's mom strolled into the kitchen. "Right on time." She kissed her son's cheek. "Please tell me you brought—" she eyed the food, still in their boxes and wrappers—"good job."

"Honey, more coffee?" Emily Grant poured herself a cup.

"I'm all set, dear," Eric replied.

"Chantal, why don't you come to the gym with Dad and me?" Cooper asked as he sat at the table.

"No thanks." His sister sat beside Geoffrey.

With the sliced quiche in hand, Cooper's mom eased into a chair. While everyone dug in, Cooper glanced at his sister. He wasn't surprised she declined his invitation. Chantal rarely left the house.

The conversations continued, but Cooper's mind kept jumping

to Danielle and their steamy parking lot kiss. He was hoping to see her at the gym, but he'd never run into her on a Sunday.

"Cooper, I've got a new business venture I want to talk to you about," Geoffrey said.

"Sounds great," Cooper replied, his thoughts still dwelling on Danielle.

"Unfortunately, I've gotta reschedule our lunch date this week," Geoffrey continued.

Cooper was up to his eyeballs with work, so he suggested they get together for dinner, instead.

"Dinner works," Geoffrey replied. "I'll text you some dates and we'll set it up."

When they finished eating, Geoffrey helped clean up. "I'm taking off." As was customary with Geoffrey, hugs all around, for everyone. "I know I say this all the time, but you're my family. Love you guys."

"We love you, too," his mom said, before Geoffrey showed himself out.

Not five minutes later, the door from the garage opened, and Tessa Grant scurried into the house. "Good morning, fam! I'm starving." She whizzed over and eyed the kitchen table. "Please tell me you saved me food."

Cooper's mom hugged her granddaughter. "Of course, we did."

She plunked down next to Chantal and grinned at her. "Hi, Auntie."

Chantal laughed. "Hey, niecey."

Tessa's gaze flitted around the table. "Hash browns?"

Cooper's mom set a box on her granddaughter's plate. "You want me to heat those for you?"

"Nope." Tessa popped up. "But I need ketchup."

Tessa had graduated college earlier that year, and lived in an apartment with two roommates, but spent a lot of her free time with her grandparents. Tessa's mom and dad had separated when her mom moved to Richmond for work last year, but her dad—Cooper's older brother by eight years—had stayed in Northern Virginia. They'd gotten married and had Tessa while in college. She had her mom's dark hair, her dad's light eyes and his height.

As a child of a Black woman and a White man, Tessa had first encountered racism in middle school when a boy made a derogatory comment at recess. During a Grant family dinner, a young Tessa had relayed their conversation.

She'd told the boy, "If you don't like me because I'm half Black and half White, that's on you. If you don't like me because I've been mean to you, that's on me."

"What did he say?" her mom has asked.

"My friends were waiting for me, so I ran to play with them. But it was on him, for sure."

As withdrawn as Cooper's sister had become in the past few years, his niece had always been the exact opposite. Outgoing, always positive, and brimming with confidence.

"Chantal and I are highlighting each other's hair, today," Tessa said between bites. "Then, you should come shopping with me, Auntie. My fave boutique is having a flash sale."

"I don't know," Chantal murmured.

"That sounds fun," Cooper's mom said. "You should go with Tessa, Chantal."

"What's the latest?" Cooper asked his niece.

"I got a new job," Tessa said. "No, wait, I already told you that. I've been working at Shannon's Shelters for three months."

"How's it going?" Cooper asked.

"I love it! The woman who runs them offers so many hands-on classes and workshops to help residents get back on their feet."

"Knowing you," Cooper said, "you'll be running those shelters before long."

Tessa giggled. "Oh, Chantal, we should sign you up for that dating site. I'm meeting so many guys."

"Tessa," warned Cooper's mom. "You be careful."

"I am, Gammy. But people don't date like they did when you and Pop Pop were young."

Cooper pushed out of his chair. "Dad, you ready to hit the gym?"

"All set." His dad wheeled over to his mom and kissed her, then regarded his daughter and granddaughter. "You two want to come with Cooper and me?"

"Nope," Tessa replied.

"I'm okay, Dad," Chantal said.

His sister was anything *but* okay, but Cooper had stopped pushing her a while ago.

Once outside in the driveway, Cooper asked his dad, "You driving, or am I?"

"You."

After his dad pulled himself into the Jeep, Cooper stored the lightweight chair, and slid in beside him. Cooper and his dad had always been close.

On the way to the gym, Cooper said, "So, I got a promotion at the job I can't talk about."

His dad chuckled. "Congratulations, son. I'm proud of you. What *can* you tell me?"

"I'm co-running the organization for a while."

"That was fast. What is it about you and management?"

"I know. I can't get away from it, but I'm still feet on the ground. Please don't say—"

"Coop, it pains me to keep anything from Mom, but I have never told her anything you confide in me."

"So, she still thinks I'm a virgin?"

His dad laughed. "I think she might have figured that one out on her own."

They drove for a few minutes in silence.

"I heard from my lawyer about Renfrow's parole," his dad said. "Denied."

"Good." Cooper didn't smile. Smiling meant a victory. Keeping Renfrow in prison was a necessity, like oxygen.

"At some point, he's going to be released, you know that, don't you?"

"No, I don't," Cooper replied.

"Why don't you let it go, son? I don't want to live with grudges, so I forgave Renfrow and set myself free."

Cooper pulled up to the gym, parked in a handicapped spot, and hung his dad's tag on the mirror. "I don't live in the past. The past lives in me. I can't unsee that day, no matter how much therapy I've had and how relieved I am that you're living your best life. The hatred drives me forward. I feel like I'm living life for me *and* for Alan."

"That's a burden he would never want for you."

Cooper was done talking. He wanted to take his frustration out on a punching bag, or escape reality by climbing a damn rock wall. He opened the Jeep door and turned back to his father. "I love you, Dad, but I'm not like you."

"You're more like me than you know."

Cooper pulled the chair from the back and opened it up. While his dad was independent and preferred to do things himself, he liked when Cooper helped him stand upright. Cooper stood like a statue while his dad used Cooper's shoulders to pull himself up. Seeing his dad standing tall always put a lump in his throat.

"You look good, Dad."

"I miss this." On a sigh, Cooper helped lower his dad into his chair. Once situated, he rolled himself toward the entrance. Cooper bit back the emotion, closed the car door, and followed his dad inside.

"Hey, guys," Naomi said from behind the counter. "There's my favorite member."

Naomi had managed the gym with the previous owner. When she'd expressed interest in staying on, Cooper accepted her offer. Cooper made changes that were more inclusive of people with physical challenges. Rather than increase membership fees, he paid for the changes himself.

"You changed your hair," his dad said. "Looks great."

Naomi had removed her cornrows and was sporting a stylish Afro. "Thanks, I love it. Your massage is in an hour," Naomi replied before addressing Cooper. "One of our kickboxing teachers had to cut back on his hours, so I'm trialing someone new for the beginner's class."

"Thanks for handling that," Cooper said.

He and his dad entered the weight room and the two men split up. Cooper had a lot of pent-up energy. No matter how much weight he lifted, he couldn't shake the monkey off his back. His thoughts jumped from Salimov to Danielle.

When father and son finished, they headed into the shower to rinse away the sweat, then on to the swimming pool. His dad could manage just fine, but Cooper liked to swim nearby. After his dad used the lift to lower himself in, he started swimming laps.

Cooper swam in the same lap lane. After several laps, his dad said, "Coop, please stop hovering."

"You told me I should never swim alone, so I'm not."

That made his dad smile before he swam away.

Of all the workouts, Cooper was the worst at swimming. But he pushed onward, one stroke at a time. His dad, on the other hand, moved freely and with grace, his strong arms propelling him forward.

Breathing hard, Cooper pulled up beside his dad. "You're on fire this morning."

"It's a good day, so I'm taking advantage of it."

After swimming more laps than he wanted, Cooper pushed out, then turned around to check on his dad. He wasn't there. A jolt of anxiety had him scanning the area. His father had moved over to a different lane and was doing the breast stroke.

On a calming breath, Cooper toweled off. When his dad was done, he went for his massage while Cooper made his way to the rock wall. The one place where Cooper could finally let the tension go. There was something very freeing about climbing to the top of a structure. Here, there was no room for wandering thoughts. After harnessing himself in, he started climbing. One hand, one foot at a time, he made his way to the top. There were two different walls—one being steeper and more challenging than the other—and he got a good workout climbing both.

When he returned to the lobby, his chest warmed while his pulse kicked up. His dad was talking to Danielle. He glanced around for Naomi who was busy signing up a new member.

He checked her out before he could stop himself. Danielle was wearing a cut-off white T-shirt over a black sports bra and light, baggy sweat pants. Despite imagining Danielle naked a number of times, seeing her in workout gear was his hot button. All muscle—with abs of steel—and yet completely feminine at the same time.

"Here's my son," his dad said with a broad smile.

"Hi," Danielle said.

"We've met." Cooper hitched a brow. "Feeling better, today?"

As she nodded, a hint of a smile tugged on her full lips, sending a surge of desire powering through him.

Naomi joined them. "Danielle, I've got some paperwork for you to sign. Cooper, this is our new kickboxing instructor."

"This is *your* gym?" Danielle blurted.

"Fly the Coop is my baby," Cooper replied.

"I thought you worked for the FBI," she said.

"I left."

Danielle held his gaze for a few beats. "Why?"

"I wanted to own a gym."

As Danielle signed the forms, her lips curved upward. *What's so amusing about me leaving the Bureau?* Rather than push her, he let it go. The less he talked about law enforcement, the less he was questioned.

When Danielle finished signing, she said, "It was good to meet you, Eric." Then, she slid her gaze to Cooper. "You should offer a line dancing class for beginners and teach it yourself." With a wink, she left with Naomi. His gaze stayed cemented on her until she disappeared around the corner. When he turned back to his dad, he was grinning.

"Please, no, Dad."

"I haven't said a word," his dad protested.

As Cooper was driving his dad home, Eric said, "Do you know Danielle from the gym?"

"I met her through Stryker and Emerson. She's Emerson's best friend."

"What's her story?"

Cooper chuffed out a laugh. "Her *story*?"

"Yeah, what does she do? Is she seeing anyone?"

"She works for Stryker. I have no idea if she's seeing anyone." His thoughts drifted to their steamy kiss, how she felt in his arms, then, how she bolted on him. Maybe she was seeing someone. Tension ran down his back. He didn't like that, at all.

"Cooper? What do you think about that?"

"I'm sorry, Dad. Say it again."

"Why don't you find out if she's seeing anyone and ask her out? She was friendly."

"She's not friendly with me, but she sure is gorgeous."

"You need someone athletic, someone smart. And, of course, someone who wants children."

Cooper laughed. "Mom is completely chill about me finding someone."

"Who do you think puts me up to these questions?"

Cooper glanced over. "Seriously?"

"She thinks you're too picky, but I get where you're coming from."

"I'll let you know if I pursue things with her." Cooper turned into his parents' neighborhood.

"It never hurts to try," his dad said. "Trying and—"

"I know, Dad. Trying and failing is better than not trying at all."

As Cooper parked in the driveway, he wondered if his dad was right about Danielle. She was definitely the type of woman he should go after. If she was seeing someone or it didn't work out, at least he'd have an answer, rather than wondering "What if…"

DANIELLE

Danielle hadn't connected Cooper to her gym, Fly the Coop Extreme Sports.

A few months ago, she'd gotten an email that the gym had changed owners. She hadn't even bothered opening it. Up until a month ago, she'd stopped working out altogether because she wasn't in the right mental state, despite knowing that working out would put her in a better frame of mind.

When she'd seen him there before, she assumed he was a member.
I give him props for not boasting about it.
Then, she thought about all the upgrades he'd made, especially the ones that accommodated people with disabilities. He'd added braille signs everywhere, there were ramps galore, sliding glass doors in the front, the lift in the swimming pool, every television had closed caption turned on, and there were several additional handicapped parking spots near the entrance.

Her heart warmed at the changes he'd made.

She and Naomi entered the kickboxing studio and excitement coursed through her. She loved this cardio workout and couldn't wait to teach it. As she got busy wrapping her hands, she realized she needed to demonstrate the wrapping technique. Normally on auto pilot, she removed the wrap and set everything on the floor in front of her. She was excited that there were a few young people, some middle-aged, and a few seniors. Twelve students, total.

Naomi walked to the front of the room. "Hi, everyone. I'm Naomi, the gym manager. We've had a lot of interest in kickboxing, so Danielle Fox is going to be working with all of you going forward."

"What happened to the guy?" asked a man in the back.

"He's still on staff," Naomi replied.

"I don't want a female instructor," said the man.

"Sir, give me a chance," Danielle said. "If you don't like my teaching style, you can find someone—"

"Sorry, honey, but I'm out." The man collected his things and left.

"Let me tell you a little about my kickboxing background," Danielle began. "I started four years ago because I wanted to do something besides run. I'm afraid of heights, so climbing isn't for me, and I'm not a strong swimmer. I love working out with weights, but just to tone. My first kickboxing class was taught by someone who wasn't the right fit for me. She was too fast and didn't take the time to slow it down so we could learn how to kickbox the right way. When I found a different teacher, I fell in love with the sport. I hope you'll feel the same way."

Naomi offered an encouraging smile and returned to the back of the room.

Danielle set expectations, then added, "You know yourself and your physical limits. Do what makes you feel comfortable. This is our first class together, not our tenth."

She led them through a warm up, then jumped into some basic kicks and punches. Next, she added ten minutes of cardio that included jumping rope, jumping jacks, and push-ups. At the end, she led a cool down, then demonstrated how to properly wrap their hands. The fifty-minute class flew by. By the end, everyone was perspiring.

"I'll stick around for a few if you have questions," she offered.

After the students filed out, Naomi said, "Great job. How many classes can you teach?"

"My schedule's packed, right now, so just this one."

"Welcome to Fly the Coop," Naomi said with a smile. "Cooper will be thrilled you're on staff. I'll let him know the next time I see him."

Danielle would tell him herself. Now that she'd learned he wasn't with the FBI, she was going to make damn sure she saw him again.

As soon as possible.

6

A LITTLE LATE-NIGHT FUN

COOPER

Monday morning, Cooper was finishing up his first team meeting to a packed conference room.

"My takeaway is to make sure we bring a Cyber Operative on board ASAP," he said. "What else?"

He was met with silence.

"A couple of things about my management style," he said. "Open door. Twenty-four seven."

"He means that," Slash added. "I called him at midnight on Saturday and he took my call."

Providence popped her head in. "Good morning, everyone. Cooper, when you have a minute."

"We're done," he replied.

She waited while the team of eighteen filed out, then she eased down at the conference table. "How was your first staff meeting?"

"Good."

"Anything I need to know about?"

"We need a hacker," Cooper said.

"Yeah, it's on my list. Can the Operatives make due with our Internet Research team?"

"Not for hacking. Why don't you hire someone from Stryker's company?"

"I hate poaching, especially from my own cousin," she replied.

"It's one hacker. We don't even know if he's got anyone who's a fit. You want me to take the lead on this?"

"No, I'll call him, today." Providence paused. "I need you to take the lead on a case. I know you're stretched to the max, but it's important."

His stomach dropped. He didn't have time to take on another case. "It doesn't sound like I have a choice."

"I got a call from the White House." She leaned back, crossed her legs. "The Bureau was handling a case, but the President pushed it to ALPHA. One of his senior advisors was murdered, execution style, a few nights ago. This is the fourth murder with a similar MO in the past three months."

"Secret Service must be shitting themselves."

Providence smiled. "I'm sure they are, but from what I learned, the President isn't at risk."

Cooper flipped open his laptop and logged in to ALPHA. "I hung on to a few cases, but I'll reassign them."

"Who are you thinking of pulling onto your team for this one?"

"Herrera," he replied. "Slash or Emerson would be a strong addition."

She pushed out of the chair. "Thanks for taking this one on. I marked it Dead Man Talking."

"Thanks for hiring a hacker."

After Providence left, Cooper collected his laptop and empty water bottle before heading toward the lunch room. *I love my job, but I don't love that I'm gonna be married to it.*

While he should've been thrilled he was singled out to handle a case that was pulled from the Bureau, he wasn't. As far as he was concerned, it was one more psychopath that had to be hunted down and arrested—or eliminated. Killing someone didn't sweeten the pot for him. He'd seen too many innocent people get arrested for crimes they didn't commit, and too many guilty ones get away with their heinous acts over and over again.

Herrera moseyed in. "Hey, man, how's it going?"

"I got assigned a special case and guess who I picked to work it with me?"

Herrera pointed at himself with both thumbs. "You know I love working with you. You wanna give me access to it?"

"Give me a few," he said, filling his bottle. "I want to read through it, first."

After grabbing a sandwich from a nearby restaurant, Cooper returned to his office and reassigned all his cases, except Salimov, which he'd secretly taken with him when he left the Bureau. Then, he read up on his newest project.

The Dead Man Talking killer was good. So good, in fact, that there wasn't any evidence pointing law enforcement in any particular direction. One by one, he reviewed each of the four cases. The first victim was a CEO of a Maryland-based pharma company. The second was a DC college prof. Victim number three was the owner of a chain of hotels in the DMV. The latest victim was Stu Sisson, longtime politico and advisor to the President.

Three of the men were White, one was Black. Ages ranged from forty-five to sixty-three. They were all wealthy, all successful, and all active in their communities. On the surface, they looked like upstanding citizens, but as the afternoon ticked by, Cooper found that all four men had two things in common.

First, multiple women had accused each of them of sexual harassment and sexual assault. The agent who'd been working the case had learned that there'd been collateral damage. Numerous women had committed suicide, over a dozen had died from drug overdoses, a handful had been vilified in the press, and one had been stabbed to death, but her case had gone cold.

Second, the police had found a half sheet of crumpled computer paper shoved inside each victim's mouth with what appeared to be their typed confessions. They all started with, "I'm a dead man talking." The killer also included victims' names, the crimes the men had been accused of committing, and links to chat rooms where victims connected with each other.

"I've got a vigilante on my hands," Cooper grumbled before picking up his desk phone and calling Emerson.

"I need you to work a serial killer case with me and Herrera," he said.

"Aren't you supposed to be managing us?" Emerson asked.

"Providence asked me to take lead on this one."

"Whatcha need?"

"I'll give you access to the file. It's called, Dead Man Talking. Are you in, tomorrow?"

"All day," she replied.

It was almost six and he couldn't spend another minute sitting. "I need to blow off some steam. You guys using your gym membership?"

"Stryker and I go early in the morning," Emerson replied. "I'll review the file tonight."

"Enjoy the light reading. No real leads, but we'll catch him."

On the way out, he stopped in Herrera's office, but he'd already left. He typed out a text. "Can you meet me and Emerson tomorrow to discuss the case?"

Dots appeared, then a reply. "Afternoon works," Herrera replied.

"I gave you access," Cooper texted. "Case is Dead Man Talking."

Herrera replied with a thumbs-up emoji.

Cooper jumped in his Jeep and headed for his gym. After an intense workout with weights, the treadmill, and an exhausting kickboxing class, he left. He needed to do payroll, but not until he had something to eat. And take-out wasn't gonna cut it.

He pulled into his garage, cut the engine, and headed inside. His home was his sanctuary. He'd purchased an older home in McLean and had spent the past few years renovating it. He loved doing the work himself, especially when he didn't have a clue how. He'd watch videos, talk to employees at the hardware store, and teach himself.

After a quick shower, he fired up the grill on his back deck. Then, back inside for food. He sliced zucchini, halved asparagus, and chopped scallions, then tossed them, plus a handful of cherry tomatoes onto a piece of foil, drizzled avocado oil over everything, then wrapped them up. He placed the vegetables, along with four chicken thighs, onto the flame. Back in the house for potatoes. One sweet, one Russet. After heating them in the microwave, he tossed those on the grill.

He popped open a cold brew and drank down half the bottle.

With his dinner cooked, he opened his laptop. As he ate, he returned work emails. At ten o'clock, he was back at the gym doing payroll. On his way out, he ran into a member whose name he could never remember.

"Hey, Cooper, you're here late." She fell in line with him as he made his way toward the front desk.

"Did you take a class tonight?" he asked.

"Rock climbing for beginners. You wanna hang out sometime? Grab a beer or chill at my place?"

"Thanks, but work is slamming me pretty hard."

"Do you have another job or something?"

Cooper wasn't used to keeping his real job a secret. *Way to go, dummy.* "I'm a... a health consultant," he lied.

As he passed the front desk, Naomi waved him over.

"Cool. Can I hire you?" she asked.

"I work with companies." He flicked his gaze to Naomi, but the member stood there grinning up at him. Wasn't the first time he'd gotten hit on at his gym. "Have a good night."

When she left, Naomi pulled a small package from under the desk. "For you."

The return address was a P.O. box in DC. "Everything okay, today?" he asked her.

"All good. Membership is slowing, so I'm going to mock-up a few ads to bring in new clientele. I'll run the budget by you for approval."

"Sounds good."

"Hey, Danielle," Naomi said. "Good class?"

Cooper glanced over his shoulder and a surge of adrenaline had him biting back a moan. *Whoa, she's hot.* Her skin glistened with sweat, her face was flush with color, and her long hair had been pulled into a messy ponytail. Heat traversed his chest while he soaked up her beauty. Seeing her had fast become the best part of his day, hands down.

I gotta spend some time with her.

"How ya doin'?" he asked her.

"Brutal kickboxing class," she replied.

The instructor walked over, his gym bag slung over his shoulder. "Great job, Danielle." Then, he tossed Cooper a nod. "You were smart to bring Danielle on board as an instructor. She's got wicked kickboxing skills."

"Naomi gets the credit for Danielle," Cooper replied.

The instructor headed out and Naomi said, "I'm gonna check the club for stragglers."

"You want help?" both Danielle and Cooper asked.

"I'd love some," Naomi replied. "Cooper, if you can check the men's locker room, and Danielle, if you want to check the rock-climbing room, that would be great."

Naomi locked the entrance and the three of them took off. As if drawn to each other, Cooper and Danielle fell in line. "You wanna climb a wall?" Cooper asked.

"No way," she replied.

He stopped in front of the men's. "I'll meet you in the rock room." He flashed her a smile before heading inside.

After confirming the restroom and locker room were empty, he told Naomi she could take off. "I'm gonna rock climb with Danielle."

He entered the rock room to find Danielle staring up at the massive structure. Another jolt of energy careened through him. He studied the sexy curve of her ass, the way her mussed ponytail hung lopsided down her back. His reaction to her was off the fucking charts.

"Climbing is an adrenaline rush, but it's the perfect escape. No room for daydreaming." He held out a harness.

Fear flashed in her eyes and she backed away. "I'll watch you."

"Watching isn't doing."

"I keep both feet on the ground."

After harnessing himself up, he climbed several feet, then turned back. "The view is great up here. You sure you don't want a lesson?"

"View's pretty good from down here," she replied. The unexpected playfulness in her voice had him climbing back down. The pull to be near her was much stronger than his need to climb a wall.

"Come here," he commanded.

Her gaze darkened as she made her way over. "Put your hand on the rock, but keep your feet on the ground."

"You're not gonna lift me up or anything, are you?" she asked.

"No, I don't mess around with climbing." He took her hand and another zing ripped through him. He wanted to pull her close and kiss her fingers, one at a time. Slowly, he guided her hand to the rock. With his hand over hers, he murmured, "Great job."

The intensity in her gaze had him grinding out a groan. Intense blue eyes stared up at him.

"My heart is pounding so hard right now," she whispered. "Just thinking about climbing freaks me out."

The energy passing between them was palpable, the desire to kiss her hijacking his thoughts. He leaned close, the desire burning through him.

"I can't stop myself," she whispered before plowing into him.

The explosion of desire had him groaning into her welcoming mouth. She wrapped her hands around his neck and she deepened the kiss. They pressed their bodies flush against each other while her throaty moan turned him hard.

There was something raw and untamed in the way they pawed each other. The sounds coming out of him were foreign, hungry sounds that he couldn't control. She was turning him into a savage beast. He broke away, gasping for breath.

"I need you," he said. "Need to pleasure you, need to be inside you. You're making me crazy."

Rather than back away, like she did from the wall, she lunged into him, thrusting her tongue into his mouth while she raked her fingers through his hair.

"Same," she whispered.

Cooper slowed them down, then pressed his mouth to hers in a long, tender kiss. "I want to fuck you, right now, but that's not happening."

"Ohgod, why not?"

"I don't have condoms, but I don't need one for what I'm about to do."

She ran her fingers down his whiskered cheek. "What did you have in mind?"

"You, coming in my mouth."

She shuddered in a sharp breath. "Oh. My. God."

"Is that a yes or a no?"

"It's a definite yes, but where?"

Cooper jumped on his phone. "The surveillance cameras are off in here." Then, he flicked his gaze to her. "Take off your pants."

DANIELLE

Danielle was trembling with anticipation, her insides burning with desire. She was completely turned on by Cooper, but she didn't do hookups. Ever.

What would Claire-Marie do? She'd go for it and have zero regrets.

"I don't want you to think this is more—"

He stopped her with another searing kiss, the kind that turned her panties wet. Her moans were guttural and desperate, breathing jagged. The kiss continued, his tongue firm and hard one minute, soft and tender the next. And those lips... Cooper Grant was the absolute best kisser.

When he slowed the kiss down, she broke away, panting hard.

"You take my pants off me," she demanded.

Cooper knelt in front of her and her heart stuttered. He was male perfection. Handsome, cool, sexy, strong...and he was kneeling at her feet. He removed her shoes, but left her socks on.

Her heart was pounding out of her chest when he pressed his lips to her abs and kissed her. "You. Are. So. Fucking. Sexy."

As if he had nothing but time, he tugged down her sweats and ran his finger inside the edge of her panties. She was dying for his mouth on her, desperate to feel his hands on her body, while she turned over total control to him. He slid down her panties, then he helped her step out of her clothing. When he nuzzled between her legs, she whimpered.

"You smell good," he murmured.

Then, he stood, captured her face in his hands and kissed her. Slow, tender pecks, again and again. The tease had her insides throbbing for a release while she floated in his strong arms. To her disappointment, he didn't strip her bare. Her nipples were hard, aching and pushing against her sports bra. She wanted to tear off her T-shirt, rip off her bra and shove her nipple into his mouth. Then, she would take his cock inside her and ride him, hard and fast until she climaxed around his long, thick shaft.

Never before had she wanted to fuck someone with such a ferocious need.

"I cannot wait to taste you." The huskiness in his deep voice had her moaning again. "Lie down on the mat."

Finding her voice, she asked, "Don't you want me naked?"

He pulled her close and kissed her, then he placed her hand over his cock. "If you're naked, I'm naked *and* inside you. Your shirt stays on."

"Then, you take *your* shirt off," she said. "If I'm half naked, so are you."

His devilish smile slayed her. She kissed him, then pulled his shirt over his head. And she did what she'd been thinking about for months. She ran her palms down those glorious pecs and over the moguls of his abs.

After pressing her lips to his shoulder, she breathed him in. His scent was intoxicating. He was a man she could get lost in for hours and hours. She did not deserve this moment of happiness, of extreme arousal, but there he was. Broad chest, bulging biceps and beautifully sculpted triceps.

She ran her fingers down his shoulders, then around to his back. More hardened muscles beneath warm, smooth skin. Her insides ached for him in a way that scared her. Their connection was electrifying.

"Do I pass the Danielle inspection?" She loved the playfulness in his voice.

"The top half of you barely squeaks by, but I can't make my final evaluation until I can see your bare ass."

He chuffed out a hearty laugh. "Next time."

"No," she blurted. "No next time. This is a one off—"

Another panty-melting kiss stopped her. When he had her panting with uncontrollable need, he scooped her into his arms and laid her on the mat. With a lustful gleam in his eyes, he said, "I've been imagining this for a while… a long while."

He positioned himself between her legs, nudging them apart. She bent her knees and propped her head on her arm so she could see. Cooper Grant between her legs was a fantasy she wanted to remember.

Lowering his face, he pressed his mouth to her belly and kissed her skin. One kiss at a time, he made his way down to her core. The throbbing between her legs was overwhelming. Desperate to touch him, she reached down and caressed his shoulder.

He peered into her eyes one more time before he ran his tongue over her swollen nib. She moaned, the pleasure of his warm breath and hot tongue so delicious. Then, he ran his finger along her opening, again and again, as if familiarizing himself with her folds, her femininity. The sensation sent tingles ripping through her and she spread her legs wider.

"You're going to make me come pretty fast," she whispered. "I'm kinda dying for you."

"Then, I'll make you wait while I tease your orgasm out of you." His voice had dropped, the throaty need sending desire spiraling through her.

He licked and fingered her, taking his time to swirl her clit with the slightest pressure from his tongue. As her excitement continued to build, her breaths came faster and she started gyrating beneath him. The growls and groans he pulled from her sounded foreign. His touch had turned her into a wild animal. When she fisted his hair and pushed his mouth against her, he began licking and sucking with fervor.

"Oh, Cooper, I'm gonna—" She cried out, shuddering and convulsing while wave after wave of ecstasy rocked her.

When she stilled, he murmured, "You are so fucking sexy."

Her eyes fluttered open. "Kiss me, Cooper."

He was on her, kissing her with a passion that had her

groaning, loudly. She wrapped her arms around him, fisting his hair while his erection pressed against her.

She wanted him in her mouth. She wanted him inside her, taking her over and over until she succumbed to the glorious pleasure all over again.

He slowed the kiss, finishing with a soft peck on her lips.

"Wow," she uttered.

"Yes, you are," he replied.

Danielle was flying high, soaring above the clouds, desperate to cling to this magical moment just a little longer. Reality was filled with guilt and loss and anger and vengeance.

After staring into his eyes, and soaking up all that male beauty, she whispered, "My turn."

Instead of rolling over, he pushed off the floor. She lay there staring up at him, his thick boner tenting his sweatpants.

What the hell?

"That was a gift," he said.

She stood, hitched her hands on her hips, stared into his eyes. "You don't want me?"

He placed her hand against his thick shaft. "I'm dying for you."

She caressed his cock. "Let me take care of you."

His guttural groan landed between her legs and she sucked down a breath. "This wasn't a hookup." He dipped down, kissed her. "Consider it a preview."

Her smile broke free. This was the first man who put her sexual needs above his own. "Thank you. No one's ever put me first."

He cupped her chin. "You will always come first." With a smirk, he collected her clothes.

She was beyond intrigued. Cooper Grant was different from any other man she'd ever met.

While they dressed, he asked, "Will I see you at Jericho's Halloween party on Saturday?"

"Maybe."

"Need a ride?"

After tying her shoes, she strolled toward the door and turned back to him. "I'll let you know."

Emerson had made sure she was on the list for Jericho's Halloween bash, but she hadn't planned on going. Now, there was no way she would miss it.

"You still owe me a line dance and a rock climb," he said as they walked toward the front desk.

Cooper turned the surveillance system back on before collecting the package from the front counter. She shouldered her gym bag as he set the alarm.

Once outside, he said, "Where'd you park?"

"In the lot."

"That's helpful." His sarcasm had her biting back a smile.

He walked her to her car but he didn't kiss her goodbye. Fine by her. They'd had a little late-night fun. No harm in that, and no need to read too much into it.

Back at home, she didn't rush to the shower. She wanted to keep Cooper's scent on her just a little while longer.

Though she didn't want to return to reality, she hadn't seen any online articles about Stu Sisson's murder, so she scoured the news feeds. As she skimmed headlines, she found one.

White House Advisor Killed in Home Invasion

Home invasion? This makes no sense.

Not only was it a lie, the article was little more than a blurb. There was no mention of the crumpled piece of paper or previous crimes with the same MO.

Why would they bury the murder?

And then, it hit her like a brick to the head. Even in death, law enforcement was protecting these powerful men while they worked quietly behind the scenes, searching for her. Danielle needed to watch her six, because there was no one else who would.

COOPER

On the drive home, Cooper's aching boner finally stood down. He'd have to relieve himself in the shower, which would be a pathetic second to being with Danielle. His reaction to her was insane. He couldn't control himself, couldn't stop staring at her. Had to touch her, kiss her, loved making her unravel beneath him. He was beyond attracted to her and was going full throttle to let her know he wanted more. And not just more sex. More time with her, more getting to know her.

It was after midnight when he pulled into his garage.

After dropping his keys on the counter and the gym bag on the floor, he eyed the package. The return address offered nothing more than a DC P.O. box. He slit open the box and opened the lid. The stench made him grimace. Inside the box was a decaying rat.

"What the fuck," he ground out.

Is this from Salimov?

7

THE INTERVIEW

DANIELLE

Danielle was busy at work, typing an email to her contact at the CIA, when her phone buzzed with an incoming text. She glanced over and a twinge of disappointment flitted through her. She'd hoped it was from Cooper. Two days had passed since their gym hookup and she hadn't gotten a single text from him. To be fair, she hadn't sent one, either.

"Hey, Danielle, it's Lori Shannon," Lori had texted. "I loved catching up with you at the reunion! Did you want to set a date to teach a workshop? We'd love to have you."

Danielle checked her schedule. "Sunday works for me," she texted back.

"How's one o'clock?"

"Perfect," Danielle replied.

"Sounds great. Our residents are going to love this!"

Knock-knock-knock.

Stryker stood in her office doorway.

"C'mon in," Danielle said.

After shutting her office door, he eased into the chair. "How's it goin'?" The divot between his brows was deeper than usual. Popping in to chat was not his thing.

"Whatcha need?"

"A hacker," he replied.

"Well, you've come to the right place." She did not have a clue what he was talking about, but rather than pummel him with questions, she sipped her iced tea and waited.

"You're one of the best hackers I've ever known and one of my smartest hires." The skin on the back of her neck prickled. *Is he about to fire me?* "I'm providing a short list of potential hires for a company that's looking to bring a hacker on board."

She released the breath she didn't realize she'd been holding. "Oh, sure. I can make a few recommendations."

"I was thinking of you," he replied.

"*Me*? What are you talking about?"

Knock-knock-knock.

"Come in," Danielle replied.

One of the receptionists from the first floor poked her head in. "Sorry to interrupt, but Mr. Grant is here to see you."

"Is he downstairs?" Stryker asked.

"No, I brought him up. He's in the conference room."

"Give me a coupla minutes," Stryker replied.

"Actually, he's here to see Danielle."

Danielle's heart skipped a beat. "Can you escort him down here in a few minutes, please?"

After a tight nod, the employee shut the door.

"Let me get to the point," Stryker said. "I'm recommending three people for this job, and you're one of them. Before you pass because it sounds like a step backward, it's not. I'd hate to lose you, but you deserve this opportunity. I'm confident you'd bring a lot of value to this group."

"Okay." Danielle was still lost. "Can you tell me *anything*?"

"The organization is run by two people I trust completely and the work they do is interesting, relevant, vital to the country's safety, and can be dangerous."

The last word caught her ear and she perked up. "Dangerous how?"

"You'll learn more tomorrow."

"Is it local?"

"Tysons."

"Who else are you recommending?"

"I can't say. And you can't discuss this with anyone."

She raised her eyebrows. "You didn't need to say that."

Stryker chuckled. "Right. You're tight lipped."

"When's the interview?"

"As early as tomorrow, if you're interested."

Danielle wasn't interested, but she was curious. She loved working at Truman CyberSecurity, but if she declined, she'd never know what she'd passed up. And she might even love the new job more. "I'll speak to them."

"I'll text you the address. What time works for you?"

"Ten. Thanks for thinking of me."

Tap-tap-tap.

"Come in," Danielle said.

Cooper breezed inside holding a giant bouquet of flowers. Danielle's brain shorted while butterflies fluttered in her belly. The effect he had on her was mind blowing. Normally chill around guys, heat warmed her cheeks.

The instant they locked gazes, his turned primal. She tried not to gawk, but Cooper in those tailored threads was the best eye candy she had ever seen. He rocked his dark, blue suit, white dress shirt, and bright pink tie. The tailored clothes clung to him, accentuating his best parts.

He has no bad parts. That man is total male perfection.

Stryker pushed out of the chair and extended his hand.

"Yo, bro," Cooper said, clasping Stryker's hand and pulling him in.

"You didn't have to bring me flowers," Stryker said.

Cooper laughed. "Idiot." He turned his full attention on Danielle. "Got a minute?"

"Sure," she replied.

At the door, Stryker glanced back at Danielle. "I'll text you the info." He shut the door, leaving her alone with Cooper.

She glanced from his eyes to his mouth. *So freakin' handsome.* Needing to be close to him, she sauntered around her desk. What she *really* wanted to do was jump in his arms and kiss him senseless.

Chill, woman.

With her gaze cemented on his, she said, "Do you want to sit? Or can I get you something to drink? We've got—"

He snaked his arm around her, pulled her close, and kissed her. Tingles exploded through her.

"I brought you flowers," he murmured, inches away.

"They're beautiful," she whispered. But she wasn't talking about the flowers. She was talking about his eyes. Clear and bright and intense. Exactly the way she liked them.

"Do you have a vase?" he whispered. His phone binged, but he ignored it.

"I'm sure there's one around here." She caressed his arm, appreciating how the suit hugged his massive muscles.

"Do you want me to take care of you? I mean…take care of the flowers for you?" He kissed her again.

He was teasing her…and it was working. Desire burned through her like a five-alarm fire. Her physical reaction to him was crazy good. She'd never been this loopy over a man in her life. She had to get control over herself, so she kissed him once, then stepped back. She hated putting distance between them, but, if she didn't, she'd be dry humping him in no time.

He offered her the bouquet.

"Thank you." She took it, pausing to appreciate his gift. It was an array of vibrant fall flowers. Peach and red roses, bright orange and yellow mums, and a smattering of green leaves. She pressed her nose to one of the roses and breathed deep. Her eyes fluttered closed as the delicious aroma flooded her senses.

"Smells so good," she said.

"Like you," he murmured. His phone rang and he slipped his hand into his pants pocket to silence it.

"I had fun the other night," she said.

"Me, too." His phone binged again.

"I had no idea gym owners were so busy," she said. "Or that they got this dressed up."

"I had a meeting. You coming to the gym, later?"

"Not tonight." She'd be busy researching her next target.

"I'll be there if you change your mind." He flashed a smile and, then, he was gone.

After a calming breath, she took several seconds to steady herself. Then, she headed to the break room in search of a vase.

She liked him enough to step out of her comfort zone and get to know this former lawman turned gym owner.

I like him... I like him a lot.

COOPER

Cooper had driven out the Dulles Toll Road for work, but he'd swung by Truman CyberSecurity to see Danielle. The moment he laid eyes on her, he couldn't resist the pull. Taking her in his arms soothed his demons, but it wasn't nearly enough. He wanted to whisk her away for the day, but the pressure to solve his latest case was monopolizing his every waking moment.

Once in his car, Cooper called Herrera back. "What's the word?"

"I talked to the university president," Herrera said. "The professor who was murdered had been accused of giving A's in exchange for sex. There're lawsuits, a student committed suicide, a bunch of them transferred. It's a total cluster. So much collateral damage."

"We're gonna have to interview everyone," Cooper bit out. "Everyone's a suspect until we start ruling them out."

"How'd you do at the pharma?" Herrera asked.

"Crash and burn. They're trying to distance themselves from the CEO. The VP claimed she had no idea what the CEO had been up to. She wasn't aware of the lawsuits. Their legal counsel was so damn tight-lipped. He kept telling me that it was a horrible tragedy and they wanted to move past it so they could focus on what they do best. Manufacturing health."

Herrera laughed. "Marketing at its best."

"They want to bury the problem because their stock took a nosedive."

"Their unwillingness to cooperate isn't helping us find the killer," Cooper said.

"No, it's not."

Cooper hung up and drove back to ALPHA thinking about the case. The victims had two things in common. The manipulative, predatory way they treated women, and the killer.

Then, his mind jumped to Danielle. He hadn't stopped thinking about her since their hookup at the gym. But he needed more than a sexual relationship and he wanted to make sure she knew that. As he pulled into the parking lot, he made a commitment to pursue Danielle with a vengeance.

Cooper spent the rest of the afternoon in the conference room with Emerson and Herrera. Herrera had taken the college prof and the pharma CEO— though Cooper had done the interview for him—Emerson had taken the hotel owner and was analyzing the video surveillance, and Cooper was following up on the murder of White House advisor, Stu Sisson.

They'd taped enlarged copies of the notes from the dead men's mouths onto a wall and were comparing them to one another.

"They all start with, 'I'm a Dead Man Talking,'" Emerson said.

"They each confess to crimes they'd previously denied," Herrera said. "And the list includes some of their victims, along with links to chat rooms."

Cooper compared the crime scene photos from Stu Sisson's condo to the crime scenes from the other three victims. Each man had been shot between the eyes. No casings found. No sign of a struggle or forced entry. Police reports noted that nothing had been taken. One of the victims—the hotel owner—didn't have a home surveillance system. The other three did, but their systems had been off at the time of their murders.

"Emerson, were you able to review surveillance from the traffic cams in the area?"

"There isn't any," she replied. "Not within a three or four block area of each victim's home. The cameras went dark for a three-hour period. That's when the men were killed."

"Seems like more than a coincidence, don't you think?" Cooper quipped.

"Any of Stryker's hacking skills rub off on you?" Herrera asked her.

"Unfortunately, not," Emerson replied. "But I'm working with Lily from the Internet Research Team. She's been pouring over the video from the surrounding area with me."

"Find anything?" Cooper asked.

"No," she replied. "It's super slow-going. Do you know how many Ford F-150s there are? A lot. There are Camry's everywhere, too. There's also the possibility that the killer switched vehicles, so that makes it even more of a challenge."

"I've got a meeting with the White House Chief of Staff, tomorrow," Cooper said. "I'm hoping he'll talk to me about Sisson."

"No one's willing to talk," Herrera said.

"They're afraid they're going to be accused of something, so they're distancing themselves from the victims," Emerson said. "You know, guilty by association."

"If we find the killer, we might not be the heroes," Cooper said. "If these men are guilty of all these crimes, the public could get behind the vigilante."

"Can you blame them?" Herrera said. "For the first time in my life, I'm not sure I want to catch him."

"I hear you," Cooper said, "but we have to follow procedure, no matter how we feel." He picked up a photo of Sisson. "We need to talk to the living victims, the women who accused these men. That's gonna take a while, too."

Cooper was adept at putting himself in the killer's shoes, thinking like they did and seeing the world through their eyes, but this killer was cunning and methodical, and left no traceable evidence. Though annoyed, Cooper never expected they'd solve this anytime soon.

He was headed to his car when Providence caught up with him. "I've lined up interviews tomorrow for a hacker."

"That's great."

"Will you be around? I'd love your thoughts on the candidates."

"What time?"

"Ten, twelve, and one thirty."

"Maybe the last one," Cooper replied. "I'm at the White House in the morning."

"Good luck, tomorrow."

"We're gonna need way more than luck to catch this killer." Cooper jumped in his Jeep and headed straight to his gym, where he pushed himself, hard, in the lap lanes. Back and forth he swam, hoping to burn through the frustration. Not tonight, though. The serial killer was out there, probably hunting his next victim, and Salimov was dropping women behind dumpsters and getting away with it.

If he got word that Salimov would be alone, again, he'd go

after him. If these women could end up dead, why couldn't Salimov?

After beating the hell out of a punching bag, then climbing both rock walls in search of his Zen moment—but not finding it—he checked the kickboxing room for Danielle. When he struck out there, too, he bolted.

At home, he dug his burner phone out of his safe and made a call.

On the third ring, the woman answered. "Hello, Cooper."

"Anything new on Salimov?"

"No small talk? Aren't you going to ask me how I've been?"

"You answered, you must be alive."

Her smoker's chuckle was thick with phlegm. "I'm sorry you and I haven't gotten closer over the years."

He had no interest in cozying up to a longtime informant. "I need information, Marta. And you're looking to get paid for that information. Our relationship is simple, let's keep it that way. I'm short on time—"

"You can't rush the art of seduction," she said. "Salimov was supposed to go to Russia, but he didn't. All I know is that it wasn't a good time for him to fly back."

"What else?"

"He mentioned taking a cruise around the holidays."

"Big fucking deal." This call was a total time suck.

"It might be," she bit back. "He's motivated by money and sex. When I find out which, I'll call you."

"I need to know the next time his fucking entourage isn't holding his dick."

"Don't hold your breath. His schedule is heavy with embassy events and he never goes alone."

"What about his club?" Cooper pressed.

"Two women were killed there, so he's not going back for a while."

"Find out where he's hanging out *now*. Can you do that?"

"Cooper, relax. I'll ask around. Maybe we get together for a drink?"

"Just get me that info." Cooper snapped the burner shut and headed downstairs to the kitchen to fire up his laptop. *That was a waste of time I don't fucking have.*

As acting head of Ops, he needed to know about every active mission. After jumping on to ALPHA's secure site, he skimmed the files. There were dozens, but two caught his eye.

EXTERMINATORS
BLACK OPS

Cooper opened the Exterminators file. As he read through it, his brain shorted. "No fucking way."

<u>Execution-Style</u>
Sinclair Develin
Dakota Luck
Stryker Truman – Will partner with Operative Emerson Easton

<u>Snipers</u>
Jericho Savage

There were other people on the list he didn't know, but he couldn't get past the ones he did. Dakota co-ran ALPHA, so no surprise there. Seeing Sin's name wasn't a shocker, either. The brothers were extremely close.

But Stryker?

Muscles running along Cooper's shoulders tensed. He and Stryker had been friends since grade school. *You think you know someone.*

Stryker had mentioned that he helped his cousin Providence with occasional hacking. He never said *anything* about being an

Operative. Everything at ALPHA was on a need-to-know basis and, clearly, Cooper didn't need to know.

Well, I fuckin' need to know now.

There were links associated with each Operative, so Cooper clicked on Stryker's and read about a serial rapist in Portland, Maine that he, Dakota, and Sin had taken out. These men were titans of industry by day and ruthless killers when the sun went down.

His chest tightened with betrayal. He'd been with ALPHA for six months and Stryker hadn't said a word to him. Not one fucking word.

He'd learned Jericho was an ALPHA sniper days after Cooper had started working there, but not because he'd bumped into Jericho at HQ. Jericho had told him because Jericho's loyalty was second to none.

Never had he suspected Stryker capable of being an assassin.

Welcome to a very elite club, Cooper.

He would confront Stryker when he wasn't so damn angry.

Pushing out of the chair, Cooper strode to his built-in liquor cabinet and pulled out a bottle of Pappy Van Winkle and a lowball glass. After pouring two fingers' worth, he tossed it back, appreciating the raw burn down to his guts. He poured more of the luxury bourbon and returned to his laptop. As he sunk onto the cushioned stool, he clicked on the **BLACK OPS** file. A window popped up.

Access Denied

Curiosity had him trying to access the file a different way. Again, he was denied.

It was after midnight. Despite the late hour, he continued reading about some of the other missions his friends had handled over the years. Little by little, the fury lifted. If these exterminators could kill the worst of the worst, why couldn't he?

Going forward, there'd be nothing—and no one—to stop him from taking out Salimov.

To make things easier, he would hunt him alone.

Fueled with determination, he cloaked his IP address and got to work. Killing Ivan Salimov had just become his number one priority.

I'm coming after you, Salimov, and I'm gonna take you out myself, execution style.

DANIELLE

At nine forty-five in the morning, Danielle pulled up to ALPHA MEAT PACKING and stared at the signage.

Are you for real? This has gotta be a joke.

But Stryker wasn't a prankster. The job opportunity had to be legit. She had no idea why a meat packing company would need a highly qualified hacker.

I'll tell them it isn't the right fit, then get to the office.

The large warehouse structure had front-facing reflective windows and a locked front door. She rang the doorbell and identified herself to the woman on the other end of the intercom. The door clicked, she crossed the threshold, and entered the blandest reception area she'd ever seen.

"Welcome to ALPHA," said the receptionist. "Ms. Luck will be out shortly."

As in, Lady Luck? I could use some right about now.

There was no artwork on the walls, no company brochures or business cards on the counter. She glanced over the counter at the receptionist's workspace. No photos, no papers of any kind. Just an open laptop.

She was the only guest, but that didn't come as a surprise. No one else from TCS would be stupid enough to bother with this interview.

A few moments later, a tall, pretty woman with short hair and a friendly smile walked over.

"Hello, Danielle, I'm Providence Luck. So good to meet you."

She seems nice enough. Maybe the HR screener?

Providence led her down a short hallway and into a nondescript office. Two executive desks faced each other. One was completely bare, the other had a closed laptop on it. There were no pictures, no books, no artwork on the walls. Another bland room.

Too weird.

Providence closed her office door. "Let's sit at the conference table."

There was an NDA on the table and a ballpoint pen.

After they sat, Providence said, "Stryker speaks very highly of you. Before I can tell you anything about the position, I need you to sign this." Providence slid the paper in front of Danielle.

"Ms. Luck—"

"Providence."

"Providence, I appreciate Stryker's recommendation, but this isn't the right fit. I'm not sure what kinds of meat you process here, but I have to pass."

"I felt the same way," Providence said with a knowing smile. "Sign it, then we'll chat. If after five minutes, you're still not interested, I'll walk you out. Is that fair?"

Danielle liked Providence. She was convincing without being pushy. As she signed the NDA, she asked, "What do you do here?"

"We're a top secret, quasi-government operation that hunts down America's most dangerous criminals or fugitives."

Those words had rolled off Providence's tongue so swiftly that Danielle needed an extra second to let that sink in. "So, no meat?"

Providence chuckled. "No meat. Our Operatives' primary

targets are serial murderers, rapists, and child molesters. You know, the real slime of society. We either arrest them or take them out."

Danielle just stared at her. "I'm sorry, do you mean your Operatives kill them?" She wanted to laugh, then run like hell. She'd just killed Stu Sisson. Murder number four made her a serial killer. She'd love to get a look at *their* most wanted list.

"Yes, sometimes."

This was surreal. "And you're looking to hire a hacker?"

"That's right. We had one, but he retired. We have a very proficient Internet Team, but they aren't hackers. We really need about five, but we don't have the budget for that. Stryker said you're one of the best hackers he's ever met, and a great manager. He doesn't want to lose you, but he's always been very good to me."

"How do you know him?"

"He's my cousin, but we're like siblings. When we were kids, he moved in with my family."

"I'm pretty surprised," Danielle said. "I wasn't expecting anything like this."

"No one ever is," Providence said with a hint of pride in her voice. "We're one of the country's best-kept secrets. We've got close to twenty Operatives, a small team of Internet researchers, and a few other management types. Technically, we're a part of the Department of Justice, but you'll never find us on an org chart. We report directly to the President."

"Who would I be working with?"

"All the Operatives, but the head of Ops would decide which cases were higher priority."

"Travel?"

"Not at this time."

"What about a trial period, so if things didn't work out, I could return to TCS?"

"I can't do that." Providence's desk phone rang and she excused herself to answer it. "Everything okay?" She listened. "I'm in the middle of an interview, so I can't answer that. The news article said Sisson died in a home invasion." She listened again. "Yes, that's a good idea. We'll talk when you get back here."

Danielle's heart was thumping out of her chest. She had to land this job to ensure she *wasn't* caught.

There was no other option.

"Sorry about that," Providence said, sitting back down. "Where were we?"

"I'm very interested in being considered for the position. As much as I love working at TCS, I'm ready for a change. What would you like to know about my hacker skills?"

An hour later, Providence concluded the interview.

"How can I follow up with you if I have questions?" Danielle asked.

Providence retrieved a business card from her desk drawer. "My cover is my marketing company. I check email and phone messages regularly."

Providence Luck
Luck Marketing

There was a phone number and an email address, along with a website.

"Would I have a cover?" Danielle asked.

"Absolutely. Every employee has one. Let me walk you back to our *very upscale* lobby."

Danielle appreciated Providence's humor as she was escorted out.

"I hope you decide I'm the best fit and would make a good addition to your team. If not, I appreciate your time and wish you the best." After a strong handshake, Danielle left.

If she got the job, she'd be on the inside. If she didn't get hired, at least she now knew what she was up against. The best of the best hunting the most dangerous criminals in the country.

And I'm one of them.

8

SWANKY

COOPER

Cooper's White House meeting with the Chief of Staff had been pushed back, but while he waited, arrangements had been made for Cooper to talk with someone from the President's legal team. That meeting had been another dead end.

Two hours later, Cooper was ushered into the Chief of Staff's office. "Craig O'Leary. It's good to meet you, Mr. Grant."

Cooper shook O'Leary's hand. "You, as well," he said, easing into one of the leather chairs across his desk.

The office was very formal with photos, awards of appreciation, law books and a tall stack of folders and papers on a side table. For all Cooper cared, they could've met on a park bench. He was there to find out about a dead man who reported to the President, and the controversy surrounding the note in Stu Sisson's mouth.

"Mr. O'Leary, I'm following up on Mr. Sisson's death."

"Tragic what happened, wasn't it?" O'Leary pressed a buzzer on his desk. "Can I get a pot of coffee and two mugs, please?" He eyed Cooper. "Cream or sugar?"

"Nothing for me."

"Just one mug," O'Leary said. "Hold my calls for ten."

Ten damn minutes wasn't going to help move Cooper's case along.

"We appreciate that ALPHA has taken over this case," O'Leary said. "We've managed to keep this story from blowing up in the press. A staffer wrote a very vague press release characterizing it as a random home invasion. The less the public knows about this, the better. You know what I mean?"

"Why don't you tell me what you mean?" Cooper asked. "Just so that I'm clear."

"The President's approval ratings are strong right now. We're heading into midterm elections with the House. If the details of Sisson's murder get out—and I'm sure they will, because no one in this city can keep their damn mouths shut—we're concerned his ratings will plummet. He wasn't personally close to Sisson, but Sisson *was* part of the President's inner circle."

"What can you tell me about Mr. Sisson? His conduct at work, his character?"

"Not a damn thing."

Tap-tap-tap.

The door opened, a man entered with a carafe and a mug on a tray. He filled the empty mug with coffee and left, closing the door behind him.

"So, you never saw Sisson behave inappropriately around a staffer?" Cooper pressed.

"No."

Cooper's patience was being tested. "Did he say anything unprofessional, insulting, out of line?"

"Sometimes, he would make a joke that he found funny, but others didn't. He was one of several senior advisors. Sisson's area was the economy. It's a dry subject, Mr. Grant. He would offer his counsel and he would leave."

Cooper studied O'Leary. He could've been lying, but how the

hell would he know? He'd met the man five minutes ago. He had no idea who was friendly with whom and he didn't have the time to try to extract information from a man who claimed to know nothing.

"Who can I speak with about Sisson's conduct and his character?"

"Jeri is his—*was*—his longtime assistant." O'Leary thumbed through his phone, then made a call. "Jeri, it's Craig O'Leary. I have a gentleman here from—" O'Leary regarded Cooper.

"FBI," Cooper said.

At least he knew not to blurt out "ALPHA".

Since ALPHA Operatives couldn't disclose their organization, they were issued IDs for most of the federal government's three-letter agencies. For this investigation, he needed his FBI badge, which he found ironic. He'd left the FBI, only to use his FBI badge to hide his true line of work.

"I have an FBI agent asking about Stu," O'Leary continued. "Would you have a few minutes to talk to him? Great, I'll send him over." O'Leary hung up and brought Cooper into the hallway, pointed him toward Jeri's office, and shook his hand.

"Sorry I couldn't be more help. I hope you catch the guy."

With help like this, we're never gonna find him.

Cooper made his way through the busy White House hallways to Jeri's office. She greeted him with a tight smile. "Have a seat," she said.

"Cooper Grant, FBI." He flashed his badge and she nodded in acknowledgment. "I'm investigating Mr. Sisson's death."

"I worked for him for twenty-four years. We kinda grew up together."

"What can you tell me about his character?"

Jeri shut her office door. When she returned to her chair, some of the color had drained from her cheeks. "I read the press release by our communications team about his murder being a result of a random home invasion." She shook her head. "That's a cover up."

Finally.

Cooper leaned back, crossed his ankle over his thigh. "What do you know?"

"Stu was a ladies' man." She straightened her glasses. "The first year I worked for him, we slept together. Once. It was a mistake and I resigned the next day. He told me that he regretted what had happened, but he asked me to stay. From that point forward, we were a team. It's like what happened had bonded us." She shrugged. "Makes no sense, but that's the way it was. Over the years, I noticed he was flirty with female staff. Sometimes, he'd say something that was inappropriate. It went on like that for decades. One evening, about" —she paused— "three, maybe four years ago, I had to stop by his condo to drop off some papers. He wasn't alone and the woman wasn't his wife. I didn't ask him anything, but the next day, he told me he'd been interviewing her for an internship."

"You didn't believe him?"

"He was wearing a silk lounging robe and silk pants. Plus, they'd been drinking. No, I didn't believe him."

"Did you ever see that woman again?"

"Yes. She got an internship, but I don't think it lasted. In recent years, the climate has changed. Women have become more empowered. They refuse to be silenced." Jeri smiled. "I'm happy to see the world continues to evolve."

"Are you speaking in generalities or about things here in Mr. Sisson's office?" Cooper's phone rang and he silenced it.

"There were threats of lawsuits. One came in, then several more. There was a seven-month period when it felt like there were new ones every day. They were all settled out of court. A few didn't materialize."

"Can you provide me with any names?"

Jeri shook her head. "Unfortunately, no. The lawsuits were passed on to the legal team. I do know that those women had to sign NDAs."

"Can you speak off the record?" Cooper pushed.

"There was one woman. I'll never forget her. Abigail Spencer. She refused to sign the NDA and she sent a few threatening letters to Stu."

"Did you read them?"

"I did."

"And?"

"She threatened to expose him for sexual assault, claiming that their relations weren't consensual. That he drugged her and had sex with her."

"What happened to Ms. Spencer?"

"I don't know."

"I appreciate your talking to me." Cooper jotted his phone number down for her. "If you think of anything else—"

She stood. "I don't know what happened between Stu and all those women. I hope you find out."

Before leaving the White House, Cooper typed several notes on his phone. Sounded like there might have been a long list of women who wanted revenge against Sisson. While one of those women could be Sisson's killer, it didn't mean she'd killed the other three men.

By the time Cooper arrived back at ALPHA, he was convinced that the killer was going after powerful men who were above the law or untouchable, and the only way to stop them from committing these crimes was to murder them.

How the hell am I supposed to find a vigilante if I don't know his method for finding his victims?

Cooper entered the building and made his way over to the Internet Team. The six-person crew spent most of their days hunting for information online. It was tedious, but it was much faster than doing it the old-fashioned way. On foot.

"Hey, Cooper, whatcha need?" Lily asked as he sat in the chair beside her desk. "You want to fill out a work req?" She set a tablet on the corner of her desk.

"No. There are hundreds of online chat rooms, right?"

"Thousands," she replied.

"If someone is going after perps who've gotten away with crimes against women, what types of chat rooms—"

"Victims' rooms."

"And there are probably ones specific to this area."

Lily held out the tablet. "Yes, I'm sure there are. Fill out the form and I'll see what I can find for you."

Cooper completed the request form. "How long will this take?"

She checked the main schedule. "A few days."

"Thanks for your help." Cooper returned to his office. He re-read the notes extracted from the victims' mouths and found Abigail Spencer's name on Stu Sisson's note, but none of the others. As he re-read each of them, he didn't see a single name that repeated.

I'm chasing a fucking ghost.

DANIELLE

At nine in the evening, Danielle approached the maître d' stand at the upscale members-only club and held her phone under the scanner. The light turned green and she sashayed out of the posh lounge and into the main dining room. Swanky was DC's premier club for the uber wealthy, and Danielle was there to stage a chance meeting with Ivan Salimov.

After hacking into his online calendar, she'd begun the daily ritual of monitoring his schedule. There were a lot of embassy-related events and other work-related functions. When he added Swanky to his itinerary, she hacked into the upscale club and created a fake membership for herself.

Dim lighting and soft music set the club's tone, while stunning artwork and expensive-looking sculptures were perfectly placed.

If Danielle had been there for fun, she would have admired the sparkly crystal chandeliers dangling from the ceiling and the small ones bathing every cozy booth in amber light. She would have appreciated the wood paneled walls that gave the club an old-style vibe, along with the stunning bar that had been buffed to a dazzling brilliance while smooth jazz floated down from hidden speakers in the ceiling.

But she was there to do a job, so after walking the entire restaurant, she found a seat at the corner of the bar in the main dining room that afforded her a bird's eye view of the main dining room and also of the hallway that led to the smaller, private rooms and restrooms.

Swanky also had a surveillance system, which she'd deactivated just before she'd left her house. According to Salimov's personal calendar, he was due to arrive at nine thirty.

Tonight, she was an eye-catching bombshell in a platinum updo. Smokey eyes, dark lipstick, and a tight, sparkly dress that accentuated her cleavage. She'd finished her look with her signature brown contact lenses and four-inch stilettos. Standing five feet eleven, she felt like an Amazon.

She ordered a sparkling water with lemon and kept her conversation with the bartender to a minimum. Danielle wanted to blend in. Calling attention to herself would only jar someone's memory when the police—or in this case, ALPHA—went looking for her.

She sipped her drink and glanced around while the room continued filling up.

Months ago, when Danielle first learned about victim chat groups, Salimov's name kept popping up. From what the women were posting, he was in a category of evil all his own. He loved women, but he did *not* love the word "No".

So, he did whatever he wanted to them and with them. His power and position allowed him to get away with it over and over again. He harassed women at the Russian Embassy, he harassed them at meetings, at his children's private schools. There were claims that he offered them career opportunities in exchange for sexual favors. Dozens and dozens of women accused him of rape. And there were hundreds of posted warnings. One in particular had caught her eye.

If you're alone with Salimov, watch the hell out. He's a predator and he'll figure out a way to get what he wants from you, usually while you're pinned beneath him.

As was often the case, Salimov used his power like a shield. His wealth opened doors, his friends were politically and professionally well-connected. But he was a generous donor to charitable causes, so that created his false sense of goodness. He painted himself as a man of the world, hoping to bring the two countries closer together through his continued efforts.

Because his network was chock-full of other power-hungry men, these women were finding it impossible to fight against a pack. Most lawsuits had been thrown out of court. A very few had settlements. Some women had committed suicide and a surprising number had gone missing.

It had been heartbreaking for Danielle to read their stories. While she didn't necessarily believe all of them, she couldn't dismiss them, either. Why would so many women lie?

She couldn't wait to take this monster down.

A man slid onto the chair beside her. She wasn't interested in chatting, but she didn't want to be a total bitch. Less was more. Blending into the background was her goal, until Salimov arrived, but it was somewhat hard to do in a sparkly silver dress and bright platinum hair.

"How ya doin'?" he asked.

"Doing alright," she replied.

"I've never seen you here before. Are you alone?"

"My friends are running late. Are you alone?"

"Not anymore."

That was a line she'd never heard before. She needed to keep the small talk to a minimum. The less he remembered about her, the better. Leaning close, she murmured, "I'm off the market. Sorry. I just don't want to waste your time."

"Thanks for the heads up." He collected his drink and moved on.

Danielle peered around as two men were ushered to a four-top in the corner. A punch of adrenaline shot through her. Salimov leered at the hostess. As Danielle had expected, his brute of a bodyguard was by his side. A server bustled over and took their drink order.

Salimov was busy texting and the other man was staring at the menu. Relaxing against the back of the leather stool, she had nothing but time.

Booze was delivered and his security detail ordered something from the menu. The men sipped their drinks and chatted. They finished their first drinks and the server brought them seconds, along with two appetizers.

Twenty long minutes later, Salimov pushed out of his seat and headed down the hallway. This was the moment Danielle had been waiting for. She abandoned her lookout spot and meandered in the direction of the restrooms. Either Salimov was going to the bathroom, or he was headed into a private dining room.

She caught him disappearing into the men's room. With her burner in hand, she waited at the beginning of the hallway. A few seconds later, the door of the women's room opened. She didn't move. A moment after that, a man exited the men's room. Again, she remained in place.

When Salimov exited, she sauntered in his direction, head down, pretending to send a text.

Bam!

She banged her shoulder into him. "Oh, my goodness, I'm so sorry." She touched his shoulder. "Are you okay?"

A flash of anger darkened his eyes. When she smiled at him, his furrowed brows were replaced with a creepy smile. "Are *you* hurt?" She picked up on his thick Russian accent.

She squeezed his arm. "You are a strong man, but no, I'm not hurt. Thank you for asking."

As he started to move past her, she blurted, "Can I buy you a drink to make it up to you?" She hated that she was laying it on so thick, but she couldn't let him get away.

"Of course," he replied.

She slipped her arm around his large one and stared into his flat eyes. "Mne nravitsya tvoy aktsent. I love your accent."

"Ty govorish' po-russki? You speak Russian?" he asked.

"Ochen' malo. Very little."

"Very nice. You speak well."

He led her to his four top. The other man glanced up, then shifted his attention to her. He didn't seem surprised that Salimov had returned with someone, but he didn't appear to like the interruption.

No matter. She was in, and there was no way in hell she was giving up her front row seat.

Salimov pulled out the corner chair and she eased down, arching her back a little as she did so. He sat beside her.

"I'm Ursula."

"Ivan." Salimov's gaze dropped to her cleavage. "Are you new member or guest?"

"I'm a member, but I haven't been here in a while." She glanced over at the guard. "Who's he?"

"A friend," Salimov replied.

The server appeared and Salimov asked what she was drinking. "Sparkling water." The waiter took their orders and left.

"You don't drink?" he asked.

"I have an early interview tomorrow and I cannot—absolutely cannot—be hungover. I need this job, bad."

"What do you do?" He glanced at her breasts again.

"I'm an executive assistant. My last boss fired me because I kept showing up late for work, probably because I'm such a party girl. Anyhoo, I can't screw this up." With a demure smile, she shrugged one shoulder. "If I land this job, I'm celebrating big time. A bottle of champagne, and I'm partying all night long."

Salimov chuckled. "I'd like to be around for that celebration."

"Sounds like a date." She unearthed her burner from her clutch. "What's your number?"

The two men exchanged quick glances.

"I wish I could," Salimov said, "but I'm married."

"No problem," she said. "I'm just looking for a good time. No strings." Danielle dropped a ten on the table. "I'm sorry I banged into you. Thanks for being so nice about it."

When she stood, he ogled her bare thighs.

"Sit," he blurted. "Your drink hasn't come."

She relaxed into the cushioned chair. "What do you do for a living?"

"I work for Russian Embassy," Salimov replied.

"Got any job openings over there?" She paused while the server set down their drinks.

"Perhaps." Salimov raised his glass. "To your interview."

They clinked glasses and she sipped the chilled water, letting the carbonation cool her dry throat.

"I don't normally meet real men like you," she said. "My last boyfriend was really just a boy. Men my age can be so immature."

"How old are you?" Salimov asked.

"Twenty-five," she lied. "You sure you don't want to exchange numbers, Ivan?" She nibbled her lower lip and tilted her head down in a show of submission. It took all her willpower not to vomit all over him.

"I help you find job, if interview doesn't work out," he replied.

She placed her hand briefly on his thigh. "Thank you so much." She rattled off her phone number. He entered it into his phone, along with a text. Her burner buzzed with his incoming message.

She drank down more of the water before she stood. "See you soon."

"Do skorogo. Until next time," he said.

"I look forward to it."

Once outside, the chilly October air whipped through her. There were a few people milling near the entrance, but other than that, the parking lot was quiet.

She walked over to her bike, opened the saddle bag and pulled out her leathers. Off came her stilettos—*ah, relief*—which she dropped in the side bag. She tugged on the leather pants, slipped into the jacket and her riding boots, then pulled on her helmet. Once on her Ninja, she started the engine and took off.

Her heart was pounding faster than usual as she rode home. Of all the men she'd targeted, Ivan Salimov was the most dangerous.As soon as she pulled into her garage and cut the engine, relief flooded her. Her goal was to meet Salimov and exchange phone numbers. Goal achieved.

In her kitchen, she checked the burner. Nothing from him beyond his initial text that said, "Ivan." Not wanting to act overly zealous, she didn't reply. Instead, she checked her personal phone. She had a text from Emerson, one from Stryker, and one from Cooper.

Seeing the one from Cooper sent excitement skittering through her. "Can't stop thinking about you," he texted.

She melted. He was being so transparent with her. Then, the guilt of who she'd become slinked back in and her shoulders dropped. "Me, too," she replied.

"Can I take you to Jericho's on Saturday?" he texted her.

What was the harm in going with him? *Him driving me home.* She thought about being with him at the gym. The way he'd kissed her, the way he'd taken care of her without expecting anything in return. Her insides started thrumming. If he drove her home, she'd invite him in.

Casual sex wasn't her thing. *I haven't had sex in so long, I don't know what my thing is. So what if it's just sex? C'mon, have a little fun.*

After wrestling with her thoughts, she decided to go for it. "Sure," she replied. "What time?"

"How's nine?" he replied.

"Perfect. See you then."

Next, she read Emerson's text. "Can we pick you up Saturday for Jericho's Halloween party?"

"Thank you, Emmy. Cooper is taking me." Danielle added a heart emoji.

Then, she read Stryker's text. "I heard you had a strong interview. Great job."

"Thanks," she replied. "I was pretty surprised by what I learned. Glad I didn't decline."

Emerson replied. "If I wear my Wonder Woman costume, will you wear your Black Widow?"

"Absolutely! Great idea."

With phone in hand, she set her house alarm and headed upstairs.

Danielle was living two completely different lives that were in stark contrast to each other. As she stepped into the shower to wash off the stench of Salimov, she wondered how much time she had before ALPHA Operatives caught up with her.

THE FOLLOWING AFTERNOON, Danielle was sitting in Stryker's Friday staff meeting when Providence Luck called. Normally, she would ignore a call during his meeting, but she'd been dying to find out if she got the job.

"Excuse me," she said as she hurried out of the conference room. "Danielle Fox," she answered.

"Hello, Danielle, it's Providence Luck. Is now a good time?"

"Yes," she replied.

"I enjoyed talking to you yesterday and I wanted to thank you for your interest in ALPHA. It was a difficult decision—Stryker sent us excellent candidates." Danielle held her breath. "The position is yours. Congratulations!"

A heady combination of relief and anxiety coursed through her. "That's fantastic, but also bittersweet. I've worked for Stryker since graduating college."

"He's an excellent boss. I feel a little guilty about stealing you away from him."

Danielle could relate. She felt a little guilty about her reason for accepting the position. "Is my start date still on Monday?"

"Yes, but I need to run a background check," Providence explained. "Unless there's a hiccup, Monday is ideal."

She shuddered. "Well, I have a top-secret clearance, so it shouldn't be necessary."

"It's standard procedure," Providence explained. "Plus, I need to let Stryker know. He's going to want to make an announcement that today's your last day. Let's discuss your cover."

"I just got a part-time job teaching kickboxing. Would that work?"

"Your cover needs to be full-time. Why don't you tell your coworkers you've taken a job with me at my marketing company?"

"Doing what?"

"VP of Operations, then do what I do, and change the subject. Turn the conversation to them."

"That'll work," Danielle replied. "Stryker's finishing up his staff meeting, so I'll tell him after."

"I look forward to seeing you on Monday. You're going to make a terrific addition to the team." Providence hung up and Danielle sighed. Leaving TCS would be gut-wrenching.

Steeling her spine, she returned to the conference room.

"I was just wrapping up the meeting," Stryker said to her. "Anything on your mind, Fox?"

A lump formed in her throat. "I'm good, thanks."

"What? No snide remark or comment?"

"Not today, boss."

When the meeting ended, Danielle funneled out with everyone else. Her heart was breaking. She loved her job and would never have even considered leaving. But she had to keep her enemies closer. The only way to do that was by working on the inside.

Back in her office, she reminded herself that she wasn't sweet Danielle who thought the best of everyone and would *never* have casual sex with someone. She'd turned into a vigilante who rooted out evil and eliminated it. Someone who *did* have casual sex with someone... and would probably do it again.

I took the job at ALPHA to make sure I don't get caught.

A moment later, Stryker appeared in her doorway. "Got a minute?"

"Of course."

He closed the door, sat across from her desk. "I heard you're leaving us for a Veep spot at Luck Marketing. Sounds like a great opportunity. Congratulations."

A lump formed in her throat. "Thank you."

"I only have myself to blame," he said. "I could have given Providence anyone and she would never have known what she was missing. I gave her the best and she took it. I'm gonna miss you."

Tears filled her eyes. She'd never cried at work, ever. One slid down her cheek and she swiped it away. "Sorry," she whispered. "This is so unprofessional." She wiped another tear. "Is Emerson coming by? I was hoping to tell—"

"You can't. You can't tell anyone where you work."

"Oh, right," she replied.

"You're a VP, now, remember that going forward." He pushed out of the chair. "We can tell the executive team together, and then, you can tell your pods, or I can tell everyone Monday. Now is better. Monday looks like you got fired."

She sucked in a ragged breath. "Let's tell them together."

Ten minutes later, the executive team knew. This time, she'd been able to contain her emotion and even pasted on a smile. After Danielle told her pods, Stryker sent out a company-wide email congratulating Danielle on her new position. Several employees stopped by to wish her well.

Before she left, she called her clients and let them know. As she shut down her computer for the last time, she choked back a sob. It was killing her to leave. She brought her laptop down to Stryker's office.

"Thank you for being one of the good guys," she said to him.

Strangely, that made him laugh. "I've been called a lot of things, but never a good guy. Thanks for being such a model employee and manager."

"This is difficult for me."

He extended his hand and she shook it. "You're gonna love your new work family at Luck Marketing. I'll see you tomorrow at Jericho's. Now, we can be friends, so, really, your leaving is a good thing."

"I am curious about one thing," she said. "How do you even know about that organization?"

"I've done some hacking for Providence."

"So, you don't know what they do?"

Silence.

"You *do* know what they do," Danielle said.

"I know Providence needed the best hacker I have, and that's you. See you tomorrow, Fox."

Her lips lifted in a subtle smile.

He knows about ALPHA. And now, I do, too.

9

STAY WITH ME

COOPER

Cooper rang the doorbell, anticipation coursing through him. Danielle had become a permanent fixture in his brain and he could not wait to spend the evening with her.

The door opened and a stunning Danielle, dressed as the superhero Black Widow, greeted him. Costume aside, she took his breath away every damn time. Heat warmed his chest while they stared into each other's eyes.

"Hi," he said. His voice had dropped, the desire to kiss her was front and center.

"Hi." Her gaze pierced his. "You wanna come in?"

He stepped into her home and she shut the door behind him.

"Wow, you're the sexiest Avenger I've ever seen," he murmured.

She did a slow three-sixty and he soaked her up. From the form-fitting jumpsuit that accentuated her curves, to the thigh-high boots that clung to her toned legs, she was off-the-charts hot. But it was the belt with the holster that caught his eye. "Packing heat?"

"I gotta defend myself against the villains who're after me." She pulled out the gun and displayed the orange tip. "It's a toy." She walked around him. "You look fantastic in that tux. Talk about wow. Who are you supposed to be?"

"I'm Bond. James Bond."

He'd paired his black tuxedo with a white shirt, black cummerbund and a black bow tie. It wasn't a creative costume, but he'd been slammed on time.

Her smile sent energy surging through him. "Nice. Maybe I should've dressed as Pussy Galore." Without missing a beat, she continued, "I'm ready, if you wanna take off."

He draped his arms over her shoulders and peered into her eyes. "I'm ready. So. Damn. Ready. I can't wait until later when I strip you out of that sexy costume and make you squirm with pleasure."

Her breath hitched. "You do *not* hold back, do you?"

"I've been waiting six months for you." He leaned close. "So, yeah, I'm ready to take off. You gonna let loose with me?"

She stood on her toes and wrapped her arms around him. Nose to nose, she murmured, "Yes. I. Am."

Her warm breath on his cheeks lured him closer until his lips brushed against hers. Desire took hold, but he was in total control. "Ready to do the cowboy hustle?"

"Uh-huh," she whispered. "Are you the cowboy and is that code?"

He smiled. "That's the line dance I taught you."

"Right." Her voice was quiet and breathy, just the way he liked it. She dropped a light kiss on his lips. "I'm ready," she whispered before breaking away from him.

So am I.

Once outside, he appreciated the brisk night air. Being around Danielle was like stepping into a furnace. He was burning for her in all the ways that made him a man.

As they made his way to his car, parked half in her driveway, half on the street, she said, "This is so nice."

"It's a '66 Corvette, completely restored." He opened the passenger door and waited while she slid into the bucket seat. As he walked around to the driver's side, a white van whizzed by. Cooper jumped out of the way.

"Slow the hell down!" he yelled.

He slid in beside Danielle. "It's probably safer to stay in tonight."

"Trust me, it's way, way, way more dangerous in there."

"You gonna show me who's boss with some of your kickboxing moves?"

She smiled. "I've got some moves, all right." He glanced over and was rewarded with another spike of energy.

If they continued with the sexual innuendos, he'd have blue balls in no time. He fired up the Corvette and revved the engine a couple of times before backing out of the driveway.

After he pulled out of her neighborhood, she said, "I was surprised you left the FBI."

"It was time."

"That's it?"

Tell her the truth.

"I'd done something that went against protocol. The higher ups wanted to ship my ass to Nevada. It's a beautiful state and I've got nothing against moving west, but I've got family and close friends here. I wasn't willing to move. Plus, most of my days were spent in meetings, anyway."

"Not a lot of rock walls to climb in a conference room."

"Owning the gym is a better fit." At the red light, they turned toward each other. The kiss happened so quickly, he hadn't processed it until she slid her tongue into his mouth. Then, he was processing it so hard, he didn't hear the horns blaring behind them.

She broke the wet kiss, and he hit the gas.

"You're trouble, Danielle Fox."

"Who, me? I'm just a lil' ole Avenger girl, sitting quietly in my seat." Her faux southern accent was laced with playfulness.

He wanted to wrap his hand around her thigh and stroke her muscular leg. Instead, he gripped the steering wheel. If she said yes later, there would be plenty of time to touch those glorious thighs…

Even though Jericho's party was invitation-only, the parking lot was already packed, so he drove around back. As they made their way toward the front door, he threaded his fingers through hers. She pulled him to a stop, pressed her body against his, then her lips to his.

Her searing kiss sent desire streaking through him while his junk firmed in his pants.

"I'm out of control around you," she murmured. "I want to do every dirty thing—"

He snaked his arms around her and kissed her like he'd been dying to do from the second she opened her front door. She groaned into him and he tightened his hold. Their kiss was hard and rough, then soft and gentle. And so fucking phenomenal.

When it ended, she murmured, "Put your hands on my ass."

He did *exactly* as instructed. "They're stuck there now."

Her adorable smile sent him flying to the moon. He caressed her rounded backside while she stared into his eyes. "We don't have to go in," he said. "Last chance to bail."

"Bail on line dancing? No way." With a playful gleam in her eyes, she clasped his hand and strode toward the front doors. After yanking one open, she gestured for him to walk through.

He held the door. "Go ahead."

"What's wrong with my holding the door for you?" she asked.

"Because I want to do that for you."

"I'll open the door for you and you can do *everything else* for me." Her sultry smile sent a wave of desire blasting through him.

With a grin, he walked inside, then turned to pull her close. "I can't wait," he said. "I cannot fucking wait."

The music was loud, the room thick with costumed people laughing, drinking, and talking. Holding Danielle's hand, he led her through the main dining room, veering into a smaller one toward the back of the restaurant.

Jericho's private party for close friends only.

Despite being pissed at Stryker for keeping his ALPHA status a secret, he wasn't going to ruin the moment, or detract from his Danielle-high by pulling Stryker aside to hash it out.

As he surveyed the crowd, he found Jericho and laughed out loud.

"What?" Danielle asked.

"Jericho's costume."

No surprise that he was Thor. At least he was clothed. Last year, he'd gone as Tarzan and worn a damn loin cloth. Jericho caught Cooper's eye and made his way over.

"Yo, bro, who the hell are you?" Jericho boomed.

"Bond, James Bond," Cooper replied, in his best Bond voice.

Jericho chuffed out a laugh. "Hey, Danielle, you look great." He arched an eyebrow at Cooper. "Danielle's wearing a *real* costume. You're just trying to look good."

"I'm not trying," Cooper retorted. "I succeeded." He shifted his attention to Danielle. "You gonna back me on this or what?"

She bit back a smile. "He *does* look good."

Jericho laughed. "Yeah, okay. I'm not sure you're a reliable source. So, guys, drinks and food are on me."

"That's awesome," Danielle said.

"Thanks, brother," Cooper echoed.

Cooper's niece, Tessa, bounded over. "Hey, Uncle." Then, she gave Jericho the once-over. "Not running around mostly naked is going to be a huge disappointment for your groupies." She laughed. "Guess what I am?"

"A cat," Jericho deadpanned.

"Ding, ding, ding! What gave it away?"

"The tail, the ears, the painted whiskers," Jericho replied. One of his waitstaff interrupted and Jericho stepped away to talk to him.

While studying Cooper's costume, Tessa scrounged up her face. "What are you?"

"Bond, James Bond."

Tessa laughed before regarding Danielle. "I'm Cooper's favorite niece, Tessa Grant."

"I'm Danielle Fox."

Tessa was tall and slender with light eyes and dark brown hair. Her smile was contagious as was her positive energy. Danielle liked her immediately.

"You two coulda dressed like brother and sister," Tessa said. "You're one of those couples who looks soooo cute together."

"Oh, we're not a couple," Danielle blurted.

"We are, tonight," Cooper pushed back.

"How do you guys know each other?" Tessa asked.

"Do you know Stryker Truman?" Danielle asked.

"Oh, sure, he's my uncle's closest friend."

"His fiancée, Emerson, is my best friend," Danielle explained. "We met through them."

"I'll grab us some drinks," Cooper said. "What can I get everyone?"

"Wine spritzer," Tessa replied. "Are you getting a martini, shaken, not stirred?"

"I was thinking of getting a beer," he replied.

She made a face at him. "You gotta have a martini, duh!"

"What are you drinking?" he asked Danielle.

"I'll have a sip of yours. I don't want to drink much." The subtle upturn of her mouth had him kissing her cheek before he took off into the crowd.

While waiting for a bartender, Stryker pulled up alongside him. "Hey, great costume. You gotta be Bond."

Stryker was dressed as a pirate, complete with an eye patch and pirate hat.

"Ahoy, matey, have ye found ye treasure trove?" Cooper asked.

"Found her, gonna marry her," Stryker said with a smile. "Where's Danielle?"

"Jericho's private room. Where's Emerson?"

Their conversation paused while the bartender took their orders.

"Probably with Danielle," Stryker replied.

"I saw an 'eyes only' list at work." Though Cooper wasn't going to say anything, he had to get it out.

Stryker cracked a smile. "Oh, yeah? See anything interesting?"

"Hell, yeah. Why didn't you tell me?"

"You just said it yourself. 'Eyes only'. As soon as you got promoted, I knew you'd see it."

"I was pissed," Cooper said, collecting the drinks. "Now, I'm just looking forward to working with you."

Stryker threw his arm around him. "Yup, I knew you would be. It's not personal, Coop, you know that, my brother."

With drinks in hand, the two men made their way back to the private room. As Stryker predicted, Emerson had joined the conversation with Danielle and Tessa.

Cooper offered the first swig of beer to Danielle. "I'm good, thanks."

Standing beside her wasn't enough. He had to touch her, but he wanted to keep things chill. Rather than slink his arm around her waist, he clasped her hand. She threaded her fingers through his and gave him a gentle squeeze.

"You look great!" Emerson said to Cooper. "Very suave, Mr. Bond."

"Right back atcha, Wonder Woman."

"I'm so excited," Tessa said. "Danielle is teaching a computer workshop at my shelter."

"On computer safety," Danielle added.

"That's cool," Cooper said. "When's that?"

"Tomorrow afternoon," Danielle replied.

"You ready to line dance?" Cooper asked.

Her smoldering gaze drilled into his. "I'm *definitely* ready."

The energy whirled around them while they stayed locked on each other. After an extra beat, she regarded the others. "Come with us."

"I'm going to find my friend," Tessa said and took off into the crowded room.

"I'm in," Emerson said.

"I go where my woman goes," Stryker replied.

As Danielle led them down the hall, he loved that she hadn't let go of his hand. His head was buzzing from being around her. Tonight, felt different, like they were vibing on a whole different level.

His chemical reaction to her was beyond addictive.

In the dance room, they found a spot in the back. After letting go of his hand, she watched for several seconds before joining in.

He was impressed. He wasn't familiar with the line dance, so he faked it until it started making sense. One quarter turn in and Cooper was admiring Danielle's curvy ass.

Front, back, sideways, she was a beautiful woman. He liked her better as a blonde, but the red wig made the costume more authentic. The song ended and another one began. Three line dances later, the DJ announced he was taking a break.

Seconds into the slow country ballad, she was in his arms, while her soft fingers tickled the back of his neck, above his collar.

"I love your touch," he murmured, while holding her flush against him.

She pressed him with a tender kiss, then peered into his eyes. "Me, too."

Cooper lost track of time, the music faded into the background, as did the other couples dancing nearby. All he could see was Danielle, her dark blue eyes locked on his. He breathed her in and exhaled a rumbling growl. Her natural scent was making him hungry with desire.

The song ended, and she whispered, "Let's take a break."

This time, they found each other's hands and left the dance floor. Back in the small dining room, a server stopped by to take their drink order.

The woman he'd met the night Danielle didn't show sauntered over. "Hey, Cooper."

"How you doin', Suzette?"

"Is this the woman you were telling me about?" Suzette asked.

"Sure is. This is Danielle. Danielle, Suzette."

"Hi," Danielle said. "I love your costume."

Suzette was a vampire. Her detailed costume included a high-collared cape and fangs.

"You're my favorite Avenger. Very cool." Suzette glanced from one to the other. "He must really like you," she said to Danielle. "You two look cute together. Happy Halloween." Suzette moved on.

"What was that about?" Danielle asked.

"She stopped by the booth the night you didn't."

"And you told her about me?"

He peered into her eyes. "I did."

Her lips lifted into a Mona Lisa smile, but she said nothing.

"You liked hearing that, didn't you?" he asked, pulling her close.

"I like you." Her voice was almost inaudible, but the look in her eyes told him plenty.

He kissed her. "That's what I've been waiting to hear."

"Excuse me," said the server. She handed Cooper a beer and a martini, then gave Danielle a bottle of water. "The martini is from Jericho."

"That's perfect," Danielle added.

Cooper caught Jericho's eye and raised his glass. Jericho gave him a thumbs-up. "Now you look like Bond," he hollered across the room.

Cooper toasted Danielle. "To a Halloween we'll never forget."

He drained half his beer while she chugged her water. When finished, he asked her if she wanted to dance. She shook her head.

"Do you want to find Emerson?" he asked.

"No."

He pulled her close. "What do you want to do, Danielle?"

"I want to take you home with me."

There was nowhere else he wanted to go.

Rather than lead her through the restaurant, they left through the back door. The second the fire door slammed shut, they were on each other. The kiss was fierce and frenzied and filled with a chaotic need. Danielle was raking her fingers down his back while he cemented his hands on her ass and squeezed.

She ground into him, the intensity of her momentum pushing him against the building. The raw sounds coming out of her were like a feral animal. He was out of his mind for her. He ended the kiss, clasped her hand, and strode to his car.

"We've got too much clothing on," he grumbled.

"Does that mean you're going to strip me of my superhero costume, Mr. Bond?"

He pressed his mouth to hers and kissed her. Long, deep, and so damn satisfying. "Yes, I am, Ms. Romanoff."

Confusion flashed in her eyes. "I forgot. I'm Natasha Romanoff. I swear, I'm buzzing so hard from being around you. No alcohol needed."

That, he could relate to. He was flying high on Danielle. Just Danielle.

He opened the passenger door and she slipped inside his car.

Seconds later, they were on the road. The difference between the ride to Jericho Road and the one now, was that his hand was superglued to her thigh.

At the traffic light, she leaned over and kissed his cheek. "I am so attracted to you, it's insane."

"Same."

She ran her tongue over his ear and nibbled his lobe. The light turned green and he eased forward, but the pulsing desire had him groaning through the pleasure.

When he pulled in her driveway, mostly filled with her car, she said, "You should park in one of the visitor spots across the street. Your car could get hit if you leave it sticking out in the road. Normally, people drive pretty slowly around here, but the crazies are out tonight."

After parking, they walked with purpose to her townhouse. She opened her front door, then turned back. "Will you come in?"

"Hell, yeah." He followed her inside.

She bolted the door, activated the alarm, and leaned up to kiss him on the corner of his mouth. "I want you," she whispered. "In my bed. Do you want that?"

"I want you, so damn badly."

This time, when she clasped his hand, hers was trembling. As she headed toward the stairs, he pulled her back.

"Are you afraid?"

"Terrified," she replied.

"We can take this slowly."

"I haven't been with anyone in a while and I haven't been vulnerable—not really—since my sister died. I'm not terrified *of* you. I'm scared of letting myself feel anything but anger."

"I get that," he said. "We go at your pace and do what makes you comfortable. Okay?"

"Thank you."

She hadn't stopped shaking, so he pulled her close and hugged her. "All you have to say is stop, at any point, and I will."

"I'm not going to want to stop," she whispered. "I'm sure of that."

DANIELLE

The desire to be intimate with Cooper was overshadowing any logical thought. She was thrumming on such an intense level that taking him inside her was her *only* option. But she couldn't let this be anything more than a physical connection. Locking down her emotions was a smarter choice.

Her life was complicated and filled with vengeance. When she got arrested, she would never want him getting caught up in her crimes. For tonight, she would give herself full permission to be with him. No backsliding, no guilt, no regret.

In her bedroom, she placed his hand on her breast. "Undress me," she said, though she could not stop shaking.

He dipped down and kissed her. One tender kiss, then another. Instead of tearing off her costume, he pulled off her wig and unpinned her hair. Then, with a light touch, he combed his fingers through her hair. "There you are."

He kissed her again while his hands roamed freely over her back. She craved his touch more than she needed air, anticipation skittering through her while her insides throbbed with unrelenting desire. She couldn't wait to feel the luxurious slide as he entered her.

"Ohgod, I need you in me."

"We're gonna get there, Danielle," he murmured before kissing her again.

She'd never been with a man who exuded so much control. His gaze hovered on hers while he unhooked her belt and let it fall to the carpet, then slowly unzipped her costume. Instead of removing it, he ran his fingers down her chest, between her breasts to her abs.

"So beautiful." He kissed her bare chest, letting his lips linger on her heated skin.

"Mmm," she whispered.

He removed his tuxedo jacket, then the cummerbund and bow tie. She was so mesmerized by his strip show that she stopped shaking.

Desperate to touch him, to lay hands on his body, she unbuttoned his dress shirt and pulled it off his strong, striated shoulders, then ran her fingertips over his perfectly sculpted pecs while he removed the cufflinks before shedding his shirt.

"Mmmm, you are a beast," she murmured, stepping close and kissing his chest.

Zing after zing of arousal zipped through her while her insides hummed with relentless need.

"Let's get you out of that costume," he said and knelt at her feet. "Hold on to me."

She grasped his sinewy shoulders while he removed her boots. Then, he ran his hands up and down her thighs, still trapped inside the latex costume, while he pressed his face to her crotch and released a low growl.

As he rose, he murmured, "I loved tasting you and I can't wait to do it again."

She was overheating, her desire turning her into a fireball. With his gaze cemented on hers, he stretched the costume away from her shoulders and peeled it down her arms and torso until it rested at her hips. Planning ahead, she'd worn black, lace panties, but no bra.

His gaze dropped to her breasts and he released a moan. "Your breasts are beautiful."

He dipped down to kiss the swell of one breast, then the other. "Talk to me, Danielle. Are you okay?"

"Yes, I love that. I want you to touch me, lick me, kiss me, and fuck me so good."

He knelt on one knee and, with the skill of a sculptor defining the curves of his creation, freed her of her costume before rising to lock eyes with her.

"You are a goddess." His husky voice ripped through her as he caressed her pussy with one hand and fondled her nipple with the other.

On a throaty moan, she became laser-focused on getting him naked. After removing his pants, she was rewarded with his massive boner.

"I see you went commando." She curled her fingers around his shaft. "May I?"

"Anything you want."

"What I *want* is to suck you." Saying those words empowered her.

"I've thought about your mouth on my cock for months."

Leaning in, she licked the head. "You taste good." Her eyes fluttered closed and she cradled his balls in one hand while taking him into her mouth.

"Mygod, you feel so fucking good," he bit out.

She licked and sucked, taking him further into her mouth until he hit the back of her throat. She loved bringing him so much pleasure, loved his moans of approval, how he was oozing with so much wetness.

The more she sucked, the more out of her mind she was with lust, unable to slow herself down. Again, and again, she would take him into her mouth and suck, then pull him out. Their groans filled her ears with deliciously dirty sounds until his cock turned rock hard and his balls drew up tight in her hands.

"Danielle, I'm gonna come."

When she lightened her touch, but increased her speed, he erupted in ecstasy and she eagerly swallowed him down. Once his orgasm ended, she slid her mouth off him.

As she rose, she kissed his granite abs, his steel pecs and sculpted shoulders. He was strong, muscular and a strikingly beautiful man. If things had been different, she would have given her heart permission to explore something with him. She'd be crazy not to.

But her life had taken a dark turn and she couldn't risk getting close to him. It was smarter to end things before they got started. Pushing him away was going to be gut wrenching, but absolutely necessary.

When she kissed him, her heart broke.

Not for what they had, but for what could never be.

10

KABOOM!

COOPER

Cooper was out of his mind over Danielle and not just because his had been blown. Rather than get ahead of himself, he'd take things slow. Less was more when it came to her, of that he was certain.

"Mygod, you're talented," he murmured. "I need to be inside you, but I'm going to spend time getting to know the girls before I eat you."

"Will I get flowers after, again?"

Her smarmy expression made him laugh.

She clasped his hand, led him to her bed, and threw back the linens. One tug, and they tumbled onto the mattress.

When he planked over her and kissed her, their collective moans sent streams of desire pounding through him. She threaded her arms around him, stroking his back with soft fingertips. Kissing Danielle was something he could *not* get enough of.

Breaking away, he nuzzled her neck.

"So good," she murmured.

When he kissed her breast, then her nipple, her breath hitched. The instant he took her pert nub into his mouth, she released a raspy groan. "Oh, that feels incredible."

He sucked and nibbled, raked his tongue across her flesh, sucking harder. The more he sucked, the more he wanted her. She was moaning and moving beneath him, but he hadn't even reached down to stroke her beautiful pussy, still hidden behind the lace undies.

He gave equal time to her beautiful mounds before trailing kisses to her muscular abs. "You're so damn sexy, you know that?"

Her eyes fluttered open and they shared a moment of connectedness before he continued on. After tugging off her panties, he admired her closely-trimmed pubic hair.

"I got caught off guard last time," she said.

He loved that she'd thought about being with him. "You're sexy both ways."

He buried his face between her legs and licked her opening. She pushed off the bed and moaned into him. "Hard and fast, Cooper. I'm so ready for you."

She bent her knees and shuddered in a deep breath. He slid his hands under her ass, lifted her off the linens and tasted that sweet, sweet pussy juice. She couldn't lay still, her body undulating beneath him while her whimpers and moans turned him hard, again.

She fisted the sheets in one hand and thrust her fingers into his hair with the other while he licked and tongued her soaked flesh. As he slid two fingers inside her, her sounds turned guttural. "Cooper, Ohgod. Coooooooooper," she cried out as she bucked beneath him.

She climaxed hard while he nursed her through it. When she stopped, he slowed and finished with a tender kiss on her soft folds.

"Kiss me," she commanded.

When he did, she latched her arms and legs around him and tongued him, hard, while her sexy gasps and groans filled the air.

She stopped. "You feel hard."

"I am hard."

Her lids were heavy, her smile relaxed. "Inside me." She gestured toward the night table. "Condoms in the drawer."

He grabbed a foil packet and rolled on the condom. "Top or bottom?"

"In."

He chuffed out a laugh. From the bottom, she guided him to her opening and lifted off the bed to meet him. The euphoric slide had him groaning while her husky sounds made him crazy with need. Once inside her, he stilled.

Gazing into her eyes soothed him like nothing he'd ever known. There was something about being connected to her that distracted his demons and assuaged his anger. As if she could sense his calmness, she ran soft fingers through his hair.

"You feel good," she whispered.

The feeling went beyond good. She felt right. "You do, too."

When he started moving, she moved against him, creating more friction.

"Harder," she murmured. "Take me." She bucked beneath him, palmed his ass, and held him inside her. "I want raw, dirty fucking."

Harder and faster he pumped, while she moaned and moved beneath him. He repositioned enough to suck her swollen nipple and she cried out, then started convulsing beneath him.

"Yes, yessssss," she groaned.

Her insides squeezed his shaft and the orgasm shot out of him, the ecstasy drowning him in wave after wave of glorious pleasure.

His mouth found hers and they shared another searing kiss, their tongues stroking each other's with wild abandon. Hard, fast, and so damn intense.

When he opened his eyes, she was waiting. "Was that good for you?" she whispered.

He tipped her chin toward him. "You're as good as it gets, Danielle Fox. Was that good for you?"

"Meh." Her sweet smile halted his breath.

He chuffed out a laugh. "I'll try harder, next time."

Sadness flashed in her eyes. "Now's not a good time for a relationship, for me."

He didn't like hearing that, at all. "Okay."

"I want to keep things casual between us."

He was liking that even less. "Why?"

"It's better that way."

His sex high was fading too damn fast. This was *not* the direction he wanted them to go. Pulling off her, he leaned against the propped pillows.

"Sounds like you want that, too," she continued.

He ran through his options. Agree or speak his mind. Cooper was never one to stay silent, especially when he felt strongly about something.

"I *don't* want that," he said.

"I…um…it's just that…I can't." Breaking eye contact, she whispered, "I'm sorry."

Fuck.

He hated, fucking hated, what he was going to say next. "I've done the casual thing and I'm over those. You're a special woman, Danielle. I don't want to walk from this, but if you're looking for an occasional fuck, I gotta pass."

Her eyes widened and she stared at him for what seemed like forever.

When she didn't respond, he pushed out of bed. "I'm gonna take off." Agitation slithered through him as he soldiered into the bathroom.

How in the fucking hell did this happen?

He cleaned off and returned to the bedroom to get dressed. Already in sweatpants, Danielle was pulling on a sweatshirt.

Pain slashed through his chest. He hated that she'd shut them down before they'd even gotten liftoff.

KABOOM!

A flash of light illuminated the room as it shook.

She whirled toward him. "What was that?"

"Sounded like an explosion."

They both hurried to her bedroom window. She yanked up the blinds and he zeroed in on the car engulfed in flames across the street.

"What the hell!" he exclaimed.

"Oh, no! Your car is on fire!"

He grabbed his phone and dialed 9-1-1. After putting the phone on speaker, he tugged on his pants.

"What's your emergency?" asked the operator.

"My car is on fire." He pulled on his dress shirt.

"Where is your car, sir?" asked the dispatcher.

"Parked across the street," he replied.

"I have fire extinguishers," Danielle blurted.

Based on the intensity of the blaze, he doubted they'd make a difference.

They hurried down the hallway. After pulling one out of her hall closet, she said, "I've got another in the kitchen."

"What's your address?" asked the operator.

Danielle told her before they bolted down the stairs. He waited by her front door while she raced into her kitchen, returning with a second fire extinguisher.

After unalarming, they rushed outside. Despite being barefoot, she hurried down to the sidewalk.

Danielle turned back. "Pull my door closed."

"I've gotta go," Cooper said to the dispatcher.

"Is the car empty?" asked the operator.

Cooper couldn't tell from across the street. "No idea."

"Is there anyone around?" the operator asked.

"Several neighbors have come outside, but no one is close enough to be in danger." The operator wanted Cooper to stay on the phone until first responders arrived, but he was done.

"First responders are still four minutes out."

"We've got extinguishers and we're gonna try to kill the blaze. Thanks for your help." Cooper hung up and ran over to his car. Danielle had already pulled the pin and was spraying his car with foam.

He joined her and together they tried to smother the flames. By the time the fire engine pulled up, the damage was done. His car was totaled. But he wasn't thinking about the vehicle. He was focused totally on the woman by his side.

"You're not supposed to run *toward* a fire," he said.

"I wasn't gonna stand by and watch your car burn without *trying* to put it out."

"Thank you for your efforts." After setting down the canister, he snapped several pictures of his totaled Corvette.

A firewoman approached. "Everyone okay?"

"Yeah," Cooper said while the firefighters sprayed the hell out of his now-charred vehicle.

After he explained what had happened, the first responder asked, "Do you think there was a leak in the fuel line?"

"Doubtful," Cooper replied before taking the fire extinguisher from Danielle and setting it down.

"Any reason to believe this was intentionally set?" she asked.

Cooper thought about the dead rat. *Salimov*. No way was he telling them about Salimov. "No."

A fireman approached them. "Looks like the fire started when the gas tank exploded. Any fuel leaks?"

"No," Cooper said, trying to keep his frustration under wraps.

"We'll call for techs," the firewoman said. "Can I get your contact information for the investigator?"

Cooper rattled it off.

"An officer will stay until they show up," she explained.

After thanking her, Cooper grasped Danielle's hand and headed back toward her house.

Danielle's next-door neighbors were standing out front. "Danielle, what happened?"

"My friend's car caught on fire."

"You weren't in it, were you?" one of them asked.

"No, we were inside."

"Glad you weren't hurt." The neighbors retreated into their house.

As Danielle continued up her front lawn, Cooper noticed she was limping. He picked her up, carried her inside and deposited her onto the kitchen counter. There, he lifted her foot. "You got some pebbles under your skin."

"I'm fine."

He turned on the kitchen faucet. "I'm gonna clean your foot. Play with my hair. You seem to like that," he said, and winked.

"Boy, you're a cocky one."

He adjusted the water temperature, then got busy cleaning her injury. She flinched. "You've got a pebble that doesn't want to come out."

She squeezed his shoulder while he worked it out, then he kissed her foot and checked her other one. That one was pebble free. "Got Band-Aids?"

She pointed. "In that cupboard."

He pulled out the box, along with first-aid ointment. He liked taking care of her. "All patched up. You were a good patient."

"Thank you, Doctor Feel Good." They stared into each other's eyes. Despite the anger flowing through him, she had this angelic effect on him. And yet, the longer he looked at her, the more he wanted her.

That's not happening.

Disappointment settled into his bones.

He picked her up, set her on the floor.

"I've got a doorbell surveillance camera," she said. "Let's check it out."

They relocated to her living room sofa. He purposefully put space between them, but after pulling up the camera, she scooted close. With her thigh pressed against his, he fought the urge to wrap her in his arms and love her all over again. His body refused the message his brain had received.

That's not happening. She shut us down.

"When the firefighter asked if you thought this was arson, you said no," she said. "Were you being honest?"

"Why would you ask that?"

"Because you said your car was in great shape. It doesn't make sense that it would explode a few hours after driving it."

"Let's see if your camera caught anything."

Danielle tapped the recording. Even with a clear line of sight across the street, Cooper hadn't parked near a streetlight and the area was dark. Then, there was movement near the Corvette, but he couldn't be sure it was a person or the shadow of a swaying tree branch. There was a small flame and, seconds later, the car exploded.

"Motherfucker," Cooper bit out. "They must've stuffed something flammable into my gas tank and lit it." He shoved off the sofa and rubbed his tight neck.

"So, it *was* arson," she said. "Who would do this to you?"

Salimov.

If this was Salimov, he needed to keep her safe.

"Can I confide in you?"

"Of course."

"I got a package at the gym with a fake return address. Inside was a decomposing rat."

Her eyes grew large. "Well, you've definitely pissed off someone. Anyone come to mind? What about someone from the gym?"

He shook his head. "I made a bunch of upgrades, but I didn't raise monthly fees. I haven't fired anyone. Naomi hasn't mentioned anything about an angry member."

"What about when you were with the FBI?" she prodded.

"Could be," he replied.

Danielle replayed the video. "I'm pretty decent with computers. I can help you."

"Thanks for the offer, but you've got a lot going on." *Should I tell her about Salimov? The less she knows, the better.* "I'm concerned about you."

"Me? I'm not in danger."

"You live alone and that makes you an easy target."

"They're coming after you, not me. I can take care of myself."

His phone rang. "Cooper Grant," he answered.

"Mr. Grant, this is Vic Bakerson. I'm the arson investigator following up on your case. I'm here with your vehicle. Are you nearby?"

"Be right out." Cooper hung up and regarded Danielle. He didn't like that she'd gotten sucked into his mess, but he loved having her by his side. "Shoes, first."

Her eyes softened. "I'll grab them from upstairs."

This time, they pulled on their shoes before heading back outside. Seeing the blackened heap made him sick to his stomach.

After introductions, the arson investigator said, "One of my techs found a charred rag with what smells like accelerant. We'll have your car towed to the impound lot so we can run further tests. Do you live over there?"

"I do," Danielle replied.

"Do you have a surveillance camera?"

"On my doorbell," she replied. "We saw someone, but the resolution is too blurry to see anything relevant. I can forward it to you."

"Please do," Investigator Bakerson replied. "Mr. Grant, can you think of anyone who could have done this to you? A co-worker, someone you were in a romantic relationship with, even someone you got into an argument with in a parking lot?"

"No, no one," he lied.

"Call me if you think of anyone." Bakerson handed him a business card. "I'll be in touch."

Cooper eyed the remains of his vehicle one more time. As he and Danielle walked across the street, he glanced around. It was impossible to know if someone was hiding nearby, watching them.

He closed her front door. "Do you have anyone you can stay with until we figure out who did this?"

"I'm surprised you aren't insisting I move into *your* house." She was leaning her backside against the door. He rested his arm on the door, above her, dipped down, and kissed her.

"If I insisted, would you?" he murmured.

Her lips tugged up, ever so slightly. "No."

Concern had him scraping his fingers over his scruffy jaw. "There is someone who could've done this. I went after him pretty hard when I was at the Bureau. He's extremely dangerous and I'm not okay leaving you here alone."

"Who is it? I can do some online digging."

"I've already involved you enough. Please, let me keep you safe. How 'bout I ask my friend to install a security system for you?"

"I have a security system." She pushed up on her toes. "How 'bout this? I'll let you know if I change my mind."

He captured her face in his hands and he kissed her. One soft, lingering kiss that had him biting back a groan. Kissing Danielle could have easily become his great escape…if she hadn't pushed him away.

But she did.

"I'm gonna grab my clothes and head out." As he broke away from her, he glimpsed a flash of sadness in her eyes.

A sliver of hope took hold. Maybe she did like him enough to see him again.

"Let me drive you home," she said.

"Will you stay?"

"No, Cooper, I *won't*." This time, frustration tinged her tone.

He hated backing off, but he would. On the way upstairs, he opened his ride share app and requested a pick up.

Back on the first floor, Cooper found Danielle on her laptop in the kitchen. She walked him to the front door. He pulled her close, but instead of kissing her, he hugged her goodbye. "You're a very special woman, Danielle. Take care of yourself, okay?"

"You, too."

Walking away from her was hard.

Too damn hard.

It was after four in the morning and Cooper was fired up over what had happened. But more than that, he hated leaving Danielle alone. He couldn't insist she leave her home, couldn't force her to move in with him, either.

On the short ride home, he flipped to the picture of the dead rat and then to the pictures of his car. As he thought back to some of the people he'd testified against as an agent, no one came to mind.

Not one single person.

But someone hated him enough to strike twice. And that someone had to be Salimov.

Next time, I'll be ready for you, asshole.

11

WELCOME TO ALPHA

DANIELLE

Sunday morning, Danielle drove the short distance to Shannon's Shelter in Alexandria, consumed with thoughts of Cooper. Line dancing with Cooper, kissing Cooper, and Cooper in her bed. The way he held her in his arms, the way he moved inside her.

Her body came alive and she exhaled a moan.

Despite what had happened to his car, and the possible danger he was in, she hadn't come down from the high of being with him.

Cooper Grant was definitely someone she would have jumped at the chance to date. He pushed all of her buttons...and buttons she didn't even know needed pushing.

You can help him for hacking, but you can't get close to him.

As she parked at the shelter, her heart ached for what could never be.

She exited her car, grabbed her computer bag from the back seat, and set her sights on the stand-alone, four-story building that took up half a city block. After entering, she walked over to the horseshoe-shaped information desk.

"Hi, I'm Danielle Fox. I'm teaching a class on Internet safety."

"Welcome to Shannon's. I'm Val." She picked up the desk phone and dialed. After a moment, Val hung up. "Lori didn't answer. I'll track her down."

While waiting, Danielle meandered around the lobby. Glass cases lined one of the walls and she read the inscriptions on the awards and plaques from the City of Alexandria for the work Shannon's Shelters were doing in the DMV.

Val sidled over. "I can bring you back now."

She led Danielle back to Lori Shannon's office where a man stood on a ladder while Lori handed him a fluorescent light bulb.

Lori offered a friendly smile. "Good to see you, Danielle. We've got a full house for your workshop."

"That's great," Danielle replied.

The man climbed down. "How ya doin'?" he asked Danielle.

"This is Billy, our handyman," Lori said. "I couldn't run the shelter without him."

Wearing a flannel shirt and overalls, Billy was short with a clean-shaven head, and a scruffy beard and mustache. His eyes were shaded behind blue tinted glasses.

Tessa Grant appeared in the doorway.

"And this is Tessa, our Facilities Manager," Lori said. "She'll help you out during your class."

Tessa gave Danielle a little wave. "Ready?"

"Thank you, again, Danielle," Lori said.

On a nod, Danielle left with Tessa. "Did you have fun last night?" Tessa asked as she escorted Danielle down the hall.

Too much fun.

"Absolutely. How 'bout you?"

"I had a blast." She led Danielle into a large meeting room. "We house over a hundred women, just at this location, and there was a huge interest in your class. We took the first fifty registrants, so we're hoping you'll come back and teach the rest of our residents."

"Of course. How long have you been working here?"

"A few months," Tessa replied, bringing Danielle to the front of the room. There were already several women sitting at the cafeteria-style tables.

"Do you need help setting up?" Tessa asked.

"Thanks, I'm good."

"I'm going to make an announcement that you're here. Be back in a second." Tessa scurried out.

A moment later, Tessa's voice boomed through the speakers as she invited residents who'd registered for the computer class to join her in the large meeting room. Residents filed in, some with laptops, others with notebooks, and some with just themselves.

Danielle set up the slide show, then waited. A few seconds later, Tessa returned.

"I'll introduce you," Tessa said.

With mic in hand, she addressed the residents from the front of the room. "Happy Sunday, everyone. Thanks for taking the time to join us for an awesome class on Internet safety. I'm Tessa Grant, your Facilities Manager. Today, we're lucky enough to have computer expert, Danielle Fox. Let's give her a Shannon's Shelter welcome."

After a warm applause, Danielle introduced herself. "I work for—" She didn't work for Truman CyberSecurity any longer. "I work for a small marketing company, helping keep the organization safe from Internet hacking. I've got a presentation, but please ask questions as we go."

She walked the class through the basics, showing the residents how to keep personal information on the Internet safe, how to spot fake websites, and how to avoid Internet scams, especially romance scams.

At some point, Billy the handyman sauntered in and watched from the back of the room. He stayed until the end, but didn't ask any questions. When the workshop ended, several residents waited to speak to Danielle. One of them was Val, the woman who'd greeted her at the front desk.

"That was totes helpful," Val said. "I fell for an online romance scam. The guy scammed me out of my savings."

"I'm sorry to hear that," Danielle said. "It happens a lot."

"Thanks for your time and expertise," Val said as Tessa pulled up alongside her.

"Val's a high school teacher," Tessa explained.

"Unfortunately, I lost my job," Val said. "I'm grateful the shelter had room for me."

"Although I'm Facilities, I've been working with our in-house career placement counselor to help Val find a teaching job." Tessa threw her arm around Val. "She's my bud."

Tessa was one of the sweetest people Danielle had ever met.

"Try some of those suggestions," Danielle said to Val. "And you can let me know how they go the next time I'm here."

On their way to the lobby, Tessa gave Danielle a tour of the facility. "We receive a lot of donations and we've got some super wealthy patrons," Tessa explained. "The residents are given so much support to get back on their feet."

As they passed Lori's office, Danielle stopped to say goodbye. She and Billy were standing nose to nose, speaking in whispers.

"Sorry to interrupt," Danielle said.

Lori jerked her head up, then backed away from Billy. "Hey, Danielle, how'd it go?"

"Great," Danielle replied. "Thanks for having me."

"Did you want to schedule your workshop for the rest of our residents?" Lori asked.

"Next Sunday works, same time."

"Perfect," Lori said. "See you then and thanks so much."

Tessa escorted Danielle to the lobby. "If the residents have follow-up questions, can I text them to you?"

"Of course."

After she and Tessa exchanged numbers, Danielle showed herself out. As she was making her way toward her car, Billy sidled beside her, startling her.

"Danielle, right?" he asked.

"Uh-huh." She stopped in front of her car.

"I'm terrible with computers," he said. "Could I join your next workshop?"

"It's fine by me," she replied. "But you'd have to check with Lori on that."

"Oh, she won't mind," Billy said. "She lets me do whatever. You have a nice day." On a nod, he headed back toward the building.

A shudder ran through her as she slipped into her car. There was something about Billy's unblinking stare that creeped her out.

That evening, as she was getting ready for bed, her phone buzzed with an incoming text and her heart leapt when she saw it was from Cooper.

"I heard you taught an awesome computer class at the shelter. How are you doing?"

"I'm good," she replied. "Making any headway with your stalker?"

"Been searching my old FBI cases," he texted back. "No one stands out."

"How do you still have access to those?"

No dots appeared.

After brushing her teeth, she entered her walk-in closet to choose an outfit for her first day at ALPHA. After deciding on a smart-looking pantsuit—tapered black pants and a waist-high jacket that she'd pair with a bright pink camisole—she checked her phone.

Still nothing from Cooper.

It's better this way.

Before getting into bed, she double-checked her house alarm and confirmed her front and back doors were bolted. Rather than leave her gun in her safe, she slid it under the other pillow.

She'd never been scared in her home before, but the car fire was a bold move by a person with a definite grudge. She hoped she hadn't made a mistake by staying there alone.

With her phone in hand, she slipped under the covers, but she didn't turn off the night table lamp. Claire-Marie floated into her thoughts. Her sister had been so trusting of everyone.

I used to be like that, too. I could crash at Emerson and Stryker's if I'm too scared to stay here.

Bing!

"Sorry about that," Cooper texted. "I've got a buddy at the Bureau who's helping me out. I'm concerned about you being alone."

"I'm fine," she lied. "Sleep well."

She turned out the light, but when sleep wouldn't come, she pulled her burner from her safe and crafted a text to Salimov. "It's Ursula, the one who bumped into you at Swanky. Unfortunately, I didn't get that job. I'm hoping you can help me."

It was after eleven. She didn't expect to hear from him, but within seconds, dots appeared.

"How's Wednesday?" he texted. "Dinner at eight?"

"I'd love that," she replied. "Where?"

"Swanky."

"Looking forward to it." After sending the text, she snapped her burner shut and locked it back in her safe.

Before getting back into bed, she peeked out her window. The street was quiet. For the first time since Emerson had moved out, Danielle didn't feel safe in her own home.

COOPER

Cooper's problem kept him up half the damn night tossing and turning. In a word… Danielle. While Salimov had managed to piss him off, he wasn't afraid. What concerned him was that Danielle had gotten caught up in his mess.

She's vulnerable living alone.

Most times, he worked out his problems on his own, but in this case, he needed advice from a close friend. If he talked to Stryker, Stryker would tell Emerson, and she'd tell Danielle. The last thing he wanted to do was disrespect Danielle by telling her boss. This time, Stryker wasn't an option.

He needed someone lowkey. And when it came to chill, Jericho was his man.

On the way to work, Cooper rapped on Jericho's front door. When he didn't answer, Cooper called him.

"Yo," Jericho answered, his voice groggy.

"I'm out front. Let me in."

"Too damn early." Jericho hung up.

Too many seconds passed before Jericho opened his front door wearing sweatpants. "What the hell do you want and why do you want it at seven in the damn morning?"

Cooper held out a coffee.

"Oh, yeah, like that's gonna do it. I own four restaurants and I got a coffee machine in my own damn kitchen." On a grunt, Jericho swung the door wide and Cooper breezed in.

"I've got a problem," Cooper said as Jericho shut the door and headed for his family room.

Jericho lived in one of the most sought-after neighborhoods in McLean. The estate boasted six bedrooms and even more baths. If Jericho weren't taking care of his family, he would have been perfectly happy living in a cave, in the middle of a dark forest. But he lived in a palace because his family came first.

Jericho lay on his family room floor. "My back's jacked the hell up."

"Have you gotten a massage at my gym?"

"Not yet."

"Did you do any of those stretching exercises I told you to do?"

"Also, a no."

Cooper laid down next to him and demonstrated one of the stretches. "Do it with me, dummy."

After Jericho finished glaring at him, he did the exercises. Ten minutes later, Jericho pushed off the floor. And smiled. "Thank you."

"You're so damn stubborn. I know what I'm talking about. I own a gym."

"You own a gym because that's your cover."

"But, I majored in Kinesiology."

"You had, like, two majors and three minors. Your fancy degrees don't impress me."

Cooper laughed. "I'm not here to impress you, I need your help."

Jericho swiped the coffee cup off the side table. "C'mon, let's go outside."

It was a chilly November morning, but Jericho kept his house super warm. Not for him. He did it for his grandmother.

"Where's Gram?" Cooper asked. "She's always up early."

"She and my aunt are on a cruise."

"Where's everyone else?"

"Who the hell knows. I was sleeping." Jericho leaned against the chair rail in his screened porch while Cooper eased onto the sofa. "What's going on?"

"I got someone stalking me," Cooper said. "He sent me a dead rat, then torched the Corvette."

"Not the Vette. I love that car."

"I spent yesterday reviewing my old cases. No one stood out."

"Okay."

"It's Salimov."

Jericho stared at him, a scowl on his sleepy face. "Did you poke the bear, Coop?"

Cooper bit back a smile. Jericho knew him too well. "It's not me I'm worried about."

"Danielle?"

"How'd you know?"

"I don't need a college degree to see what's happening between you two. You're a smitten kitten." Jericho's deep laugh rumbled like an earthquake.

"My car got torched at her place, after your party. She lives alone."

"Gimme two secs." Jericho left, only to return a few seconds later with a hair tie. He pulled his wild hair into a neat ponytail, then into a bun.

"Ask Hawk to put protection on her."

"I'd have to tell her." Cooper sipped the lukewarm drink.

"So?"

"Too invasive, plus, she told me she doesn't want to see me again."

Jericho stroked his beard. "I thought she was into you."

"She is, but she doesn't want to get close to me."

"Women make no sense to me... at all."

"I think her sister's death messed her up. I like her and I don't want to push. I can be pretty intense."

Jericho threw his head back and chuffed out a hearty laugh. "I give you props for knowing yourself. Is her home secure?"

"Not enough."

"Pay for a major upgrade. Get her Hawk's deluxe package with the barking German Shepherd. That would scare the hell outta anyone."

"Great idea." He paused. "How're my investments?"

"Never better. I'm adding a wine cellar at Carole Jean's and I'm talking to a broker about buying a fifth location for a family-style Mexican eatery."

"You need cash?"

"I'll take the investment. The wine cellar will be around a mil."

"Why so much?"

"Because I never do anything half-assed."

Cooper chuckled. "No, you don't." He stood. "I gotta get to work. Providence hired a hacker and they're starting today."

"Who is it?"

"No idea." He pulled Jericho in for a hug. "I'll call Hawk on my way to work."

The men walked through the house. At Jericho's front door, Cooper said, "Thanks for your help. Do those back exercises and get a damn massage. Everything at my gym is free for you."

"Thanks, bro." Jericho shut his front door and Cooper headed down the driveway toward his Jeep.

Before hopping in, he glanced around. A few cars were parked at the curb, but Cooper didn't see anyone watching him.

As he drove past one car, he thought he saw someone leaning down in the front seat. At the stop sign, he backtracked to check it out, but the car was gone.

He made a call. "Yo, baby," Hawk answered.

"Hey, bro, I need your help."

DANIELLE

Butterflies fluttered in Danielle's stomach as she drove into ALPHA's parking lot. Her nerves were a combination of not sleeping well—because every damn creak in her house had her jerking awake—and not knowing what to expect, especially when it came to the Operative hunting her down.

As she approached the front door, she hoped she'd made the right decision. After ringing the buzzer, the door clicked open. The friendly receptionist escorted her to Providence's office.

With a warm smile, Providence rounded her desk and shook Danielle's hand. "Welcome to ALPHA. We're so excited you're part of our team."

Providence's kind words, along with her friendly expression helped settle her down.

I'm gonna be fine.

"Would you like some coffee?"

"I'm good, thanks."

Providence closed her office door. "Before I bring you to HR, there're a couple of things to go over."

After the women got comfortable at the conference table, Providence said, "You're working for the most secret organization in the country. If that information ever got into the wrong hands, you'd be a potential target for kidnapping and ransom. Because of that, you need eyes on you at all times."

Ohgod, no.

"Our Operatives don't get a choice, but you do. You can choose to have a tiny microchip inserted into the back of your neck or we can download an app to your phone that works like any Geolocating app, but it's more sophisticated."

Danielle swallowed down the anxiety. "I wasn't expecting that."

"No one does, and no one much likes it, but it's protocol. Which do you want?"

There was no way she was letting them insert a chip into her neck. She had her sights on Salimov and she wasn't backing down. "The app."

"We have a mentor program, so I'm going to hand you off to someone. Today might not be what you're expecting, so if things become overwhelming, take a moment for yourself. My door is always open."

Danielle didn't like when people spoke around a subject, but she wasn't about to push back on day one with her new boss. "Okay."

"You report directly to me," Providence continued, "but the head of operations will decide which projects you take on. Before I take you to HR, what questions do you have for me?"

"Nothing now."

Providence stood. "Okay, then, let's get you to HR."

Forty-five minutes later, Danielle was officially an ALPHA employee. She'd filled out more online forms than the new patient packet at a doctor's office and she'd signed four more NDAs. Then, she handed over her phone while the HR manager downloaded an app that required her to create an entirely new password that was so secure, she wondered if she'd even be able to remember it.

"What's your legend?" asked the HR manager.

"I'm VP of Operations for Luck Marketing."

"That's always a safe one." She pulled out a camera. "I'll take your picture so we can add it to Luck's website."

The woman snapped a few pics, then let Danielle select one.

"Your legend will be live by the end of the day," said the HR manager. "Any questions?"

"None."

"Let me see if your mentor's ready." She dialed a four-digit extension. "Good morning. Can I bring Danielle Fox to you?" After listening, she hung up.

"Your mentor will be right down." Then, the manager offered a smile. "This is the most exciting job you can never tell anyone about. I love working here, but I hate keeping it a secret from my family, even though it's for their own protection." Then, she laughed. "And I'm just in HR! I don't know half the things that go on with the Operatives, but I know it's exciting."

Knock-knock.

"C'mon in."

The door opened and Emerson walked in. Danielle's brain screeched to a halt while she stared at her best friend.

"Hi, Danny, blah-blah-blah-blah. I'm so happy blah-blah-blah-blah-blah-blah mentor. Ready to blah-blah-blah-blah-blah-blah?"

Danielle saw Emerson's mouth moving and she heard sound, but she couldn't make sense of it.

"Blah-blah-blah my office," Emerson said.

Walking on rubber legs down the corridor, Danielle stayed close to Emerson. They passed a man who said, "Good morning."

Danielle might've said something in return. Then again, maybe not.

After rounding the corner, Emerson pulled to a stop in the quiet hallway in front of a woman. "Lily, this is Danielle Fox, our new hacker. Danny, this is Lily."

Danielle's ears were working, again.

Lily extended her hand. "Welcome to ALPHA. I'm on the Internet Research Team and we have been *dying* for a new hacker. You're going to be the most popular person around here."

Danielle offered what she hoped was a friendly smile. "I look forward to working with you."

Lily continued in the opposite direction, but Danielle didn't move. Emerson looped her arm around Danielle's and ushered her into an office at the end of the hallway.

After closing the door, Emerson dropped into one of the guest chairs. Danielle sat beside her and took in her surroundings.

"My office," Emerson said.

Another drab work space. Desk, executive chair, two guest chairs. A fake plant, no windows. Emerson did have a pretty desk lamp that gave her office a homey feel. There were no photos of her and Stryker, or their cat, Pima.

"I know this is a shock," Emerson said. "How are you doing?"

Now, Danielle had questions. A lot of them, but they were jumbled in her head, clogging up her ability to think clearly, or to speak.

"I'm sorry I had to lie to you," Emerson continued. "I'm am ALPHA Operative and—"

"Working for Stryker is your cover," Danielle said, finding her voice as the fog in her head slowly started to lift.

"Right." Emerson's sweet smile was so familiar to Danielle. "Congratulations on being hired. I just found out this morning and I couldn't wait to see you. I asked to mentor you, but if you'd rather work with someone else, that's totally okay."

"How long have you worked here?"

"Six months. I resigned as a detective to come here."

"Does Stryker work here, too?"

"No, he really does run TCS."

Danielle regarded her closest friend in the world. "This explains a lot. I knew you were lying about work because you were never there. Nothing made sense, until now."

"It was killing me." Emerson leaned over and hugged her. "You're our only hacker, so things are going to be crazy busy for you." She glanced at the time. "Why don't I take you around and introduce you to everyone?" Emerson rose. "Let's start with your office. As you can see, you can't bring in any photos. It was weird, at first, but everything we do is top-secret, so if the building was ever raided, there can't be anything here that could ID us."

"Makes sense." Danielle followed Emerson out.

Emerson introduced her to the Internet team, led by Lily. Rather than have their own offices, the team worked in cubicles, separated by partitions. Then, Emerson showed Danielle her office, which was near the Internet team.

Continuing down the hall, Emerson said, "This is where the Operatives work." A woman with purple hair stepped out of her office.

"Hey, Slash, this is our new hacker, Danielle Fox."

"Dude, I need your help, like, yesterday."

Emerson laughed. "I said you'd be crazy busy."

"Welcome to ALPHA," Slash said.

Danielle met a dozen more Operatives before Emerson brought her into the lunch room. She pulled two bottles of water from the refrigerator and handed one to Danielle.

As Danielle unscrewed the bottle and drank down half, Lily hurried in and over to Emerson. "Sorry to interrupt your tour, but I've got some good news about our Dead Man Talking case."

Danielle jerked her head in Lily's direction and her mouth went bone dry.

"Can I borrow you for a second?" Lily asked.

"Lily has been helping me with a case that you're probably going to be tasked with," Emerson explained.

"I saw a motorcycle at every single crime scene," Lily blurted.

Emerson's elated expression fell away. "First, great work, Lily, but we've seen F-150s and Camrys in every crime-scene video as well. Why is this any different?"

"I think it might be the *exact same* motorcycle." Then, Lily regarded Danielle. "I cannot wait for you to help us with this case."

Danielle had stopped breathing.

COOPER

Cooper had spent the last twenty minutes studying the surveillance videos. The man looked like Andy Driskoll, and he sounded like Andy Driskoll, but Cooper needed confirmation it *was* Driskoll. And he could only get that from seeing Driskoll up close and personal.

Driskoll was wanted in eight states. His rap sheet included carjacking—with the victims still in their vehicles—grand theft, twelve rape charges, and seventeen counts of murder. Seven of his closest relatives had been gunned down during a holiday party and his killing sprees ranged from late-night mini-marts to murdering a bunch of guys playing football in a park. He changed his looks as frequently as he changed his residence. And he could blend into a crowd so well, he'd been nicknamed Mr. Invisible.

Driskoll had been caught twice and released twice.

Cooper wanted to find this man because he was the slime of the earth, but he *needed* to find him because he was closely connected to Salimov. A reliable informant had collected information on Driskoll that included several pictures of the two men chatting on a park bench, walking down a bustling city street, even standing in line for ice cream at a shopping mall. Some of the pictures were local to the DC area, but Salimov and Driskoll had been spotted as far south as New Orleans and as far north as New York City. This hit was strategic. Cooper wanted to send a message to Salimov that he was *not* backing down. But if Cooper was going after him, he would need backup.

These latest videos put Driskoll in Myrtle Beach, South Carolina. He'd been traveling with a man, most likely security, and a woman.

He pulled out his cell phone, dialed the number.

"Yo," Jericho answered.

"I need an advance man."

"Talk to me."

After Cooper gave Jericho the lowdown, Jericho said, "I'm in. I'll drive down and get intel."

"You don't want the ALPHA jet?"

"Nah."

"Bring someone with you," Cooper said.

"I do recon alone. Who else you including?"

"Stryker and Herrera. I haven't talked to either of them—"

"You taking the ALPHA jet?"

"Yeah. We gotta move on this." Cooper checked his schedule. "How's Thursday?"

"Hold on." A few seconds later, Jericho said, "That works."

"I'll send you the file," Cooper said before ending the call.

Cooper called Stryker. "I got a kill mission."

"Go," Stryker said.

"It's Driskoll."

"Where?"

"Myrtle Beach."

Knock-knock-knock.

"Hold on," he told Stryker. "Come in."

The door opened and Emerson walked in. "Got a second?"

Cooper waved her in. "I'm back," he said to Stryker.

"Who's in?" Stryker asked.

"Me, Jericho. I'm asking Herrera."

"I'll do it. File?"

"Hold on." After a few keystrokes, he gave Stryker and Jericho access. "Done."

Emerson stepped aside and Danielle Fox crossed the threshold. In that second, everything in Cooper's universe shifted... his worlds had collided.

What the hell?

"I gotta go." Cooper disconnected.

He'd checked her out before he'd realized he'd done it. She looked stunning in a simple black pantsuit and a clingy pink top. She'd pulled her hair into a relaxed ponytail. When his gaze met hers, she was waiting.

What's she doing here and how in the hell did she even get buzzed into the building? Why would Emerson breach protocol—Oh, fuck. Fuck me. Danielle's our new hacker.

He had to play this cool. Otherwise, he'd look like a damn fool. Pushing down his surprise with what he hoped was a pleasant smile, he rounded his desk.

"Welcome to ALPHA, Danielle." He extended his hand.

When she slipped her warm, soft palm into his, the electrifying connection sent jolts of energy powering through him.

Providence appeared in the doorway. "Oh, good, you two have met. Danielle, how's your morning going?"

"Great, thank you."

"Cooper, now that you've got your hacker, the Operatives will be reaching out to her for help. Work closely with Danielle to make sure she's not overloaded."

"Of course," he replied, his attention cemented on Danielle.

"I'm here if you need me," Providence said before moving on.

Of all the hackers in the DC area, why did it have to be Danielle Fox?

It wasn't bad enough that she had rejected him. He had to see her every damn day *and* work closely with her. Even if she hadn't pushed him away, she'd be off limits, now. He'd never had a workplace romance and he wasn't about to start now. Dakota and Providence were testament that intimate relationships were permitted, but anything beyond a platonic friendship had to be documented with HR. It was bad enough that he had a chip in his neck. He didn't want one inserted into his dick as well.

His Monday morning just took a major nosedive in which he saw no way to recover. Frustration burned down to his guts. Going forward, Danielle Fox was an ALPHA team member, just like everyone else.

Only, she wasn't like everyone else. She was a beautiful, headstrong, independent, brilliant woman he desperately wanted to get to know better.

"Cooper, do you want her for the rest of the morning?" Emerson asked.

Yes, I do.

Cooper wanted her for the morning, the afternoon, and the evening. The *entire* evening.

"Did you take Danielle on a tour of the building and introduce her to everyone?" he asked.

"We got as far as your office," Emerson replied.

"Why don't you finish the tour?" Cooper asked. "I'll decide which cases need her immediate attention." He regarded Danielle and that familiar hit of adrenaline pounded through him.

This is going to be fucking torture.

"We could definitely use her help with the Dead Man Talking case," Emerson said. "We'll be in my office when you're ready for her."

I was ready for her the minute she walked through the door.

"I look forward to working with you, Danielle."

"Me, too," she replied.

Her expression gave nothing away. She did *not* look as exasperated as he felt. She wasn't smiling too big, but she wasn't frowning at him, either. She looked like she was there to do a job and appeared unfazed by the fact that he was running ALPHA.

"Pull the door closed," he said.

Once alone in his office, he sat at his desk and checked email. He had sixty-three unread ones from the weekend. The Driskoll case had snared his attention and he hadn't seen the one Providence had sent him Sunday night.

Subject Line: New Hacker

Of all the candidates I interviewed, Danielle Fox was the most qualified. She has accepted the position of Lead Hacker and will start Monday. I'm confident she'll make an excellent addition to your team. First thing Monday, I'll see if Emerson wants to be her onboarding mentor. If you have an issue with that, let me know. Please bring Danielle up to speed on the high-profile cases, and the ones where your team is chasing the most violent offenders.
I'm here if you have questions.

A growl shot from the back of his throat. Rather than dwell on what he couldn't control, he turned his attention to what he could. Which cases needed Danielle's immediate attention? At the top of his list was Dead Man Talking.

If anyone could help them find this killer, he was confident Danielle could.

12

STALLED

DANIELLE

Danielle was grateful she had a strong stomach. If she hadn't, she would have spent her first morning at ALPHA in the restroom.

It wasn't because she'd be working on a case to catch herself. She was prepared for that. What completely rocked her world was learning Emerson worked there and Cooper was running the damn show. Going forward, she would no longer accept what people told her as the absolute truth.

After Emerson finished taking Danielle around, she got her set up on her desktop and laptop. While Danielle had been cleared for top-secret work because of her previous job, she'd still been on the outside looking in. Working at ALPHA put her smack-dab in the middle of everything.

"Here's where you can view all the cases," Emerson explained. "I only have access to my own cases or any cases I'm working on with other Operatives."

When Danielle clicked on the ALL CASES file, a window popped up.

Access Denied

Emerson handed Danielle a notebook and pen. "We have chips in our necks, but we still use paper and pen." Emerson chuckled. "Let's make a list of everything we should talk to Cooper about."

Danielle jotted a note about getting access to all the files.

"What's the Dead Man Talking case?" Danielle asked, trying to sound nonchalant.

"Ooooeee, that's a hot one," Emerson said. "Someone is killing powerful, wealthy men and shoving notes in their mouths confessing to some of their crimes."

"Wow." Anxiety made Danielle's heart pound too damn hard. Emerson would hate her forever once she learned the truth.

"Yeah, a serial vigilante."

Oh, boy. "Why is ALPHA handling it?"

"The last victim was an advisor to the President, so the White House insisted ALPHA work it. In addition to managing ops, Cooper's taken the lead on that one."

Ohgod, this is so bad. "Who's working with him?"

"I am, plus Antonio Herrera. He goes by Herrera. You met him earlier."

Danielle's stomach dropped as she pushed out of her chair. "I need to use the restroom. Back in a flash."

Emerson was by her side in seconds. "I'll go, too." She smiled at Danielle. "I'm so, so happy you work here. You have no idea."

Danielle had needed a moment alone, which was so not happening. While washing their hands, Emerson said, "It's after one. I'm starving. Are you?"

Danielle had lost her appetite hours ago.

"It's your first day, so ALPHA picks up the tab. We can grab Italian at a nearby restaurant and bring it back here. You good with that?"

Danielle offered a tight nod. On the way to the restaurant, Danielle said, "Can I tell you something in confidence?"

"Of course." Emerson turned down a side street.

"Cooper and I got together after Jericho's Halloween party."

Emerson grinned at her. "And?"

"That's it."

"What do you mean, 'That's it'? How was it? Are you going to see him again? He's had a thing for you since the night we went to Raphael's."

"I told him I couldn't see him again."

Emerson pulled into the restaurant parking lot. "He must've hated hearing that."

"He did, but it doesn't matter. I can't see him now that he's my boss."

"You can, you just have to document it with HR. But why couldn't you see him again, I mean, before he became your boss?"

"Doesn't matter."

"It does to me. Is it because of Claire-Marie?"

She nodded.

Emerson reached out and clasped her hand. "How can I help, Danny?"

"You just did," Danielle replied. "I feel better knowing I can confide in you."

"Always." Emerson squeezed her hand. "Maybe you'll change your mind once you start working with him."

"No way. Dating the boss at my new job is so *not* cool."

"He's super smart, very level-headed, and a natural leader. Since he's been here, he's solved two of our hardest cases by getting into the mind of the killer."

"That's great." A wave of nausea had Danielle pushing out of the car, grateful for the cool November air.

I'm going to prison, and Cooper Grant is going to put me there.

COOPER

Leaning against the doorframe, Cooper glanced around the lunch room, in search of his target. When his gaze settled on Danielle, he couldn't look away. She was surrounded by excited employees interested in getting to know their new hacker. He couldn't blame them. He felt the same way, only he couldn't hover like a starstruck teen with a backstage pass.

He'd taken a moment to read through her resume. She'd worked her way up through the ranks at Stryker's company because she was hard working, a talented hacker, and a well-liked manager. He was about to put her to the test.

Slash said something and Danielle laughed. The joy on her face chased away the agitation he carried around with him day in and day out. That's how powerful of an effect she had on him.

"Hey, guys," he said. "Everyone getting to know Danielle?"

"She's a wicked-good hacker," Slash said. "She's too modest to admit it, but she's gonna slay it."

"Glad you approve." He regarded Danielle. "When you're finished, we'll work in my office."

"I'm done," she replied. "Thanks for making me feel so welcome," Danielle said to the group. "I hope I can live up to the hype."

After discarding her trash, she filled her water bottle, then left with him. Walking down the hall, he could feel this invisible force tugging him closer. Pushing that out, he said, "How's your first day going?"

"It's been…" She paused. "Revealing." Her voice sounded tighter than he remembered.

"I give you props. You're handling everything like a pro." He glanced over at her. Her eyebrows were knitted together and she was nibbling on her lip. Maybe she wasn't doing as well as he thought. "Let's grab your laptop," he added as they rounded the corner.

After she did, they continued in silence to his office. He left his office door open, on purpose.

"Before we begin," he said, "I want you to feel comfortable working with me. I don't want you to be concerned about being alone with me or on edge that I'm going to say something inappropriate because of what happened between us. Or, that I'll ask you out again. I'm going to treat you with the same respect I show everyone."

Her shoulders relaxed. "Thanks for saying that. I do feel comfortable with you, and I don't want things to be awkward between us either. I meant it when I told you I'd be happy to help you with whoever's stalking you."

"I appreciate that." He gestured to one of the conference table chairs and he sat beside her. "Right now, I want to bring you up to speed on several of our more high-profile cases."

Cooper dragged his gaze to her laptop and helped her navigate through the various online files. She had access to a lot of them, but not everything.

"When Emerson and I were working together, she had me click on the ALL CASES link, but I couldn't open that," she explained.

"You only have access to the cases you're working and I spent the morning figuring out where you're needed most. As we go through those, I'll give you permission to view. Sound good?"

Her pretty smile sent a streak of white-hot energy burning through him. "Absolutely."

"Let's start with our top-priority case, the Dead Man Talking killer, DMT, for short." Cooper pulled up the crime scene photos from Stu Sisson's condo. "This is Stu Sisson, a former advisor to the President." Then, he brought her up to speed on his conversation with the White House Chief of Staff, along with Sisson's longtime assistant. "The killer leaves a crumpled note of confession in each of the victims' mouths."

He stopped. She'd gone sheet-white.

"I'm sorry, Danielle. I'm plowing through this. Are the crime scene photos too much?"

"I'm fine. Really."

He regarded her for an extra second before pulling up the note. "Over the years, there have been multiple formal complaints and lawsuits filed against the victim, just like the three prior victims. Most lawsuits were settled out of court, others were dropped altogether. Some of the women were later found dead, or had committed suicide. Despite our personal opinions, we've got a job to do and that's to find the vigilante and bring him to justice."

"What do *you* think about this?" she asked.

He loved the way she peered into his eyes. It was as if she was trying to read his thoughts.

Good thing she couldn't do that. Not all of them were G-rated.

"These men are monsters, but we need to catch the vigilante before he kills again. Starting tomorrow, can you hack into the surveillance cameras near each of the crime scenes to confirm if the motorcycles Lily spotted are the same one?"

"I can start the process." Her fingers trembled as she jotted down a note. "It's not like I tap a few keys and I'm in."

He offered what he hoped was an encouraging smile. "I know this might take some time."

"I'll do my best." Her strained voice caught his ear.

"I'll give you access to the case."

He was totally into working with her, but he hated the tension rolling off her. He was concerned she might not be okay working with him. If she couldn't relax, he'd have to offload everything to Emerson. The muscles running down his shoulders turned to lead at the thought, but he'd do what was in her best interest, regardless of how he felt.

After he'd given her access to the files she needed, he closed his laptop. "What questions do you have?"

"None, now," she replied.

"I'm available if you need anything." With the meeting over, he returned to his desk.

Rather than collect her laptop and leave, she went right over to him. "I want to help you find the person stalking you," she murmured.

"I don't think that's a good idea."

She furrowed her brow. "Why not? Don't you think I can help you?"

"I know you can, but my personal interest in you hasn't changed."

"I see." She was staring so hard at him, the desire to kiss her had him biting back a groan.

"I think you're in danger," she murmured, "and I wouldn't want anything bad to happen to you."

There it was. Her truth. She had feelings for him, despite whatever issues she was struggling with. Or, maybe, he was reading her all wrong.

"Danielle, do you blame yourself for your sister's death?"

Her expression faltered, then she hugged herself. The desire to comfort her was stronger than his commitment to act like a professional. He pulled her into his arms and held her. She relaxed into him for a few glorious seconds and every damn problem in his world disappeared. Salimov didn't matter. Neither did Renfrow. His vengeance drifted away on a raft, leaving only still waters for miles and miles.

She broke away from him. "I'm sorry, Cooper. I'm acting so unprofessional."

"I'm going to close the door so I can talk to you. If you're uncomfortable with that, we'll invite Emerson to join us."

"I trust you. If I didn't, I never would have invited you into my bed," she whispered.

As he closed his office door, thoughts of them entwined in an intimate embrace flashed in his mind. Forcing that out, he sat behind his desk. He hated the distance because she looked like she was in pain, but he was her boss and he had to act like one.

"Please sit." He gestured to one of his guest chairs.

She did.

"Danielle, why are you blaming yourself?"

"I didn't protect my sister and she died."

"She was killed by a psychopath who manipulated her to gain her trust. He took advantage of that trust and, then, he violated it." She didn't respond, so he continued. "Good people make terrible decisions every day. Most of the time, nothing bad happens. Sometimes bad things do, and on occasion, the absolute worst thing imaginable does."

"I know."

"What can I do to help you work through your grief and anger?"

Again, she furrowed her brow. "How did you know I was angry?"

"Years ago, my brother was killed. Even though I couldn't have prevented it, I've been angry most of my life."

"We're more alike than I realized," she whispered. "What happened to your brother?"

Knock-knock.

"Come in."

Emerson opened the door. When she saw Danielle, she grinned. "There she is! I'm taking off, but I wanted to check in before I left." After a second, her smile dropped. She entered the office and shut the door.

"Danny, what's wrong?" Emerson sat in the chair beside Danielle.

"I've been blaming myself for Claire-Marie's death." Danielle was speaking so quietly, Cooper had to lean forward to hear her.

Emerson hugged her, then took her hand. "Honey, it's not your fault."

"I'm going to give you two some privacy." Cooper slid his laptop into his computer bag, then stood.

Danielle smiled up at him. "Thank you for your

professionalism and kindness today. My offer to help you still stands."

"Thank you. I hope we didn't overload you."

"I'll be ready to dive in, first thing tomorrow."

"Emerson, pull my door closed when you leave." Cooper left, shutting the door behind him.

DANIELLE

Danielle shifted in the chair. "I know we've talked about Claire-Marie's death so many times you're sick of hearing about it."

"We can talk about it for as long as you need until you feel better," Emerson replied.

Danielle smiled. "Thank you for being so amazing. When I saw the crime scene pictures of Stu Sisson, I kind of flipped out a little."

"That's understandable. You want to talk about why you're blaming yourself?"

"I feel like I could have stopped Claire-Marie from going to that photo shoot, or gone with her, or asked you to come with us."

Emerson's sweet smile assuaged Danielle's angry soul. "No one could have stopped your sister. She was a free spirit and a very trusting woman. Are you replaying the situation with a different outcome?"

"Yeah, how'd you know?"

"I did that after Doug died, even though I wasn't even working his case with him. My therapist told me that's one of the ways people can process loss. Everyone is different. There's no right or wrong way."

While staring at the floor, she murmured, "There *are* wrong ways to process death."

"Like what?"

Killing bad guys so they don't hurt anyone else.

Danielle shrugged. "I'm rambling. It's been a great first day, but I'm pretty beat."

"You want to grab some dinner?"

"I'm gonna drop in on a kickboxing class, then go home and make myself a big bowl of pasta."

"If you want me to spend a few days with you—"

"You are so good to me." Danielle rose. "Thank you for listening and for being there."

"Always," Emerson replied.

Grateful for the love, Danielle hugged her friend, then returned to her office. She slipped her laptop into her satchel and left. Despite her only having access to certain files, she had a feeling that, if she wanted, she could hack into all of them.

Her first day at her new job would have been great, except for the myriad of surprises. Emerson, Cooper, then learning that both of them were hunting her down. No doubt she'd end up in prison and lose her best friend in the process.

Even if I stopped going after these monsters, I'm still guilty of committing four murders.

After an intense workout in her kickboxing class, she left the gym. If Cooper was there, she didn't see him. Back at her house, she re-alarmed as soon as she got inside. Then, she showered and made herself that pasta, pausing a few times to peek out her window. The neighborhood was quiet.

Once she'd eaten, she went into her closet, opened her safe, and checked her burner. There were two messages from Salimov. The first one had come in during the day.

"I might have job for you. We talk at dinner."

When she hadn't responded, he sent another. "Wed, 8 at Swanky still work for you?"

She typed out a response. "Yes, Swanky on Wed." And she sent it.

Dots appeared, then his message. "Excellent."

Here we go...

She returned the burner to the safe, then went into her kitchen and logged into her ALPHA laptop. As she started reading the Dead Man Talking case, she released a long sigh of relief.

There were scarce clues and no evidence, though she knew she was working on borrowed time.

COOPER

Wednesday afternoon, Cooper was reviewing the Dead Man Talking case with Danielle, Emerson, and Herrera in the conference room. Much to his disappointment, Danielle hadn't made any headway. For the past two days, she'd been trying to access the surveillance systems of residences and businesses along the motorcycle's route. So far, that trail had gone cold.

Cooper's frustration was growing with each passing day. The bright spot in this case was that Danielle had confirmed Lily's findings. A black motorcycle with a blurred license plate had been in the vicinity of all four murders.

"I'm going to step away from the case, tomorrow, and focus on a different one," Danielle explained. "I feel like I'm already behind, and I can make up for my lack of progress if I move on."

"Understood," Cooper replied. "Herrera, do you have any updates?"

Herrera had been questioning some of Sisson's victims. Most had signed NDAs and couldn't talk about Sisson, but he had spoken to Abigail Spencer, the woman Sisson's assistant had mentioned to Cooper.

"It was tough to hear," Herrera said. "Sisson was championing her onboarding with one of the senators, when he suggested they meet so he could help her prep for her interview. He sexually assaulted her, then threatened to hurt her and her family if she talked to anyone."

"Men like these make me want to never find the vigilante," Cooper mumbled under his breath. "Sorry, disregard."

"I feel the same way," Emerson said. "But we have a job to do, right? I think I might have made some headway. I've got the cell phone records from the first two men killed and I'm going to start working on those after our meeting."

"The White House is putting the pressure on us to come up with a list of suspects," Cooper explained. "They must be watching too many crime shows because Providence and I have told them that clues don't just fall out of the sky."

"I'm sorry I can't ID the motorcycle," Danielle said.

"I agree with your strategy," Cooper said. "Move on to a different case and circle back to this in a few days. Sometimes time away is a good thing."

Except when it came to Danielle. Then, it was a very, very bad thing. She'd been head down in her office the past two days. He'd stopped by a couple of times to check in with her, but he was forcing himself to treat her like he treated everyone else on his team.

Only, she wasn't like anyone else on his team.

Seeing her was the absolute highlight of his day. There was no close second when Danielle was in a room. She had a powerful effect on him, in the best way possible. It wasn't just that he found her so incredibly beautiful or that she smelled like a flower garden after a rainstorm. She had a quality about her—a mix of confidence and humility that he found so damn appealing.

"Before I forget, I need help with Friday's team-building event." His gaze flitted between Emerson and Herrera.

"I'll help you," Danielle and Emerson replied in unison.

"What do you need?" Danielle followed up with.

What he needed was her.

He held her gaze for a beat too long, appreciating how she'd worn her hair up in a twist, the loose tendrils framing her face. Every time he glanced in her direction, he'd get an adrenaline hit. Being around her was both invigorating and frustrating as hell.

"I've rented Paintball Playland in Chantilly, from noon 'til four," he told Danielle. "Can you confirm that?"

"Of course." She made a note. "Under what name?"

"Fly the Coop Extreme Sports," Cooper replied.

"Emerson, can you get a final head count for paintball and for dinner?" Cooper asked. "So far, we've got eighteen who are playing and twenty-three for dinner."

"Reservations are at Carole Jean's, right?" Emerson asked.

"Why not Jericho Road or Raphael's?" Herrera asked.

"Jericho Road is closed for a wedding reception on Friday," Cooper explained. "Carole Jean's has a private dining room that can accommodate all of us. Remind them that dinner is at eight. Herrera, can you split the paintball teams into two? And make them evenly balanced."

Herrera chuckled. "No worries."

When the meeting ended, Cooper asked Danielle to stay behind.

The second they were alone, the energy in the room shifted. The air became charged with a strong magnetic pull he had to fight against. He wanted to go to her, wrap her in his arms, and tell her how much he loved seeing her every day. But seeing her wasn't enough. He wanted to ask her out, cook her dinner, take her on a relaxing boat ride. It didn't matter what they did, as long as they were together.

"Settling in okay?" he asked.

"Absolutely." She held his gaze for an extra beat. "Did you hear back from the arson investigator?"

Cooper nodded. "The rag was soaked in a flammable liquid. They've opened a case, but I doubt they'll find anything. I've been rethinking your offer to help me find the person who's stalking me."

Her face lit up, sending a blast of heat through him. "I'd be happy to help you. Maybe one night this week?"

"My schedule's packed this week, but I've got time over the weekend."

Her reaction was subtle, but he caught it. There was a slight tug on her lips and her cheeks pinkened. "That'll work," she murmured.

The look in her eyes, coupled with the desire to be close to her, had him swallowing down the burgeoning desire. He wanted to touch her so damn badly. Take her hand in his and kiss her fingertips, or lean close and feel her lips on his. Hell, he'd even settle for a damn handshake.

"We can figure out a time at Friday night's dinner."

After she collected her laptop and left, he raked his hands through his hair.

How the hell am I supposed to keep my distance when all I want is her by my side?

He left his office and found Herrera in his. After shutting the door, he waited until his coworker hung up.

"Whatcha need?" Herrera asked.

"When you split the paintball teams, put Danielle on my team."

Herrera chuckled. "You got it bad for her, don't you?"

"That obvious?"

"You've been keepin' things chill, except for now. I put clues together for a living. This one's a no-brainer."

"If only it were that easy to solve the DMT case."

"You know, sometimes those killers have a knack for hiding in plain sight," Herrera replied.

DANIELLE

As Danielle finished getting ready for her evening with Salimov, she pushed Cooper from her thoughts to focus on her next mark. One was such a good man, the other beyond evil.

She opened her safe and switched out her personal phone for her burner, then pulled out her Glock. Though she had no intention of leaving with Salimov, Ursula never went anywhere without her sidearm.

After tucking it into her jacket pocket, she returned to the bathroom to check herself. No blonde hairs were sticking out below her wig's platinum-blonde updo, and her brown contact lenses were in place. She'd dressed in leather pants, a white shirt, and leather jacket. She'd been debating how many shirt buttons to leave open, so she unfastened the second button, then buttoned it back up.

Tonight, was recon only, but she'd hacked into Swanky's surveillance system and shut down their cameras. If someone on their security team realized the cameras were off, there was a good chance they'd turn them back on. Danielle had a backup plan for that, as well. She'd also turned off the traffic cameras in the area.

Back on the first floor, she set the house alarm, and walked into her single-car garage. There, she pulled on her riding boots and helmet, then her leather gloves. As she rode to the club, she got into character. Ursula was a free spirit, like her sister had been. Ursula was looking for a job, maybe even a good time. Whatever it took to lure these predators into her web.

She parked in Swanky's lot, locked up her helmet, tucked her riding gloves into the side satchel, and sashayed inside.

The hostess led her to a table. She'd arrived early on purpose, since she told Salimov how she'd gotten fired from her last job for being late all the time. This was Ursula's best attempt at showing him that she really, really needed a job.

Not long after, Salimov was escorted to the table.

"Hello, Ivan."

He gave her a brief once over and frowned.

Not enough skin for you?

"How have you been?" he asked after sitting across from her.

"I'm about to take a nanny job if I don't find something more suitable. I don't like children, so it's definitely not a good fit. But a girl's gotta eat, right?"

The server took their drink orders, returning promptly with his scotch and her sparkling water.

"Tonight, we share bottle of wine," Salimov said.

"Trying to get me drunk and take advantage of me?" She forced a laugh.

His smile did not touch his eyes. Had she struck a chord with him?

Moving on, she said, "Tell me about this possible job you have for me."

"Ursula, why all business? You are beautiful woman. I want to get to know you."

She leaned forward. "Are you trying to help me find a job or get into my pants?"

"What's wrong with having more than one goal?"

She had to play this carefully. If she stormed off in a huff, she'd ruin her chances of seeing him again. If she seemed overly eager, he might expect her to leave with him. "I like to prioritize my goals. First, we work, then we play. Why don't you help me find a job, first, then I can show you my gratitude?"

His lips split into a menacing grin that sent shivers down her spine. "A reward after we work, no?"

I'm going to reward you with a bullet between your eyes.

13

PASSION UNLEASHED

COOPER

Cooper had planned his evening down to the minute. Dinner with Geoffrey, home to prep, on the plane by midnight, land in Myrtle Beach at one thirty in the morning. Mission goes down by four, he and his crew are back in the DMV the next morning.

As he was parking at the restaurant, his phone rang. It was Jericho.

"Hey," Cooper answered. "What's the word?"

"It's Driskoll, confirmed," Jericho said.

"Is he alone?"

"He's got a woman and a coupla guys with him. One's his guard. Never leaves him alone. Waits outside the can for him."

"Who's the other?"

"No idea. I ran his face through Stryker's IDware, but I'm not getting a hit."

"You got photos you can upload to the portal?"

"Doing it."

Geoffrey's Rolls Royce pulled into the parking lot. He got out and headed toward the restaurant.

"I'll do recon on the flight," Cooper said.

"You're cutting it close," Jericho said.

"I got this."

"Safe travels." The line went dead and Cooper exited his Jeep.

Swanky was an over-the-top members-only restaurant that catered to the elite. Since Geoffrey had a financial stake in the eatery, he liked stopping by to check on things. Cooper paused at the maître d' stand before being whisked to Geoffrey's private booth. He was busy flirting with the server when Cooper eased down across from him.

The woman giggled. "Mr. Edelman, you're so funny." She eyed Cooper. "Is this your brother?"

"My son," Geoffrey replied.

Rather than correct him, Cooper let it go. Geoffrey liked touting himself as something of a family man. For some reason, he thought it impressed the ladies.

"What can I get you to drink?" she asked.

"A gin martini, one olive," Geoffrey said. "Use the Nolet's Reserve and do *not* bruise the gin."

"Yes, sir." She regarded Cooper.

"Whiskey, neat," Cooper replied.

"Is Macallan acceptable?" she asked.

"It's fine," Cooper replied.

"Would you like an appetizer?" she asked.

"I don't," Geoffrey said. "Coop?"

Cooper had worked through lunch. "Yeah, surprise me." Then, he glanced over at Geoffrey. "I'm ready to order."

"What's the rush? We just sat down."

"I'm gonna gnaw on this table if I don't eat."

Geoffrey chuckled. "I'll have the mahi-mahi."

"Excellent choice, Mr. Edelman. And you, sir?"

"What does the chef recommend?"

"Chicken marsala or the pan-seared salmon," she replied.

Cooper was hungry enough to eat both. As if Geoffrey could read his mind, he said, "Let's get both."

Cooper chuckled. "I'll take the salmon."

The server said she'd be back with their drinks and left.

Cooper looked forward to his get together with Geoffrey, a monthly event since he'd graduated from the Naval Academy. The two men talked about their investments, market trends, and the latest financial fad to hit the Internet. Geoffrey always had a cautionary tale about an investment he'd made that had gone south, or he'd share a story about a chance meeting with someone that had resulted in a great business opportunity.

They rarely talked about the women they were seeing. Cooper hadn't dated anyone seriously in a while. Geoffrey was a dating machine, never staying with one woman more than a few months.

As the two men discussed the latest trends with cryptocurrency, the server returned with their drinks. "I put a rush on the order."

"Thank you," Cooper said, before turning back to Geoffrey.

"You should get her number, hook up with her," Geoffrey said after the waitress left.

"I'll pass."

"Seeing someone?"

"Not at the moment." Cooper wasn't ready to talk about Danielle, mostly because there *was* no Danielle. It was easy to redirect the conversation with Geoffrey, so he said, "My net worth just hit a hundred and ten mil."

A beaming Geoffrey raised his martini glass. "Congratulations, that's fantastic. I'm very proud of you." He swallowed down a mouthful of gin.

Cooper sipped the top-shelf liquor. "I want to talk to you about an investment I'm thinking of selling."

The conversation about wealth and investments continued,

while the attentive server delivered their sundried tomato garlic butter bruschetta appetizer, and then their entrees.

After plates were cleared, Geoffrey's phone rang. "Excuse me." He answered. After listening, a shadow darkened his eyes. "Hold on." He pushed out of his chair. "Cooper, I have to take this."

As Geoffrey made his way toward the lounge, the server returned. "Any dessert or an after-dinner drink?"

Cooper needed to take off. He had left little time to prep for his mission, then get to the airport. He pulled out his credit card. "Just the check."

She took the card and left.

After downing the last swig of his liquor, he glanced around the room. Swanky was filled with men in suits and women in dresses. A party of ten dressed in tuxes and gowns were seated nearby. Cooper's thoughts jumped to Danielle and how elegant she looked with her hair up.

She looks phenomenal in everything... or nothing at all.

As that large group cleared out, his gaze settled on a man across the room facing him. Hair on the back of Cooper's neck prickled.

No fucking way. That's Salimov.

There he was, but Cooper couldn't do a damn thing about it. His stomach dropped while his hands curled into fists. Every muscle in his body wanted to walk over to that table, pull out his Glock, and fire at will.

The blonde seated across from Salimov rose and began weaving her way through the maze of tables toward the back of the restaurant. Her leather pants hugged her muscular thighs. Her leather jacket hung open, revealing a simple white shirt. Based on his knowledge of Salimov, the woman wasn't his wife or his mistress.

Another potential victim.

As she passed him, their eyes met. A jolt of electricity surged through him. Despite the platinum hair, that woman was Danielle. He was certain of it.

She kept going and vanished down the hallway toward the restrooms.

What the fucking hell is she doing with Salimov?

His training kept him calm, but his mind was racing with possibilities, none of them good. If she left with him, she'd be putting herself at the mercy of a monster. He thought he knew her. Clearly, he did not. Not at all.

He refocused his thoughts on getting her the hell out of there.

Geoffrey returned to the table. "Cooper, I'm sorry, but I have to leave."

"No problem," Cooper bit out, his thoughts still tethered to Danielle.

"We'll talk soon." Geoffrey took off toward the front door.

The server returned with Cooper's credit card. He signed, left her a generous tip, and stashed his card.

The server handed him a folded napkin. "My number."

As he rose, he glanced in Salimov's direction and confirmed it was the diplomat. Fortunately, Salimov was head down on his phone. Cooper left the napkin before powering down the hallway toward the ladies' room, rage nipping at his heels.

As he stood guard outside, he eyed the fire alarm on the wall and emergency exit at the end of the hall. He would be long gone by the time anyone had figured out what had happened. If the surveillance cameras caught him, he'd deal with that. Better to ask for forgiveness than permission.

A woman exited and startled when she saw Cooper looming at the entrance. "Oh, you scared me."

"I'm waiting for my girlfriend. Did you see a pretty blonde in black leather?"

Just then, the door flew open and Danielle stood there, her gaze cemented on Cooper. She didn't look surprised. She looked fucking furious.

"There you are, honey," Cooper said before tossing a nod at the other woman. "I found her."

"Have a good evening," the woman said before heading toward the dining room.

With a firm grip on Danielle's arm, he ushered her toward the back exit.

"What the hell are you doing?" she ground out, the anger in her voice catching Cooper's ear.

"Saving your damn life," he replied, before pulling the fire alarm.

The siren blasted the air as Cooper pushed through the back door, triggering the emergency alarm. Moving with urgency, he escorted her to his Jeep. "Get in."

"Get lost, Cooper. I don't work for you after hours."

"This isn't about being your boss, for fuck's sake. That guy you're with is Ivan Salimov. He's extremely dangerous. Get in the fucking car."

He opened the door and glared at her. A few seconds passed before she got in. The fury he worked so hard to keep in check was ready to explode out of him in a torrent of rage.

She's safe.

He sped away as people started filtering through the front door. Agitation streamed through him and he had to focus on his breathing to calm himself down. He was hunting Salimov to take him out and the one—*the one*—woman he was interested in, was having dinner with him.

There was no rock wall high enough that could take this enragement away. He said nothing as he drove. After several blocks, he stopped at a red light and realized he had no idea where he was headed.

"If you keep driving west, we'll eventually end up in California. Salimov won't be able to get to me there." Her voice was thick with sarcasm.

"Did you drive to Swanky?"

She pursed her lips.

"Tell me Salimov doesn't know where you live."

More silence.

"He doesn't."

The light turned green and Cooper pushed through the intersection. The silence was deafening, but he did not give a fuck. Not one single fuck. He drove until he'd arrived at her house. Per usual, her car was parked in the driveway, so he pulled in and tapped her bumper with his.

She pushed out of the Jeep and stormed up her driveway, punched the code into the garage keypad and waited while the door opened.

So much for a 'thank you'.

In the garage, she turned. "I'm having a drink," she bit out. "Do you want one?"

Why the hell not?

He followed her through the empty garage and inside. He would have asked why she didn't park her car in there, but that seemed pretty fucking irrelevant, at the moment. As the garage door closed, she deactivated the house alarm.

In her kitchen, she hitched her hand on her hip. "What do you want?" Pregnant pause. "To drink, I mean. What do you want to drink?"

"Hard liquor."

She opened a cupboard. The bottle of Maker's Mark was on the top shelf and out of her direct reach.

"Can I get that for you or is that also a violation of fucking with Danielle's life?"

She growled so hard at him, he almost laughed. Strange, how he wanted to do something nice for her and this was how she showed her appreciation. She set out two glasses, he pulled down the bottle and poured in the alcohol.

She raised her glass. "Mind your own damn business, Cooper." And she tossed back a hearty mouthful.

He downed half the whiskey. "Did you hack into my work file?"

The surprise in her eyes gave him her answer. She had not.

"What? Absolutely not."

"Why were you with him?"

Silence. Cold, biting, glaring silence.

"What I do in my private life is none of your business."

"It damn well is when the person you're with is a fucking monster." He tossed back the rest of the booze.

"It's not like I do a background check on every guy I meet in a bar."

Her eyebrow arched. It was subtle, but that could have been a lie. At this point, he wasn't sure what to believe.

"Are you into stranger sex?" he pressed.

She downed another mouthful. "Maybe."

He was utterly confused. "You tell me you're gutted over not protecting your sister, but you've become her. You were having dinner with a predator."

"Fuck you, Cooper Grant."

"You want a stranger? I can be that guy who fucks you for his own needs and doesn't put you first. Doesn't give a damn about pleasuring you. At least with me, you know I'm not gonna hurt you. That I won't rape you and completely tank your life."

DANIELLE

Danielle plowed into him and kissed him with everything she had. And he kissed her back with an intensity that left her panting. The kiss was filled with a fury that turned into no-holds-barred lust. She raked her fingers down his back and bit his earlobe. Their frenzied groans and gasps fueled their passion. She couldn't slow down, had to get him inside her. A mix of hatred and gratitude consumed her.

Their clothing came off in a tornado of flying garments. Frisson after frisson of desire had her grinding into him and raking her tongue over his. His hard-muscled body had her soaked with need.

His eyelids were hooded while he sucked down a lung-filling breath. She eyed his massive chest and jutting cock before soaking up his gorgeous face.

She was on fire for him. Out of control burning, blazing, crazy lust. She was also raging angry with him for pulling her out of that restaurant. But buried beneath the anger was a woman who now knew this man would walk through fire to protect her. Because he'd just done that.

"Sit on the sofa." She left him to grab the box of condoms from her bedroom.

When she returned, she slunk over to him, mounted him, and tossed the box on the cushion next to them. She'd left the wig on, but she'd removed her tinted contact lenses.

"You want stranger sex?" he asked. "I'm all in."

The condom was on in seconds. She rose up and placed his massive shaft at her opening. Inch by glorious inch, her tender flesh expanded around his massive cock until he was rooted deep inside her. An explosion of pleasure had her crying out, hijacking her ability to think.

Her need wasn't for some random guy. She wanted him and only him. And that scared the hell out of her. She was setting herself up for a colossal loss. Pain slashed at her heart.

"Where'd you go?" he murmured between kisses.

"I'm right here. No talking. Just fucking. It's a hookup and we're fucking for pleasure. That's all you need to do."

"You sure about that?" he asked, as if she'd just dared him.

"Yes."

"Get on the floor. I'm gonna fuck you from behind."

She dropped down, he knelt behind her, then tunneled back inside. She cried out, the overwhelming explosion of pleasure chasing away her demons. His grunts and groans were gritty, like she'd given him permission to unleash his own inner wild.

"Fuck, fuck, you feel good," he said, his husky voice making her wetter still.

The intensity of his thrusts, coupled with his sexy sounds, had awakened something inside her she didn't know existed. He turned her into a savage beast overcome with lust.

He reached around, fondled her breast, massaged and pinched her nipple. She cried out. "You're gonna make me come." Her breathing was erratic and she was spiraling toward an orgasm.

He slowed his thrusting down, but he powered all the way to her end, then did it again. On the third pass, he roared out his climax while he poured himself into her.

Her own orgasm was triggered by his. Wave after wave of euphoria washed over her, drowning her in absolute glory.

Something she did not deserve.

She was a killer. She was one of the bad guys. And she was being rewarded by the one man who was hunting her.

He didn't pull out. Instead, he leaned over and hugged her. Then, he kissed her back and slowly withdrew. Sated, all she could do was roll onto her back and lay on the floor, boneless. The second they stared into each other's eyes, she knew.

She knew how she felt. She could fall in love with this man. If her life had been on a different track going in a completely different direction, she would have.

He shook his head, but there was a just-fucked gleam in his eyes that kept her anchored on his handsome face. When he lay on her, she *didn't* want to wrap her arms around him. She *didn't* want to kiss him again and again, either. And she sure as fuck *didn't* want him to fold her into his arms, breathe deep, and release a long, satisfying sigh.

Yet, they did all of those things. The absolute worst thing he did was capture her heart, fully and completely.

There was no way this would end well. No way at all.

Their embrace sparked another fiery kiss that slowly tapered to a series of tender pecks. Then, his smile made her heart leap. She tried not to smile. Again, her body was working independently of her brain. She smiled back.

"There she is." After he kissed her forehead, he peered into her eyes. "What am I going to do with you, Danielle? I mean, seriously."

"This sex thing was just a blip. You know, a one-off."

"Are you lying to me or to yourself? Because I like you, despite your dangerous behavior. And I'm gonna pursue you. You've been warned."

She wanted to crawl into his lap and hide there forever. This sexy, intelligent, hardworking, good guy wanted her, and only her. She should be floating on a fluffy cloud, but she was mired in angst.

"Thank you for the hookup," she said. "You can go now."

He laughed. "You like me. I see it in your eyes. Your fingers are in my hair again."

She jerked her hand off his head and nudged him off her. As he moved away, he kissed her tummy.

"You've got the abs of a beast." He stood. "And the face of an angel. Do you really want me to go?"

Of course not.

She stayed silent.

"While you sort that out, I'm gonna shower. Why don't you take off that wig and shower with me?"

He held out his hands. It was like he'd thrown her a life raft in the middle of a raging sea. She placed her hands in his and he pulled her to her feet. When he kissed her again, her entire universe clicked into place.

Hand in hand, they went up the stairs and into her bathroom.

He kissed her bare shoulder and caressed her backside. His touch left her breathless, yet, around him, she breathed easier. It was a heady combination that defied logic.

While he removed the condom, she pulled off the wig. He turned on the faucet while she removed hair clips. Simple, irrelevant tasks that had her feeling like they were a couple.

Only we aren't. This was a hookup to throw him off my trail.

Her heart dipped. She liked this man.

After removing her diamond heart necklace, she joined him in the shower. The hot water felt glorious on her back, but it was his arms around her that felt like heaven. Being doted on by Cooper was like a dream she never wanted to wake from. He lathered her hair and massaged her scalp. Hard, strong fingers working their magic on her head.

As she rinsed away the soap, he kissed her nipple. Her eyes fluttered open while he kissed and gently sucked her hard nib. First one, then the other.

"I neglected the girls during our role play fuck or whatever the hell that was."

Then, with strong, soothing hands, he washed her body. After she rinsed off, he cupped her core. Her insides came alive and she nuzzled his neck. Large fingers entered her folds and she clung to him. He was spoiling her with another round of ecstasy.

While pleasuring her, his mouth found hers. The way he kissed her had her panting and moaning with delight. The way he fondled her clit—gently, at first, then with increased pressure and speed—had her roaring toward a release. When the orgasm ripped through her, she gripped him for support, kissed him hard, and climaxed into his protective hand.

There was something so intimate about being in the shower with him that tears pricked her eyes and flowed down her cheeks. Tears that she didn't realize she had left to cry. Only, these weren't from grief, they were from joy. Something she never ever thought she'd feel again.

The hollow place in her heart was letting him in... just a little.

He kissed her softly. "I'm right here."

Her ugly sobs were gut-wrenching and freeing at the same time. And, then, they were over. She lifted her tear-streaked face to his. "You're right. I do like you. But I'm not the person you think I am."

Pushing out of his arms, she squeezed the bodywash onto her palm and created a sudsy mountain, which she rubbed onto Cooper's chest. Touching him was like a present she didn't deserve, yet she would appreciate every dip, every striation, every damn thing about him while she could.

As she ran her fingers over his abs, she leaned up and kissed him. Their chemistry was unstoppable and insatiable. When she stroked his hard shaft, he moaned.

"I love your touch," he murmured.

I love touching you, Cooper.

Careful not to get suds near his opening, she took her time bringing him the ultimate pleasure.

When she finished, she pulled him close and kissed him like it was the last time she would feel his lips pressed to hers.

She dressed for him in a cut-off T-shirt and loose sweats. He pulled on his pants and shirt. Then, she made them hot toddies and they huddled close on the floor by her roaring gas fireplace.

"We need to talk," Cooper said.

He was right, they did.

COOPER

"Salimov is dangerous," he began. "Why were you with him?"

She pursed her lips.

"Were you going to have stranger sex with him?"

"No."

He regarded her for a minute. "Are you going to see him again?"

"It's not what you think."

He sipped the spiked tea before setting the mug on the hearth. "Despite your unwillingness to confide in me, I'm going to tell you something I haven't told *anyone*, not even Stryker."

"Okay," she replied.

"Six years ago, my younger sister, Chantal, got a job as an event planner. After a couple of years, she was promoted to account manager. One of her accounts was the Russian Embassy, where she met Salimov." Cooper stopped. This was always gut-wrenching for him to talk about, but Danielle needed to know how evil Salimov was.

When she ran a gentle hand down his back, her soothing touch spurred him on.

"Salimov started sexually harassing her, but he threatened to get her fired if she told anyone. Then, one night, he raped her. More than once." His chest tightened, the anger rushing to the surface, like it always did.

"Ohgod, no," Danielle whispered.

"That time, he told her if she said anything to anyone, he'd hurt her *and* her family. That's when she quit her job and refused to leave the house. She lost a lot of weight. When she finally confided in my mom, my family hired a lawyer and went after Salimov. He denied everything. Every fucking thing. I was with the Bureau and tried going after him myself, more than once. Salimov has a lot of powerful friends in Washington. The last time I went after him, the State Department told my boss I needed to stand down. They tried to ship me off to Nevada by promoting me. Fortunately, Stryker stepped in and I got hired into ALPHA."

After a long pause, he said, "I hate Salimov with everything I have." Cooper pushed off the floor and paced. "And there's not a fucking thing I can do about it."

Danielle went to him and held him. "I'm sorry for what he did to your sister. He's a monster and he has got to be stopped."

"Now, do you understand why I was so furious when I saw you with him?"

She kissed him. "Thank you for stepping in."

"There's one more thing." A shadow darkened his eyes. "I don't have confirmation, but I think he's behind the dead rat and my torched Vette."

"Ohmygod, seriously?"

"He caught me on a stakeout and he's sending me a very clear message. Please, Danielle, stay away from him." He broke away from her. "I hate to leave you, but I gotta go."

Sadness flashed in her eyes. "Why?"

"I've got a kill job."

DANIELLE

She stared at him. Had she even heard him correctly. "Did you say kill?"

"Yeah."

"Are you taking out Salimov?"

"I can't touch him."

"But you're an Operative."

"Even Operatives have fucking rules."

At her front door, he held her in his arms. "I'm flying to South Carolina, back sometime tomorrow, but I'll be working from home. Stay away from Salimov. He's a predator with an army to protect him. You can't win."

"I understand."

He kissed her. "See you at work on Friday. You better bring your A-game for paintball."

"Good luck on your mission."

He opened the door, glanced back. "Stay out of trouble."

On a smile, she closed and bolted her door, set her house alarm, then headed into the family room to collect her leathers and fish her burner phone from her pocket. As she'd expected, there was a text from Salimov.

"I lost you in the chaos," Salimov texted. "Sorry our evening was cut short."

"Me, too," she texted him back. "Let's plan to get together again, real soon."

Thinking about what Salimov had done to Cooper's sister made her blood boil. Despite Cooper's warning, she was going to take out the son of a bitch herself, first chance she got.

Cooper can't go after Salimov, but I can... and there's no one to stop me.

14

THE ALPHA KILL

COOPER

At quarter past midnight, Cooper boarded ALPHA's private jet to find Stryker and Sinclair Develin already on board.

"Welcome to the party," Stryker said. "We were starting to think you'd bailed. Don't you check your phone?"

Sin rose. He and Cooper hugged it out. "It's been a while," Cooper said. "Where's Herrera?"

"I'm his fill-in," Sin said.

"I'll let the pilot know we're ready." Cooper dropped his duffel, spoke with the pilot and returned to sit facing both men. Like him, they were wearing all black. Per these types of missions, he'd left his personal cell phone and his ID at home. Instead, he had a burner he'd use, then ditch after the kill.

The Cessna Citation X+ was a sleek, sophisticated mid-sized jet with seating for eight, arranged in two pods of two rear-facing and two forward-facing seats in each one. As the bird taxied toward the runway, Cooper buckled in.

"I called you a half dozen times," Stryker said. "Where were you?"

"I had an issue I had to deal with."

Stryker and Sin exchanged glances. "A woman," they both said.

Cooper bit back a smile. "It's complicated." Now was *not* the time to talk about Danielle. He needed to get focused. "Whatcha got for me?"

"Herrera backed out because Estrella wasn't feeling well," Stryker explained. "He couldn't get in touch with you, so he called me. I hit Sin up and, lucky for us, he was available."

"Thanks for stepping up," Cooper said to Sin as the plane lifted off.

"Happy to take out the bottom feeders," Sin replied.

"Jericho called me, after he couldn't find you," Stryker continued. "He said we caught a break *and* we have a problem. The woman and the man we couldn't ID left. But two guys joined Driskoll."

"Who?" Cooper asked.

"Driskoll's brother and a Russian with a long rap sheet," Sin replied.

"Koslov?"

Sin nodded. "How'd you know?"

"Koslov cleans up Salimov's messes." Cooper cracked a brief smile. "I look forward to taking out all three of 'em."

They spent the next hour going over specs. Everything from mission goal to what could go wrong and how they'd handle it. Then, he spent the remaining thirty minutes trying to clear his mind. Any mistake during the mission could cost him his life, or worse, the life of a crew member.

But he couldn't reconcile seeing Danielle with Salimov. What was with her disguise and the stranger sex? So many unanswered questions. If Danielle was hiding something, he'd uncover it. As the plane touched down at Myrtle Beach International Airport, Cooper turned his full attention to the kill.

Jericho was waiting when they entered the General Aviation

terminal, a stand-alone building not far from the main terminal. "I'll prep you in the car," was all he said.

They walked in silence through the building, seeing no one but the night janitor.

As they approached the ALPHA SUV, Cooper noticed the license plate was covered with a plastic deflector that blurred the tags. Before sliding into the passenger seat, he glanced around. Impossible to know if Driskoll or his guys were staked out in the lot, but he didn't give a fuck if they were being tracked. Driskoll and his team of yes-men were finished. Cooper was confident of that.

"Driskoll's brother was an easy mark," Jericho began as he drove toward the airport exit. "Dude's a talker and Driskoll's front man. After several drinks and a coupla games of pool, he told me Driskoll and Koslov have been running drugs across the border, then selling 'em up and down the East Coast. Driskoll's old lady is tired of livin' in hotels, so he's gonna buy her a beachfront condo. The day she left to visit her sister, he spent his at a fortune teller's house that fronts a brothel. Man's a saint."

Sin chuckled.

"What's your cover?" Cooper asked.

"Name's Brick and I work for a coke dealer—a Mr. Carpuchio —in Ohio. That's you, Coop. You got an unreliable supplier and I heard Driskoll's the man."

"Any pushback?" Cooper asked.

"I flashed him ten grand and told him I needed a quarter mil worth of coke ASAP. They're meeting us at three this morning in the state park."

"Where's Koslov?" Cooper asked.

"With his nose up Driskoll's ass all the damn time," Jericho replied. "There's gonna be at least three of 'em, but they could have a second carload."

"This just got a lot more interesting," Sin said.

"Where in the park are we meeting?" Cooper asked Jericho.

"In a lot, near a shelter that's got trees behind it," Jericho replied.

"We'll drop Stryker and Sin at the location now," Cooper began. "Jericho and I will get there *after* Driskoll does. I'll be waiting in the car. Jericho, you start the convo. When I step out, we take everyone out *except* Driskoll." Cooper glanced in the back seat at Stryker and Sin. "Who's the better sniper?"

"I am," Jericho replied.

"Between Stryker and Sin," Cooper continued.

"I am," Sin replied.

"If there's a second car, they're yours. Stryker, take out Koslov, then backup Sin. Jericho, you got the brother. I'll handle Driskoll, but I won't take my kill shot until I've seen the fear in his eyes."

"Nice," Sin replied.

Jericho pulled over so they could flesh out all possibilities, especially the ones where the mission went sideways. But Cooper had every confidence in his crew. If anyone could take out these career criminals, it was them.

Cooper couldn't touch Salimov, so he'd hit the motherfucker where it would hurt the most. Those closest to him were going down, ALPHA-style.

Before Jericho pulled back onto the quiet road, they fitted the comms into their ears. After testing the devices to insure they worked, Jericho jumped on South Kings Highway and drove to the park entrance. As soon as he turned in, he killed the headlights.

"There's one entrance and one exit," Jericho said, "plus a campground. It's easy to blend in, easy for them to hide pretty much anywhere."

Using the SUV's parking lights to guide him, Jericho drove around the bend, passing the state park office, closed for the night. He pulled into a small parking lot near a restroom, left the engine running, and killed the parking lights.

"The shelter's about a quarter of a mile down the road," Jericho said. "Hide in the trees behind the building." He started to open his door.

"Stop," Cooper said. "They could be waiting to ambush us."

Cooper pulled his weapon before he and Jericho got out. They walked to the rear of the SUV, where Jericho opened the liftgate. Cooper listened for anyone approaching by vehicle or on foot. The night was silent.

After a minute, Cooper tapped on the back door. Sin and Stryker emerged, their faces concealed behind black ski masks, their hands covered in black gloves. Both men had night goggles strapped to their heads.

Jericho pulled back a blanket revealing four M4s and four Glocks. He handed each man an M4, then shoved a Glock into the back of his pants at the waist.

"Need Glocks?" Jericho asked.

"I got mine," Cooper said.

"Same for Stryker and me," Sin replied before turning to Stryker. "Let's do this."

"We got your backs," Stryker said before shouldering his weapon.

As soon as Sin and Stryker disappeared into the wooded area, Cooper got into the back seat. Jericho closed the hatch and got behind the wheel. Per their plan, they waited there in the dark for Driskoll and his guys to drive by. Cooper stayed silent, focused on the job, his gaze trained on the dark park road ahead of him. Fifteen minutes later, a car drove past.

"We got company," Jericho said.

"We see 'em," Stryker whispered, through the comm. "They're parking at the shelter. Back passenger door opened. One of the guys is heading behind the building."

"Night goggles?" Cooper asked.

"No," Sin replied. "But he's got a gun."

"I recognize him from the video," Stryker said. "It's Driskoll's bodyguard.

"From where we are, I got a clean shot," Sin said.

Jericho turned on the headlights and rolled out of the lot.

"We're on the move." Cooper's heart beat faster, the blood whooshing through him. It had been too long since he'd been on a boots-on-the-ground mission.

Jericho pulled into the shelter area and backed into a spot, leaving the headlights on to illuminate the area.

"Ready to do this?" Cooper asked Jericho.

"Born ready, baby." Jericho retrieved the duffel from the back seat, while Cooper sat tight.

"How's it goin'?" Jericho asked Driskoll and his guys.

"Hey, Brick," said Driskoll's brother. "You got the money?"

"What the fuck do you think this is?" Jericho dropped the bag on the ground. "Mr. Carpuchio flew in to make the deal, but I gotta see the coke, first."

"I don't know you. I don't trust you, neither," Driskoll said. "My guys—" he tossed a nod toward Koslov and his brother— "checked around. Nobody's ever heard of you or your boss."

"I heard you're reliable," Jericho said. "Look, bro, if you don't wanna do business, just say so."

"How do I know you ain't narcs?" Driskoll asked.

Jericho grunted. "One, I fucking hate the law and, two, 'cause I got the money. Count it. It's all there."

Koslov dropped to his knees and pulled out a wad. He pressed the stack to his face and inhaled. "Nothing like the smell of money to make my dick stiff."

"I'm more of a pussy man, myself," said Driskoll's brother and both men started laughing.

"Shut the fuck up, you idiots," Driskoll bit out. "Just check the money."

"For someone who just got laid, you're wound tight," Driskoll's brother said. "Relax, brother. If Brick's got the money, he's got it."

Driskoll unearthed a gun from his jacket pocket and pointed it at Jericho.

"Whoa, dude," Jericho said. "You gotta take it down and chill the hell out."

"We're moving out," Stryker whispered through the comm. "The guy out back's headed in your direction."

"Here we go," Cooper murmured.

He opened the vehicle door, stepped out—

BANG! BANG! BANG! BANG!

Everything happened in slow-mo, but was over in an instant.

Cooper fired his weapon, shooting Driskoll in the hand.

"Aaaaiiiieeeee!" Driskoll dropped his gun and clutched his bleeding wound. "Fuck! You shot my finger off, motherfucker!"

"Bodyguard is down," Sin said.

"Koslov down," Jericho echoed.

"Brother's down," Stryker added.

Jericho kicked Driskoll's gun out of his reach.

Jogging over, Sin and Stryker kept their weapons trained on Driskoll.

"Bodyguard's dead," Sin said.

Jericho confirmed that Driskoll's brother and Koslov were also dead.

"Where the fuck is my finger?" Driskoll bleated.

"Get on your knees." Cooper pointed his gun at Driskoll.

Driskoll dropped. "What the fuck have you done?"

"Me?" Cooper growled. "You pulled the gun. You got your guys killed."

"I thought you was narcs," Driskoll said.

Cooper stared down at Driskoll. "Wrong, stupid. We're not narcs. We're worse, much, much worse. A narc would arrest you. Me? I'm gonna blow your fucking brains out. Time to say hello to the devil himself."

Driskoll started shaking. "God, no, please no. Don't kill me."

"You got arrested for carjacking, grand theft, rape and murder. You're a fuckin' peach of a human being. You killed your family during a holiday party. Who the fuck does that? Andy Driskoll, that's who. You're done."

Cooper lifted his weapon and fired, hitting Driskoll between the eyes. Driskoll dropped.

Jericho grabbed the duffel and the stack of cash from Koslov's clenched fist. "Let's get outta here."

Sin and Stryker picked up the shell casings before all four men made their way to the SUV. The M4s were stored, the guys jumped in, and Jericho turned off the headlights. He rolled out, the parking lights guiding him toward the exit.

As soon as Jericho turned onto South Kings Highway, he flipped on his headlights and hit the gas.

Cooper unearthed his burner. "I gotta call this in." He dialed 9-1-1.

"What's your emergency?" asked the operator.

"Four drug dealers were shot at Myrtle Beach State Park, Shelter 2B. All four are down. One of 'em is Andy Driskoll. He's on the FBI's Most Wanted list."

"When you say down, do you mean injured?"

"Dead."

"How do you know this?"

"Because I saw it go down," Cooper replied. "There might be cocaine at the scene. No idea if it's laced with fentanyl."

"Sir, what's your name?"

"Good Samaritan." Cooper hung up.

He called the FBI hotline and repeated what he'd told the local emergency operator. Then, he ripped the flip phone in half.

"Everyone okay?" Cooper asked.

"All good," Stryker replied.

"Four less pieces of shit in the world," Sin said.

Jericho glanced over at him. "Love workin' with you, brother."

"Thanks for doing this with me," Cooper said to the guys.

Killing those men brought him no joy, but knowing they couldn't hurt anyone anymore did.

Jericho drove to the airport, pulled up to the General Aviation building. Stryker and Sin got out.

"You sure you don't want someone to ride back with you?" Cooper asked after exiting the SUV.

"I got six glorious hours alone," Jericho replied. "When am I ever alone? My entire family lives with me. I'm surrounded by people at work, all the fuckin' time. As much as I love you guys, I do my best thinking on road trips." He tossed them a nod. "Safe flight. I'll talk to you."

After Cooper closed the passenger door, Jericho pulled away. The three men made their way to the ALPHA jet.

Cooper was relieved Driskoll and his thugs were finished destroying lives, but the tightness in his shoulders wouldn't let up. Driskoll was a close second, but he wasn't Salimov.

He'd have no peace until Salimov was a dead man.

No peace at all.

15

PAINTBALL MAYHEM

DANIELLE

Danielle had been hunkered down in her office Friday morning, trying to hack into a home surveillance system to catch a glimpse of herself flying by on her Ninja the night of Sisson's murder. After working two different cases on Thursday, she refocused her efforts on searching for herself.

Movement caught her eye and she glanced up to see Cooper standing in her doorway. Her heart skipped a beat. She wanted to go to him, throw her arms around him, and tell him how happy she was to see him.

Since she wasn't about to do that, she offered him a smile. Hard not to when the most gorgeous man she'd ever laid eyes on was leaning against the doorframe. She loved seeing him in his work duds. The pink button-down strained against his biceps and the black pants were fitted perfectly to his strong hips and thick thighs.

Eye candy to the max.

His stance said relaxed, but the fire in his eyes made it

impossible to look away. More than anything, she wanted all that passion for herself.

He strode in and the temperature in the room shot up ten degrees. "Got a second?" His bright eyes drilled into her.

"Of course."

"Whatcha working on?"

"Dead Man Talking. I'm trying to hack into a home surveillance system so I can track the motorcycle."

A shadow darkened his gaze. "Can I see?" His voice had dropped, and she felt like his question had nothing to do with what was on her computer screen.

"I'd love to show you."

She couldn't drag herself from him as he made his way around her desk, then leaned over her shoulder to view her computer. A frisson of excitement flitted through her. She could feel the tension rolling off him while his breathing roared in her ears. The desire to touch him, kiss him, was too powerful to ignore.

They were inches away. Her breath hitched.

"Miss me?" he whispered.

God, yes, so much. "Were you gone?"

Biting back a smile, he caressed her hand still on the mouse. "I missed you."

Her heart took off in her chest. His honesty was killing her and she would die a thousand deaths when he learned her truth.

"Making any progress?" he asked.

"Not really. Some of these systems store the videos for a period of time, like twenty-four hours, some store it on the cloud. This could take a while."

He was so close, she inhaled his delicious scent. A mix of shampoo and coffee and Cooper. He smelled like someone she could get lost in and never want to find her way out.

Lily rushed into her office. "I got the model of the motorcycle. It's a Kawasaki Ninja 400."

Cooper straightened up. "Great work, Lily. Let's run a search to find the owner."

"We can do that?" Danielle blurted.

"Oh, yeah, it's awesome," Lily replied. "I can show you—"

"I'll show her," Cooper interjected.

"I'm going to lunch, then I'm changing for paintball. I can't wait!" With a grin, Lily hurried out.

"Let's start in Virginia," Cooper said.

God, no.

"Why don't you show me how to do it in DC?"

A low, gravelly growl rolled out of him, hitting her smack between her legs, which she crossed. She really needed to get a handle on her raging libido.

"I meant, let's pull the data in DC. I'll do Maryland and Virginia, then start drilling down on the motorcycle owners."

His smile, coupled with a husky chuckle, turned her inside out. "You definitely missed me." He pulled a chair around and eased down beside her. "I'll definitely show you how to do it, and then you can do all the drilling you want."

I would love that.

He guided her on the steps to access the data from the Department of Motor Vehicles in DC. There were thousands of registered motorcycle owners. The anxiety that churned her stomach settled down, a little. It could take weeks to scrub this list. They'd have to do the same for the registered owners in Virginia and Maryland, too.

Maybe I've bought myself some time.

"Let's hope the bike is registered in the DC metro area," Danielle said. "It could be registered elsewhere."

Instead of leaving, he leaned back and let his gaze drift over her face. Staring at him was her favorite thing to do.

"You ready for paintball?"

She nodded.

"Did you see the team list?"

Cooper up close made her squirm in her chair. "Uh-huh."

"We're on the same team," he continued. "Interested in being my partner in crime?"

Hell, yeah. "Sure."

"Have you ever fired a gun?"

That felt like a question that could come back to bite her in the ass, but she wanted him to know she could pull her weight. "I'll be okay."

He ran the back of his index finger down her cheek and her skin tingled from his touch. "You want to ride with me?"

"Okay." She wanted to kiss him so, so badly.

"I'm going to grab a sandwich. You want something?"

What she wanted was sitting right next to her. "I brought something from home." She leaned back. "I'll run these reports before we leave."

He moved the guest chair back, then held her gaze for an extra second.

"Go," she said, "or I won't get this done."

He placed both palms on her desk and leaned down. "Leaving you is the hardest thing I do." He winked, then he was gone.

Danielle sucked down a breath. She was out of control around him and over her head.

Focus, dammit, focus.

After draining her water bottle, she ran the Virginia report. There were thousands of motorcycle owners in Virginia. She resorted, alphabetically, and scanned the list.

Fox, Claire-Marie | Kawasaki Ninja 400

When her sister had died, Danielle had stored the bike in her garage. At first, it was a keepsake, which morphed into a curiosity, then an avid interest. Several motorcycle lessons later, she was hooked. Riding freed her and gave her a private way to honor her sister.

After Danielle downloaded the list to a spreadsheet, she deleted her sister's name and corresponding information. Then, she compiled the data for the Maryland motorcycle owners. Once she had all three lists, she emailed Lily and let her know they could start scrubbing them on Monday.

Tap-tap-tap.

Emerson walked in, carrying two lunch containers. "How's week one been for you?"

Murder isn't bad enough. Now, I can add tampering with evidence to my list of crimes.

"What did you say?" Danielle eyed their lunch boxes. "Yes, I am starving. Let's eat!"

Emerson's brows puckered for a second before she sat.

"Are you nervous about paintball?" Emerson asked as she unearthed her sandwich.

"No, Cooper asked me if I wanted to be his partner."

"I mean about using a gun. You've never even fired one before."

"It's paintball," Danielle replied. "How difficult can it be?"

COOPER

The day was overcast, the air crisp. While the immediate area of Paintball Playland was free of fallen leaves, the surrounding woods were not and a crisp layer covered the ground. That would help when listening for an opponent, but hurt when Cooper didn't want to make a sound.

He tightened Danielle's helmet before handing it back to her. "Try this."

She put it on. "Much better. Thanks."

He was well aware she could tighten her own helmet, but he liked doting on her.

Cooper had played paintball a number of times. It was a fast-paced, high-energy game that required endurance, patience, and a decent aim. He was doing it for team-building and to give everyone an afternoon off from their intense jobs.

There were two teams of ten each, and most players had decided to pair up as a strategy. As it turned out, he and Danielle had both dressed in camouflage pants and shirts. She'd pulled her hair into a ponytail and secured it in place so it wasn't flying around.

He hoped partnering with her hadn't been a mistake. Even in her fatigues, Danielle Fox was a total babe. This game required concentration, not a beautiful distraction. What struck him most was how seriously she was taking the game. She had no nervous giggles, she didn't say anything disparaging about how she wouldn't be able to pull her weight or how he'd have to do most of the work.

"This'll be fun." He pulled on his helmet as she tugged on her gloves.

"I'm glad we're partners," she said.

He loved how she was slowly opening up to him. "Me, too."

Once all twenty players had arrived, Cooper explained the rules, then suggested a short practice round. As it turned out, there were some very competitive ALPHA employees running around the woods that afternoon.

Before the game began, Danielle slipped her hand around Cooper's arm and pulled him close to huddle. "We should take out the weakest teams, first, then go after the fiercer ones. You good with that?"

More than actually winning, he loved how she hadn't removed her hand from his arm.

"I should lead us in," he said.

"No," she pushed back. "You should have my back."

Who the hell is this woman?

The game started, and Danielle took off toward the woods, Cooper close on her heels. She stopped behind a large Oak tree, her chest rising and falling as she caught her breath. She peeked around the trunk. "I see Mark and Kevin. They're coming our way. I'll take out Mark. On three."

On three, they both jumped out and fired. Cooper struck Kevin on his shoulder. Danielle hit Mark in the center of his chest.

That's impressive.

Cooper led the next mission. Danielle had wanted to climb a tree, but there wasn't enough foliage to hide her, so they came out firing hard and took the next team by surprise. Two by two, they shut down their opponents.

As they closed in on Herrera and Slash, Slash spotted them. The battle was fierce, but they hit them before fleeing deeper into the woods.

Then, Cooper glimpsed Emerson crouched behind a pile of cut logs from a downed tree. He gestured to Danielle. She stepped behind Cooper. "Her partner is coming up behind us. I got him, you take her out."

In a flash of brightly-colored paintballs, they fired a deluge of rounds. Danielle hit Stryker in his stomach and on his mask before she took several to her midsection and legs. Emerson was hit in the head and had several splotches on her legs. Cooper was covered in a spray of paint on his upper chest and shoulders.

Laughing hard, Stryker bent over to catch his breath.

Cooper regarded the three of them. Stryker was his oldest friend in the world. Emerson was Stryker's forever person. When he slid his gaze to Danielle, he knew.

He was falling in love with her. He knew himself well enough to know what he liked and what he didn't. He'd been searching for *the one*. The one who would take his breath away, be his equal in some ways, and his partner in all ways.

Danielle—laughing, covered in paint splotches, and hugging her best friend—was that person.

"Where'd you come from?" Cooper asked Stryker. "You weren't even on the damn list."

"He was my secret weapon," Emerson replied. "There was no way I could beat you without him."

"You were so damn surprised when you saw it was me," Stryker said and started laughing again.

"We were definitely evenly matched," Cooper said. "But I gotta say, Danielle, you were phenomenal. Where'd you learn to shoot like that?"

"Beginner's luck," she replied. "I'm sure I could never replicate that."

There was one thing Cooper was certain of... Danielle Fox was full of hidden talents and lots of surprises.

They headed back toward the main play area where Herrera and a few other Operatives had set up a firing range. There were three movable targets, so everyone formed three lines of seven. One by one, they fired at the human cutout. The first round was easy since Herrera had set them back forty feet. After everyone had had a turn, the targets were moved farther away. The ratio of hits was still higher than misses, but Cooper expected that from his Operatives.

Danielle stepped up, aimed, and released a few rounds.

Bang! Bang! Bang!

All three dead center. Cooper and Stryker exchanged glances.

Emerson applauded. "Way to go, Danny. We should be partners, next. We'd blow these guys away."

The third round was set into the woods. Everyone on the Internet Team missed the targets, and several of the Operatives did as well. Danielle stepped up, lifted the weapon, and eyed the mark. She missed the first two, then hit the next several. Two in the chest, one in the shoulder and two between the target's eyes.

Danielle was a mystery. There was no way she could hit the target that many times without practice... lots of practice.

Next up, a game of paintball Capture the Flag. By that time, everyone was starting to tire, but the group rallied and put forth their best efforts. Cooper loved how the teams pulled together, rooting for each other, and having a great time bonding.

When the event was over, Cooper called everyone together. "Thanks for a great afternoon. I hope everyone had fun."

"A total blast," Slash said.

"This was awesome," Lily added.

"Today was paid for by the organization, so please thank Providence. Dinner is on me."

The group erupted in hoots and hollers. As everyone made their way back to their cars, Danielle fell in line beside him.

"That was so much fun." She'd removed her helmet and the ends of her hair were covered in pink paint splotches.

"I'm glad you had a good time. Thanks for having my back, today."

"Thanks for having mine."

"Next time you go to the firing range, take me with you," he said.

Silence.

At his Jeep, she turned back to him. "I don't know what you're talking about."

After they got in, he said, "You're talented enough to be a sniper."

She laughed. "I like being a hacker, but thanks for the compliment."

They returned to ALPHA's parking lot. He hated saying goodbye to her, even if just for a little while.

"Save me a seat next to you," she said before jumping into her car.

He flashed her a smile. That was already part of his plan.

DANIELLE

Danielle entered her home through her garage and glanced over at her Ninja. Yesterday, after work, she'd returned to Swanky to pick it up, wishing she didn't have to leave it out in the open for so long. But when Cooper had ushered her into his Jeep, she'd been left with no other choice.

After a shower, she dressed in her favorite black halter dress. It was sophisticated and a little sexy. Rather than leave her hair down, she pulled it all over one shoulder, and secured it with a large clip.

As she combed mascara onto her lashes, she wondered if hitting all the targets had been a mistake. In addition to taking motorcycle lessons, she'd also taken a gun safety class and two on marksmanship. Today, was the first time she'd done anything outside the firing range.

I did a good job holding my own... maybe too good.

When she finished getting ready, Danielle slipped into heels and hurried downstairs.

Friday traffic slowed her down and she got to the Tysons restaurant at seven fifteen. She entered the upscale eatery and bit back a gasp. Carole Jean's was first class, all the way. Rich burgundy walls made the white linen tablecloths pop. Framed oil paintings adorned the walls and glowing candles on every table gave the restaurant a romantic vibe.

The amber lighting and teardrop chandeliers caught her attention as the maître d' led her through the large dining room. As she passed a table, the man glanced up at her, and her heart jumped into her throat. It was Ivan Salimov.

Do not turn around.

She held her breath as she walked down the hallway and into the private dining room. Feeling exposed without her Ursula disguise, she hoped he hadn't recognized her.

Five round tables filled the sizeable room. As she was standing there, trying to come up with a plan if Salimov walked in, Cooper appeared by her side.

"You look stunning," he whispered. "I saved you a seat."

As they made their way to his table, Emerson waved. Grateful for that lifeline, Danielle walked toward her friend.

"Is this place amazing or what?" Emerson said to her.

Operating on auto-pilot while she obsessed over Salimov, Danielle eased down between her and Cooper. Relieved Cooper didn't seat her, she didn't want anyone to suspect anything. But if the night ended the way she hoped, they'd have to disclose their "situation" to HR.

The exquisite room boasted backlit copper-paneled walls. A roaring gas fireplace on the back wall created a brilliant glow only made brighter from the shiny copper walls. The atmosphere was both cozy and provocative, but Danielle couldn't tear her gaze from the doorway. It swung open and she startled.

Herrera walked in and Cooper waved him over.

Calm down. Salimov didn't recognize you.

Had Cooper seen Salimov? If he knew Salimov was seated in the main dining room, he would be orchestrating a kill, not chatting about their fun afternoon of paintball.

The waitstaff appeared and, like synchronized swimmers, introduced themselves to their assigned tables. Bottles of pinot noir and sauvignon blanc were offered while another attendant rattled off the evening's specials. Danielle hadn't planned on drinking, but she needed a little wine to take the edge off.

When the server mentioned the fish of the day and its side of pasta, she chose the white wine. Her mouth watered while the server filled her glass. Though she wanted to guzzle it down, she didn't.

Cooper stood and raised his wine goblet. "Team, can I get your attention?"

Conversations were paused while everyone turned in his direction. "You're a smart group of hard-working employees and I appreciate your efforts, every single day. Today was a fun way to spend the afternoon. Thanks to those who played paintball and to everyone for being here tonight."

As everyone clinked glasses and drank, Cooper sat back down. After tapping his glass to Danielle's, he held her gaze before he pressed the crystal goblet to his mouth, tipped the glass, and sipped.

She could watch him all day long. His quiet confidence paired with an equal dose of suave was the *perfect* distraction.

Danielle swallowed down a mouthful of wine, then one more, hoping it would help settle her nerves. Salads were delivered and conversations resumed. Before their entrees had arrived, Emerson whispered, "Will you go to the bathroom with me?"

Ohgod. She did *not* want to run into Salimov.

"Of course."

Danielle let out a little sigh as they entered the nearby restroom. Though she was curious if Salimov was still out there, she wasn't going near that main dining room. She needed to keep Cooper out of there, as well.

Danielle checked her makeup, while Emerson walked into a private-room toilet and shut the door.

A middle-aged woman with dark hair walked in, her phone pressed against her ear. "Ivan uyezzhayet po delam v dekabre, poetomu ya lechu domoy."

Danielle flicked her gaze to the woman. *That's Russian. Is that Salimov's wife?* The woman was speaking too fast for Danielle to catch anything more than the word Ivan and what she thought might be the word December.

Rather than stare at her, Danielle pulled out her lip gloss and rolled it on.

The woman walked into a private-room toilet and shut the door, as Emerson emerged from hers.

"You should check out the chandelier in there," Emerson said. "It's pink. You'd totally love it."

"Uh-huh."

Emerson frowned. "What's wrong? You look like you're going to be sick."

"I'm good," Danielle murmured. "You all set?" Without waiting for an answer, she looped her arm around Emerson's and hurried out, keeping her head down until they'd returned to the private dining room.

Emerson pulled her to a stop. "What is up with you? Seriously, you're acting like a wreck."

Danielle forced a smile. "I'm beyond starving and our entrees are being served. We should get back to the table."

Providence was right. Redirecting the conversation did work, and not just for talking about her job. After sitting, she glanced in Cooper's direction and that familiar punch of adrenaline made her heart soar.

They shared a smile, and in that brief moment, everything was right in her dark, dark world.

While the team was enjoying their desserts and after-dinner liqueurs, Cooper's phone rang. "Excuse me." He stepped away from the table and answered. When he returned, he just sat there. He didn't finish his dessert. He didn't engage in any of the conversations at the table.

His face was drained of color. He looked like someone had died.

Danielle leaned close. "Are you okay?" she whispered.

"No," he replied. "No, I'm not."

16

SHOCKING NEWS

COOPER

While joyous chatter and laughter filled the room, Cooper wanted to scream. He needed to be alone, to process the news, but he couldn't walk out on his team. For the moment, he would push aside his fury and his concern for his family and he would get through dinner.

Danielle's soft touch snapped him back to the moment. "Stryker and Emerson are taking off."

Everyone stopped by to thank him and let him know how much fun they had. Once the room cleared, Cooper sat back down. Even after signing the credit card receipt, he didn't move. He felt like a caged bird.

Danielle had been sitting quietly. Though he'd barely acknowledged her, having her by his side was a godsend.

"I'd like to help," she murmured.

Concerned eyes met his. She took his hands and held them in her lap. As she caressed his fingers, she offered a sweet smile.

She needs to know.

"I told you my brother was killed," he began.

"I remember."

"He died in a school shooting." Cooper fucking hated talking about this. Every time he did, he ripped open a wound that had never healed.

Soft arms wrapped him in a hug. He didn't deserve her warm body pressed to his. He didn't deserve her compassion when his own brother's life had been cut short. Pain pelted Cooper's chest, the sorrow still so raw, all these years later.

"My dad was signing Alan back in after an orthodontist appointment. This lunatic walked into the front office and opened fire. My brother was killed, right away. Somehow, the bullets missed my dad and he lunged for the semi-automatic. That's when Renfrow shot him."

Sad eyes stared into his. "I'm so sorry," she murmured.

"My dad never walked again."

The decades of pain never subsided. Ever.

"How old were you and your brother?"

"I was in seventh grade. Alan was in sixth. We'd just moved to Maryland for my dad's work, but after it happened, I refused to leave the house. Despite my dad's challenges, my parents decided to move back to our old neighborhood in Northern Virginia, near where Stryker lived with his family. Being back with old friends and away from that nightmare, I felt like I could go back to school."

Soft fingers stroked his hand. "I'm sorry for what your family has been through."

"The motherfucker who did this, William Renfrow, was convicted and sent to prison. Four years ago, he was up for parole. Dozens of victims and their families showed up to speak out and his parole was denied. A few weeks ago, I went to his third parole hearing. I was the *only* one who showed. Even my dad told me to let it go." Cooper gritted his teeth. "I will never fucking let it go."

Cooper felt like he was going to suffocate if he didn't move. He kissed Danielle's hand, then stood and raked his hands through his hair. He paced, then gripped the back of the chair.

"My dad called to let me know Renfrow escaped."

Danielle's eyes grew wide. "Oh, no!"

"They think he stabbed himself or had someone stab him. He was taken to a hospital, where he got stitched up. As he was being transported back, he attacked the driver and the van crashed. The driver was killed. Renfrow escaped. All this happened after the hearing. My dad's lawyer just found out and called him."

"Do you think your family's in danger?"

"I don't know what to think," Cooper said. "But I'm not going to sit around and do nothing."

He unearthed his phone, called his dad back. "What are you guys going to do about this?"

"Nothing, Cooper," his dad replied. "Renfrow isn't interested in coming after me, but Mom and I are worried about you."

"Me?"

"You're the reason he didn't get paroled."

The dead rat and his burned Corvette popped into his thoughts. *It was Renfrow, not Salimov.*

"Has your home security system alerted you to anyone hanging around the house at night?" Cooper asked.

"No. You?"

"I'm good, Dad," he lied to keep his parents from worrying. "I'll check in with you tomorrow." Cooper hung up and fixed his gaze on Danielle.

"Renfrow is coming after me."

"What do you mean?" Danielle asked.

"The dead rat, the car explosion. I thought it was Salimov, but it's Renfrow. That makes more sense, now that I know Renfrow escaped. I can put round-the-clock protection on you—"

No!" She sprang out of her chair. "Sorry. I'm okay."

"Danielle, he knows where you live," Cooper said. "You aren't safe at home." He held out his hand. "Let's get outta here."

"Where are we going?" she asked, clasping his hand.

"My place," he replied.

"I need to swing by my house and grab a few things."

As he followed her home, he made a call. "I need your help."

"What's going on?" Hawk answered, his voice rough, like sandpaper.

"Renfrow escaped. I'm concerned for my mom and dad."

"Got it."

"They can't know we've got full protection on them."

"Discretion is my jam, babe."

"Thanks, bro."

"Watch your six." Hawk hung up.

As Cooper followed Danielle home, he thought about the rat and the explosion. He'd gotten it wrong about Salimov. Renfrow was out for revenge.

She pulled into her driveway and he parked behind her. Once inside, she turned off her security system before bolting the front door.

"I'm going to pack a bag." She vanished up the stairs and he headed toward her kitchen. Rather than turn the light on, he stood in the dark, staring through her bay window. Renfrow had been tailing him, possibly for weeks. Renfrow knew about his gym, he knew where Danielle lived. Did he know that Cooper spent most of his days driving to a large warehouse-like building with ALPHA MEAT PACKING over the front door?

Cooper gritted his teeth while he lowered the blinds. After turning on the kitchen light, he thought about their vulnerability. He wasn't afraid of Renfrow, but he was concerned for Danielle. While he wanted to put one of Hawk's guys on her, he wouldn't. She'd said no and he would honor her decision. Despite the shit storm raining down on him, he was developing real feelings for her. The last thing he needed was to ruin it by going behind her back. He hated that she was vulnerable, but maybe she'd agree to let him drive her to work and the gym, too. That might be a fair compromise.

We gotta hide her car.

As Danielle entered the kitchen, he opened the door leading into her garage. The motion triggered the light and he stared at a large, black motorcycle parked inside.

What the hell?

He turned back to her. "You ride?"

"The bike was my sister's."

She hadn't answered his question, so he pressed her. "Do you ride?"

"I kept it as a reminder of how she lived life on the edge. What are you doing in my garage, anyway?"

"If you won't let me hire protection for you, I thought we'd hide your car in here and I'd drive you to work and the gym."

She furrowed her brows. "For real? Don't you think you're taking this to the extreme?"

Her expression was a mix of surprise and frustration. Not what he would have expected, but maybe she thought he was being too controlling.

"I'll stay with you, tonight," she said, tugging him away from the garage and closing the door. "But driving me everywhere is insane."

Cooper pulled her into his arms. "I've got a lunatic after me who stabbed himself to get outta prison. He crashed the prison van and escaped. I appreciate that you're independent and don't want a babysitter, but we're not dealing with a sane person."

Her phone buzzed, then buzzed again. She grabbed it off the counter. "My doorbell cam detected motion."

Ding dong.

Cooper killed the kitchen light, pulled his Glock from the back of his pants. "Lay flat on the floor," he whispered.

He strode into the foyer and killed that light, too, but he wasn't opening the front door until he could get a visual.

Rather than listen to him, Danielle had removed her stilettos and was hurrying up the stairs. He peeked out the living room window, but saw no one. Relieved neither car was on fire, he needed access to the camera for a bird's-eye view.

Danielle raced back down the stairs, a firearm in her hand. The surprises kept on coming with her. She hurried into the foyer and stood against the wall, her gun at the ready.

He stood beside her. "Show me the surveillance videos."

She pulled out her phone. The first video showed a man in dark clothes, his face hidden behind a ski mask, walking through the front yard, a package in hand. He set it down, rang the doorbell, and sauntered away.

"Brazen motherfucker," Cooper bit out. "If I open the door, he could open fire or throw a grenade into the house. If I pick up the box, it might explode."

"What about asking ALPHA to handle it?"

"If ALPHA learns about this, I'll be placed on leave. On the other hand, I'm putting the entire organization at risk if they think I'm being followed."

"I won't say a word. Your secret is safe with me." She crossed her heart.

That sweet gesture made him smile. He slid his arm around her waist, pulled her close, and kissed her. "You're a one-of-a-kind woman. You just crossed your heart with one hand while holding a gun in the other." He kissed her again before he unearthed his phone.

"Who are you calling?"

"Someone who can tell us if there's a bomb inside that package without the entire fucking town finding out." He dialed.

"Again?" Hawk answered. "Dammit, Coop, it's midnight. I'm about to… I'm not at home."

"I'm at Danielle's and someone just dropped a box out front. I need your bomb-detecting robot."

"Gimme the address."

After Cooper rattled it off, he said, "Bring her with you."

Hawk barked out a raspy laugh before the line went dead.

Cooper clasped Danielle's hand and led her into the kitchen. Rather than turn on a light, they sat at the table, in darkness, and set their weapons down.

"I'm sorry," he said as he stroked her hand. "I've dragged you into this mess."

She moved onto his lap. "There was no dragging." She kissed him. "I like being with you... so much. I want to enjoy every minute we have together before—" She stilled.

"Finish that sentence."

She kissed his temple. "Things might not work out for us, you know, long-term, so we'll live for the now. Even if it means sitting in my dark kitchen waiting for your friend to check a package. I would rather be with you than any other man I've ever met."

I feel the exact same way.

He captured her face in his hands and kissed her softly. "What happened to you only wanting casual hookups?"

Her sweet smile calmed his angry soul.

"I didn't mean that," she said. "I like you so much, but—" She steeled her spine.

"But, what?"

"Nothing," she replied, pausing to kiss him.

Despite what they were dealing with, he loved that they were facing it together.

"This feels different," he murmured.

"For me, too," she whispered.

"Seeing your Glock explains a lot," he said.

She tensed. "What do you mean?"

"You killed it at paintball. You were hitting the targets like a pro."

She ran soft fingers through his hair. "It was luck and adrenaline."

"So, what's with the weapon?"

She shrugged. "Protection. I live alone."

Cooper's phone rang. It was Hawk. "I'm here," he answered.

"Robot's headed to your front door." Hawk hung up.

Several moments later, his phone buzzed with a text from Hawk. "All clear."

They went outside to find Hawk holding the package, a look of disgust on his unshaven face. His T-shirt was grungy, his jeans tattered, and his dark hair mussed.

"Thanks for doing this," Cooper said.

"I got your six, even if it was at the worst possible moment." A grin split his lips before he held out the box and his smile fell away. "Dead rat. I got a guy watching your parents' house. You want round-the-clock protection, too?"

"No." Cooper took the box, but didn't open it. "This is Danielle."

"I'm Hawk. You got a nice place, but you can't stay here. It's not secure. I installed Coop's system, so I know he's safe." He squeezed Cooper's shoulder. "Gotta go home and take care of unfinished biz. Love ya." On a throaty chuckle, he strolled toward his truck.

Cooper opened the lid. Inside was another dead rat. This time, there was a note.

**Every rat has a mate.
Looks like I found yours.**

His blood ran ice cold.

17

COOPER'S BABY

DANIELLE

Danielle had become one of the hunted... again. A shiver streaked through her and she hugged herself. It was bad enough that Cooper and Emerson were looking for the DMT killer, but now she had some escapee after her, too.

The universe is telling me to stop taking out evil by putting a target on my back.

Cooper set the box outside, brought Danielle inside, and shut the front door. In the darkened foyer, he tipped her chin toward him and smiled down at her. She wanted to smile back, but she was mired in conflict. Where would she live? If she stayed with Emerson and Stryker, she'd be risking their safety. Staying in a hotel wasn't a viable option, either.

"I'm sorry you've gotten sucked into this," Cooper said. "I'll kill Renfrow before I let him lay one fucking finger on you."

"Your friend, Hawk, is right. I'm not safe here."

"You'll stay with me."

"Wait! What? No, that's crazy. I mean, it's very nice, but I'd be imposing. Plus—"

He stopped her with a kiss. A melt-her-panties-off kiss. Her insides jump started, she flung her arms around him, and she groaned into him. When the kiss ended, she whispered, "Okay."

What choice did she have?

She would stay the weekend and figure out next steps. Staying with him sounded cozy, too cozy. Would she put a hold on Salimov? She was so close to taking him out. So close, she could visualize that bullet piercing his skull, sucking the destructive life out of him.

Ending his reign of terror against the innocent.

"Danielle. *Danielle.*"

She blinked several times.

"Whoa, woman, where'd you go?"

"Sorry, my mind wandered." She took a few steps toward the stairs. "I'm going to grab a few more things. Back in a sec."

She trotted upstairs and into her closet, where she pulled out an overnight bag. She hadn't checked her burner all day, so she opened the safe. A text from Salimov was waiting.

"I'm free Sunday night for job help," Salimov texted. "You?"

"Yes," she texted back. "Where?"

Even at this late hour, dots appeared. *Come on, come on.* She glanced into her bedroom, but no sign of Cooper.

"The embassy owns townhouse in DC. We meet there, eight thirty." He added the address.

"Why can't we meet during normal biz hours?" she texted back.

"You want help? Sunday night."

Monster.

"See you then," she texted as Cooper appeared in the closet doorway.

"I don't want to rush you—" he said.

She dropped the burner into the duffle, shut the door to the safe, and stood. Then, she pulled a couple of random outfits off hangers and shoved them into the bag. "All ready."

When her gaze met his, he was eyeing the duffle. Then, he glanced at the safe.

He saw the burner.

"You want me to take that for you?" he asked.

"I got it. Let's go."

She grabbed her personal laptop, set her alarm, and left her house feeling conflicted. On one hand, she wanted to stay and protect her home, but she wasn't safe there by herself.

As she followed Cooper back to his place, she thought about Salimov. She wasn't confident she'd be able to pull off a kill while staying with Cooper.

Unless, I come up with a reason to be gone, tomorrow, so I can prep. But I'd have to leave Cooper on Sunday night.

After mulling her options, she decided to cancel with Salimov. There would be no way she could do it without arousing Cooper's suspicions.

Cooper pulled into a neighborhood and stopped at the curb. Her phone rang. It was him.

"Hey," she answered.

"I'm making sure we aren't being followed."

"Smart." She glanced in the mirror. They were alone on the street. After a moment, he said, "All clear." He hung up and drove on.

He made a few more turns before pulling into the driveway of a beautiful two-story, stone-front home in McLean. The double-wide garage door opened and Cooper drove in. There was plenty of room, so she pulled in beside him.

As soon as she cut the engine, the garage door closed silently behind them. She exited and pulled her overnight bags from the back seat. He was by her side, shouldering them before he walked over to the door. In addition to a small camera mounted in the corner of the ceiling, there was a scanner that captured Cooper's retina, like the one at ALPHA.

"This is definitely a better security system than mine," she said.

As soon as he stepped inside, light illuminated the spacious mudroom. On the wall across from the washer and dryer were built-in storage compartments and a closed door.

"Security system off," Cooper commanded and the beeping stopped.

"Hello, Cooper," replied the computerized female voice. "System off."

"Wow, that's impressive," Danielle said.

"It recognizes me visually and it knows my voice. Hawk has some cool gadgets. Let me get your coat." After hanging her coat in the mudroom closet, he said, "I'll show you around."

"Wait," she said. "Can you show me a picture of this Renfrow guy? I want to see if I can—"

"It's Friday, no, it's Saturday after one in the morning. We can hunt for that asshole tomorrow. I'm going to show you around, then do something just for you. Whatever you want. A hot bath, a massage, maybe you'd like a series of relaxing, mind-blowing orgasms."

She adored him. It was that simple. What man would put aside his own problems to focus on her? Her smile was filled with gratitude. "Thank you, but no. You've got so much going on and—"

"You just got uprooted from your home because of me," he murmured. "Plus, you are the best distraction."

Without waiting for her reply, he clasped her hand, kissed her nose, then led her down the hall, stopping in front of an open door. "Bathroom," he said and flashed her an adorable smile.

She couldn't believe he was this composed after what they'd just been through. Her nerves were shot. The dead rat saddened her, but that note made her angry as hell.

When he led her into his office, the light turned on automatically.

"Wow, this is so nice." She admired the dark built-in cabinets and bookshelves that spanned an entire wall, the drawer-free desk in the same dark-grain wood. A throw rug lay over the dark wood flooring, and a deep-red upholstered chair with ottoman sat in the corner. But it was the modern light dangling from the ceiling that captured her attention.

"I've got a thing for chandeliers and unusual lights," she said, "and that is absolutely stunning."

"You're stunning," he replied. "That's a light."

Twenty lamp shades of various sizes, with LED lights buried inside, hung from wires that dangled from the ceiling fixture. As she dragged her gaze to the wall of built-ins, she walked over and examined the framed photos on display.

There was one of him with Stryker, Jericho, Hawk, and another man cutting a ribbon in front of Carole Jean's. There were several pictures of his family. One, in particular, caught her eye. Cooper's dad was standing on a beach holding two toddlers in his arms while a young boy stood by his side. Everyone was smiling so big, it made Danielle happy, yet sad, to see it. She lifted the photo. "Which one is you?"

"That's me," he said, pointing, "and that's Alan. He was ten months younger than me. We were best buds, did everything together. That's my older brother, Henry, Tessa's dad. My baby sister, Chantal, wasn't born yet and my mom was taking the picture."

Her heart broke for his family in the same way it broke for her own. So much evil existed. No matter how hard she tried, she would never be able to eliminate all of it.

"You have a beautiful family."

He held out his hand and she eagerly placed hers in his. Holding his hand was fast becoming one of her favorite things to do. He led her down the hall and into his stunning kitchen. As dark and manly as his office had been, his kitchen was bright white cabinets, white marble countertops and top-brand stainless-steel appliances. Her eyes hovered on the teardrop pendant lights that hung over the center island.

"This is pretty big for one person. You sure you aren't hiding a wife and children around here?"

"If I had a wife, I wouldn't have invited you back here to rub oil all over your naked body."

"Touché." That was a test. She was thrilled he'd passed.

When he went to retrieve her bags from the mudroom, she continued on the tour by herself. She passed by his living room and sunroom, then waited at the bottom of the staircase.

When he rounded the corner, she felt like she'd found a home for her heart. That, like the picture from his childhood, made her happy *and* sad. She wouldn't be able to have her fairy-tale ending with her Prince Charming from a prison cell.

He interrupted her thoughts with a kiss. "What's happening in that beautiful head of yours?"

"Just thinking about stuff."

"Anything you want to tell me about?"

"Nothing now."

"Activate alarm," he said in a commanding tone.

Beep, beep, beep. "Alarm on," replied the computerized voice.

They walked up the steps and he showed her the guest rooms. Like the rest of his home, they were lovely. "Is one of these my bedroom until we figure out our plan?"

He stopped outside the closed double doors at the end of the hall. "I want you in my bed with me," he said without reservation. "But that's your call."

She was conflicted. She *should* sleep in one of the other bedrooms, alone. But her heart wanted to be near him, as close as two people could be. As she stood there, immobilized by the war raging in her head, he opened one of the bedroom doors and the lights flicked on.

"Fireplace on," he said, and flames roared to life.

He set down her bags. "There's a chandelier in the bathroom you might want to see before you reject this room."

When she saw it, she smiled. It was simple, elegant, and very sparkly.

"I'm hoping that light is your tipping point." He slipped his hands around her waist and rested them on her ass.

"Aren't you angry about Renfrow?"

"Furious," he replied and kissed her.

"But you aren't acting like it."

"No," he said and kissed her again. "We're safe, we're together, and I promised you something relaxing. I hate what Renfrow did to my family, and I would gladly take him out, but having you here with me, now, is all I care about."

His kiss was tender, his arms held her tightly. She felt safe and adored. And like the luckiest woman in the world.

"I want to stay here with you," she murmured.

There was a shopping bag on his bathroom vanity. "I was hoping you'd say that. I got us a little something."

Inside was a bottle of massage oil and a box of condoms.

"I haven't stopped thinking about you." He stepped behind her, wrapped his arms around her, and kissed the back of her neck until she trembled with arousal. "I love how you feel in my arms, how seeing you at work is the best part of my day, how everything feels right when we're together."

She stared at him in the mirror. "I wish I could promise you that things will always be this good."

He turned her toward him. "Life doesn't hand out guarantees. I'm grateful you're with me, now."

Pressing herself close, she kissed him.

"As beautiful and sexy as you look, I think it's time we got you out of that dress." He collected the oil and the box of condoms before they returned to his bedroom.

He closed both bedroom doors. "Lights on low."

The lights dimmed. "Lights lowered," said the computer.

After removing each other's clothing, he cradled her in his arms and laid her in his bed like she was a porcelain doll.

Cooper had this amazing way of capturing her complete attention with the intensity in his eyes or the power in his kiss. When he covered her body with his, he became her entire world. Nothing mattered, except him.

"Roll over," he murmured.

"You don't have to—"

He pressed his mouth to hers and deepened their embrace. When the kiss ended, he said, "Do this… for me."

She kissed him, ran the backs of her fingers down his cheek. "I don't deserve you." She rolled onto her stomach.

After dotting her back with several tender kisses, he caressed her skin, running his strong hands down her back and over her buttocks. The stress started melting away. When he massaged her with the almond-scented oil, she released a long, soul-cleansing sigh.

"Never have I ever been spoiled like this," she whispered.

"Never have I ever had anyone this special who I wanted to spoil," he replied.

As if he had nothing but time and energy, he massaged out the knots in her back and along her shoulders.

"Are you awake," he whispered in her ear.

She smiled. "Uh-huh."

"Time to roll over."

Feeling completely relaxed, she rolled onto her back and smiled up at him.

"That was my goal," he said. "I saw that look the night we met."

"I was pretty tipsy at Raphael's."

"You were happy and chatty and so damn interested in the chandelier over the table."

She laughed. "I've got a thing for lights."

"And my hair."

"You've got great hair. Thick and blond, just the way I like it." Then, she eyed his massive boner. "Your friend's not bad, either."

He dipped down, kissed her. "We'll get there, if that's what you want." He filled his palm with oil, rubbed his hands together, and coated her chest with liquid. His slow, rhythmic caresses both stimulated and relaxed her. He had this magical ability to massage away the stress, leaving only desire. He massaged her abs, her thighs, her calves, and, when he rubbed her feet, she started moaning.

"I can add amazing hands to my list of things I like about you," she murmured.

"What else do you like about me?" She loved the gleam in his eyes.

"You are the best—*the best*—kisser. Like, wow. I love kissing you."

That made him smile. "It's not me. It's us."

"You think?"

He nodded. "I don't think… I *know*."

When he finished, she pushed up on elbows. Completely relaxed, she could barely think. "Your turn."

"Next time." Then, his gaze turned heated. "Would my lady like a happy ending?"

She grinned at him. "Only if the gentleman gets one, too."

"It would be hard for me not to, with you."

He rolled on a condom, but he didn't go inside her. Instead, he planked over her and pressed his lips to hers. His kisses were addictive. The kissing deepened until they were both moaning from pent-up passion. She spread her legs and wrapped her hands around his shaft.

"Make me happy, Cooper."

He stole her breath when he slid inside her, the euphoria sending her flying high. She loved stroking his muscular back, his soft hair, his massive arms. The strength of his thrusts had her panting with need while she wrapped her legs around his back and trapped him. He repositioned so he could take her nipple into his mouth and tease her tender flesh with his tongue.

"I'm gonna come, but I want us to come, together," she said.

"I'll come with you," he murmured. "Don't close your eyes. Stay with me."

The orgasm started deep inside her, moving its way through her until it burst forth, sending spasms of pleasure careening through her. She shook beneath him, clinging to him like she was at the top of a rock wall, while they peered into each other's eyes.

The ecstasy overwhelmed her while he groaned through his release. She never wanted to float back to earth. She wanted to hide in his beautiful home, forever.

But this wasn't a fairy tale, and she wasn't a damsel in distress waiting for a prince to rescue her from the castle. She was a fearless woman on a mission, hunting down evil and taking out the bad guys, one at a time.

He snuggled close, then rolled them sideways so his full weight didn't crush her. For a long time, they stared into each other's eyes, as if under the same magical spell.

"You," he whispered.

"Us," she replied with a kiss.

Even though this fantasy would be short lived, she was going to enjoy every single moment of it. Cooper Grant was a special, special man.

In the moment, she could see in his eyes that he felt the same way about her.

Pity it couldn't last forever.

COOPER

The following morning, Cooper woke to Danielle splayed over him. He didn't want to wake her, but his arm was dead asleep. As he slowly pulled away from her, she lifted her head and peered down at him.

Her mussed hair and sleepy smile had him forgetting every bad thing.

"Ah, so it wasn't a dream," she said, her voice groggy. She kissed him. "Good morning."

He kissed her back. "Sleep okay?"

"The best sleep I've had in a long, long time." She sat up and the linens collected around her waist. He appreciated her soft, rounded shoulders, beautiful breasts and strong abs. Leaning over, he kissed each nipple. She slipped her hand into his hair and caressed his scalp. "I haven't been completely honest."

He pushed onto his elbow. "What about?"

"I wasn't sleeping so great after the car explosion," she said. "I've never been scared in my own home, but I was concerned."

His chest tightened. He hated that she'd been scared. "I'm sorry. You can tell me anything, okay? I won't judge, and I keep secrets. Ask Tessa. She tells me all her boyfriend problems and I have never broken her trust." He'd been stroking her thigh and her muscles tensed.

Danielle might look like an angel, but she was wrapped pretty tightly.

"Relax," he said, caressing her leg. "I won't let anything happen to you."

She leaned down, kissed him again. "Let's find this Renfrow before he finds us again." She pushed out of bed, walked over to his side, pulled back the linens, and held out her hand.

When he placed his into hers, he knew he'd kill to keep her safe.

After getting ready, they ate cereal at the kitchen island while he searched for a picture of Renfrow. He found one and spun his laptop toward her.

"Is that current?" she asked.

"No, but he doesn't look much different. Older, maybe a few pounds heavier."

"So, he's got dark hair, parted on the side. Any facial hair?"

"No."

"How tall is he?"

"Five seven, five eight."

She dragged her laptop over, and started to hunt for him via an ancestry website. "I'm looking for relatives he might have gone to stay with. Do you know if he's married or has children?"

He stopped chewing. "At the parole hearing, he mentioned he had someone in his life and he'd be living with her."

"Would your dad's lawyer know? Could we call someone at the prison and ask?"

He called his dad's attorney who said he'd check and get back to him. He called the prison, but the records clerk didn't work weekends. He pushed off the cushioned stool. "You eat eggs?"

"Sure," she replied, still on her computer.

Despite her efforts, they made no progress on Renfrow's whereabouts. He didn't have any social media accounts under his name, but Cooper never expected he'd be *that* stupid.

"I ran that picture using Stryker's IDware," she said, "but I didn't get any hits."

"I appreciate the help." He served her two fried eggs. "When I find the son of a bitch— and I will—I'll show him what twenty years of pent-up rage looks like."

When they finished breakfast, they slogged through Saturday traffic to the gym. Cooper scanned their surroundings. "Renfrow could be fucking anywhere," he bit out.

She laid her hand on his thigh, gave him a squeeze. "We'll be vigilant."

"Do you mind if I join your kickboxing class?" he asked.

"I'm not sure what I could teach you, but I'd love to have you there."

He parked at the gym and they went inside.

The class was almost full. After Cooper found a spot in the front, Danielle welcomed everyone, then started with a warm up.

He loved watching her lead the group, loved seeing her walking around to offer an assist.

"Looking good, Grant," she said with a smile.

She returned to the front of the room. "Let's partner up for some sparring. Remember, sparring is an opportunity to learn and improve."

People began pairing off. Cooper walked over to Danielle. "Spar with me."

"I was going to walk around and observe."

"I'll be waiting after you make your rounds."

He moved over to one of the training dummies in the corner and began jabbing and kicking. The harder he hit, the angrier he got. Rather than helping, the fighting only riled him up more. He hated being out of control, hated that Danielle was at risk. And he fucking hated that his family was so vulnerable.

She appeared by his side and he stopped. He was sweating and breathing hard.

"I definitely think the dummy is sufficiently annihilated," she said.

They moved out of the corner and began circling each other. Her gloved hands were protecting her face, but then she swung around and kicked him. He blocked her with his arm. The jabs and crosses continued with a few additional kicks. She was strong and fast, but he was holding back. No way would he unleash his full power on her. Despite her power and agility, he was double her size.

The sparring ended, they fist bumped each other. "Great job," she said. "Thanks for going easy on me. I know you're a beast."

"So are you," he replied.

Danielle finished the class with cool downs.

"You're a natural," he said as they removed their gloves and finger wraps. "I'm going to climb a wall. Come with me."

When they entered the rock-climbing room, she hung back. He returned to her and said, "Please put the harness on."

"What for?"

"One step closer to tackling that wall."

She looked up. "I'm not climbing that thing."

"Trust me," he whispered.

He helped her attach the harness, then attached his own.

"I'm good," she replied.

"You can do it."

She released a growl.

"Use that fear."

"Ugh," she bit out and walked over to the wall. "I'm here."

He stood by her side and explained the value of pushing with legs versus pulling with arms, then he demonstrated by placing his foot on a low stud. "Try it."

She did.

He reached up and, as he did so, he pushed using his grounded foot. Then, he turned back and instructed her. She did it.

"Nice job," he said. "Can you reach up to this hold?"

She did. "I'm shaking like crazy."

"You did well, today," he said. "I'm going up a little higher, but you can step back down."

To his delight, she pushed with her foot and grabbed another hold. She made it a quarter of the way up the wall before she said, "I'm done."

He climbed back down with her, staying close and offering words of encouragement. When her feet were on the mat, she was smiling pretty hard.

He high-fived her, then pulled her close and kissed her cheek. "You gotta be proud of yourself."

"Thank you for helping me," she said.

He loved that she'd pushed past her fear. "One step at a time, right? Isn't that how we get anywhere in life?"

"I don't deserve you," she whispered under her breath.

It pained him to hear her say that. "You gotta stop saying that, Danielle. It's not true."

Her brows were locked in a downward slope and she was nibbling her lower lip. Something had her on edge, but beyond Renfrow, he had no idea what. "You wanna talk about it?"

"No," she replied. "I wanna watch you climb the wall, so I can see you flex those big, sexy muscles."

After removing her harness, she stepped out of the way. He turned back to the wall and started to climb. The higher he got, the more relaxed he felt. At the top, he peered out through the floor-to-ceiling window. This wasn't like mountain climbing, but it would work in the moment.

Back on the floor, he removed the harness and scanned the room. She was waiting, her gaze glued to his. As if pulled by an invisible force, he went to her. The closer he got, the better he felt. He stopped inches away.

"You're sexy," she whispered. "And so brave."

He skimmed her backside. "We'll get you to the top of that wall."

"I'm not so sure about that."

"Ready to head out?"

They stopped at the front desk. Naomi had nothing to report and no packages for him.

On the way back to his house, his phone rang. It was Tessa. "Hey, Tessa, you're on speaker and Danielle's with me."

"Hey, Uncle Coop. Danielle, I saw you on the schedule tomorrow at the shelter," Tessa said. "The residents who took your class loved it, and the next group can't wait."

"I'm looking forward to it," Danielle replied.

"Uncle Cooper, are you going to Gammy and Pop Pop's for game night? Please, please say yes. Oh, and you *have* to bring Danielle."

Cooper and Danielle exchanged glances. "I'll be there," Cooper replied.

"Danielle?" Tessa asked.

"Of course," Danielle replied. "Game night sounds fun."

"Yay! Oh, and Gammy is making ribs and a bunch of sides, so she said to come hungry. Love you!" Tessa hung up.

"She's a ball of energy," Cooper said.

"You don't have to bring me just because I'm staying with you."

"I want you with me. You're gonna love my family." After a beat, he said, "What about yours? Where are your mom and dad?"

"After my sister died, my parents moved to Atlanta to be near my older brother. He and his wife are expecting their third child."

"How are they doing?"

"You mean, since Claire-Marie's death?"

He nodded.

"Being around their grandkids helps, but they're still really sad."

He grasped her hand, kissed her finger. "I'm sure they are. Have you visited them since they moved?"

"No. I might fly down for Thanksgiving. If I don't, then definitely Christmas."

It had to be hard not having family nearby. Cooper was close to his. He glanced over and caught the sadness in her eyes. Despite his being stalked, he wanted to do something fun with her. As he drove toward home, a plan took hold.

"It's a beautiful day. We're going to take the next few hours and play."

"Play? Are you kidding? We've got to find Renfrow."

He drove into his neighborhood and pulled over to make sure they weren't being followed. "Fuck Renfrow," he said. When no one turned down the street, he drove home.

They went inside and upstairs to change.

"What should I wear?" she asked.

"Layers. We're going to be inside and outside."

She sidled close, stood on her toes, and draped her arms over his shoulders. "I love surprises."

After a kiss that left him eager for more, she broke away to get ready. Since she didn't have a lot of clothes with her, he grabbed an extra sweatshirt for her. When he saw what she was wearing, he chuckled.

She regarded him, then laughed. "Oh, no, we're wearing the same thing."

Both had changed into tattered jeans and black shirts. He, in a T-shirt, and she, in a tank top. She was holding a sweater and a sweatshirt.

"You look hot," he said, threading his arms around her.

She tilted her face toward his. "So do you."

"It might be windy, so bring a hair tie and your Converse are perfect." One, chaste kiss, and they were out the door, sailing around the beltway and hopping on Route 50, heading east.

"I have no idea where we're going, but I cannot wait to get there." She clasped his hand and kissed it before setting them in her lap.

He loved having her by his side, loved getting to know her. Unfortunately, he couldn't shake the image of her on that flip phone she kept in her safe. His gut told him it was a burner. The image of her with Salimov popped into his thoughts and he glanced over at her. He wanted to ask her about the phone. She was living in his home and sleeping in his bed. If she was working with Salimov—

There's no way she's doing that.

He pushed out the nauseating thought as he drove into the parking lot of the marina.

"Oh, wow," she exclaimed. "Are we going for a boat ride?"

The excitement and joy in her eyes took his breath away.

When he brought her to his boat slip, she gasped. His forty-foot yacht could accommodate as many as ten overnight guests.

"This is Freedom," he said as he brought her on board.

"She's beautiful."

"Make yourself at home," he said. "I'm going to ready the vessel."

Boating was another sport he loved. Though it was a brisk fall day, he'd fire up the heater and wrap her in a blanket if she got cold.

After Danielle stepped inside, he started the blower and turned on all the yacht's electronics. A few minutes later, he checked the engine compartment. Having smelled no fumes, he fired up the twin diesel engines. Once he untied the boat from its moorings, he found Danielle sitting in the co-captain's chair with a huge smile plastered on her face. He pulled a blanket from belowdecks and wrapped it around her shoulders.

"It might get cold on the bay."

She leaned up and kissed him. "Thank you. You take such good care of me."

He took his seat in the captain's chair, eased out of the slip, then motored slowly through the no wake zone. Once they'd cleared the channel and were in the bay, he thrust the throttles two-thirds of the way forward. The engines roared, the boat surged forward and, in seconds, they were at cruising speed and on plane.

"This is awesome!" Danielle exclaimed.

He boated up and down the Severn River, past the Naval Academy, and down Annapolis' Ego Alley. The narrow waterway gave boaters a place where they could dock their vessel, hop out, and enjoy a meal at the restaurants that lined both sides. Lots of times, boaters drove through simply because it was the place to see *and* be seen, hence the name.

The hard part was maneuvering his ship at the end of the inlet. He'd done it enough times to know just where to reverse the port engine to make the turn easily.

She stood beside him, wrapped her arm around his waist and rested her head on his shoulder. "Thank you for sharing this with me. I don't *ever* want to leave. This is the perfect escape."

Cooper put his arm around her, kissed the top of her head. He wished he could motor away to an island for two, bask in the sun, and make love to his beautiful woman all day.

But someone had to catch Renfrow *and* stop the vigilante... and that someone was him.

18

GAME NIGHT WITH THE GRANTS

DANIELLE

Danielle didn't have time to make a dish to bring to game night, so she asked Cooper to stop at a toy store on the way to his parents' house where she bought a few board games.

Her heart was pounding pretty fast as Cooper pushed open the front door and waited while she entered their home.

"Hey, guys," Cooper called as he brought her into the kitchen.

His mom and dad were sitting at the kitchen table, laughing hysterically, while Tessa was demonstrating her best twerking moves.

Danielle pulled up a song on her phone, and Tessa began dancing around the kitchen. When the song ended, Tessa took a bow and everyone applauded.

Tessa bounded over, hugged Cooper, then Danielle. "I was showing Gammy and Pop Pop how to twerk."

Still laughing, Cooper's mom rose from her seat. "Hi, Danielle, I'm Emily, Cooper's mom. It's lovely to meet you."

"You, too, Emily," Danielle replied. "Hi, Eric, good to see you."

"Looks like you came prepared for game night," Eric said.

"These are for you guys." Danielle set the games on the kitchen table. "Cooper didn't think you had any of these."

"That was so nice of you," Emily said.

Tessa examined each of them. "I've never played Catan, but I've heard tons about it."

A petite blonde walked into the room and Tessa hurried over to her. "This is my Aunt Chantal."

"Hi, Chantal. I'm Danielle."

"Hi." Chantal barely smiled and didn't hold Danielle's gaze longer than a few seconds.

While Tessa was vibrant and all smiles, Chantal was very withdrawn.

"I thought my dad was coming over tonight," Tessa said to Danielle. "He's Uncle Cooper's brother. But he can't make it." She shrugged. "His loss."

Tessa twirled her way over to Cooper's mom, who'd opened the oven to check on the ribs. The delicious scent of savory meat wafted in Danielle's direction.

"That smells so good," Danielle said. "What can I do to help?"

Emily pulled slaw, potato salad, and a garden salad from the refrigerator, then a bubbling mac-n-cheese from the oven. "Tessa, why don't you and Danielle set the table? Chantal, can you help with drinks?"

Danielle spied Cooper sitting next to his dad, the two men talking in hushed tones, no doubt about Renfrow. The kitchen was a bustle of activity until everyone's plates had been filled. Emily prepared a plate for herself and one for Eric.

"Thank you, dear," Eric said. "I could have done that."

With a sweet smile, Emily patted his back affectionately before sitting beside him.

"Dad, you don't have a salad." Chantal scooped salad into a small bowl, then returned to the table.

While they ate, Danielle loved seeing Cooper interact with his family. He asked a lot of questions, trying to draw his timid sister into the conversation. Danielle's heart broke for Chantal. She reminded her of a wounded baby bird, no longer able to fly. Danielle wanted to swaddle her in a blanket and nurse her back to health.

"Cooper, how do you and Danielle know each other?" his mom asked.

"Danielle and Emerson—Stryker's fiancée—are best friends," Cooper explained. "And Danielle teaches kickboxing part-time at my gym."

"Very nice," said his mom.

"Danielle is the computer expert I told you about, Gammy," Tessa said. "She taught my residents a class on Internet safety and she's coming back tomorrow, right, Danielle?"

"Absolutely," Danielle replied. "Will I see you tomorrow?"

"Of course," Tessa beamed.

"You sound as busy as Cooper," Emily added.

"The kickboxing class is just once a week," Danielle volunteered. "I used to work at Stryker's company full-time, but now I—" she temporarily forgot her cover— "I manage online security at a marketing firm." Then, she redirected the conversation. "Where do you guys work?"

"I'm an architect," Emily said. "Our firm does mostly residential projects."

"Chantal and I run a marketing company," Cooper's dad said. "We probably know a lot of the same people."

"I just started working there, so I don't know anyone outside our small office," Danielle replied.

Change the subject.

"Chantal, I haven't seen you at Cooper's gym," Danielle said. "Do you rock climb like your brother?"

Chantal's chest rose as she inhaled a deep breath. "We've got a small workout room, here, that I use."

"I'm terrified of heights," Danielle shared. "Your brother has been helping me get over my phobia. Yesterday, I climbed a few feet off the ground. Have you ever tried kickboxing?"

"No, but I've seen videos," Chantal replied. "It looks fun."

"It's a great workout and it's also good for confidence and self-defense. I'd love it if you came to my class."

"Thanks, but I'm pretty busy."

Danielle slid her gaze to Cooper, then back to Chantal. "What if I came over here and taught you some basic moves?"

Chantal's expression lifted. "Really, you would do that?"

"I'd love to," Danielle replied. "We can set a date before I leave."

"And I'll grab you a set of gloves and some wraps for your hands," Cooper volunteered.

After dinner, Danielle asked Chantal if she could see the in-house gym. "Do you want to come with us, Tessa?"

"I'm gonna check out the games you brought," Tessa replied.

In silence, Chantal led Danielle to the other side of the house and into their home gym. The spare bedroom house a treadmill in one corner, hand weights and workout bands, and an elliptical across the room. For a small space, they'd certainly made the most of it.

"This is awesome," Danielle said. "One of the things I like about Cooper's gym is that there are mirrors on the walls of the workout studios. That helps us make sure we're doing things correctly."

"Uh-huh."

"We can make this room work for the basics of kickboxing, like warm-up exercises and jabs and punches, but if we decide to spar, we'll need more space."

"I don't leave the house much," Chantal murmured.

"No worries. We'll figure out how to make it work."

"I get anxious when I go out, unless I walk around the neighborhood with my mom."

"If you decide you want to go to Cooper's gym, I wouldn't leave you, not even if you went to the restroom."

Chantal laughed, then her joyous expression fell away. "Someone hurt me and I don't trust people anymore."

"I'm sorry. Life is tough sometimes, huh?"

"I wish it had never happened."

"Sounds like it was pretty bad."

Chantal nodded.

Danielle stayed silent, but Chantal didn't say anything more.

"If you use the pain and the anger, even the fear, to overcome that hardship, you'll take back your power and your life."

Silence.

"Can you say that again?" Chantal asked.

"Use that pain and anger and fear to overcome your hardship so you can take back your power and your life. If you don't, the person or people who hurt you have all the power. No asshole deserves that."

Chantal's lips turned up, just a little. "You're cool."

Danielle smiled. "Actually, I'm a total mess."

Chantal laughed as Cooper walked into the room. His expression brightened when he saw his sister laughing. "You two look like you're having fun."

"I'm going to write down what you said in my journal," Chantal said. "Don't start the board game without me." She scurried out.

Cooper stepped close. "What was that all about?"

"She told me someone hurt her and she doesn't leave the house. I suggested she use the pain and anger and fear to take back her life."

"Nice. Do you think it helped?"

"I hope so, but I'm definitely *not* the best person to be giving advice." She pasted on a smile. "Let's see what game Tessa picked."

Cooper pulled her into his arms, then kissed her forehead. "Thank you for spending time with my sister."

Danielle loved game night with the Grants. They were an easygoing family who made her feel welcome. As the evening wore on, the guilt crept back in. They would feel deceived once she got arrested for her crimes. Rather than get in her head about the future, she focused on this wonderful man and his kind family.

When game night ended, Danielle made plans to teach Chantal basic kickboxing in her home.

"Thank you both so much for having me," she said to Cooper's mom and dad.

"It was our pleasure," Emily said. "Thanks for the games."

"I'll see you at the gym," Eric said, "and cheer you on as you climb the wall."

"Three feet at a time," Danielle said and laughed.

"Progress is progress," Eric replied. "That's what counts."

Tessa hugged her. "See you tomorrow, Danielle." Then, she hugged Cooper. "Love you, Uncle."

On the ride home, Danielle said, "Your family's great."

In the dark car, he held her hand. "If you're not careful, the entire Grant family will fall in love with you."

Until they learn the ruthless truth about me.

EARLY SUNDAY MORNING, Danielle hacked into the records system of the prison where Renfrow had been jailed. He hadn't had any visitors in the days leading up to his hearing.

"I'm sorry, Cooper," she said, shutting her laptop. "I can't find a single relative of Renfrow's and it doesn't look like he had any recent visitors." After pushing off the sofa, she slid her laptop into her computer satchel. "I'll see you later."

Cooper had been working alongside her. "Where are you going?"

"To the shelter."

He rose. "I'll go with you."

Gazing up at him, she stroked his massive arms, appreciating his hard triceps and bulging biceps. "No, you're not. I'm going to the shelter and you are *not* going with me. I will be fine."

"Do you have a chip in your neck?"

"Ohmygod, are you going to track me?"

"I would check on your whereabouts."

"I have the phone app," she replied. "After the workshop, I'm having lunch with Lori Shannon."

Her chest tightened. She hated lying to him, but if she could steal away for a few hours, she could plan her evening with Salimov. After meeting Chantal, she was more determined than ever to take him out.

His phone rang. "It's Naomi," he replied before answering. As he listened, his brow furrowed. "I'll be there in twenty." He hung up.

"One of the washing machines flooded at the gym and it sounds pretty bad."

"Oh, no. Good luck with that." She kissed him, then headed toward the door. "Can you close the garage door after I leave?"

"I'll get you a remote." He handed her one from a kitchen drawer, then gave her the eight-digit code to turn off the home security system. "That was Alan's birthday." He pulled her into his arms and hugged her. "Be careful out there."

"You, too."

He walked her into the garage and waited while she drove away.

As she drove to the shelter, she considered canceling with Salimov. Then, she thought about Chantal and the pain he'd caused her and countless other women.

By the time she pulled up to the shelter, her mind was made up.

He'll be my last and final target.

When she walked inside, Tessa was manning reception. To her surprise, Tessa didn't greet her with her normal exuberance. With microphone in hand, she announced that the workshop was starting and told Danielle she'd be back to facilitate as soon as she could find someone to handle the phones.

"Where's your friend, Val?" Danielle asked.

A shadow darkened Tessa's light eyes. "She left."

"Isn't that a good thing?"

"Every resident goes through the program, then graduates. Val was only halfway through, and we'd been talking about her maybe moving in with me. It's not like her to ghost." Tessa glanced around. "I'm, like, worried about her."

Billy moseyed into reception, dressed in overalls and a blue shirt, the ceiling lights reflecting off his shiny head. "Hey, Danielle."

"Hi, Billy."

He pushed his tinted glasses back onto the bridge of his nose. "I'll take you to the conference room."

Danielle glanced at Tessa.

Tessa nodded. "I'll be there as soon as I can."

As Danielle walked down the corridor with Billy, he asked how her day was going. "It's fine. How 'bout you?"

"Never better," he said. "You live around here?"

"Not too far." As Danielle walked into the conference room and over to the table at the front of the room, Billy stayed by her side. "Need help setting up?"

"I'm good," she said, plugging her laptop into the projector. "Is Lori here?"

"She's coming in later today. I'm gonna hang around to help if you need anything." He moseyed to the back of the room.

Rather than wait for Tessa to kick off the workshop, Danielle introduced herself, then discussed the agenda. The room was more crowded this time and she saw a handful of women from the first class.

"Let's start with some basic questions about Internet safety. Who has social media accounts?"

Most everyone raised their hands.

"Who uses a dating site?"

Again, the majority of women raised their hands.

"Okay, so let's talk about how we can protect ourselves, our personal information, and our safety while we meet people online."

They were a very attentive audience. When the class ended, several asked questions. The room emptied, leaving her alone with Billy, who made his way to the front.

"You're good with computers," he said.

"I know enough to make me dangerous," she said with a chuckle.

"What do you mean?" he asked as she shouldered her computer bag.

"Nothing, really." She headed out and he tagged along.

"Are you coming back to teach another course?" he asked.

"I can, if Lori wants me to."

He escorted her to the lobby. "Stay safe out there. Sounds like there're lots of creeps on the Internet." Billy shuffled away and Danielle flicked her gaze to Tessa.

Tessa sprang out of the chair and around reception. "He's weird," she whispered. "I'm sorry I left you with him, but I couldn't find anyone to work the front desk. How'd it go?"

"Great," Danielle replied. "If Lori needs me to teach another class, or do any kind of follow-up, let me know."

"I'll walk you out," Tessa said.

On the sidewalk, outside the building, Tessa said, "I'm worried about Val. This isn't the first time one of the residents vanished."

"What do you mean *vanished*?"

"They're here one day, then, they're gone. Their things are gone and the roster says they're no longer a resident."

"What does Lori say about that?" Danielle asked.

"She told me that sometimes it doesn't work out. Residents don't have to stay for the entire program. Some leave on their own. Sometimes a family member will check them out early. She wasn't worried at all."

"Why are you?"

"Val would never leave without saying goodbye to me. She hasn't replied to any of my texts and her voicemail is full." Tessa, normally so smiley and energetic, stood there wringing her hands. "You're good with computers. Can you help me find her?"

"Of course," Danielle replied. She didn't have the time to do this, but she couldn't say no. Though she assumed Val had left the shelter, she wouldn't ignore Tessa's plea for help.

The angst on Tessa's face subsided and she hugged Danielle. To her surprise, Tessa was trembling. "Thank you."

Tessa retreated inside and Danielle jumped in her car. As she drove past the front of the building, she spotted Billy smoking. He'd removed his tinted glasses and was leaning against the building. He waved as she drove by.

Danielle's next step was risky. She needed to go home and prep for her evening with Salimov, but Cooper could be tracking her via the app. If he was, she'd tell him her afternoon plans with Lori had changed.

She drove down her street, relieved her home look undisturbed. With her Glock in hand, she hurried inside and got to work. After hacking into DC's transportation system, she programmed the traffic cameras to turn off during a three-hour window that evening. Then, she spent way too much time searching for the embassy townhome's surveillance system, only to conclude there *were* no cameras in the townhouse.

Makes sense. If there's no video, there's no evidence of him molesting anyone.

Danielle had been working so intently, she didn't realize she was sitting in the dark. It was just before six. She confirmed her front door was bolted and she turned on her security system.

She needed to check in with Cooper. To her surprise, her phone battery was dead. Her charger was at Cooper's, but she found a spare. Seconds after she plugged it in, it started buzzing with incoming texts and missed calls.

Tessa had texted her Val's contact information.

Emerson had texted her about hanging out that evening.

"I'm back from the gym," Cooper had texted at four thirty. "Are you still out with Lori?"

Twenty minutes after that text, Cooper sent another. "Tessa said you left hours ago, without Lori. I checked the app and you're offline. Call me."

He'd called her twice.

She started to call him, but stopped. *What am I going to tell him I've been doing all afternoon?* As she started to call him, her phone rang. It was Cooper.

"Hey," she answered. "I'm at my place and I didn't realize my phone had died."

Silence.

"Cooper?"

"I'm here." And he was totally pissed off. "You want to tell me what's going on with you."

"I wanted to be in my house," she replied.

"What the hell for? You're not safe there."

This time, she didn't respond.

"Jericho invited the guys over for poker night," he said. "I told him no—"

"You should go. It sounds fun."

"How can I fucking relax if you're there and Renfrow knows where you live?"

"Is Stryker going to the party?"

"Yeah."

"Perfect," she said. "I'll go to Emerson's."

Her idea was met with silence. This time, she waited, hoping he'd agree to her plan.

"I'll come over."

"I needed some alone time. Everything is happening so fast with us. I stopped by to grab a few things and time got away from me."

Through the silence, his anger was palpable.

"Make sure your phone is charged," he ground out.

"It's charging, now."

"I'll see you tonight." He hung up.

She stared out the window into pitch-black darkness, the streetlights shining like beacons of hope. Fueled with determination, she pushed off the stool and headed upstairs to change.

It's time, Salimov. I'm coming for you.

19

THE HIT AND THE MISTAKE

COOPER

Cooper tossed his cards on the table. "I'm out."

He loved poker night with his boys, but he couldn't concentrate. He kept thinking about Danielle and her bizarre behavior. She knew Renfrow was dangerous, she'd seen his destruction firsthand, yet she insisted on spending the afternoon alone at her townhouse… without even checking in with him.

He eyed the guys chilling around Jericho's poker table. Stryker had the best poker face. He could've been holding all four aces or a bunch of nothing. Jericho was king of multitasking. Between his sister and brothers wandering in and out, and his phone constantly buzzing, it was a wonder he had a life, at all. And then, there was Hawk. He wore a smirk all the damn time. He coulda been getting blown under the table, that's how relaxed he looked.

Jericho's finished basement was large enough to house a billiards table, a ping-pong table, a jukebox, a pinball station, and an arcade basketball game.

On the other side of the room was a live-in suite, complete

with a bedroom, bath, and sitting room. There was always someone crashing there.

"You got someone living in the guest suite?" Cooper asked.

"Nah," Jericho replied. "The strays I usually take in haven't come around lately, but it's almost the holidays, so I expect a full house."

After a pause, Cooper asked, "Am I being too controlling?"

"No," Stryker replied. "Renfrow's dangerous."

"You said Danielle thinks things are moving too fast," Jericho said while replying to a text. "Give her space."

"Dawg, do what I do," Hawk said. "Nothing." His lips split into a smile. "I can barely control my own behavior. Why in the hell would I try to control a woman's? Hell, I don't even understand 'em most of the time."

The guys laughed.

Earlier, Cooper checked the ALPHA app. Danielle was still at her place. Checking up on her felt like stalking, which was definitely not his style. So, he'd shoved his phone in his jacket pocket and hadn't checked since. But his head was pounding and he hadn't been able to focus on the card game.

If anything happens to her...

His chest grew tight.

The guys showed their hands and Stryker pulled over the chips. "Hawk, I heard from all the guys, but you. Are you in my wedding, or what?"

"Why wouldn't I be?" Hawk replied.

Jericho chuckled. "Hawk, you keep things simple, don't you?"

"When have I ever said no to you guys?" Hawk asked. "I haven't, so I figured you'd know I was in."

"He's got a point," Cooper said, coming to his defense.

"You sent us a text asking if we'd be in your wedding, but you got no date yet," Hawk pressed.

Feeling restless, Cooper pushed out of his chair. "I'm playing pool. Who's in?"

Hawk stood. "I gotcha." Then, he smirked at Stryker. "Like I said... I have *never* said no to my boys."

DANIELLE

Danielle shifted on the living room chair of the embassy's townhouse. Salimov was sipping a vodka and eye-fucking her pretty hard. In addition to her platinum-blonde wig and her brown contact lenses, she'd worn a pair of jeans, a shirt, and her leather jacket. She suspected he didn't appreciate how clothed she was.

The first few minutes, Salimov tried to convince her to have a drink with him… and take off her jacket. When he failed on both counts, he suggested they sit in the living room, where he launched into a rant about the importance of him. According to the wall clock, she'd been there for eight minutes. He was a large man, which posed a challenge, but if she could secure him, she'd have the upper hand.

He finished his vodka, set his empty glass on the table. "Enough small talk. You here for a job, yes?"

She nodded.

"I like you, Ursula, so I have two opportunities. One pays fifty grand. I give you name of business associate and you talk to him."

"What kind of job is it?"

"Assistant." He leaned back. "The second job pays one fifty, plus bonus."

"Doing what?"

"My personal executive. You travel with me. You entertain Russian friends."

Ohgod, he would traffic me.

"I want to get to know you better," he continued. "We go

upstairs, see if I like. That's your real interview. If yes, job is yours."

Her eyes grew wide. "You can't be serious."

"Why not? It's a job. You need job, no?"

"I need a *real* job, Ivan. You know, one where I actually work."

"You work with me. I have meetings. You come with. I have trips. You travel. See the country, the world. I have exciting life. I have much money. You need money, yes?"

"What else would I do besides be your whore?"

He chuckled. "Americans are so crass. I get lecture about consent." This time, he rolled his eyes. "You work for me, that means you consent, no?"

"What *else* would I do for you?" Playing the part, she feigned frustration.

"I find you tasks."

"Do you have other personal executives?"

"That is not your concern."

"You have a wife."

"I have mistress, too. Ivan has big need. Many women to satisfy me." He pushed out of the chair. "You interested? You come. If not, you leave."

"I didn't think I'd be having sex with you."

"You come here at night. What the fuck you think would happen?"

"I *thought* you were going to interview me."

Salimov threw his head back and laughed. "Interview happens on bed."

If she could tie him down, she'd have the edge. She pulled the BDSM bed restraints from her bag. "I *had* planned on going to my kink club later, but I'll stay and fuck you if I can use these."

"Not first time. Tonight, I control."

She shook her head. "You like blow jobs?"

His freakish smile made her stomach clench. "Of course."

"I give very good head. You have your rules. I have mine."

He eyed the restraints. "You are excellent negotiator, Ursula. I agree."

She shouldered her handbag.

"Why do you need that?"

"Condoms for fucking after I suck you."

"I have."

"I use latex-free and ribbed, for me. We use mine."

"When will Ivan get his way?"

"When you come in my mouth," she replied dryly.

At the foot of the stairs, he gestured for her to walk ahead of him.

"You, first." She needed eyes on him at all times. If he attacked her from behind, it was all over.

"I want to admire your ass on way up."

"Once we're upstairs, you get to admire my *naked* ass." She fisted her hand on her hip. "Or should we continue to argue about it?"

"Very strong-willed. You must be tamed. Ivan is boss. You *will* learn that."

Her fingers twitched for her weapon. She couldn't wait to silence him.

Before heading up, he grabbed her ass, and her skin crawled with what felt like a hundred spiders.

"End of hallway," he said as he lumbered forward.

He entered a bedroom with Russian décor and a queen bed. To her relief, the curtains were drawn.

When he stroked her breast, she could taste the bile. "Get naked," he ordered.

"Remove your pants and get on the bed," she replied.

"You want to work for me, you do what I say. Take off fucking clothes." His tone was abrupt while his beady eyes drilled into her. Then, he started tugging off her jacket. "Are you fucking deaf?"

She jerked away from him, but he lunged for her, wrapping his large hands around her neck. Clawing at his fingers, she forced hers under his and yanked hard, then kneed him in the groin.

"Aaaaiiieee!" The second he released her, she shoved him back, then delivered a powerful kick to his chest that left him splayed on the bed. Groaning, he rolled onto his side, holding his crotch.

She pulled her Glock, pointed it at his face. "Don't move or I'll blow your fucking brains out."

His eyes widened, then he composed himself. "Ursula, no need for gun."

She couldn't use the restraints because he'd overpower her. Since he wasn't held down on the bed, she couldn't attach the silencer, either.

"How many women have you raped? How many others have you trafficked? How many lives have you ruined? Do you even fucking know?"

He said nothing.

"Answer my questions."

"I help women," he replied, pushing up on his elbow. "Give them jobs, take care of them."

"You're a monster who's manipulated and abused women for decades. Chantal Grant used to work for you. Remember her? You raped her, repeatedly, then threatened her if she told anyone. This is for her and all the other women you hurt. Rot in hell, Salimov."

He started pushing off the bed.

BANG!

The bullet pierced his cheek.

BANG!

She hit him between the eyes and he fell backward onto the bed.

Without the silencer, the gunshots blasted through the quiet night. An urge to flee had adrenaline charging through her, but she had to stick with her plan. She watched his chest. It was still.

Another predator dead.

She shoved the Glock into her pocket, pulled on her gloves and extracted the wadded-up note from her bag. After opening his mouth, she shoved it halfway in. She threw both casings into her bag, turned out the bedroom light, and hurried down the stairs.

On the first floor, she slipped out the front door, head down as she walked down the sidewalk, and around Salimov's end unit.

It was another half block before she arrived at her Ninja, parked at the curb. A couple was strolling toward her, hand-in hand. If she pulled out her leather pants, she'd only attract attention, so she turned away and unlocked her helmet.

"I love your bike," said the woman.

Dammit.

Danielle pulled on her helmet, but didn't turn to face them. "Thanks."

"Is that a Ninja?" she asked.

After flipping down the tinted visor, Danielle mounted her bike. Rather than speak, she gave a thumbs-up.

"I would love to learn how to ride," continued the woman. "Can I sit on your bike, you know, like, just for fun? Maybe even take a few pics?"

Danielle had to get the hell out of there. After starting the Ninja, she glanced over her shoulder and pulled into traffic. Not stopping to chat was equally as problematic as chatting it up. She needed to blend in, not stand out.

Let it go.

A block later, she pulled to the curb, tugged her leather pants over her jeans and swapped her heels for riding boots. Next, she slid her weapon into the side satchel. In order to keep her face hidden, she didn't flip up the visor.

As she rode toward home, she had this nagging feeling she'd left something at Salimov's.

COOPER

Cooper and Stryker were playing a game of arcade basketball when Stryker's phone buzzed. He pulled it from his pocket and laughed, then sent off a quick text.

"You gotta see this." Stryker showed Cooper the photos on his phone.

Their cat, Pima, had climbed up the two-story curtains in the living room. Emerson's text read, "He won't climb down. Can't tell if he's stuck or stubborn. Not calling the FD."

Stryker had texted back, "Idiot cat."

Cooper chuckled. "What did she and Danielle do tonight?"

"I didn't know Danielle was with her."

Ah, fuck. "Check with Emerson."

"Not sure if I want to go there, Coop."

"Just do it."

Stryker shot off a text. Within seconds, Stryker read Emerson's reply out loud. "I just got home from dinner at my mom and dad's. I wanted Danny to come with me, but I never heard back from her."

Cooper shook his head.

"Your problem is you like her." Hawk moseyed over to look at the picture of Pima clinging to the curtains. "I gotta get me a cat or two. They're hilarious."

"They're insane," Stryker said and both men laughed.

"Talk to her," Jericho said joining their conversation.

"I fucking hate talking," Hawk blurted. "When a woman tells me she wants to talk, I'm outta there. Adios, sayonara, bye-bye."

"She worked for me for *years*," Stryker added, "and I didn't know she and Emerson were best friends until that night at Raphael's. Bro, if you want answers, you gotta *ask* her what's going on?"

Cooper unearthed his phone and checked the ALPHA app. Danielle was still at home. "Alright, guys, I'm taking off."

"Me, too," Stryker said.

"I'm in no rush," Hawk said. "Got any women we can call?" he asked Jericho.

Jericho's hearty laugh made Cooper chuckle. "Thinking with your wee little man again?" Cooper asked.

"He always comes first," Hawk replied, before pulling Cooper in for a bro-hug. "Tell her you love her and see what happens."

Cooper laughed. "Stick with your day job, Hawk. Jericho, thanks for having us over. My place, next time."

Cooper and Stryker headed out. In the driveway, Stryker said, "If you're good at anything, it's getting to the truth."

Twenty minutes later, Cooper drove down Danielle's quiet street. Her home was dark and her car was parked in the driveway. He parked, jumped out, and rang the doorbell.

No answer.

He called her. Also, no answer.

Was she out with friends and someone else drove? Was she inside asleep? Had Renfrow gotten in and she was either hurt or—

He banged on her front door. "Danielle! Danielle!"

He bolted into her yard and stared up at her house. No lights flicked on. Emerson might have a key and she'd know the code to turn off the house alarm. As adrenaline pounded through him, he unearthed his phone as the garage door opened and a motorcycle rode up the driveway.

A woman he assumed was Danielle, dressed in black leathers and wearing a black helmet with a tinted visor, parked in the garage. He strode in after her. She cut the engine and removed her helmet, revealing her platinum-blond wig.

A growl rumbled out of him. He had no idea what the fuck was going on with her, but he was done. She was lying, leading a double life, maybe even spending the evening with Salimov. The possibilities were endless and, clearly, none of his fucking business.

"I came over because I was concerned Renfrow had gotten to

you. You seem fine. I'll ask Hawk to install a security system tomorrow."

She dismounted, but she didn't go to him. "It's not what you think."

"I don't know what to think."

"Do you want to come in?"

"Not really, but I don't want you walking into your house alone at night with a madman on the loose."

She waited for the garage door to close before she stepped inside and turned off her security system. "If someone had broken in, my alarm would have gone off."

In her kitchen, she pulled two glasses, then the Maker's Mark. "Can you pour? I'll be right back."

She strode out, leaving him standing there wondering who the fuck she really was. And whether or not he cared to find out.

DANIELLE

After closing her bedroom door, Danielle stood there trying to figure out how to fix this mess. She had been so focused on offing Salimov, she'd given no thought to Cooper showing up. But there he was concerned for her safety. Her heart was breaking, but she had to end things with him. It was smarter that way.

In her bathroom, she turned on the shower, removed her wig and stripped down. While waiting for the water to heat up, she spotted a trickle of dried blood on her neck. Something had irritated her skin, then broken through.

Salimov must've scratched me.

Her heart necklace wasn't on the bathroom vanity. Bolting into her bedroom, she checked the dresser. Not there, either.

Ohgod, no!

She'd forgotten to remove the necklace before she went to

Salimov's and it had come off in the struggle. While her mind raced, she stepped into the shower. As she stood there under the hot spray, she ran through her options. Tell Cooper the truth and turn herself in. Say nothing and hope the necklace never turns up.

My prints are all over that necklace.

Her heart sank. It was over. She'd finally made that critical mistake.

As she washed Salimov down the drain, she thought about how to move forward. Her heart was tugging her in a direction she couldn't go. She had to sever ties with Cooper to ensure he wasn't linked to her when he arrested her for Salimov's murder.

She dried off and dressed in yoga pants and a cut-off T-shirt. She should have been wrecked over killing Salimov, but she was not.

Walking down the stairs, she started shaking. Finding love was never, ever, part of her plan.

Steeling her spine, she found Cooper sitting in the living room sipping the whiskey.

"We need to talk," he said.

The moment she'd been dreading since her killing spree began.

20

ANOTHER DEAD MAN TALKS

COOPER

He rose and went to her. It about killed him, but he didn't touch her, didn't kiss her hello, either. She wasn't his, despite what he had thought. But he felt an obligation to keep her safe and out of harm's way.

"I'm not one to lead with emotions, but I did with you," he said.

"I'm glad you did," she whispered, though he barely heard her. "I haven't been honest with you and you deserve to know the truth."

"My head is pounding and I don't want to get into anything when I'm angry. You should stay at my place until I hire Hawk's company to install security here."

"I'll grab something to wear for work." Her rueful expression sliced through him. She left the room, returning with a garment bag and a backpack. The sadness in her eyes was more than he could stand. He took the items from her and stared into her eyes. "This is not how I envisioned us."

"I kinda did, but not for the reasons you might think. You're a forever kind of man and you deserve that type of woman."

"I thought you were."

"I used to be, but I'm not anymore."

What the hell?

"Danielle, I—it's late. We'll talk tomorrow."

As she followed him home, he let go of his anger to uncover his own truth. He'd been scared Renfrow had killed her, like he'd killed his brother.

In reality, Danielle didn't owe him an explanation. Their relationship was just getting started. He would never have suggested she move in so quickly, but he wanted to protect her.

Then, why didn't I have Hawk install her system? Because I wanted her to move in. I want to keep her safe and I'm angry as fuck because I don't know where I stand with her.

As he pulled into his garage, he knew what he had to do. He had to apologize. They walked into his kitchen and he set down her things.

"You want something to drink?" he asked.

"Water's fine."

He poured two glasses, suggested they sit in the family room. As she made her way to the lone chair in the corner, he said, "Danielle, I'm sorry for being an ass."

She whirled toward him, her brows pinched together. "What?"

He went to her, took her glass, and set them both on the end table, then scooped her up and sat on the sofa with her nestled in his lap.

"I'm sorry." He hugged her and breathed for the first time all day. Really breathed. She clung to him so hard, he wanted to keep her there forever.

After a long moment, he peered into her eyes. They were moist. He kissed her cheek, then wiped the lone tear that had streaked down her beautiful face.

"I haven't been honest with you, either," he said.

She clasped his hand and threaded her fingers through his. This moment felt so fucking right. He had to tell her, even if she didn't feel the same. Then, he would let her go, if that's what she wanted.

"I got scared as fuck when you didn't answer your phone or your front door. I thought Renfrow had gotten to you. I thought he'd killed you to get back at me."

She kissed him softly, once. "Thank you for telling me," she whispered.

"You have a right to your privacy and your own life. I'm sorry if I came across as an overbearing, controlling prick. I'm falling in love with you and I *don't* want to push you away."

Her smile was like a stunning sunset at the end of a long, hard day, filling his heart with joy.

"I'm falling in love with you, too," she said. "If things were different, this would be the best day of my entire life. But I'm not going to let us happen. I'm not someone you can get close to."

He was stunned and confused. In those few seconds, she'd lifted his spirit to the heavens, then tossed him into a lava-spewing volcano.

"You aren't making sense to me."

"I know, but it all will soon, I'm sure of it." She pushed off his lap and held out her hand. "Let's go to sleep. I want to be in your arms, but I can stay in the spare bedroom."

At the top of the stairs, she said, "I wasn't with anyone sexually, tonight, or any other time since we got together. I would never do that to you… to us."

Resisting her was impossible. He pulled her into his arms and held her there for several glorious seconds.

Hand in hand, they made their way to his bedroom. Clothes were shed and they snuggled beneath the blankets, finding refuge in each other's arms, their naked bodies pressed close.

"We'll talk tomorrow," he murmured.

Her kiss was tender, but over too soon. "Thank you."

As she rolled away from him, he spotted a bruise and a cut on her neck.

"Hey, you hurt yourself," he said.

"It's nothing."

He pushed out of bed. "Lemme see if I've got something to put on that." After rummaging through his bathroom, he found first-aid ointment. Back in bed, he gently covered her reddened skin with medicine.

"Lights out," he said.

The room darkened. "Goodnight, Cooper," said the computer.

He spooned behind her, wrapping his arm around her and pulling her snug against him.

"I love you, Cooper," she whispered. "And I'm sorry."

He kissed her bare shoulder. "I love you, too, Danielle, and I'm sorry."

The next morning, she said very little as they readied for work.

"I'm gonna take my car," she said. "I don't want anyone seeing us driving in together and I'll make sure I'm not followed."

She was out the door before he could say goodbye.

Cooper's morning was spent in meetings and digging out of emails. Early afternoon, he, Herrera, and Emerson had been hunkered down in the conference room, combing through the MVA records for the mysterious Ninja.

Tap-tap.

Providence entered the room, closed the door behind her, then studied the photos pinned on the cork board wall. "How's the case coming along?"

"Painfully slow," Emerson replied.

"He took out his fifth victim," Providence said.

"Fuck," Cooper bit out.

"I second that," Herrera uttered.

"Who's the vic?" Cooper asked.

"Ivan Salimov," Providence replied.

Cooper's brain skidded to a screeching halt.

"Same MO," Providence continued. "Salimov had a typed note

stuffed in his mouth with the names of some of his alleged victims."

"What else?" Emerson asked.

"He was found at a townhome owned by the embassy," Providence began. "His wife called the police at two in the morning when he hadn't come home. She told them he had a meeting there, last night. They found him dead with the note in his mouth. Bring your FBI badges and head over there now. I'll text you the address. Cooper, stop by my office on your way out."

She left the conference room and Cooper pushed to his feet. "Who's with me?"

"I can't," Herrera said. "I've got another case I'm working on."

Emerson rose. "I'm in."

Cooper didn't need three guesses why Providence wanted to speak to him. He entered her office, shut the door. Instead of sitting, he stood, arms crossed.

"You weren't shy about how much you hated Salimov, so an alibi would help."

"I didn't kill him," Cooper bit out. "And I'm insulted you'd even ask me for one. I was playing poker at Jericho's. Check with Stryker, unless you think he, Jericho, and Hawk were in on it, too."

"I'm sorry," Providence said. "The White House is pressing me and I have nothing new to tell them."

"I'm glad he's dead, but I didn't pull the trigger."

Thirty minutes later, Cooper stared down at Salimov's cold, dead body while Emerson spoke with someone from the crime scene unit.

One of the bullets had pierced Salimov's left cheek, but the second was a clean shot between his eyes. Already gloved up, Cooper lifted Salimov's fingers. His fingernails had been trimmed short, but that didn't mean trace amounts of skin or blood wouldn't be found if there had been a struggle.

One of the crime scene techs walked over. "No signs of forced entry."

"What did the surveillance cameras pick up?" Cooper asked.

"There aren't any, inside or out."

Cooper regarded Salimov, again. "That says something, right there."

Cooper walked the entire home. The place was filled with expensive-looking artwork and sculptures. Nothing was out of place, not even a throw pillow on any of the sofas. After retracing his steps, he returned to the bedroom.

Staring intently at Salimov, the weight of the cases bore down on him.

He got on his hands and knees and peered under the bed. Nothing. Using his gloved hands, he felt around. There wasn't even the back of a damn earring.

As he was leaving the bedroom, something shiny caught his eye. Tucked beside the leg of the dresser was a heart-shaped pendant. He scooped it up and, with it, came a gold chain. One of the links had been pulled apart, thus ripping the necklace in two. He stared at the heart-shaped pendant fitted with brilliant, round diamonds.

No fucking way.

It looked just like the necklace Danielle wore.

This can't be hers.

Using his phone, he searched the Internet for diamond necklaces. The open-heart style was extremely popular. It could have belonged to any number of women Salimov lured into the bedroom or an overnight guest of the embassy.

Cooper reflected on yesterday. Danielle didn't have lunch with Lori Shannon and she hadn't spent the evening with Emerson either. When she rode in, on her bike, she was wearing that light-blonde wig.

Who rides a black motorcycle, dressed in black, in the damn dark? Someone who doesn't want to be seen, that's who.

He ran through everything, item by item. Danielle had been wearing the same blonde wig with Salimov at Swanky. The traffic cams had all been deactivated in a three-block radius of every crime scene—only a sophisticated hacker could pull that off. Lily had identified a Ninja motorcycle in the vicinity of each murder. Danielle had offered to run the motor vehicle reports, then volunteered to work with Lily on scrubbing those lists. Then, there was the flip phone she'd been using when he found her in her closet.

Nausea overtook him and he put his hand on the wall to steady himself. After it passed and his mind cleared, he couldn't ignore the clues. Cooper needed answers and he knew where to find them. Before leaving, he shoved the jewelry into his pocket and checked in with Emerson.

"I'm going to see if the neighbors saw or heard anything," she said.

"I'll see you back at the office." Cooper left with a potentially critical piece of evidence buried in his pocket.

No matter how hard he wanted to hide the truth, it would come out… it always did.

As he drove back to ALPHA, he thought about what Danielle had said when he told her he was falling in love with her.

"If things were different, this would be the best day of my entire life. But I'm not going to let us happen. I'm not someone you can get close to."

"She's taking these men out."

He turned down a side street a few blocks from ALPHA and pulled over. After confirming no one was following him, he drove to the office.

Once inside, he went directly to Danielle's office. She and Lily were working together, each poring over their laptops.

"Hey," he said from the doorway.

Danielle glanced up. A mix of emotions crossed her face, then she swallowed, hard. "We heard about Salimov from Providence."

"We've got a determined vigilante on our hands," he said.

She held his gaze as he walked in.

"What are you two working on?" he asked.

"Providence asked us to focus on the Dead Man Talking case," Lily explained, "so we're reviewing cell phone records for the first four victims."

"And?" Cooper asked.

"Nothing, yet," Danielle replied.

Lily popped out of her chair. "Be right back." She scooted out, leaving Cooper alone with Danielle.

"What are you doing after work?" he asked.

"I was actually going to put in some extra time, here, then head over to the gym. You?"

He'd been staring at her, trying to reconcile how she was killing these men by herself. It must have taken a tremendous amount of courage to take them on alone. Even at ALPHA, kill missions were carried out by teams.

"Hello, where'd you go?" she asked, crashing in on his thoughts.

He raked his hand through his hair. "Sorry. What'd you say?"

"I asked what you were doing after work."

"I don't know," he replied. "I'll be in my office if you need me."

On his way there, he found Lily in the lunch room eating a yogurt. "I was taking a break."

"Relax, Lily. I'm not here to micromanage you."

"I was in at six and my eyes hurt from staring—"

"Lily, you're fine. When you get a minute, forward me the motor vehicle records Danielle emailed you."

"I can do it, now." She recycled her empty yogurt container.

"I only need Virginia. Don't copy anyone when you send it over."

He returned to his office, shut the door, and jumped online to pull the records of licensed motorcyclists in Virginia. As the program compiled the data, he ran through the evidence one more time.

All five murdered men had several things in common. They were powerful and wealthy. They were all being sued by multiple victims, but the lawsuits were handled out of court or the cases had been dropped. None of them had been arrested. Cooper knew, firsthand, that Salimov wasn't going to get arrested. He ran with a powerful pack who looked out for their own. Power was a hard thing to achieve and, once these men had it, they would do whatever necessary to keep it.

If Danielle was the vigilante, she'd risked her own life to put an end to theirs.

A surge of loyalty filled him. He was *not* going to let her take the fall for what she'd done, but before he jumped into planning mode, he needed to know the truth.

When the data was ready for viewing, he downloaded, then sorted. As he skimmed the pages of names, he stilled on one.

Fox, Claire-Marie | Kawasaki Ninja 400

His email pinged with a new one from Lily. He scanned the Virginia list, but Claire-Marie's name had been removed. Danielle had scrubbed that list before sharing it with Lily.

Cooper was certain he had found the killer.

I'm in love with a vigilante.

DANIELLE

Danielle should have been floating on air. Cooper was in love with her, and she with him. But she'd spent the entire day hiding out in her office. Her stomach was tied in knots so badly, she'd bailed on lunch, hours earlier.

Emerson entered her office. "Ivan Salimov, the Russian diplomat, is the vigilante's latest victim."

"I heard. Were there any clues found at the crime scene?" Danielle held her breath.

"The techs are still there. Do you know anything about this Salimov?"

A ton. "What do you mean?"

"Supposedly, he was a real predator, like, the worst of the worst."

"I'd heard that about him," Danielle admitted. "When will you hear back about any evidence found at the crime scene?"

"Hopefully soon," Emerson replied. "They were combing through that place pretty good."

Danielle swallowed the plum-sized lump in her throat.

"Are you making any progress?" Emerson asked.

"Not really."

"Ugh, well, maybe we'll catch a break and blow this case wide open." Emerson left.

Alone in her office, Danielle rubbed her chest, but the ache wouldn't stop.

I need to tell Cooper the truth. Tonight.

At six o'clock, her phone rang. It was Naomi from the gym. "Hey, Naomi."

"Hi, Danielle, the kickboxing instructor isn't feeling well. Any chance you could teach tonight's intermediate class?"

"I'd be happy to."

"Great! It starts at eight forty." Naomi hung up and Danielle went looking for Cooper.

He wasn't in his office or the lunch room. Most everyone had left for the evening. Since Providence's office door was closed, she assumed he was in a meeting.

He's probably making plans to arrest me.

On her way out, she texted him. "Naomi needs kickboxing sub. Going to your place to change, then to gym. See you later."

Danielle felt like a trapped animal and needed to get out of the office, so she could breathe. She made sure she wasn't followed before pulling down Cooper's street and parking in his garage. If things had been different, she would have loved living there with him. After changing into sweats, she returned to the kitchen where she made two salads, ate hers and put his in the fridge.

On his kitchen island, she left him a note.

I made you a salad. I need to talk to you. It's important.
I love you, Danielle

Instead of feeling anxious, a weight lifted off her. What she had done was wrong, but she didn't regret her actions.

Teaching the kickboxing class was a total distraction, and she was grateful for the mental break. Feeling better than she had all day, Danielle waited until the room cleared before she beat the hell out of a punching bag. When finished, she laid on the mat and stared up at the ceiling.

I've gotta tell him everything... all of it.

After several minutes, she pushed off the floor and checked her phone, hoping for a text from him.

"I'm at the gym," he texted. "Find me when your class is over."

Her heart clenched. She would accept the consequences for her actions, but she would never, ever get over losing Cooper.

Time to face the cold, hard truth.

21

TAKEN

COOPER

After a monstrous lift, Cooper pushed himself hard in the pool. Didn't matter what he did, the tension would *not* release. Despite where the evidence pointed, he would not desert Danielle, no matter what the consequences. She did to Salimov what he could not. As far as he was concerned, he would put his career on the line to protect her. That's how strongly he felt about the woman he loved. But... he was having a hard time wrapping his brain around Danielle's vigilantism.

When he made his way to the front desk, Naomi was saying goodbye to a member and locking the front door from the inside. "How's it goin'?" she asked.

"Never fucking better," Cooper grumbled to himself.

"Sorry, I didn't catch that."

"You can take off," he said. "I'll close up."

"Thanks." Naomi grabbed her bag. "Women's locker room is empty. Danielle's in the kickboxing studio."

As Cooper approached the studio, Danielle exited. Their eyes met and the familiar surge of attraction powered through him. No denying he was in love with her, but as a lawman, he was wrought with conflict.

"Hey," she said.

Her ponytail was askew and long tendrils framed her face while the divot between her eyebrows was deeper than normal. The desire to touch her had him tucking her flyaways behind her ear.

"We need to talk," he said.

"As soon as we get home—I mean, back to your place."

"Home." Unable to stop himself, he dropped a kiss on her lips.

Sadness flashed in her eyes. "I'll check the women's—"

"Naomi already did," he replied. "Can you check the rock walls while I do the men's?"

"Sure." Danielle leaned up, kissed his cheek, then headed toward the climbing room.

I can't arrest her. There's no fucking way that's gonna happen.

The locker room was empty, so he headed toward the rock wall room.

THUD!

Something had banged against the emergency exit at the end of the hallway. *What the hell was that?*

BAM! BAM! BAM!

His phone was in his gym bag, at the front desk, so he couldn't check the surveillance camera over the door.

"Cooper, I forgot my gym bag," said the muffled male voice.

He pushed open the door. Someone grabbed him, yanked him outside, then fired a taser.

"Aaaaaiiiieeeee!"

Cooper crashed to the ground, incapacitated by the searing pain. A towel was held against his face...and everything faded to black.

DANIELLE

With her gym bag slung over her shoulder, Danielle exited the rock wall room as the emergency exit slammed shut.

"Cooper?"

He didn't respond.

"Cooper?" she yelled.

She hurried over and pushed open the back exit as a white passenger van sped away.

Ohmygod.

A crumpled towel lay on the ground a few feet away. She pulled the fire door shut and ran to the front desk.

Naomi was gone. She didn't know how to use the surveillance system, and it would take too long to hack in. Panic surged through her.

Get it together. NOW.

She grabbed Cooper's duffel and left, making sure the front door was locked from the outside. In her car, she unearthed her ALPHA laptop and jumped online. She tried accessing the geolocation system that displayed the Operatives locations.

Access Denied

Fuck.

She scrounged through Cooper's gym bag. *Please, please be in here.*

She grabbed his cell phone, typed in Alan's birthday. The phone unlocked. Releasing the breath she'd been holding, she opened the Geolocator App, tapped on his name, and watched as the blip headed North on Route 7. Minutes mattered, but Danielle couldn't go flying down the road after him.

A feeling of confidence came over her. *I can do this. I can save him.*

Fueled with determination, she sped home and scrambled

upstairs to change. After pulling on her leathers, she grabbed her Glock out of her safe. Back in her garage, she stepped into her boots, turned both their phones on silent, then pulled up the Geolocator App on his.

The blip had stopped moving. Cooper was in Great Falls.

She started the directions, pulled on her helmet and gloves, and coasted to the street. When the garage door closed, she revved the Ninja's engine and popped the clutch, sending her screaming into the unknown.

I will save him or I will die trying.

COOPER

Cooper opened his eyes. He was lying on the floor of a prison cell. He sat up and took in his surroundings. *What the hell is this?*

The room was no bigger than his walk-in closet. A cot was pushed against the far wall, a sink nearby. No toilet. The floor was covered in wood laminate that continued beyond the iron bars.

Outside the cell, a folding chair sat empty in a room the size of a small bedroom. While the cell's walls were cold, gray cinderblocks, the room walls were bright white. There were no windows, only one interior door that was closed. Recessed ceiling lights were set on low.

Where the fuck am I?

He didn't see any surveillance cameras anywhere. He went for his phone, but it was in his gym bag. His last memory was being hit by a taser after opening the back door to his gym.

Danielle!

Concern had him pushing to his feet. Had she been taken, too? Pacing the small cell, anger coursed through him. He would kill the motherfucker if he laid one finger on her. He shook the cell bars, but they were cemented into the floor. The padlock was industrial strength. It didn't budge either. The minutes ticked by. There was no escape, no way out. His concern for Danielle had morphed into full-blown fury.

The door opened. A short White guy sauntered in, a smug expression on his face, a water bottle in his hand. His shaved head was in stark contrast to his dark beard and mustache. His eyes were shaded behind blue tinted glasses. He wore a T-shirt, jeans, and a jacket.

Who the hell is he?

"Today is a great fuckin' day," the man said. "Don'tcha think?"

Cooper did not.

The man dragged the chair out of Cooper's long reach, spun it around, and squatted onto it. "I've been fantasizing about this moment for so many years, it doesn't seem real."

Cooper searched his face while rage surged through him, like a violent hurricane on an unstoppable path of destruction.

"You don't recognize me, do ya?" asked the stranger.

"No idea, motherfucker."

If he could get him to come closer, he'd wrap his hands around his neck and squeeze the life out of him.

"I'm William Renfrow."

Cooper blanked. This man looked nothing like Renfrow.

Then, the man removed his tinted glasses and held them up. "This was the best purchase I ever made. I put these on, I become a completely different guy. You can't see my eyes, you can't see me, right, pretty boy?"

Fuck.

It *was* Renfrow, out for revenge. His shaved head and facial hair made him unrecognizable. A low growl rumbled out of Cooper.

After pocketing the glasses, Renfrow leered at him. "I was getting paroled, but you showed up with your expensive suit and your polished speech. You changed their minds and I got fucked, again."

"You fucked yourself." Cooper's voice dripped with hatred.

"I was twenty-one when it all went down. I was a kid."

Cooper glared at him, his hands curled into tight fists. "No. My brother was a kid. You were a killing machine."

An eerie grin filled Renfrow's face. "I was all-powerful that day, wasn't I? People cowered in fear or dropped at my feet. What a fuckin' high. I relived that day for years."

Cooper stared in disbelief.

"My only regret is getting caught," Renfrow uttered.

Fury had Cooper shaking the prison bars, but they didn't budge. "You killed children, you fucking monster!"

Renfrow threw his head back and laughed, then he glowered at Cooper. "You are *never* getting out. You're going to die in this cell. Slowly, day by day. I can't wait to watch you suffer, like I did for all those years. Then, when you're gone, I'm going after your girl."

Stepping back from the bars, Cooper glared at Renfrow. This was much worse than he imagined.

"She's a stunning woman," Renfrow continued. "She's got an ass wiggle that's fun to watch. I got a girl, so I don't want to fuck her, but I'll kill her 'cause I can. Who's got the power now, asshole?"

Cooper would bargain for Danielle's life, but anything he said in the moment would be a knee-jerk reaction. Silence would be a stronger choice.

"Don't you wanna know how I broke outta the slammer?" Renfrow asked.

Cooper said nothing.

"Well, I'll tell ya. I walked into that hearing smellin' freedom and I left with your stench all over me. So, I staged a fight, got myself stabbed." He lifted his shirt, pointed to a four-inch scar on his abdomen. "This was my ticket outta that hellhole. On the trip back, I got to the driver and he crashed the van."

Silence.

"You're not a curious person, are ya?" Renfrow cracked open

the bottle of water and chugged some down. "This was the breakout of the century. I'm gonna go down as a mastermind, like Houdini. The great escape. Renfrow vanishes, never to be seen again."

Renfrow drank down more water.

"I followed you," Renfrow continued. "You got a sweet life, Mr. Bigshot. I kinda hated blowing up your Vette. It woulda made a nice get-out-of-jail present, but I'm gonna keep that sweet yacht of yours. I'm gonna sail away and live somewhere warm with lots of tanned cuties running around."

He's been hiding in plain sight.

Cooper's temples were pounding. The anger coursing through him was preventing him from thinking clearly. He retreated to the dark corner of the cell, leaned against the wall and crossed his arms.

"You givin' up, already?" Renfrow asked with a snicker. "That was easy. I'm gonna stay with you tonight, make sure you get settled in. You got a sink to pee in. Bucket's for your shits." His eerie smile made Cooper's stomach clench. "It's almost Thanksgiving. I gotta lot to be thankful for, this year."

DANIELLE

Twenty minutes later, Danielle pulled down the street in the Great Falls neighborhood. The homes were set back, their long driveways leading to large estate homes.

She killed the motorcycle headlight and continued until she reached the address. Once there, she cut the engine and stashed the bike and her helmet behind large bushes at the beginning of the property. She shoved their phones in her pocket, drew her weapon, and took off on foot.

The home was dark, so she ran around back, staying light on

her feet, careful not to crunch the fallen leaves. A white passenger van was parked in the driveway. Its rear doors had been left open, along with one of the garage doors.

Entering through the garage, she cracked open the interior door, fully expecting to set off the security system.

Silence.

Inhaling a calming breath, she stepped into the dark house. As her eyes adjusted, she glanced around the spacious kitchen. No Cooper.

Without making a sound, she closed the door and tiptoed through the expansive first floor. As she rounded a corner, light illuminated the floor and she skulked over. The basement light was on, the door wide open.

One ninja-like step at a time, she headed downstairs, her Glock at the ready. The unknown awaited her. Her heart was racing, but she wasn't backing down. She loved Cooper and she would die trying to save him.

Buoyed by that thought, she peeked around the corner. The furnished basement was dark, but the light from the stairs was enough for her to see a billiard table. As she edged around the corner, more light shone from the bottom of a closed door.

Despite her nerves, she opened the door and stepped into the room. Nothing but an empty chair. She gasped when her gaze fell on the prison cell.

Cooper emerged from the shadows. "Get out, Danielle. *Now.* He'll kill you."

Ignoring him, she ran over and yanked on the padlock. "How do I get you out of—"

"On your six!" Cooper shouted.

As Danielle whirled around, someone lunged for her, then a hard slap across her cheek. He grabbed for her Glock.

"No!" she screamed.

BANG!

Searing pain ripped her shoulder. With adrenaline surging

through her, she yanked the gun away, then delivered a powerful kick, sending him flying back.

The wall stopped his fall. In that split second, she recognized him.

It was Billy from the shelter.

"I'm gonna fuckin' kill ya!" he yelled, charging her, again.

BANG! BANG! BANG!

She hit him twice in the chest and once between his eyes. Blood spatter from his chest sprayed her as he dropped to the floor. His unseeing eyes glared up at her. Ignoring the throbbing pain, she felt his front pant pockets for a key. Nothing. She checked his back pockets and found it.

With trembling fingers, she unlocked the padlock. Cooper came flying out.

"You've been hit," he said.

"I'm fine," she said. "Are you okay?"

He unzipped her jacket. Her shirt was blood-soaked. "Fuck."

The energy that had been pumping through her came to abrupt end. She pressed her hand against her shoulder. "This isn't good."

"I got you," he said. "But we gotta get your jacket off."

She groaned through gritted teeth as he removed it, then, tried not to pass out while he unbuttoned her shirt to examine her injury.

The bullet had pierced her shoulder. He yanked his shift off and used it to apply pressure to her injury.

She flinched. "Ow, ow, ow."

"Breathe," he murmured.

When she did, he said, "I need a phone."

"My jacket pocket."

As he searched her pockets, she started to drift off.

"Taken… Danielle hit… hurry," she heard him say.

Then, she was tousled awake. "Danielle, open your eyes. You gotta stay with me, baby."

She opened her eyes. "I'm your baby?"

"Absolutely." His loving smile filled her with hope. "You're gonna be fine."

She nodded. "Why would Billy hurt you?"

"Who's Billy?"

"The guy I shot. He's the handyman at the shelter."

"That's William Renfrow."

Her eyes grew large. "The school shooter?"

Cooper nodded.

"He was hiding at the shelter this whole time," she said. "I had no idea." She strained to look around and flinched.

"Babe, you gotta lie still," Cooper said, applying pressure to her shoulder.

She grimaced. "What is this place?"

"A prison cell," he replied.

"In someone's house?"

"Looks that way."

"Cooper, I have to tell you something," she whispered.

"What, babe?"

"I'm the vigilante. I killed those monsters."

Dipping down, he kissed her forehead. "I know."

Despite the pain, she offered a little smile. "Karma's a bitch."

"Don't tell anyone else, okay?"

Incredulous, she stared up at him. "Aren't you going to arrest me?"

"Not if I can help it. For now, that secret stays with us."

22

ALPHA'S SAFE HOUSE

COOPER

Cooper's phone rang.

"I'm here," Dakota said. "And I'm coming in through the garage. Has the house been cleared?"

"No," Cooper replied.

A moment later, Dakota burst into the room, a Glock in his hand, his gaze flitting from Cooper to Danielle to Renfrow.

"Jericho is on his way." Dakota shoved his Glock into the back of his waist, knelt beside them. "Danielle, I'm Providence's husband Dakota Luck. Cooper and I are gonna get you outta here."

"I think I can walk."

Cooper helped her to her feet. "I can carry you."

"No, I need to do this on my own."

Both men exchanged glances. This was one strong-willed woman.

They brought her outside and into the back seat of a waiting SUV. "How'd you get here?" Cooper asked as he got in beside her.

"My bike," she replied. "I left it in the bushes at the bottom of the driveway. Key's in the ignition."

"I'll ask Stryker to pick it up for you," Cooper said.

As Dakota headed out, Cooper made a call, put it on speaker.

"Hey, bro," Stryker answered.

"You're on speaker and Danielle and Dakota are with me," Cooper said. "I got kidnapped by Renfrow, Danielle came after me. She got shot and Renfrow's down. I need her bike picked up."

"How badly is she hurt?" Stryker asked.

"Shoulder," Cooper replied.

"I'm taking her to the black site," Dakota interjected.

"Where's that?" Stryker asked.

Dakota gave him directions to a nearby location, also in Great Falls.

"Emerson and I are on our way," Stryker replied before the line went dead.

"How are you doing?" Cooper asked Danielle.

"I'm okay," she replied.

This time, Dakota made a call, put it on speaker.

"Yo," Jericho said.

"The house hasn't been cleared," Dakota began. "Don't go in alone. Stryker and Emerson are on their way. Wait for them."

Jericho chuffed out a laugh. "Wait? What the hell for? I'll clear it on my own. What else do you need?"

"Clean up and body disposal," Dakota said.

"Bring me Renfrow's phone," Cooper added.

"You get everything but the clothed body," Jericho replied. "But you won't have it for several hours. Where you gonna be?"

"Black site," Dakota replied.

"The what?" Jericho asked.

Dakota gave him directions, then hung up. Not long after, he turned down a dirt road, passing a NO TRESPASSING sign.

Cooper's phone rang. It was Emerson. "She's okay," he answered, putting the call on speaker.

"I need to hear her voice," Emerson said.

"I'm here, Emmy."

"Ohgod, you scared me so badly. We'll be there as soon as we're done with Jericho." Emerson hung up.

Dakota drove up to a dark, unmarked, one-story building that looked like an abandoned warehouse. He waited while an oversized garage door opened and he drove inside. As the door closed, Cooper helped Danielle out. The retina scanner cleared Dakota and all three entered the building. Like ALPHA HQ, the corridors were devoid of art, the place sterile and utilitarian.

"The medical team will be here, soon," Dakota said, ushering Danielle into a hospital room.

Cooper helped Danielle onto the bed, then continued applying pressure to her wound.

"You want me to relieve you?" Dakota asked.

"I got this," Cooper replied.

Dakota left, returning with several wet paper towels. He handed them to Cooper. "For blood spatter."

Cooper gently wiped Danielle's face. There was nothing he could do about her shirt.

Not long after, Dakota's phone rang. "The medical team is here." He strode out.

Cooper kissed Danielle's forehead. "How you doing?"

"I'm okay. I have a lot of questions."

He peered into her eyes. "Like what?"

"Like how long you've known it was me," she whispered.

"Shh. We'll figure this out together, once that bullet is out of you."

"Will you stay with me?"

He smiled at her. "I'm not going anywhere. My ugly mug'll be the first one you see when you wake up."

"I'm a little scared," she murmured.

"Of what?"

"Surgery."

He gaped at her. "You walked into that house to find me *alone* and you're scared to have a bullet removed?"

"I'd probably feel better if I was taking it out myself."

Dakota returned. "This is Dr. Joyce Ferguson, your surgeon, and Nurse Baker Deen, anesthetist. This is Cooper Grant and Danielle Fox."

The physician washed her hands, then stood next to Cooper. "Mr. Grant, would you mind changing spots with me?"

"Sorry, I'm a little concerned," Cooper said as he moved out of the way.

"Okay, Ms. Fox, I'm going to examine your wound, then we'll get you into surgery. You want to tell me what happened?"

"I was shot," Danielle replied.

The doctor glanced at Cooper and Dakota. "Your patient has been trained well. I get summoned in the middle of the night, always under mysterious circumstances."

After examining Danielle, the doctor said, "You're lucky the bullet landed where it did." She turned to the nurse. "I'm going to scrub up. Nurse Baker will set up your IV."

As the nurse got busy, Cooper stepped close and whispered, "I love you. You got this"

"I love you, too," she whispered back.

After Danielle was wheeled into surgery, Dakota asked Cooper, "How 'bout a drink?"

"Hell, yeah."

Once in the office, Dakota opened the credenza, pulled out two glasses and a bottle of Macallan. "How you holding up?" He poured the whisky, handed Cooper a glass.

After swallowing down a mouthful, he said, "I'm relieved Danielle will be okay, but I'm pretty fucking angry."

"You got a thing about going rogue," Dakota said. "I can relate, but you gotta get help when you're in danger. We're not just a team, we're a family."

"I made a mistake."

"It almost cost you your life and Danielle's life. Any of the Operatives would drop everything to help you."

"On one hand, I expected a lecture. But I look around here and I wonder why in the hell I didn't know about this place."

Dakota chuckled. "I save the lectures for my children, and I dropped the ball on this place. I'm sorry. I thought you knew."

"I do, now."

"When I turned everything over to you, it cleared you for the entire operation. The black site and all the files you didn't have access to."

"Not all of them," Cooper said. "I couldn't access Black Ops."

A smile filled Dakota's face. "The true gem of ALPHA." He sipped the luxury liquor. "Let me bring you up to speed."

After he did, Cooper was floored. Now, he knew *all* of ALPHA's secrets.

"I read through the files," Cooper said. "You, Sin, and Stryker were all vigilantes, at one point. Yet, none of you were arrested for your crimes."

Dakota nodded, once. "And this is relevant because…?"

"I solved the Dead Man Talking case. Danielle took out those men."

Dakota arched a brow, then leaned against the credenza. "That's impressive."

"I'm not arresting her. I understand why she did what she did. Her sister's senseless murder pushed her over the edge, whatever the cost."

Dakota nodded. "Been there."

"I want to make her an Operative," Cooper continued. "If she agrees, I'll train her myself."

"You have my complete support. ALPHA Ops is yours. Do what you think is best."

"Miss it?" Cooper asked.

"Every damn day," Dakota replied. "I love the work we do and I miss working with Providence. My business partner's husband passed and she's not ready to return to work yet."

"I'm sorry to hear that." Cooper drained his glass and stood.

As the two men headed down the hallway, Cooper said, "I'm gonna do some digging on that house."

"That prison cell was fucked up. I'll run the address through MLS and let you know what I find." Dakota stopped in front of the exit. "I'm gonna head home. Text me when Danielle is out of surgery."

"Thanks for everything," Cooper said.

"Congratulations on solving the DMT case." Dakota left and Cooper took off toward the surgical room.

He paced outside the doorway for another twenty before the surgeon exited the room. "She did great," Dr. Ferguson said, removing her surgical mask. "The bullet was lodged in some tendons, so she'll be sore for a while. I expect her to make a full recovery. Baker will be out in a moment, then you can see her."

"Thank you."

"So, what is it that you do?"

"I own a gym in Tysons."

The doctor furrowed her brows. "What is this building and who are these people who get shot in the middle of the night? I've been here several times over the years, but no one has ever told me what's really going on."

Cooper smiled. "As soon as I find out, you'll be the first one I tell."

She laughed. "One of these days, someone is going to answer all my questions. I'm gonna take off, but Baker will stay until Danielle's ready to head home. Unless there's an issue, he'll discharge her tomorrow afternoon. Can you walk me out?"

As Cooper watched the doctor drive away, Stryker rode into the garage on Danielle's Ninja, with Emerson following in her car.

"How's she doing?" Stryker asked after he removed his helmet.

"Is Danielle still in surgery?" Emerson asked.

"She's out," Cooper replied. "The nurse is with her."

Emerson hurried inside ahead of them.

"This is a great bike," Stryker said as the two men headed in. "Did you know she rode?"

"Yeah," Cooper replied. "Did you see Jericho?"

"We helped him move the body and clean the blood-stained floor. He left the van there until you tell him what to do with it."

"I'll let him know."

They stopped in front of the surgical room where Emerson was waiting. Baker popped his head out. "Who wants to go first?"

Emerson turned to Cooper. "You go."

Cooper found Danielle resting comfortably and swallowed down the anxiety that had been gripping him by the throat.

She was safe. She was going to be okay.

In that moment, she never looked so beautiful. Her sleepy smile was laced with love. He kissed her forehead. "Hello, my love. How are you feeling?"

"Here to arrest me?" she whispered.

"That all depends on you," he replied.

DANIELLE

Danielle was groggy from the sedation, but relieved Cooper was by her side. His smile made her heart flutter and her soul happy. She would relish their brief time together, no matter how brief it would be.

"It's not up to me," Danielle said.

Nurse Baker returned with a plastic cup. "Ice chips. Let's keep the chatting to a minimum, please."

"I'll feed her," Cooper said taking the cup.

He spoon-fed her a few ice chips. The cold water refreshed her dry throat, but it was the look of relief in Cooper's eyes that she loved the most. After a few spoonfuls, he told her Emerson was waiting to see her.

"What does she know?"

"Only that you were shot by Renfrow," he whispered, then dropped a soft kiss on her cheek. "And that you risked your life to save mine."

"You would have done the same," she said, her throat scratchy.

Cooper left the room and Emerson rushed in. She sat on the bed and held Danielle's hand. "How are you?"

"I'm okay," Danielle replied.

"You are so brave, Danny."

She shrugged. "Ow! Ah, wrong shoulder."

"Just relax." Emerson picked up the cup of ice. "Do you want these or should I feed you?"

"I can." Danielle took the cup from her.

"Stryker rode your bike over, but we'll drop it at your house on our way home. I still have a spare key."

"The garage door code is the same from when you lived with me," Danielle said. "Thanks for doing that."

"I have questions, for another day. Stryker wants to check on you. Is that okay?"

"Of course."

Emerson smiled. "I'm so relieved you're okay." Tears filled her eyes. "When I heard you'd been shot—"

"I'm fine and I love you."

"I love you." Emerson kissed her cheek. "I'll send Stryker in."

Stryker entered her room and sat in the chair. "You got a nice bike."

"You can borrow it whenever you want."

He chuffed out a laugh. "You get better and we'll go for a ride together."

She nodded.

They sat in silence for a minute.

"Thanks for saving him," Stryker said, breaking the silence. "I woulda been wrecked if either of you had died. You know, you coulda called for help."

"I needed to do this alone."

That made Stryker smile. "You're a beast, Fox. ALPHA's lucky to have you." He pushed out of the chair. "Nice job tonight. Get some rest."

Alone with her thoughts and her cup of ice, Danielle thought about Billy. How did he get a job at the shelter and did Lori Shannon know his true identity? And who owned that beautiful home with the basement prison cell?

She'd been pumping out the adrenaline, but now she was beat. As she started to relax, Cooper returned with the nurse.

He took the cup of ice and set it on the bedside table while the nurse checked her IV bag. "Danielle, I think you need to get up and use the bathroom," Baker said. "Can I help you?"

"I'd like Cooper, please."

"Be careful on your feet," Baker said. "You might be a little light-headed."

With Cooper's help, she went to the bathroom, then returned to bed.

"Time to rest," the nurse said. "I'll be in the break room if you need me."

When Baker left, Danielle clasped Cooper's hand. "We need to talk."

"Not now." Cooper dropped a soft kiss on her lips. "You sleep and I'll be right here when you wake."

She patted the bed. "Stay with me."

It was a tight fit, but he lay down beside her. She released a satisfied sigh. "Now, I'm happy."

Danielle's future was uncertain. The only certainty in her life was the love in her heart for the man by her side.

23

THE TRUTH, THE PACT, AND THE DEAL

DANIELLE

The following afternoon, Danielle was cleared to leave. Despite her discomfort, she was ready to get out of there. Nurse Baker gave her instructions on how to care for the wound and what she could expect over the next several days.

"The stitches will dissolve," he explained. "Your shoulder will be sore, so go easy."

Danielle thanked him and Cooper escorted him out.

Back in the room, Cooper sat on the edge of her bed. "We're alone and we need to talk."

She offered a little smile, then waggled her eyebrows. "I thought you had something else in mind, you know, being that we're alone."

He kissed her softly, held her hand, then his smile fell away.

"Oh, you want to have a serious talk," she said. "Okay, well, I can't avoid that forever."

"You did what I couldn't," he began. "You killed Salimov and I'm grateful you stopped him."

"Have you told your family he's dead?"

"No. They might have heard, since the press is all over it. I've gotta contact Sinclair Develin for damage control. What I'm looking for, from you, are answers. The truth, Danielle, to all my questions."

She caressed his fingers. After a pregnant pause, she gazed up at him. "Okay."

"I've got my assumptions, but I need to hear it from you. What triggered the killing spree?"

"After Claire-Marie was killed, I wasn't okay, which you knew. I wasn't sleeping well and, one night, I was online tooling around. I found a website for women who'd been abused. The more I looked into it, the angrier I got. So many of these victims, like Chantal, were powerless against these men. I read their stories and I felt their anguish, so I stepped up to help them. I took motorcycle lessons, created Ursula, and I hacked into their calendars to stage accidental meet ups. I couldn't save my sister, but I could stop other women from being victimized by these men."

"You could have gotten raped or killed."

"I wasn't afraid, even with Salimov. He tried overpowering me and things got a little crazy, but I was *not* going to let him win. I felt the only way those women would ever get any peace was if these men were stopped. And, from what I'd learned, none of them had even been arrested."

"You did your homework."

She offered a little smile. "I like to hack."

There was a pregnant pause before Cooper spoke. "While I understand your reasons, I can't let you go on being a lone-wolf assassin. I have a responsibility to make sure you don't."

Her stomach dropped. "Are you arresting me?"

"No. I'm going to train you to become an ALPHA Operative."

She stared at him for a few seconds, while she processed what he'd told her. "Are you for real?"

"You're not the only vigilante on the team."

She couldn't contain her surprise. "Seriously?"

"That's a story for another day. You've been through a lot." He stood. "Ready to head out?"

"Absolutely." Moving slowly, she got out of bed. Cooper helped her dress in a clean shirt and pants that Emerson had brought for her, and they left the black site.

"You good heading to my house?" he asked, once they hit the main road.

"Yes, but I'm going to need some more of my things," she replied.

"We'll swing by your house tomorrow." He paused. "I know we're still figuring us out, but I need to be straight-up honest with you. I want you to move in with me. I love seeing you every day, but we're gonna take this at your pace. Will you think about it?"

"I love how transparent you are with me. Yes, I'll think about it." After a few seconds, she said, "I'm sorry for my lies and for the secrets."

"Thank you," he replied.

When they drove down his street, Danielle said, "Emmy's here. And whose truck is that?"

"Jericho's." He pulled into his two-car garage where her Ninja was waiting.

Inside, they found Emerson, Stryker, and Jericho sitting around the kitchen table. Emerson gently hugged her. "I made you chicken noodle soup."

"You are the best," Danielle replied.

"That sounds like baby food, to me," Jericho said, pulling carry-out bags from the fridge. "I got food from Jericho Road. Ribs. Potatoes. *Real* food."

While everyone ate, Cooper said, "I don't always ask for help, but I will going forward."

"We love you, brother, and we're here for you," Jericho said.

"Any updates on my kidnapping and who gave Renfrow access to that house?" Cooper asked.

"Dakota looked up the house in the MLS," Stryker replied. "It's owned by Fantasea Ventures, Inc. Has been for a couple of decades."

"That's strange," Danielle said.

Jericho set a cell phone on the table. "Renfrow's. No password. Lori Shannon texted him."

Cooper read Lori's texts out loud.

"Where are you?"
"It's been hours. What's going on?"
"You took off with the shelter van!?! What the hell is wrong with you?"

"Sounds like she wasn't involved in your kidnapping," Danielle said, "or she's leaving the texts as a cover up."

"Good point," Cooper said. "Renfrow said he was going to keep me there until I died, which makes me think the house is always empty."

"Danny, what's Renfrow's relationship with Lori Shannon?" Emerson asked.

"He worked for her as the shelter's handyman, but they looked close. I walked into her office after my computer class and they were huddled together. She jumped away from him when she saw me."

"I hacked into Renfrow's prison records," Stryker said. "A month before his parole hearing, he had a visitor. She wore sunglasses, a baseball cap pulled low, and a scarf around her neck. My IDware couldn't make her."

"The house's bedroom closets were filled with designer gowns with the price tags still on them," Emerson said. "There was a lot of makeup in the bathrooms. I found an old backpack in a closet with a cell phone. I asked the Internet Team to check it out."

"I called Hawk," Cooper said. "He's installing cameras at the house tonight."

"That prison cell could be a BDSM confinement cell," Stryker added.

"I would never have thought of that," Danielle said.

"That's a relief," Cooper said, and everyone laughed. "What's the story on the van?"

"Owned by the shelter," Jericho explained. "It's been scrubbed and moved to the Union Station parking lot. Keys are under the seat and Hawk is fitting it with a tracking device."

"Nice work," Cooper said.

"I'll stop by the shelter tomorrow," Danielle said.

"You talked to Lori Shannon for a while at the reunion," Emerson said. "Hopefully, she sees you as a friend."

"If she had anything to do with Cooper's kidnapping, I'll find out," Danielle added.

"What about your sling?" Stryker asked.

"A kickboxing injury," Danielle replied.

"In addition to my kidnapping, I've got something else I need everyone's help with," Cooper continued.

"So, what? Now, you're piling on?" Stryker asked with a smile.

Cooper laughed, then the smile faded. "This is serious and confidential."

"Everything we do is top-secret," Stryker said.

"This stays with the five of us." Cooper eyed everyone at the table. "I solved the Dead Man Talking case."

"That's great," Emerson said. "Who's our perp?"

"It's Danielle," Cooper said.

Oh, no. Danielle stilled.

All heads turned in her direction. Their stares were agonizing, as was the silence that accompanied them.

Jericho broke the silence. "I did *not* see that comin'."

"Whoa," Emerson said. "I can't believe it. *You're* the vigilante?"

Danielle shuddered in a breath. "I am."

Cooper jumped in. "I think we'd all agree that, while what Danielle did was wrong, those predators had to be stopped." The team nodded in agreement. "Danielle's quickly become a valuable contributor at ALPHA as a hacker. Now that we know about her other skills, I've decided to make her an Operative. I'll be training her myself."

"Welcome to the *real* ALPHA," Stryker said.

"The murder cases will go cold," Cooper continued.

"What about the White House?" Emerson asked.

"I'll handle that," Cooper replied. "The Chief of Staff is concerned about the President's ratings' approval if word got out about Sisson. They've already buried Sisson's murder and distanced themselves from him."

Emerson slipped her arm around Danielle's shoulder. "Working together is gonna be awesome."

"Thank you for being so accepting of me," Danielle said. "What I did was wrong—"

"Been there," Stryker said.

"Guilty," Jericho added.

"Me, too," Emerson chimed in.

Danielle regarded each of them. She couldn't believe what she'd just heard.

"Thank you all for your efforts," Cooper said, before pushing out of his chair. "I'm calling the White House. Stryker, get Sin to deep six Salimov's death with the press."

"You got it," Stryker replied.

"I'm gone." Jericho stood. "Let me know what you dig up." He pulled Cooper in for a bear hug. "Coop, watch your six. Danielle, welcome to the club."

"We'll walk you out," Cooper said and all three men left the room.

Emerson took Danielle's hands. "I want to tell you the real story behind my brother's death and who killed the person responsible for taking Doug's life."

When Emerson finished confiding her greatest secret, the two friends hugged. "Thank you for trusting me," Danielle said.

"You're my sister-friend, and now we *really* have no secrets." Emerson smiled. "You're gonna make a freakin' awesome Operative."

Emotion welled up and tears rolled down Danielle's cheeks. Since Claire-Marie's murder, she'd felt isolated, alone, and filled with uncontrollable rage. She wiped her wet cheeks and smiled at her best friend. "No matter what I've done, you love me."

"No matter what *I've* done, you love me back."

COOPER

Cooper called the White House Chief of Staff's office. "Cooper Grant for Craig O'Leary."

A moment later, O'Leary came on the line. "Tell me you've got good news."

"The problem's been resolved."

"So, you arrested the killer?" O'Leary asked.

"Eliminated."

"Even better. Nice work, Mr. Grant. Thanks for the update." O'Leary hung up.

"Done," Cooper said to Stryker.

"That was easy," Stryker replied.

"His priority is the President. Sisson didn't matter to him."

Stryker called Sin, hit the speaker button.

"Hold on," Sin answered.

The line went quiet. A moment later, Sin said, "I'm here."

"Coop's with me. We need media blackout for Salimov."

"What a piece of shit he was," Sin said. "Consider it done."

"And we need you to make sure the Russian Embassy and the State Department don't press the issue," Cooper added.

"Here's what I'll do," Sin said. "I'll tell my embassy contact I'm the only thing stopping the State Department from opening an inquiry into Salimov. Then, I'll call my contact at State and let him know I'm not going public with their cover-up of Salimov."

Cooper smiled. "That's perfect."

"I'll scare them, then threaten them," Sin continued. "When they need my help because they've fucked up again—and they will—I'll tell them *not* to call me. Power is a beautiful thing, especially when I have it all."

Cooper and Stryker laughed.

"Thank you," Cooper said.

"Anytime, brother." The line went dead.

Stryker slapped Cooper on the back. "You good?"

"For the moment," Cooper said as the men returned to the kitchen.

"I'm leaving," Stryker said. "Anyone need a ride?"

Emerson laughed. "I drove, so *you're* coming with *me*." She gently hugged Danielle. "Please rest and—"

"I'm going to the shelter tomorrow," Danielle replied. "I need to know if Lori was involved in Cooper's kidnapping."

"Find out what she knows about the house and the jail cell," Stryker added.

After saying their goodbyes, Cooper shut his front door and clasped Danielle's hand. He kissed her, then brought her into his family room. "How are you feeling?"

"I'm okay," she replied as they sat on the sofa. "*You* got kidnapped. How are you doing?"

"I can breathe, knowing you're okay and my family's safe, but I'm so fucking pissed about Renfrow."

"I can help with that anger." Her sweet smile soothed some of his fury.

"Tonight, you rest." He dropped a soft kiss on her lips, held her hands in his. "Before we head to bed, we need to get clear on something."

"Okay," she replied.

"The offer of Operative comes with a condition. Your killing spree is over. From now on, it's ALPHA-sanctioned kills only. Do we have a deal?"

"I'm done hunting these monsters," she said. "But I'm never going to stop protecting and fighting for women like your sister. I couldn't save mine, but maybe I can save yours."

In that moment, he'd never loved or admired anyone more than he did her.

She extended her uninjured hand. "We have a deal."

When he slipped his large hand into her smaller one, desire and warmth traveled up his arm. He adored Danielle with his entire being. She was his person, he was sure of that.

"I have a confession," she said. "I scrubbed the Virginia motor vehicle list and removed my sister's name."

"I know," he replied.

"And I wasn't working the serial killer case very hard."

"No kidding."

She leaned over and kissed him. "Starting now, I'm going to give you one hundred percent."

He put his arm around her and kissed the top of her head. "You can start tomorrow, if you feel up to it."

Despite her protests that she wasn't tired, Danielle fell asleep as soon as her head hit the pillow. Cooper lay awake in the dark, hoping he wasn't letting his personal feelings about her cloud his decision to make her an Operative.

The following morning, over breakfast, they worked out their plan. Then, he drove her to her townhome.

"Are you sure you're okay to drive with one hand?" Cooper asked as they walked into her garage.

"Positive. I'll text you when I get to the shelter, and again if I get time with Lori."

After several goodbye kisses, Danielle got behind the wheel and drove away.

There goes my person... my kick-ass biker babe... my vigilante.

DANIELLE

Thirty minutes later, Danielle parked at the shelter. "I'm here," she texted Cooper before making her way inside.

Tessa was on the phone, but greeted her with an exuberant wave. After she hung up, she bolted around the desk, but stopped short. "Oh, no! What happened?"

"Kickboxing injury."

"I didn't know you were teaching another class today."

"I'm not. I wanted to check in with Lori. Is she here?"

"She's in a meeting, but she should be out soon." Tessa stepped closer. "Have you had a chance to look for my friend, Val?"

Danielle felt terrible. With everything going on, she'd forgotten. "I'm so sorry, I haven't."

The shelter phone rang and Tessa hurried behind the desk to answer as Lori came around the corner with an older man in a tailored suit and spit-shined loafers. His short, graying hair was styled to perfection. His tanned complexion and trim physique gave him a youthful appearance.

"Danielle, hi!" Lori stopped in front of her. "I didn't know you were on the schedule, today."

She smiled. "I'm guilty of a pop in."

"That's so nice," Lori replied.

"Hello, I'm Geoffrey Edelman."

"Danielle Fox."

"Your hair is stunning," Geoffrey said to her.

"Geoffrey is our biggest donor," Lori said while wrapping her arm through his. "We're so grateful for his support."

"It's my pleasure." Geoffrey kissed Lori on her cheek. "I'm off, my dear." He regarded Danielle. "Pleasure to have met you."

"You, too," Danielle replied.

As he was leaving, he waved over his shoulder. "Goodbye, Tessa."

"What happened to your arm?" Lori asked.

"Kickboxing injury. I wanted to see if we should offer a second workshop or even a Q-and-A follow-up. The residents seemed very interested."

"Let's go to my office. I'll check the schedule."

As they passed a restroom, Danielle said, "I'll be right in."

Lori pointed down the hallway. "My office."

Danielle ducked into a stall and texted Cooper. "Heading to Lori's office."

Once in Lori's office, she sank into the guest chair while Lori hopped on her computer. "How's mid-December? I'm out of town the first Friday for ten days."

"That sounds like a vacation."

"No, it's work," Lori replied.

"Oh, you have more than one business?"

"I'm going to a conference." Lori's cell phone buzzed on her desk. She glanced over, then snatched it up. "Dammit," she murmured as a pinkish hue covered her cheeks.

"What's wrong?" Danielle asked.

"Nothing," Lori bit out, as her thumbs flew over the screen.

Danielle waited, while a few more texts were exchanged between Lori and Cooper, who was posing as Renfrow using Renfrow's phone.

"I cannot believe this," Lori murmured. "Fucking asshole."

"Well, it's definitely a man," Danielle said.

Lori set her phone down and studied Danielle. "Do you remember Billy, the handyman?"

"Oh, sure."

"We'd been seeing each other for a while," Lori confided. "He took the shelter van a couple of nights ago, but he never came back." Her eyes misted, then she cleared her throat. "He left town."

Playing along, Danielle furrowed her brows. "For good?"

"Looks that way," Lori replied.

"If I had a boyfriend and he broke up with me in a text, I'd be a mess."

"I should probably turn him in," Lori mumbled.

"Turn him in? Like, what, he's a fugitive?"

Lori had been staring at her phone. She jerked her head up. "*What?* I'm just talking to myself. He left the van at Union Station. Would you mind taking me there so I can pick it up?"

"I'd love to," Danielle said. "It'll give us more time to catch up."

Once in the lobby, Lori told Tessa she had to run a quick errand and she'd be back soon.

While that was happening, Danielle texted Cooper. "Going to US."

On the drive over, Danielle asked, "Where'd Billy go?"

"Texas."

"Well, nothing you can do about that," Danielle said. "You've got a business to run. Plus, I'm sure you meet great guys all the time."

"I run three women's shelters," Lori said. "I hardly ever meet men."

"Geoffrey seemed nice. What about him?"

Lori barked out a laugh. "We're very close, but he'd never settle for just one woman. Most men are like that, you know?"

"Did you reconnect with anyone from our reunion?" Danielle asked.

"I connected with a lot of people, but you're the only one who followed through."

"I was super happy to see you." Danielle smiled over at her. "We'll have to go out sometime. To a bar or clubbing. Are you up for that?" She drove over the bridge into DC.

"That sounds perfect," Lori replied.

"Can you keep a secret?" Danielle asked.

"It's what I do best."

"I belong to a private BDSM club," she lied. "If you're interested, you can come as my guest."

Lori's eyes widened. "Wow, I didn't expect that from you. What are you into?"

Less is more. "Mainly bondage. I've got a friend who's a Dominatrix. She's into some crazy stuff. Do you play in that space?"

"I haven't, but I'd love to check it out. I work all the time and I don't really have any girlfriends to hang with."

Danielle offered a little smile. "Well, you've got me. I'll even come get you, unless you live way out in the 'burbs."

"I'm in Georgetown."

"Perfect," she said while pulling into the parking lot at Union Station. After driving up and down several aisles, she spotted the white passenger van.

"There it is." Lori pointed. "I hope he didn't take the keys."

"I'll wait while you check."

"Thank you for helping me," Lori said. "Have a happy Thanksgiving. We'll reconnect after the holiday." After searching inside the van, she pulled out a key ring and held it up. "Got it!"

Danielle gave her a thumbs-up sign and drove off. Before pulling onto the road, she called Cooper.

"How'd it go?" he answered.

"She found the van."

"Nice job. Whad'ya learn?"

"She lives in Georgetown," Danielle said. "I wasn't sure what to say to get her talking about a house with a jail cell, so I told her I belonged to a kink club, and asked if she was into BDSM. She said she doesn't play in that space."

Silence.

"You there?" Danielle asked.

"Are you into that kind of thing?" he asked, his voice low.

"Well, I'm definitely not into prison cells. As far as BDSM, I'm vanilla, but I'm open to experimenting with the right person. What I like is dirty talk, but not all the time."

"You've never been that open with me."

"I'm done keeping secrets from you. So, what's your kink story?"

"You, in lingerie."

She smiled. "I can definitely help you with that."

"I'm gonna have a big problem if we don't change the subject."

She laughed.

"We need to disclose our personal relationship to Providence," he continued.

"That makes me happy to hear you say that."

"Me, too," he replied. "Providence wants to see you, so text me when you get here and we'll tell her together." The call ended and she hung up.

As Danielle drove to work, she thought about everything that had transpired since her sister had been killed. The path she'd taken had been extreme and some of the choices she'd made had been born of evil. She should have regretted killing those men, but she didn't.

Her thoughts drifted to Chantal. She hoped Salimov's death would bring her some peace and help her heal. Then, she thought about Cooper and how hard she'd fallen for him.

"He's the one," she whispered as she pulled into ALPHA's parking lot.

"I'm here," she texted Cooper.

She entered the building and made her way to Providence's office as Cooper rounded the corner.

That familiar zing skittered through her as they shared a loving smile.

"Ready to do this?" he asked.

"Absolutely," she replied.

Together, they headed to Providence's office. They stopped in her doorway and she glanced up from her computer.

"Can we talk to you for a minute?" Cooper asked.

"Come on in."

Cooper shut the door as Danielle eased into one of the guest chairs.

Providence eyed Danielle's sling. "You've had a busy couple of days. How are you feeling?"

"I'm good, thanks."

Cooper sat beside Danielle. "We wanted to let you know that Danielle and I are seeing each other, romantically."

"Thank you for letting me know," Providence said. "Please maintain a professional relationship while in the office and on a mission."

"Without a doubt," he replied.

"Of course," Danielle added.

"Danielle, your credentials don't qualify you to be an Operative, but you've got the skills, so Cooper is going to mentor your career. Is being an Operative something you'd like to do?"

"It is," Danielle replied. "I think I'd love it."

"Are you comfortable having Cooper as your mentor?" Providence prodded.

"Absolutely," Danielle replied.

Providence nodded. "I'm fine authorizing this arrangement. Cooper, you can't show any favoritism toward Danielle."

"Understood." He rose. "I'm going to document this with HR."

"Dakota and I make a great team," Providence said with a smile. "I have every confidence you two will, as well."

On a nod, Cooper left, shutting the door behind him.

"Congratulations on your new position," Providence began. "Until I can find your replacement, you'll have to wear two hats."

Danielle nodded.

"As an Operative, you're required to wear a tracking chip—"

"I'm good with that."

"Never go on a mission alone."

"I won't."

Providence set a small leather bag on her desk. "For you."

Danielle unzipped the bag. Inside were four different government ID badges. She extracted one and smiled when she read her alias. Ursula Jones, FBI.

"You've got a badge for State Department, another that says you're with ATF, and the CIA. As it was explained to me by my predecessor, please only use one of those badges per case."

"Where'd Jones come from?"

"My alias is Elaine Jones. Jones is an easy name to remember and just as easy to forget. You good with that?"

"Absolutely. Thank you for this opportunity."

"It's all Cooper. He believes in your abilities. After what I heard, I can understand why. Great work on the rescue."

"Thank you."

"Your Kevlar vest is in the garment bag on the back of my door. Wear it on every mission."

Danielle dropped her things in her office, stopped by HR to document her relationship with Cooper, then on to IT for her microchip.

"Cooper has it," said the IT manager.

She knocked on Cooper's open office door. When their eyes met, she felt that urgent pull to go to him. "Do you have a minute?"

"Always."

She closed his door. "You've got my chip."

He pulled a bottle of rubbing alcohol from his desk, along with a syringe. "Here's the chip."

It was the size of a gnat and floating in liquid inside the needle. She pulled her hair out of the way so he could sterilize her skin.

"Relax," he said. "You'll feel a slight pinch."

She felt a little tug on her skin, then he said, "All done." He sat on the corner of his desk. "How'd Lori take the news about Renfrow skipping town?"

"She handled it well, but probably because I was with her."

Knock-knock-knock.

"Come in."

Emerson popped her head in. "Danny, did you see Lori?"

"Let's work together in the conference room," Danielle replied, "and I'll fill you in."

Danielle shot Cooper a smile before she took off with Emerson.

"I documented our little love affair, today," Danielle whispered as they headed down the hall.

"I love that," Emerson replied, "and I'm so happy for both of you."

After Danielle grabbed her laptop, they worked side by side in the conference room for the rest of the day. Come five o'clock, they'd made little progress. Hours earlier, Danielle had removed her sling and her shoulder ached from overuse at the keyboard.

"What are we missing?" Emerson asked as she closed her laptop.

"It's like Fantasea Ventures doesn't exist." Danielle slipped her arm back into the sling. "Tomorrow, we're going to look at this from a whole new angle."

"Good idea," Emerson said. "Are you coming to our house for Thanksgiving?"

Danielle stared at her. "Lori wished me a happy Thanksgiving and I totally blanked. Is that this week?"

"It snuck up on us, didn't it? Are you spending it with Cooper?"

Cooper sauntered into the conference room. "Spending what with me?"

"Thanksgiving," Emerson replied.

"I hope so," Cooper said. "What are your plans, Danielle?"

"I always spend Thanksgiving with Emerson and her family."

"This year, Stryker and I are hosting both our families. It's going to be fun." Emerson headed toward the door. "We'd love to have you join us. Cooper, your family's welcome, too."

Emerson headed out and Danielle slid her gaze to Cooper. Those beautiful blue eyes were waiting, his gaze electrifying.

Alone with Cooper. Her absolute favorite thing in the world. He eased down beside her and she breathed in his delicious scent. "How are you holding up?"

"I'm doing great," she said.

"I'm pampering you, tonight."

"No, Cooper, you do that all the time."

"And you're fighting me on this… why?"

She smiled. "Because I want to spoil you."

"Spend Thanksgiving with me," he said. "We can have dinner with my family and dessert with Emerson, Stryker and their families."

"I would love that."

"And then, we'll spend Christmas with yours," he said without hesitation.

"Aren't you getting ahead of yourself? A lot can change in a month," she murmured.

"I know," he replied. "I could love you even more."

24

GIVING THANKS

COOPER

Cooper wanted Danielle to know how special she was to him, beyond the words he'd uttered. When they got home, he wrapped his arms around her and kissed her hello like he could *not* live without her.

"Whew," she murmured. "Wow, you are *the best* kisser."

He smiled. "No, babe, it's you."

She hugged him with her uninjured arm. "I love you."

"I love you, too." He stole one more kiss. "I'm going to make us dinner. Do you want to take a relaxing bath or snooze on the sofa?"

She laughed. "A nap?"

"Not a napper?"

"That's a definite no. You?"

"On occasion."

"Helping you make dinner will relax me."

"I think you're overdoing it with your arm."

"Probably, but I need a distraction from thinking about Lori

Shannon. Emerson and I made no progress all afternoon," she said washing her hands.

After washing up, he set the ingredients on the kitchen island. He was making Danielle her favorite meal. Chicken parmesan and a side salad.

"My comfort food." She wrapped her uninjured arm around him and hugged him. "This is so wonderful of you. You are an *amazing* man. Thank you, thank you, so much."

"Can you make a salad?" he asked, pulling a tub of mixed greens, cherry tomatoes, and a cucumber from the crisper bin.

"Give me a knife and I'm happy."

"I could read a lot into that."

She laughed. "I can't handle blood, that's why I needed a clean shot."

"I can't believe we're having this conversation," he said.

"When I hit Billy in the chest and got spattered in blood, I almost passed out."

"We're not a normal couple."

She leaned up, kissed his cheek. "No, we're not."

They made dinner listening to music on her playlist. An eclectic mix of classic rock, country, and breakout artists he'd never heard of.

While the chicken and pasta cooked, he offered her two wine choices—chianti or pinot noir. When she couldn't decide, he opened them both and poured a little of each into glasses.

After tasting them, she chose the chianti.

He added to their glasses and held his up. "To my kick-ass biker babe. You're brave, brilliant, and absolutely beautiful. I'm the luckiest guy on the planet."

She kissed him. "*I'm* the lucky one. You're smart, gorgeous, kind, determined, and you didn't arrest me." She shot him a little smile. "I adore you, Cooper Grant."

They clinked glasses, sipped the dry red, and plated their food.

"Dim the kitchen lights," he commanded.

Danielle started walking toward the light switch when the recessed and pendant lights lowered.

"Kitchen lights on low," said the computerized voice.

Danielle laughed. "I thought you were talking to me."

Cooper furrowed his brow. "Babe, I'd never bark an order at you." After a second, he added, "We'll record your voice so you can control lights, the window shades, and the security system."

"Thank you for making me feel like I belong here," she replied.

"You do belong here, Danielle."

She kissed him before they sat at the table. After taking a bite, she sighed. "This is delicious. So, so good."

"I don't want to talk about work," he said. "Tell me about you."

"Only if you tell me about *you*," she replied.

During dinner, he learned she got into trouble freshman year of high school for hacking into the school's database.

"I didn't change my grades or anyone else's," she said. "It was a big accomplishment just to be able to do that."

"I bet they didn't see it like that."

"The principal was going to suspend me, but the computer science teacher came to my rescue. He made a deal with me. In exchange for my *not* doing that again, he would tutor me for free. He was a great mentor."

"Where is he now?"

"He died a few years ago. I spoke at his funeral. He was such a good man." Then, she leaned forward. He met her halfway and kissed her. "*You're* a good man. You put your family first, your friends, too." They kissed again. "Okay, your turn. I don't even know how old you are."

"Thirty-four."

"Where'd you go to college?"

"The Naval Academy."

"Nice. Why didn't you mention that when we went boating?"

"I don't talk about myself much."

"Handsome, humble, *and* well hung."

They shared a laugh.

"What did you do after graduation?" she asked.

"I worked as an intelligence analyst with NCIS for five years, but my goal was always the FBI."

"Which you achieved," she said. "You're very goal oriented."

"Work hard, play hard." He pushed his empty plate out of the way and held out his hand. She moved her plate and placed her hand in his. "Now, I want to love hard." He smiled. "And you are very easy to love."

She batted her eyes in a playful way. "Why, thank you, kind sir."

As he pushed away from the table, he said, "Be right back. Don't go anywhere." He collected the bag from behind the sofa and set it on a chair. "For you."

She eyed the large shopping bag. "Wow, how'd you manage this?"

"I got kidnapped, but I didn't take any time off. I think that entitles me to do a little shopping."

"I got shot. Does that mean I get a week off?"

They laughed together, again.

"You're too much of a workaholic to take *any* time off," he said.

"Not true. I'd jump at the chance to spend a long weekend on your yacht."

He kissed her. "It's a date."

She peeked inside the bag and pulled out all three boxes. "You are spoiling me so much. Which should I open, first?"

He handed her one of the small jewelry boxes.

She opened it and gasped. "The necklace my sister gave me. Where'd you find it?"

"Salimov's. That's when I suspected you were the killer. The chain was broken, so I bought you a new one."

She kissed him. "Thank you for hiding the evidence. You took a huge risk for me."

"The things we do for love."

"I'm sorry I made you an accomplice."

"You didn't *make* me anything. I chose to protect you. You took out Salimov, something I couldn't do."

She pointed to the two remaining boxes. "Which one, next?"

He slid the large one close.

After opening it and pulling away the pink tissue paper, she lifted out a black lace teddy with a plunging neckline and a crotchless lower half connected by a thin line of fabric and crisscross lacing over the pubic area. "Wow, this is sexy."

"In full disclosure, that one's really a present for me."

Her lips split into a smile as she moved onto his lap, then kissed him. "Thank you. I love it." She peered into his eyes. "I don't have anything for you."

"Danielle, honey, tonight is about me showing you how much you mean to me. You're my gift."

"You are so romantic. Seriously, Cooper." She kissed him, letting her tongue find his.

When the kiss ended, he pulled the third box over to her. "Last one."

Once she'd opened the box, she stilled for so long, he peered around to look at her.

"They're stunning," she said. "I can't believe you bought me something this… this serious."

The one carat, round diamond stud earrings were surrounded by a halo of smaller diamonds, all set in platinum.

She popped them in and pulled her hair out of the way. "Do you like?"

"They look great on you."

She pressed her lips to his and kissed him again. "Let me give you a proper thank you."

They left the dishes and retreated upstairs. Danielle slipped into the bathroom to remove her sling and change into her new teddy.

When she exited, he let out a low groan. "Whoa, you are *scorching* hot." He waited, naked, in the middle of his spacious bedroom. In the few seconds that she sashayed over and wrapped her arms around him, he was more than ready.

"Looks like the whole team approves," she said.

"Where's your sling?" he asked.

"I don't need it, tonight. I just need you."

Buried under a cozy blanket by the fire, he held her in his arms and gazed into her eyes. "Dammit. I forgot a condom." He started to get up, but she wrapped her hand around his arm to stop him.

"After we got together the first time, I started taking the pill. I didn't tell you because I wanted to see how things went with us." She kissed him again. "I'm clean and I just want you."

"Same goes for me."

He loved her like she was his entire world… because she was.

DANIELLE

Danielle had never given herself to a man the way she was giving herself to Cooper. It went beyond the physical. Her soul was drawn to him in so many ways she'd never even imagined possible.

He held her in his strong arms, yet his touch was so tender. Their lovemaking was gentle, yet filled with limitless passion. All he wanted to do was please her, and she never wanted to leave the safety and love of his embrace.

"I love loving you," he whispered in the afterglow.

They shared a smile while she ran soft fingers down his cheeks. "I love you. Being with you makes me feel hopeful."

As he fell asleep holding her close, she lay awake staring at the dancing flames in the fireplace. When her sister died, her heart had hardened. Terrified of loving and losing, she had taken it upon herself to eradicate evil, but every murder only further tarnished her own soul.

Maybe it was time to let the anger go, to step into the light, and be the best version of herself that she could be.

Maybe, she told herself as she drifted to sleep.

Next morning, at work, she requested a comprehensive background check on Lori Shannon, including criminal records. While waiting on that, she searched for Fantasea Ventures, but got zero hits.

How is that possible?

Her hunt for information on the non-profit shelter took her to an IRS search page, where, she typed in "Shannon's Shelters".

Up popped links to tax returns going back five years. She clicked on a recent one.

Organization: Fantasea Ventures, Inc
Doing Business As: Shannon's Shelters
Contact: Lori Shannon, Managing Director

There's that Fantasea Ventures again. Why would a shelter and a home be owned by a holding company? Are there other companies under that organization? Does Lori own Fantasea Ventures?

As a basis for comparison, she pulled up tax forms for another non-profit in the region. The name of the charity was also its legal name. This one had no DBA.

Bing!

Lori's background check was ready. She lived in Georgetown. Relatives included her mom, in Florida, her dad in Hawaii, and a sibling in Alabama. She'd been Managing Director of Shannon's Shelters for a decade. Prior to that, she was Geoffrey Edelman's personal assistant. She hadn't returned to college after her first year because she'd taken the job with Edelman.

She had no prior convictions, no outstanding warrants. Lori Shannon was squeaky clean. There was nothing linking her to William Renfrow.

Looks like she just got mixed up with the wrong guy.

Danielle had run into another dead end.

She called Emerson. "Got a sec?"

"Be right there."

A moment later, Emerson walked in. "Find something?"

"There's nothing on Lori's background check that caught my eye, but look at this." Danielle turned her monitor toward Emerson. "The house *and* the shelters are owned by the same holding company."

Emerson read page one of the tax document. "Fantasea Ventures. Maybe Lori owns other businesses."

"I ran a basic search for Fantasea Ventures and got no hits." Danielle shook her head. "None of this makes sense to me."

"After you dropped Lori off yesterday, she went straight to the house in Great Falls. We'd locked the door leading into the house, but left the garage door open since we didn't have the code. She did *not* look happy about that door being left open."

"What'd she do when she went inside?" Danielle asked.

"She walked the entire house, including the basement, then she drove back to the shelter."

"She did tell me she's heading out of town mid-December for a conference."

"Let's invite her out for drinks and get her chatting," Emerson said.

"Great idea."

"What are her Thanksgiving plans?"

"No idea."

"See if she wants to get together on Saturday night," Emerson suggested.

Danielle typed out a text. "Do you want to join Emerson and me on Sat night for drinks?"

Dots appeared, then, Lori's text. "Yes! Sounds great!"

"Awesome!" Danielle replied. "I'll text you Saturday with the deets."

"Maybe the Thanksgiving holiday will help us," Emerson said. "Sometimes, when I step away from a case, things become clearer."

"I'm spending Thanksgiving with Cooper and his family, but we'll have dessert with you guys."

"I'd miss you if we didn't spend *some* of the day together."

"Me, too, Em."

Emerson headed toward the door. "See you Thursday."

Before turning her attention back to work, Danielle texted Cooper's sister, Chantal. "How's tonight for your first kickboxing class?"

After sending the text, she was determined to find something on Fantasea Ventures. She opened a template, started writing code. Then, she created a bot that would search the Internet for any instance of "Fantasea Ventures".

At this point, she wasn't confident she'd find anything, but she would exhaust all avenues before calling it quits. When finished, she launched the program. Results could come back in minutes, days, even weeks… or never.

While she'd been writing the bot program, a text had come in from Chantal. "You remembered. Tonight works."

"See you at eight," Danielle texted.

Chantal replied with a smiley face.

The end of the day brought no results to her search. On the way out, she stopped in Cooper's office.

His door was open, but he was on a video conference call. From the doorway, she sent him a text.

"I'm stopping by my house for clothing, yours for food, then kickboxing with Chantal."

He glanced at the text, then flicked his gaze in her direction. The love in his eyes was all the reply she needed.

She drove home, relieved she'd be safe in her house alone. After loading up her car with more clothes, she drove to Cooper's. She loved his place, especially the open flow of the first floor. After making fajitas, she ate, then unloaded her vehicle.

As she was changing into sweats, Cooper called out, "Babe, I'm home!"

She exited the bedroom and stood in the hallway overlooking the first floor. "That sounded so domestic."

He shot her a grin. "I know. I love it."

"I left food out for you. Be right down." She returned to the bedroom. Within seconds, he was by her side, pulling her in for a panty-searing kiss. Losing herself in him was effortless. When the kiss ended, his smiling eyes gazed into hers.

"You're the best part of my day, you know that?" he murmured.

"And you're mine." She broke their embrace to finish getting ready. "Does your family know Salimov is dead?"

"I told my mom and dad this afternoon. They're telling Chantal at dinner."

"Thanks for the heads up," she said before kissing him goodbye. "Be home around ten."

"I put gloves for Chantal in your car," he said.

She blew him a kiss before trotting down the stairs. Though her arm was still on the mend, she'd opted not to wear the sling. She couldn't tell the Grants the truth and she didn't want to tell Chantal it was from a kickboxing accident.

At five before eight, she rang the Grants' doorbell.

Chantal swung the door wide, a sweet smile on her face. She'd pulled her hair into a ponytail and was dressed in a T-shirt and shorts.

"Hi." Chantal eyed the boxing gloves and roll of hand wraps.

Danielle entered the house and followed Chantal down the hall into the home gym.

"Are you here by yourself?" Danielle asked.

"My parents ran to the store. You just missed them."

Danielle was surprised she was alone.

Salimov can't hurt her anymore.

"From Cooper." She handed Chantel the gloves and wraps. "Before I show you how to properly wrap your fingers, let's start with the basics. Do you have a kickboxing goal? If you don't, we can come up with one or two for you to think about."

"I'd like to become more confident in my body and increase my strength and speed."

Danielle smiled. "Those are perfect."

After taking Chantal through her stretch routine, she talked a little about the value of kickboxing. Then, they watched a brief video together and Danielle taught her the proper technique for a few beginner punches and kicks.

"When can we use the gloves?" Chantal asked at the midway point.

"Whenever you'd like to give them a try, but we aren't going to do any actual sparring."

Chantal laughed. "I hope not."

Her sweet laughter caught Danielle by surprise, the emotion catching in her throat.

At the end of the intro class, both women were breathing hard and perspiring. Danielle was impressed with how hard Chantal worked. She was fully engaged and seemed to be having fun. That, above all, was Danielle's goal for her, especially in the beginning.

"You did a great job, tonight," Danielle said. "I definitely didn't go easy on you."

"This was so much fun," Chantal said. "Other than Tessa, I don't really talk to anyone, you know, closer to my age."

"At some point, when you feel comfortable, we'll go to Cooper's gym. The beginner class I teach is filled with a nice group of people. Some young, some older. Some in better shape than others, but everyone has fun together. That's my goal for the class, and not to get injured, of course."

"Can you stay and have some lemonade or something?"

"I'd love to."

As they sat at the kitchen table sipping their drinks, Chantal said, "How much do I owe you for my lesson?"

"Nothing," Danielle replied. "It was my pleasure."

After a pregnant pause, Chantal said, "The man I told you about… someone killed him. I'm in a chat room for survivors. Anyway, everyone was talking about how this vigilante was taking out the worst predators. The ones that are untouchable. Whoever he is, he's my hero."

"How do you know it's a man? Maybe it was a woman." Danielle had blurted that before her brain had caught up with her mouth. "But, killing is wrong, even if they were monsters."

"I know, but I wish I could thank that person. Before, my mom and dad would never have been able to leave me alone, even if you were five minutes away. I hope one day that I can be as brave as you."

Danielle smiled at her. "You're a survivor, Chantal. Nothing more warrior-like than that."

Chantal stared at her for the longest time. "Thank you for saying that."

"Tragedy shapes who we are, but it doesn't define us. That's something I just learned."

"Can I ask what your tragedy is?"

"My sister was murdered by a serial killer and it messed me up pretty badly."

"I'm sorry for your loss."

Eric rolled in with Emily by his side. "Looks like you two had quite a workout," Emily said.

"It was awesome," Chantal said with a grin.

"Danielle, we're delighted you're joining us for Thanksgiving," Emily added.

"What can I bring?" Danielle asked.

"Nothing," Emily said, "but I wouldn't mind an extra set of hands in the kitchen."

"Absolutely. I look forward to it." Danielle turned to Chantal. "Text me if you have questions and watch the videos I suggested. I'll see everyone on turkey day."

Chantal walked her out. "I'm glad my brother met you."

"Me, too," Danielle replied with a smile.

She wasn't just falling in love with Cooper, she was falling in love with his entire family, too.

COOPER

Cooper loved Thanksgiving, and this one was even more special because he was sharing it with Danielle. His dad was in charge, which meant organization and delegation. While Cooper assembled the artificial tree, his dad and Tessa untangled the strings of lights.

Danielle had been in the kitchen for over an hour with his mom and sister. Joyous sounds of laughter coming from that direction had Tessa popping up from the chair.

"I'll be right back." She trotted out of the room.

Cooper glanced over at the football game before taking Tessa's place to help his dad with the lights. "How does this happen?" Cooper asked. "I thought they were neatly stored."

"Evil elves," his dad answered, straight-faced.

Cooper laughed. "Gotta be."

"Mom and I are happy you brought Danielle with you. Things must be serious if you're dragging her to a Grant event."

"I'm thinking she's the one," Cooper said.

"You seem happier. Definitely less frustrated. And Chantal admires her. It's nice to see your sister is taking an interest in kickboxing. She even talked about going to the gym sometime to take Danielle's class. That would be a big step for her."

Danielle wandered in. "I like your giant ball of Christmas lights."

Cooper's dad chuckled. "Got any patience?"

Danielle sat beside them. "I'll give it a try."

"What's the kitchen crew up to?" Cooper asked.

"Cutting, chopping, mixing, baking... and laughing. Tom turkey is browning nicely." Danielle started untangling the strands. "The stuffing just went in, along with the sweet potato casserole. There is so much food, you'll have leftovers for days."

"You two can take some home with you," Eric said as the front door chime rang out.

"Hey! Where is everyone?" Cooper's brother shouted. A few seconds later, Henry Grant stood in the doorway of the family room, his wife, Aisha, by his side.

Cooper jumped up and hugged them as Tessa, Chantal, and Cooper's mom came hurrying into the room.

"Mom! Dad!" Tessa exclaimed, throwing her arms around her parents. "What are you doing here?"

"Celebrating Thanksgiving, honey," said Aisha.

"No one told me," Tessa said, before addressing her grandmother. "Gammy, did you know?"

Cooper's mom smiled. "I was sworn to secrecy. I didn't even tell Pop Pop."

"This is the best surprise!" Tessa hugged her mom again.

Aisha Grant was a defense attorney who focused on civil rights cases. She'd been working at a DC law firm when a Richmond group reached out and offered her partner. When she left, a year ago, Henry stayed in the area, but they continued to celebrate holidays and birthdays as a family.

Cooper made the introductions.

"I'm a hugger," Aisha said.

"Bring it in," Danielle replied before the women warmly embraced.

"Hey, bro, Danielle is way too pretty to be hanging with you," Henry said.

The family ribbing continued until Cooper's mom returned to the kitchen. Tessa whispered something to Danielle and the two women left the room together.

DANIELLE

With her laptop in hand, Danielle sat down on the living room sofa. Tessa plopped down next to her.

"You must be so happy your mom and dad are here," Danielle said.

"That was such an awesome surprise. They're separated, but we still do family things together."

"Alright," Danielle said, opening her laptop. "Let's see if we can find your friend Val."

Danielle kicked off a basic background check, then started searching social media sites. As she scrolled through Val's timeline, Tessa's shoulders sagged.

"Val hasn't posted in months," Tessa explained. "She told me that picture was taken on her last day at work."

"Did Val ever mention family or any friends, like, from work?"

"Her mom and dad live in Pennsylvania and she has a brother who lives in the southwest."

While Danielle went searching for family, Tessa tapped on her phone. "I'm looking on a few of her friends' social media pages, but there's no mention of Val."

"You're *sure* she wouldn't leave without saying goodbye?" Danielle asked.

"Absolutely. She wanted to be my roommate, but she told me

she needed a job, first. There's no way she'd leave without saying goodbye, plus, where would she go?"

"What about back to Pennsylvania or to live with her brother?"

"She didn't even want her parents to know she was living at the shelter," Tessa added.

After several minutes of searching, Danielle turned the laptop toward Tessa. "I found her parents' home phone number, if you want to talk to them about her."

Tessa texted it to herself. "Just so you know, we have an exit process at the shelter that everyone goes through. A staff member interviews the resident. They provide contact information and we have a duffle bag that we give them. It has a pair of pajamas, socks, underwear, jeans and a shirt. There's a bunch of items like soap, a razor, shampoo, that kind of thing, plus a $25 gift card to a grocery store." Tessa shifted on the sofa. "I did a little snooping and I found a handful of residents from this year who didn't graduate, like Val."

"I remember you mentioning that," Danielle said.

The basic background check was ready. It showed Val's last known residence to be an apartment in Falls Church.

"That's her," Tessa said. "She told me she'd been living in Falls Church."

"Check with the property manager over there," Danielle suggested. "I can help you find the number."

Tessa sighed. "No, it's okay. Thanks for helping me."

Danielle's computer rang with an incoming video chat call. "Will you say hello to my family with me?"

"Sure."

Danielle's mom and niece's smiling faces popped on the screen. "Happy Turkey Day!" her little niece shouted with a toothless grin.

"Happy Thanksgiving, fam," Danielle replied.

After introductions, Danielle's mom asked Tessa how her

holiday was going and what kind of work she did. When their chat ended, Tessa headed toward the kitchen.

Danielle's niece went to play and her dad joined their chat.

"How's my angel doing?" he asked.

"She's turned into a devil," Danielle replied and her parents laughed.

They wouldn't be laughing if they knew the truth about me.

"How's your holiday?" Danielle asked.

"It's been lovely. It's hard not to smile around the kids," her mom said.

Danielle was relieved that her mom and dad looked better. Her sister's death had been devastating for them, but they appeared more upbeat since moving closer to Danielle's brother and his family.

"We miss having you with us, today," her mom said.

"Me, too, but I'm coming home for Christmas."

Cooper walked into the room and her heart pitter-pattered. He pointed to the sofa and she waved him over. "I want you to meet someone."

Cooper sat beside her on the sofa. "Hello, Mr. and Mrs. Fox. I'm Cooper Grant. Happy Thanksgiving."

"You, as well, Cooper," said her dad. "Call me Steve."

"And I'm Beverly."

"How's your holiday going?" Cooper asked.

As Danielle's mom and dad chatted with Cooper, she appreciated what a good conversationalist he was.

"Cooper, are you visiting over Christmas when Danielle comes home?" her dad asked.

"That sounds like an invitation to me," Cooper replied.

"Oops, maybe I should have checked with Danielle, first," her dad said.

"I'd love Cooper to spend Christmas with us," Danielle said.

Chantal wandered in. "Coop, can I borrow you?"

"My sister is in need of help, so I'm guessing it's time to string the lights on the tree."

"As in, Christmas tree?" her mom asked.

"It's a long-standing Grant tradition that while the turkey cooks, we put up the tree and the lights. The ornaments don't get hung until the weekend."

"Have a wonderful holiday and thanks for including Danielle," her mom said.

"I love that she's here with me and my family." Cooper kissed Danielle's cheek before pushing off the sofa.

"I'm going to give you and Mom a few minutes," her dad said. "I love you, honey. Have a happy holiday. I miss you. See you next month."

After her dad left, her mom smiled. "You two look very happy together."

Danielle glanced around the quiet room, while laughter and conversations floated in from the other side of the home. "I'm pretty crazy about him and, you know, I'm always so slow-going when it comes to boyfriends."

"Like I've always said, 'you know when you know.'" Her mom moved the laptop closer. "I read an article about a vigilante who's killing powerful men in your area," she murmured. "They haven't caught the guy. Are you safe?"

"Well, since I'm not a wealthy, powerful man who's preying on innocent women, I'm pretty sure I'm safe," Danielle murmured. "You don't have to worry."

"Have you run a background check on Cooper?" her mom whispered.

Danielle laughed. "I promise you, he checks out."

"I know how much you love to hack and I thought of you when I read the story about the vigilante. Most think it's a man, but some swear it's a woman. Have you done any digging to see if you can figure it out?"

Danielle bit back a smile. "No, I'm going to let the

professionals do their jobs, but I appreciate the props. If I hear anything, I'll let you know."

"I miss you, honey. Please be safe."

"I am, Mom. I love you."

"Love you, too. Can't wait to see you at Christmas."

The call ended and she closed her laptop.

As she headed toward the festive sounds of Cooper's family, she thought about Val's disappearance and Tessa's insistence that her friend would never leave without saying goodbye. A shiver skirted through her. Her gut was telling her that something was not right.

COOPER

After everyone's plates had been loaded down with food, Cooper's dad led the family in a prayer of thanks. For the first few minutes, compliments were plentiful as the family dug in and enjoyed the holiday feast.

As was a long-standing tradition in the Grant family, they always participated in a circle of thanks, usually kicked off by Tessa.

To Cooper's surprise, Chantal said, "I'd like to start the gratitude circle, this year." She paused for a brief second. "I'm grateful for Mom and Dad. They are so good to me and so patient. I'm grateful for our successful business and grateful that Dad and I work so well together, especially since we see each other *every single day*." She paused for laughter. "I'm grateful for Tessa who spends a lot of time with me, since I don't go out."

"Love you, Auntie," Tessa said.

"I'm thankful Danielle gave me a private kickboxing lesson. I hope, one day, I'm brave enough to head to Coop's gym and take her class there."

The gratitude continued around the table. When it was Henry's turn, he said, "I'm grateful for my family and my job. This year, however, I'm incredibly grateful for my wife. I'm glad we had this year apart because it made me realize what an idiot I am for not moving to Richmond with her. It turns out—I'll stop. Aisha, your turn, honey."

"I'm grateful for both my families. I'm grateful for the wonderful law firm in Richmond and for the clients who put their trust in me to help them. Professionally, it was a rewarding year and I'm so thankful for that, but personally, I missed all of you so much. About a month ago, I moved back home with Henry and I'm in the process of working out details with my old firm. I'm returning as partner, and Henry and I are thrilled about that."

"Hurray!" Tessa exclaimed before she scowled. "Why are we just now finding out?"

"Mom and I wanted a few weeks, just the two of us," Henry said. "We wanted to make sure before we told all of you."

Emily wiped the corner of her eye with her cloth napkin. "That is wonderful news. We've missed you, Aisha."

Aisha smiled. "Me, too. It's great to be home." After a pause, she said, "Your turn, Danielle."

"I'm grateful for my family and for my work family. I'm grateful to my new boss, who's also become my mentor."

"Uh-oh, Coop, you got competition." Henry waggled his eyebrows.

"I met him and I'm not threatened." Cooper winked at Danielle while his family cracked up.

"I'm *very* thankful Cooper gave me a second chance when I didn't show for our first date," Danielle added, and the entire table erupted in laughter.

"Uncle Cooper, you must really like her a lot to have asked her out again," Tessa said.

Cooper chuckled. "I do. And she was worth my wounded pride when she left me hanging."

"Thank you for welcoming me into your family," Danielle said. "Your turn," she said to Cooper.

"I'm thankful to be here, today, and for Danielle for making sure that happened."

"What does that mean?" asked his dad. "Weren't you coming?"

"I ran into a little snag and Danielle got me out of it," Cooper replied. "I'm grateful for my wonderful family and I'm thankful for a job that I love."

"Who would have thought you'd like owning a gym so much," Henry said. "You've been in law enforcement for so long, I never thought you'd leave it."

Under the table, Danielle found Cooper's hand and gave him a little squeeze.

Cooper raised his wine glass. "Here's to family."

"To family," everyone replied.

They continued eating until stomachs were stuffed. Coffee was made and desserts were set on the island, but everyone was too full to try any of them.

After Emily packaged up leftovers for Cooper and Danielle, they were saying their goodbyes when there was a knock on the front door.

"Anyone home?" Geoffrey yelled as the front door chimed.

"Kitchen," Cooper's dad called out.

Geoffrey Edelman walked in, a bottle of cognac in hand. As his gaze floated over the island, he said, "Is my timing perfect or what?" He set the bottle on the counter, walked over to Eric and kissed his cheek, then patted his back. "Happy Thanksgiving, my friend."

"Glad you could make it, after all," his dad replied.

"That bottle of Louis the thirteenth cognac cost four grand," Geoffrey said. "Who's having a glass with me?"

"One glass?" Cooper asked Danielle.

"Gotta try it," she replied.

Cooper's mom and Chantal set several small glasses on the

table and Geoffrey shared his luxury brandy. When his gaze fell on Danielle, he said, "Ah, the lady with the striking hair." Then, he regarded Cooper. "You never mentioned your friend."

"This is Danielle. Danielle, this is—"

"Geoffrey Edelman," Danielle replied. "We met at the shelter when I stopped by to see Lori this week. Good to see you."

"You, as well," Geoffrey replied.

"Geoffrey, did you eat?" his mom asked.

"I worked most of the day, so if you've got anything left, I'll make myself a plate."

Chantal stood. "I'll get out the food."

After Geoffrey finished pouring the brandy, everyone lifted their glasses. "Here's to my family," Geoffrey said. "On this special day of thanks."

Cooper savored the smooth cognac before swallowing it down. "Wow, that is fantastic."

"It's like drinking velvet," Danielle added.

Emily brought a warmed plate over and set it on the table next. Several sat back down to keep Geoffrey company, but Cooper was ready to head out, knowing Danielle wanted to spend time with Emerson.

"What had you working today?" Eric asked.

"I work every day," Geoffrey replied, before taking a bite of stuffing. "This is delicious. Who should I compliment?"

"Total group effort," Tessa answered.

"Kudos to all," Geoffrey said.

"Unfortunately, we're heading out," Cooper said.

"I'm sorry we won't get a chance to catch up. Coop, before I forget, I have to reschedule our lunch in two weeks. I'm heading out of town."

"Text me when you're back and we'll set something up."

After ten minutes of saying their goodbyes, Cooper and Danielle left, their bags of leftovers in hand.

In the car, Danielle kissed him. "Thank you so much for today. You have a wonderful family."

"They love you. Thank you for coming with me." He started the car and drove down the quiet, lamp-lit street.

"Lori Shannon told me she was heading out of town for a conference the second week of December," she said.

"So?"

"That's the same time Geoffrey is out of town. Do you think they're going somewhere, together?"

"Doubtful," Cooper replied, while sliding his hand over her thigh. "When Geoffrey's working, he's nose-down the entire time."

25

WHERE'S TESSA?

DANIELLE

Danielle and Emerson had been waiting fifteen minutes for Lori Shannon to arrive at Kaleidoscope when the server returned to check on them. "Would you like to order a small plate, while you wait?"

"I'm starving," Emerson said flipping open the menu. After selecting a couple of starters, the server flitted off to fill the order.

Danielle checked her phone, again. Nothing new from Lori. Earlier that day, she'd sent Lori a text confirming the restaurant. Lori had replied with a thumbs-up emoji. But it looked like she was a no-show.

Ten minutes later, they were chowing down on their appetizers. "We should swing by the shelter," Danielle said.

"Good idea," Emerson replied. "And that empty house, too."

"Seeing Cooper in that prison was crazy sick. I mean, that lock was real. If someone had been playing around, wouldn't the lock be plastic?"

"Not necessarily," Emerson said.

"I'll text Cooper before we leave, so the guys know where we are."

Danielle loved catching up with Emerson, just the two of them. Now that there were no secrets, their friendship was back on track.

As they were finishing up their burgers, Danielle's phone buzzed. "It's Lori." She read the text to Emerson. "I'm super bummed I couldn't make it. I had a work thing."

"You should reply," Emerson said.

"How's this, 'Emerson and I are still at the restaurant. Come join us!'" Danielle spun her phone around for Emerson to see.

"Ask her if we can meet her closer to where she is," Emerson suggested.

Danielle added that, then sent it. No dots, no response.

Emerson sighed. "I'm so suspicious of everyone, but she's probably just super busy with the shelters or whatever other businesses she has."

Danielle leaned forward in the booth. "One of Tessa's friends—a resident at the shelter—has disappeared, and Tessa asked me to see what I could find."

"And?"

Danielle shook her head. "Nothing. And she said others had, too. I don't know what to think. Let me send Cooper a text."

"Lori Shannon didn't show," she texted Cooper. "Em and I are swinging by the shelter. What's the status at the vacant house?"

Dots appeared and, then, his response. "Stryker and I checked house surveillance cams. No one is there. Do not go to house."

"Shelter only," she texted back.

After Danielle paid for dinner, she drove them to the shelter. The lobby was bathed in evening lighting and they couldn't tell if someone was sitting at the front desk.

"Let's see if she's in there," Emerson said.

They parked out front and peered through the front door. There was a woman sitting behind reception.

Knock-knock-knock.

The woman walked over to the door, but didn't open it. "Can I help you?"

"We're friends of Lori Shannon," Danielle said. "I'm Danielle Fox. I taught a computer class—"

The woman unlocked the door and opened it. "I thought I recognized you. C'mon in."

Once inside, the employee bolted the front door. "Did you say you're looking for Lori?"

"Yes," Danielle replied. "Is she here?"

"No, she's on call, but she doesn't come in on weekends. Do you want to leave her a message?"

"No, that's okay," Danielle said. "We had plans, but she didn't show. We were hoping we could convince her to have a drink with us."

"Sorry, I can't help you."

In the car, on their way to Emerson's, Danielle said, "Cooper asked me to move in with him."

"Oooh, I love that. What are you gonna do?"

"I haven't given him my answer, but I've been staying there every night."

"Life is crazy. Three months ago, you were hunting down those men, and I had to keep my job a secret from you. And here we are working a case together."

"I love that we're working together, too, Em."

A song they both loved came up on Emerson's playlist. They harmonized, the uplifting moment helping to lighten the serious mood.

When the song ended, Danielle said, "I used to be much more trusting, but I'm not anymore."

In the darkened car, Emerson nodded. "I get that."

Danielle pulled into Emerson's driveway. "Do you want to come in and hang?"

"No, I'm gonna get home to Cooper."

Emerson hugged her. "Enjoy your evening with him and try to put all of this out of your mind."

She waited until Emerson was inside before she backed out of the driveway. Before taking off, she checked her phone, but Lori never replied.

When she got back to Cooper's, she hung up her coat, then found him in the kitchen on his laptop. He pushed out of his chair and folded her into his arms. "There's my beauty." His kiss was long and gentle, his hold warm and firm. In his arms, the tension in her shoulders melted away. "I'm sorry Lori didn't show," he said.

"We stopped by the shelter, but she wasn't there."

"What can we do to redirect your attention?" He flashed her a smile. "Anything come to mind?"

Before she could answer, he whisked her into his arms, and carried her into the family room.

"Fireplace on," he commanded and the flames jumped to life. "Lights off."

"Fireplace on. Lights off," replied the computerized voice.

He set her on the floor by the hearth, then sat across from her.

"Not tonight," she said and watched his expression drop. She leaned close and kissed him. "Tonight isn't about me. It's about you. You spoil me all the time, Cooper. I want to bring *you* all the pleasure."

She rose and set the throw blanket on the floor beside him. "Get naked. I'll be right back." With an extra sway in her hips, she headed toward the stairs, but turned back before she left the room.

His searing gaze sent a thrill careening through her. She blew him a kiss and trotted up the stairs. She knew exactly what she was going to do, but first, she needed to find the perfect outfit to wear.

COOPER

Cooper shed his clothes, then propped himself against a bunch of throw pillows. The room was plenty warm, but he tossed the blanket over his hardening shaft, which tented against the soft fabric.

A moment later, she slinked into the room, her hair in a ponytail, a silky bathrobe tied at her waist, and a bottle of massage oil in her hand. Her sexy sandal stilettos gave her an extra four inches. He released a long whistle when she posed, and the bathrobe opened, revealing her beautifully muscular thighs.

"A stunning woman is headed my way," he said. "And I'm at her mercy."

She knelt in front of him and leaned close. "I'm going to take care of your dirtiest dreams, but first, I'm going to relax you." She kissed him, letting her tongue tangle with his.

Jolts of energy surged through him, the desire to drive himself inside her hijacked his thoughts.

"Tell me about a fantasy," she murmured. "A wild, dirty one."

He had the perfect one. "I'm at a bachelor party and you're the entertainment."

She kissed him harder, this time, and he groaned out his approval.

Pushing to her feet, she set her heel on his thigh, still covered by the blanket. Then, she looked around the room, as if planning the fantasy. She stepped away and offered her hand. When he placed his in hers, she pulled him to his feet.

"Sit on the sofa." After he did, she asked him if he had voice activation for music.

"I do," he replied.

"Something sexy I can dance to."

He found a sultry playlist of songs and leaned back to enjoy the spectacular show. Her sexy gyrations and shimmies turned him hard, but when she slowly started to remove her robe, his body warmed and his shaft shot to attention. She dropped it off her shoulders, revealing a black, mesh bra and matching thong. Strips of black fabric covered her nipples and pussy. Another groan ripped through him while his dick bobbed up and down.

A provocative smile touched her eyes as she slinked closer. "I can't wait until you come all over my tits."

What the hell? He liked his angel's dirty talk.

She was poetry in motion, her moves were sublime and graceful. When she turned around and backed into him, he palmed her glorious ass.

"Mmm, you feel good," he murmured.

She began straddling him. "Do you want to suck my tits?"

"Hell, yeah."

"I'm really not supposed to let clients do that," she said, sliding her index finger into her mouth as she arched her back. "We're all about looking, but no touching. But you're soooo cute, I'll break the rules for you and your friends, just this once."

"I'll make it worth your while."

"Ooooh, I love that." She slowly pushed the straps off her shoulders and the bra fell away, exposing her breasts and erect nipples. When she thrust her chest toward him, he ran his tongue over her nipple. Once, twice, and then, he sucked her tender flesh while it plumped in his mouth.

His cock was throbbing and he was eager to root himself inside her while she rode him to a release.

Her husky moan landed in his balls and he fondled her other breast, tweaking her nipple while he stroked her ass. The more he sucked her nipples, the louder she moaned. The frenzy of their foreplay was making him crazy with desire.

"Suck them harder," she commanded. "And slide your fingers inside my hot, wet pussy."

When he did, their collective moans made his balls ache with pent-up need. She began to massage his shaft, running her fingers over the top of his tip and spreading the wetness over it.

The need to fuck her had turned him into a wild beast.

"Take your fingers out," she said.

He did, then he slid both of them into his mouth and licked her juices. "You taste like more."

"Ohgod," she ground out. "I'm dying for you, but we're definitely not supposed to fuck the customers."

"If you fuck me," he said, "what about everyone else, here?"

"Oh, I'll fuck them, too."

This dirty side of Danielle was an unexpected treat.

She pushed off him. Her lids were hooded, her cheeks pink, her chest was rising and falling fast. But it was the lust in her eyes that sent another wave of wetness oozing out of him. The throbbing between his legs was agonizingly spectacular.

"Sit on the edge of the sofa so I can fuck you," she commanded.

When he did, she backed into him. He positioned himself at her opening, and she sank down on his hard shaft.

"Oh, yeah," he ground out.

"Soooo good." She grasped his thighs for support.

As soon as she started moving, he reached around and fondled her breasts. She arched into his hands while her carnal groans turned feral. Up and down, again and again, the ecstasy building at a frenetic pace.

Then, she increased her speed and cried out, "I'm a naughty girl for letting you fuck me."

The orgasm ripped through him, the waves of pulsating pleasure quieting his tortured soul. She stilled, his cock rooted deep inside her. He wrapped his arms around her and kissed each shoulder before dotting her back with several more kisses.

Moving slowly, she pulled off. He was flying high, but he needed to take care of her, his way.

He stood and folded her in his arms. Her eyes were black with lust, her breathing jagged. When she raked her fingers down his back, they came together in a violent kiss, mouths crashing together, their tongues stroking hard, their passion uncontrollable.

Panting, the kiss ended.

"Lay on the floor and spread your legs," he said.

"But I've got to fuck the next customer." He loved that she was still role playing. Despite not having any alcohol, he was definitely feeling drunk.

"You can fuck them when I've had my way with you."

As she lay by the fire, he grabbed a few tissues. "You fuck so good," he said while gently cleaning away the wetness.

"You can show me your appreciation when you tip me," she quipped, her adorable smile stealing his heart.

His kisses were intense, her breathy moans were filled with need. Planking over her, he kissed his way down her body while she writhed beneath him.

"Abs of steel," he murmured before he came to rest between her legs.

He loved how she responded to his touch, the way he licked her wet folds, and how he caressed her clit.

"The guys want to come on me while you eat me," she ground out.

Dirty Danielle was turning him hard again. When she arched off the floor, he knew she was about to come. He applied more pressure to her clit while thrusting his fingers into her dripping core.

"Yes, yessssss," she cried out, then jerked violently while he tasted her sweet, sweet come.

While she lay there catching her breath, he dotted her naked body with kisses until his mouth found hers. They wrapped their legs around each other and snuggled close. Gentle kisses and caresses replaced the moans and thrusts of moments ago.

She ran the back of her fingers down his cheeks while her gaze never left his. "Wow, that was hot. Got any more fantasies you'd like to share?"

"Your turn," he whispered. "I'm sure you've got a few dirty stories of your own."

Her sweet smile made him happy. "I do, and I can't wait to share *all* of them with you."

WEDNESDAY EVENING, COOPER had finished his advanced kickboxing class and was waiting for Danielle in the rock-climbing room. When she arrived, her face flushed from physical activity, she smiled at him from across the room.

As she made her way over, he checked her out. Danielle was checking all his boxes.

Hitching a brow at him, she stood inches away. "Like what you see?"

"Love it… and I love you," he replied. "Ready to climb?"

"I thought we were taking off after class."

"Give me three more feet, then we're out."

With a nod, she accepted the harness. He checked to make sure she secured it correctly, then fitted himself in one. "You can do it, babe."

The knot between her brows relaxed a little and she took her first step.

She stopped ten feet off the ground. "I can't go any higher. If I look down, I'll freak." Her rosy glow had gone pale.

"Look at me."

She'd been clinging to the rocks. Finally, she glanced over. "If we were at an outdoor concert and I put you on my shoulders, you'd be around nine feet in the air. Babe, you're about ten feet off the ground."

"First, I wouldn't be on your shoulders unless we were in a swimming pool, and second, this was fun, but I'm climbing back down."

She was on the ground in seconds. "Whew," she said as she removed the harness. "I feel so much better down here."

Cooper couldn't resist the urge to climb higher, so he took off toward the top of the wall. Once there, he could see out the window, but it was dark, and his own reflection shone back.

As he made his way down, Danielle pulled his ringing phone out of his duffle. "It's your mom."

"Can you answer?"

She did, as he started his descent. Back on the floor, he removed the harness and headed over to Danielle.

"We had turkey sandwiches for lunch," she said. "They were delicious. Hold on, here's Cooper." She handed him his phone.

"Hey, Mom."

"I'm sure I'm overreacting, but Tessa and I had a shopping date tonight and she didn't show."

"Did you call her?"

"I texted her. When she didn't reply, I called, but got voicemail."

"Maybe she forgot to charge her phone. Have Henry or Aisha seen her?"

"Not since Saturday."

"What about her roommates?" he asked.

"She had two, but one moved out. I have the roommates first name, but I don't have anything else."

"It's probably nothing. Let me try to find her." He hung up.

"Is Tessa missing?" Danielle asked, the concern evident in her voice.

"She was supposed to go shopping with my mom tonight, but she didn't show."

"Oh, no," Danielle said. "We gotta go."

He wrapped his hand around her arm. "Tessa's done this before."

"What do you mean?"

"Once, she took the train to New York City with some friends for a long weekend. She told my mom and dad she'd stop by on Sunday, but she didn't. Another time, she went to Cancun with friends and didn't tell anyone."

"Okay. I'll take it down a few notches." They headed toward the front of the gym.

"Need my help closing?" Cooper asked Naomi.

"I've got a couple of staffers helping me," Naomi replied.

Once outside, Danielle said, "I sent her a text."

On the way home, Cooper called her, but got voicemail.

"It's Tessa, don't leave me a message. I never check. Text me."

He hung up.

"I'll swing by the shelter in the morning," Danielle said. "Maybe she lost her phone or she's been working at one of the other locations."

In the middle of the night, when sleep wouldn't come, Cooper told Danielle he was going to geolocate Tessa's phone. They sat side by side at the kitchen island while he pulled up the FBI's proprietary software used for cell phone location.

While they waited, she made a pot of coffee and checked the surveillance cams at the house in Great Falls. The house was dark. She checked the tracking software for the shelter van and found it in the parking lot of the Maryland shelter.

When the results came back, Cooper wasn't sure what to think. The last ping came in on Monday from the Alexandria shelter. "Check this out."

Danielle pulled the stool close. "She went to work that morning, then over to the DC shelter. That afternoon, she was back in Alexandria. In the evening, her phone goes dead."

"Either it ran out of juice or she turned it off." Danielle sipped the coffee. "Let's find her roommate."

They went searching on Tessa's social media sites. After

scrolling back a few months, they found a pic of three women and a post.

The Three Musketeers are becoming the Dynamic Duo. We're going to miss KC soooo much.

Both women were tagged, so they clicked on the roommate's social media page. Meg's page didn't provide a way to contact her and she hadn't posted in months. Danielle hopped online, did a people search, and found Meg's cell phone number.

"Do you think Tessa's mentioned you to her roommate?" Danielle asked.

"No idea."

"Let's send Meg a text," Danielle suggested.

Cooper began typing. "Meg, this is Cooper Grant, Tessa's uncle. We haven't heard from Tessa in a few days. Have you seen her?" Cooper fired off the message.

It was five fifteen in the morning and no dots appeared. "Hopefully, she'll reply." Danielle pushed off the stool. "I'm going to get ready for work."

That morning, Cooper was reviewing ALPHA's open cases when Slash walked into his office. "Got a sec?"

Cooper dragged his eyes from the spreadsheet. "Whad'ya need?"

"My Salimov informant resurfaced. He told me Salimov had this thing he did four times a year and one of them was coming up."

"What does that mean?"

"Hell if I know, but my informant told me it was sketchy."

"That's useless, unless dead men really do talk."

"I ran his name through the State Department's list of international travelers. Not there."

"He's dead," Cooper said. "Wouldn't his name have been removed?"

"No idea." She shrugged, then turned on her heel. "I'll stay on it."

"Thanks for the heads up." Cooper returned to his spreadsheet. He had three teams out on assignment and another four queued up to take off. If he didn't stay organized, he wouldn't know where anyone was on any given day.

His phone buzzed. It was a text from Tessa's roommate.

"Hi, Cooper. Tessa talks about her cool uncle all the time. I saw Tessa Monday before I flew to Orlando for work. Here 'til Thurs. She's been putting in the hours at work. Maybe she crashed there."

DANIELLE

Danielle waited in the lobby for Lori Shannon while the receptionist talked to a repairman about upgrading the shelter's thermostats in addition to handling a flurry of incoming calls.

When she finally had a break, she said to Danielle, "Thanks for your patience. I'm new and we're super short-staffed."

"Where's Tessa?" Danielle asked, playing dumb.

"She resigned."

No way. "She's gone?"

"Lori said she quit on Monday." The woman's expression fell. "I liked Tessa. She was so positive and helpful. I got one whole day with her and now I'm stuck figuring things out on my own."

Danielle glanced around the large lobby. "I know where Lori's office is. I'm just gonna pop in."

"You're not supposed—" The shelter phone rang and the staffer picked it up.

Danielle took off toward Lori's office. As she walked down the hallway, she searched for what could be Tessa's office. She stepped into a dark office and flicked on the light. Nothing beyond an empty desk and bookcase.

Danielle entered another dark office, turned on the light. This office was in use. In addition to a computer and keyboard, two stacks of papers sat on the desk, along with a photo of Tessa with several residents.

Where's her phone?

She tugged on a desk drawer and it slid open. No phone.

"What are you doing?" Lori stood in the doorway, her gaze drilling into Danielle.

"There you are!" Danielle pasted on a cheery smile. "My phone is dead and I need a charger."

Lori glared at Danielle. "I have one you can borrow," she said, her tone abrupt.

Lori's chilly silence carried them down the hallway and into her office. She handed Danielle a phone charger. To keep up the ruse, Danielle plugged her phone in.

"I'm gonna be honest," Danielle said. "I'm disappointed you didn't show on Saturday, but a little peeved. You tell me you don't have any friends, so Emerson and I invite you to join us, and you blow us off."

"I had to work. You know, I don't appreciate your walking around here without an escort."

Danielle regarded Lori. "I volunteered my time here. I reached out to reconnect with you. You stand me up and you bite *my* head off. I *thought* we were friends." She unplugged her phone from the charger and shoved it into her coat pocket. "I'm gonna take off."

"Wait," Lori said. "I'm headed out of town, and my DC and Maryland Facilities Managers have to manage this one while I'm gone." She blew out an exasperated breath. "I'm feeling overwhelmed. Sorry."

"The receptionist said Tessa walked. What happened?"

"We got into it about something. It's not the first time an employee has left without giving notice."

"When are you leaving for your conference?"

"Tomorrow."

"Where is it?"

Lori glanced at her watch. "I'd love to chat, but I've got a ton to do." She rounded her desk. "I will definitely call you when I get back."

She ushered Danielle to the lobby. "Thanks for stopping by." She slowed at reception, spoke briefly to the staffer, then hurried around the corner.

Danielle didn't believe a word Lori Shannon had said. On the way back to ALPHA, she phoned Cooper, but she got voicemail.

At the office, she saw him in the conference room with several Operatives, so she filled her water bottle and returned to her office to check emails. One snagged her attention. The bot program had returned a search result for Fantasea Ventures. She clicked on the link, which took her to the Virginia Department of Wildlife Resources. Her mind blanked as she stared at the website's home page.

This has gotta be a mistake.

As she was about to close the site, she read the page's title again.

Boat Registration and Titling

Beneath that were several categories, starting with:

Registering and Titling Your Watercraft

She opened a new browser and searched for a boat registration website. Once she found one, she plugged in "Fantasea Ventures". Zero hits.

Dammit.

Then, she entered "Fantasea". This time, her search returned a long list of watercraft named Fantasea from all over the country.

The results also included the length of the vessel. The majority were thirty to forty feet in length. A yacht registered in Louisiana was over a hundred feet long, and the one in Virginia was over five-hundred-feet long.

She re-read the original email from her bot search. That search had turned up one match. Fantasea Ventures owned a 520-foot small ship named Fantasea.

What's a holding company that runs a women's shelter doing with a cruise ship?

26

THE HUNT IS ON

COOPER

That evening, Cooper was toweling off after his shower when Danielle walked into the bathroom, laptop in hand.

"Hey, baby," she said as her gaze dropped from his eyes, to his chest, then back to his eyes.

"See something you like?"

"Definitely, and if I wasn't worried about Tessa, I'd take advantage of your sexy, naked self." She set the laptop on the vanity. "We've got movement at the Great Falls house."

They watched as Lori Shannon entered the house, flicking on lights on her way upstairs. She searched one of the bedroom closets filled with gowns, then moved on, empty handed, to the next one. There, she flipped through dress after dress, pulling out three and laying them over her arm. Next, she hurried into the primary bedroom, entered the large walk-in closet and pulled several more. Down the stairs she went, out through the garage and into her car. Her visit hadn't lasted ten minutes.

Of one thing Cooper was certain—his niece was missing.

Neither he nor Danielle believed Tessa had quit her job, like Lori had claimed.

Earlier, he'd driven to Tessa's apartment, where he'd arranged for the property manager to meet him. It helped that he shared Tessa's last name and he had photos of their family to prove he wasn't some stalker. If neither of those had worked, he had his ALPHA-issued FBI badge with him, as well. Whatever the hell it took to get inside.

The place hadn't been burglarized and there were no signs she'd been taken. He found her overnight bag—the one she brought with her when she stayed with his folks—in her closet. Her toothbrush was in the bathroom. She had vanished, leaving no clues.

To say he was worried was an understatement. On his way home, he'd stopped at the police station to file a missing person's report.

Cooper walked into his bedroom, pulled on a sweatshirt and shorts before they headed downstairs and into the kitchen.

His phone rang and he snatched it up. "It's my brother." He answered, hit the speaker. "Have you heard from her?"

"No, but Aisha said you filed a missing person's report. Isn't that a little much?"

He gritted his teeth to keep from screaming at his brother. "You and Aisha saw her on Saturday. It's Wednesday. How long did *you* plan on waiting?"

"If she quit, like her boss said, maybe she hopped a flight to Mexico or something," Henry said. "She's very impulsive. C'mon, Cooper, you know that."

"If she calls you or Aisha, let me know." Cooper hung up downright pissed his brother hadn't been more concerned about his own daughter.

Cooper's phone rang again. "I don't recognize this number."

"Answer it."

He answered on speaker. "Hello?"

"Uncle Cooper, I was taken," Tessa whispered. "I'm on a ship."

Adrenaline surged through him. "Where? Where are you, Tessa?"

"I'm in Balti—Aiiieee!" The line went dead.

"Tessa! *Tessa!*"

She was gone.

"Fuck! Fuck, no."

"We've got to geolocate that device," Danielle said, the urgency in her voice catching his ear.

Cooper sprang into action. At the kitchen island, he opened his laptop, plugged the number into the program and paced while it ran. His worst fears were confirmed. His niece had been kidnapped. "I cannot fucking believe this."

"She's brilliant," Danielle said.

"*What?*"

"She found a phone and she knew to call you."

He stopped pacing and fixated on the screen. "C'mon, *c'mon*."

While they waited for the software to locate the cell origination, Danielle's fingers flew over the keyboard. "I'm looking for cruise lines docked at the Port of Baltimore."

A new window popped open on Cooper's laptop and a green light flashed in the location of the cell phone, then it went dark.

"What happened?" Cooper blurted. "Where'd it go?"

Cooper zoomed in to where he'd seen the flash. "Whoever found her turned off the phone." He continued zooming in to where he'd seen that one blip. "It's definitely Baltimore, but I don't know if it's one of several marinas or the port where the cruise ships are docked."

"There are two cruise ships docked there now, but they're commercial ships that carry over two thousand passengers." After searching further, Danielle said, "I was able to get into the Port of Baltimore's mooring database. There's an entry for Fantasea, and it's scheduled for departure tomorrow."

Fury had him growling. "I will kill whoever fucking took her."

As Cooper called Stryker, he said, "I'm putting together a team."

"I'm here," Stryker answered, his voice groggy.

"Tessa's been kidnapped."

"What?"

"She's being held on a ship in Baltimore. We think it's a small cruise ship named Fantasea, but it's unconfirmed. I need a team on standby."

"Who?"

"You, Emerson, Jericho, Hawk, Herrera, and Slash."

"I'm on it." Stryker hung up.

Cooper pounded his fist on the marble countertop. "Fuck. *Fuck!*"

"I'm gonna hack into Lori Shannon's computer," Danielle said.

Every fiber of his being wanted to take off for Baltimore and kill the motherfucker who'd kidnapped his niece. But he couldn't go alone and he couldn't lead the team without a strategy. Were they dealing with arms dealers, drug smugglers, human traffickers? Was this Shannon woman even involved? If yes, what the fuck was she up to?

His blood boiled.

While waiting for Danielle's results, he ran a trace on the phone Tessa had used. The burner had been purchased with cash from a big box store.

Another fucking dead end.

It was after two in the morning when Danielle said, "I'm in. Cooper, *Cooper*."

He flicked his attention her way. "I'm sorry, babe. What'd you say?"

"I'm in Lori's calendar. She's off starting today and she'll be back at work over a week later."

"Where's she going?"

"There's a calendar banner that says 'F.O.'. The F's gotta be Fantasea."

Cooper's phone rang. It was Stryker. He put the call on speaker. "Go."

"Team's ready."

"Stryker," Danielle said. "I need Emerson."

"I'm here," Emerson replied.

"Lori has an Ozark account where she stores her docs, but I don't know the answers to her security questions. Do you remember the name of her childhood dog?"

"Um... I'm thinking." After a pregnant pause, Emerson said, "No."

"What about her favorite teacher?"

"Who was our gym teacher? You know, the cute one. No, wait. It was our algebra teacher. She told me she thought he was hot. What was his name?"

"I didn't have him, but I know who you're talking about," Danielle replied.

"Mr.… Mr., oh, what was it?" After a second, she blurted, "Mr. Mitchell!"

Danielle typed in Mitchell, but it didn't work. Then, she typed in Mr. Mitchell. "I'm in."

"We're on standby," Emerson said. "Stryker's on the phone with Jericho now."

"We'll keep you posted." Cooper hung up.

"I found a folder called FO Res." Danielle opened it, revealing dozens of documents, each labeled with a date. She opened the one dated that day.

Together, they read the list of names, fifty-nine in total. Next to each name was a corresponding number.

Cooper scanned the list. "I recognize Jim Bruhmer and Petrov Utkin." He jumped onto his computer. "Bruhmer was the CEO of a tech company, but he stepped down after being accused of having undisclosed sexual relationships with several employees. Utkin works at the Russian Embassy. He and Salimov were close."

"There're fifty-three men and six women," Danielle said.

"Tessa's at the Port of Baltimore on a ship that's leaving tomorrow for a week-long cruise."

"How do you know?"

"I just found the itinerary."

DANIELLE

Years ago, Danielle had gone on a cruise with her family. She remembered there being a detailed schedule of things they could do once on board.

The itinerary, created by Lori Shannon, was bare bones, at best.

Friday
AM - Lori arrives
4:00-6:00pm - Boarding and Cocktails
6:30pm - Depart PoB
7:00pm - Dinner
8:00pm - Welcome & Masquerade Ball
10:00pm - Quiet Time
Saturday – Thursday (Times TBD)
Auction
Leather-n-Lace Party
Slumber Party
Poker Challenge
Water Fun
Movie Night
Ongoing - Quiet Time
Friday
11:00am - Return PoB
Saturday
Close Out Cruise

"What the hell is Quiet Time?" Danielle mumbled. "It starts on Friday evening, then it's ongoing all week. There're no port destinations or land excursions on the itinerary. So, they're cruising on the ocean for an entire week, like a booze cruise?"

He clicked back over to the guest list. "If I went on a cruise, I'd want you to come with me. There are three couples on this entire passenger list. Everyone else is traveling solo. That's odd, don't you think?"

"Maybe it's a singles' cruise."

"When I was investigating Salimov, I looked into the men in his inner circle. Petrov Utkin is married. Bruhmer's married, too, but his wife might have left him when the scandal broke."

Danielle knew what they had to do, but she wasn't sure if her plan would work. "We need to get ourselves on that ship."

"Lori will recognize you."

"Not in my disguise. I'll wear a brown wig and brown contacts, plus, if I use brown-tinted glasses, it'll be hard to see my eyes at all. Lori has never seen you. We'll need formal clothing and maybe masquerade masks for the ball."

"I want to arrest her *now*," Cooper said while scraping his hands down his scruffy cheeks.

"If we wait and get on that ship with the other passengers, we find Tessa *and* we find out what's going on."

Nonstop adrenaline had Danielle working on all thrusters. She clicked on the guest list. "What do you think those numbers are next to the passenger names?"

"My guess is suite numbers."

"Nice." She started typing in the online doc. "Your alias is Godfrey Lisk. Mine is Ursula Graves. I'll put us down for lucky number thirteen."

"That cabin's been assigned."

"That's the crew's problem." After closing the doc, Danielle went searching for more information, when a different document opened, along with a notification pop-up window.

Lori Shannon has joined the session

"Oh, crap," Danielle said. "Lori just logged in."

"Can she see you're online?"

"Yes, but I'm cloaked behind a VPN with an IP address in Las Vegas. I'm pretty confident she got an email or text from Ozark, letting her know someone in Las Vegas had logged in."

"Don't you need to get out?" he asked.

"No, I want to see where she goes."

Adrenaline pumped through Danielle while Lori viewed the guest list. The cursor hovered on Godfrey Lisk and Ursula Graves, before she moved on.

"She might have made us," Danielle said, "though she doesn't know it's us she's made."

"We've got a lot to do if we're boarding at four this afternoon."

Danielle waited for Lori to close the documents before she got out. She had every confidence that Lori had changed her password and would be on the lookout for Godfrey and Ursula when they boarded the vessel. Despite the potential danger, she wasn't scared. She was downright determined to find Tessa before that cruise ship sailed.

Pushing away from the island, Cooper regarded her. "Ready to kick this into high gear?"

"I sure as hell am," she replied.

27

FANTASEA OASIS

COOPER

At ten past four, Cooper and Danielle, posing as Godfrey Lisk and Ursula Graves, rolled up to the Port of Baltimore in an ALPHA SUV, driven by Stryker.

"There she is," Stryker said. "Fantasea Oasis." He turned to look at them. "I got you two a bon voyage gift." Stryker handed them fake driver's licenses. "Courtesy of Lily."

"These are great," Danielle said.

On the ride to Baltimore, they'd come up with their legends. Cooper and Danielle were a married couple from Potomac who'd made their wealth in the stock market. Vague but believable.

Since Danielle hadn't found any information on dress code, Cooper had worn a dark blue suit and Danielle a black pantsuit. Their weapons were hidden beneath their suit jackets.

"Our burners and comms are hidden in my suitcase," Cooper said to Stryker.

"The team is awaiting your instructions," Stryker replied.

"Chopper ready?" Cooper asked.

"Sure is. Hawk is itching to fly that baby."

A man walked past the SUV toward the ship. He, too, wore a suit, his eyes hidden behind dark sunglasses.

"I'll text you a photo of the ship's layout," Cooper said.

"As soon as you set sail, we'll be flying five miles behind you," Stryker said.

Danielle slid on her tinted glasses. "Here we go."

Acting as their chauffeur, Stryker opened the back door for Danielle, then retrieved their rolling bags and garment bag from the cargo area. Cooper slid on his shades and exited from the back seat.

"Good luck," Stryker said.

With their suitcases in tow, Cooper and Danielle made their way toward the small-ship ocean cruiser. Based on its size, Cooper guestimated she could carry between two hundred and three hundred passengers.

Stopping short of the gangplank, Cooper said, "You ready?"

"I can't wait," Danielle replied.

As they made their way toward the crew member, Cooper surveyed the vessel. If Tessa was on that ship, he would find her. He hadn't been able to save his brother, but he was damn well going to save his niece.

The day was clear, the breeze mild, but the air was biting cold. It made no sense that the cruise ship wasn't destined for a warmer harbor, but all his questions would be answered soon enough.

The man in front of them stopped to check in. The crew member, dressed in a midnight-black suit, smiled warmly. "Welcome back, sir."

"Thank you." He handed over a packet of papers.

"Your attendant is waiting inside to escort you to your suite. Please let us know what we can do to ensure your week with us is perfect."

On a nod, the passenger proceeded up the gangplank.

"Good day, sir, ma'am," said the crew member. "Who can I welcome?"

"Godfrey Lisk and Ursula Graves." Cooper had dropped his voice to a deeper register.

The staffer tapped his tablet. "You and your companion are in suite—" He paused to read something. Cooper strained to see what was on the tablet, but couldn't. "Is this your first cruise with us?"

"Yes," Cooper replied.

"And how did you hear about us?"

"A friend."

Using the stylus, the staffer made a few notes. "Thank you, sir. We don't have any activities listed for you and your—"

"Wife," he replied. "Is that a problem?"

"Not at all. Did you receive your welcome packet?"

"I don't remember seeing it," Cooper answered. "Did you, dear?" he asked Danielle.

"I did not," she replied, her Southern accent detectable without sounding forced.

"There was a small issue with—" he paused—"you'll be in suite eighteen." He pressed a button clipped to his lapel. "A welcome packet for eighteen." Then, he gestured toward the entrance. "Your butler is waiting inside. Enjoy your stay."

"Thank you," Danielle said.

They walked up the gangplank, stepped inside the ship, and were greeted by another cheery attendant.

"Good day, Mr. Lisk, Ms. Graves." The man wore a black tuxedo with tails and a personable smile. "My name is Ben and I'll be attending to you during your stay this week."

He tucked a plain blue folder under his arm, took their rolling luggage, and headed down a narrow hallway and into a waiting elevator. They ascended to the third floor and down the hall to suite eighteen.

Once inside, he set the folder on the dresser and their luggage on the racks, before hanging the garment bag in the closet. "Do you have phones with you?"

"No," they lied.

His eyebrows jutted up. "That's a first."

"Really?" Cooper asked.

"I've never met anyone who didn't bring their phone. We have a strict no picture-taking policy." He leaned close. "For obvious reasons."

What the hell does that mean?

"We work all the time," Danielle said, her Southern lilt catching Cooper's ear. "If we have our phones, we most certainly are not on vacation."

"Excellent. We don't offer Wi-Fi to guests, which they find frustrating, at first, but by the end of the week, they appreciate the break. If you need anything, press this buzzer and I will assist you." He unzipped Danielle's luggage. "While I unpack your clothing, you're welcome to tour the ship or relax in one of our four lounges." He opened her suitcase.

Cooper was relieved she'd buried her laptop.

"I'd prefer to handle my clothes," she said.

"Yes, ma'am." He regarded Cooper. "You, as well, sir?"

"Yes."

The butler opened the plain blue folder and set two keycards on the dresser. "Being that it's your maiden voyage with us, let me help you navigate." He chuckled at his pun while pulling out a few sheets of paper. "This is the activity form. Fill it out and leave it in your room. I'll collect it during turn-down service or in the morning when I tidy your suite. If you change your mind about something or want to add activities, let me know and we'll accommodate your every desire." He winked.

"Thank you," Danielle said before she and Cooper exchanged glances.

"None of this is online?" Cooper asked. "No tablets for us to use during our stay?"

"Discretion is our priority, so we don't have an online presence." He pointed to the activity sheets. "Your names aren't on this. Just the suite number. That way your privacy stays secure."

Cooper nodded. "We appreciate that."

"I have a terrible sense of direction," Danielle lied. "Is there a map of the ship's layout in that folder?"

"That, we do have." Ben pulled one out and offered it to her.

Cooper wanted to walk the ship so he could memorize the layout. "Ben, I'm more of a hands-on kinda guy. Do we have time for a tour of the ship?"

"It would be my pleasure." Ben glanced at Danielle. "You, as well, ma'am?"

"No, thank you." She held up the map. "This is perfect."

Ben handed Cooper his keycard before opening the door. "After you, sir."

Cooper kissed Danielle on her cheek. "Be back shortly, dear."

"Good day, ma'am," Ben said before pulling the door shut behind him.

Butler Ben led Cooper down to the main deck and showed him around the ship. Everything was first class all the way, but Cooper didn't give a fuck about any of that. He was there to find his niece—assuming she was there—then, arrest this Shannon woman for kidnapping. He couldn't fucking wait to do that.

Ben pointed out the custom Brazilian hardwood flooring. Cooper acknowledged it while memorizing the ship's layout. Ben slowed in one of the lounges so Cooper could collect a drink. He declined. Cooper was paraded through the lounges, the swimming pools, saunas, and hot tubs. He was shown the game room, the theatre that seated a hundred, and the formal dining room. He brought Cooper to the top of a long, winding stairway that led down to the atrium of the ship. An internal elevator opened into that open area, as well.

"This is where the masquerade party will be held this evening," Ben explained. "I call it the party of parties."

"My helicopter will be picking us up after the cruise," Cooper said. "Where can it land?"

"There's a helipad on the bow," Ben replied.

Cooper had a lot of questions, but he didn't want to reveal how little they knew about the cruise. Less was definitely more, in this case.

"How long have you worked for the cruise line?" Cooper asked.

"This is my fifth year. It's a great company that takes excellent care of its employees." He offered a friendly smile, then started the trek back to Cooper's cabin.

As they passed a stairwell heading below deck, Cooper asked about it. "The crew's quarters," Ben replied.

"How many passengers and crew does the vessel hold?"

"We have just over two hundred on this voyage," Ben said as they returned to Cooper's suite.

Outside the cabin, Cooper pulled a crisp hundred-dollar bill from his wallet. "Thank you for your time, Ben."

"Sir, that's not necessary."

"Please, I insist."

Ben slipped the bill into his pocket. "Much appreciated."

Cooper held the keycard over the door, the light turned green, and he opened it, but didn't enter. He wanted to give Danielle a heads-up that he was back. "I'm just curious… what's the split between guests and crew?"

"We have sixty-one guests this week," Ben said. "I'll be back to escort you to dinner."

"Not necessary," Cooper replied. "I'll make sure we get to the dining room on time."

"Of course, sir."

After Ben left, Cooper entered the room, locking the door behind him.

Danielle was head-down on her laptop. Had they been on vacation, he would have pulled her into his arms and loved her, then scheduled couples' massages. But he was there to find his niece, so he ignored the sweet fantasy.

"Hey, babe," Danielle said. "What did you find out?"

"There are over two hundred on the ship, but only sixty-one passengers. That's a lot of crew. We're gonna have someone in our business, twenty-four seven."

"The guests must've paid a fortune," she said. "Wi-Fi is for crew only, but I was able to hack in without leaving a trail. I also found my way into their surveillance system. There're security cams *everywhere*, except the suites. Boy, are they watching us. What do they think we're gonna do? Steal the silverware?"

"Nice work," Cooper said before unpacking their burner phones and comms. "I'm updating the team." He called Stryker.

"What's the word?" Stryker asked.

"I toured the ship and have a good sense of the layout. Danielle got into the surveillance system."

"Any sign of Tessa?"

"No. We'll update you when we have something."

"I just texted him a picture of the ship's layout," Danielle said.

"Danielle sent you a pic," Cooper said to Stryker.

"Got it," Stryker replied.

"I'll be in touch." Cooper hung up.

He hated not being in control. Hated that he had no idea where his niece was. Was she hurt? Worse? He opened the plain blue folder to try to get an angle on what the hell was going on.

Across the top of the activity sheet, was a caption:

CELEBRATE THE MAGIC OF THE HOLIDAY SEASON, WHERE ALL YOUR WISHES REALLY DO COME TRUE.

What the fuck? They got a genie on board?

The welcome letter reiterated Ben's comments about discretion and privacy. It was signed by The Staff.

As he flipped through the packet, he couldn't find a single

person's name anywhere. "They're not just protecting us," he muttered, "they're protecting themselves."

The itinerary Danielle had found in Lori's online docs was included in the packet.

Friday
4:00-6:00pm - Boarding and Cocktails
6:30pm - Depart PoB
7:00pm - Dinner
8:00pm - Welcome & Masquerade Ball
10:00pm - Quiet Time
Saturday – Thursday, Activities and Times Announced Daily
Auction
Leather-n-Lace Party
Slumber Party
Poker Challenge
Water Fun
Movie Night
Ongoing - Quiet Time
Friday
11:00am - Return PoB

Guests could sign up for a deep-tissue massage, play racquetball on two onboard courts, or take a cooking class with the ship's award-winning chef.

Agitation slithered through him. He wanted to search every damn cabin for Tessa, but he had to force himself to be patient. When the time was right, he'd unleash his pent-up fury and take them all down.

"Good afternoon," said a male voice through the intercom. "This is your captain, speaking. On behalf of the entire crew, welcome to Fantasea Oasis. I'm happy to announce that all passengers have boarded, so we'll be departing right on schedule.

Join us in any of the lounges for a bon voyage cocktail as we sail down the Patapsco River toward the Chesapeake Bay."

Cooper shot off a text to his team. "Departing."

"Copy," Hawk replied. "Boarding the bird."

His gaze fell on Danielle. She hadn't stopped working since he'd returned to the cabin. "Babe, you doing okay?"

She met his gaze. "I wrote a program to override the surveillance system and plug in a pre-recorded loop. When we find Tessa, I'll activate it so no one on their security team will see what's happening real time. I'm assuming they're holding Tessa in a cabin or somewhere a keycard is needed, so I also wrote code that will let me override the keypad and get her out."

"You're brilliant."

"This had better work. I need your laptop so I can cloak your IP address. Then, you can activate IDware."

He handed her his laptop.

A few minutes later, she handed it back to him. Cooper activated the program, uploaded a picture of Tessa, and set the IDware on search mode. Then, he paired their comms to the program, so they'd be alerted if the software found a match.

"How can the software find her if there's no surveillance where she's being held?" Cooper asked.

"It'll search the stored video going back a week," Danielle explained.

"If the files are set to self-erase after twenty-four hours, we'll never get a match." Concern shadowed his eyes.

"Don't go there," she said.

His greatest fear was that once they hit the open ocean, Tessa would be tossed overboard. His hands curled into fists while his blood turned to ice in his veins.

He pushed off the bed, shoved his laptop into his suitcase, and stared out the sliding glass door as the ship rolled out of the harbor. If he let his thoughts wander to dark places, he wouldn't be able to control his rage, so he kicked at the demons that tore at his heels.

Appearing by his side, Danielle caressed his back. He wrapped his arm around her and she cast her eyes up at his. Then, she kissed him. "If Tessa's here, we'll find her and we'll bring her home."

"I wanna kill this Shannon woman."

"So do I." She patted his back. "We should dress for dinner."

He unzipped the garment bag. "Babe, do you want the black dress or the other black dress?"

"This is a deep purple." She pulled out the full-length black dress and laid it on the bed.

He loved having her by his side, loved that they were partners on this mission. Though she was an ALPHA trainee, he trusted her with his life. How could he not? She'd already saved him once.

As she stood before him in her bra and thong, he paused to appreciate her beauty. She was a stunning woman, but he admired her courage the most. She vanished into the bathroom while he slipped into his formalwear. In order to accommodate his Glock, he wore a shoulder holster beneath his tuxedo.

When she returned to get dressed, she was wearing a different dark wig. This updo had long bangs that rested on the frames of her tinted glasses.

"Your disguise is perfect." He placed his Glock into the holster.

She pulled the thigh holster into place before she stepped into her dress, then turned so he could zip her.

He leaned forward and pressed his lips to her warm skin, then dropped a few soft kisses on her back.

Once zipped, she tucked her sidearm into the thigh holster. "I'm ready to find Tessa."

"Boots on the ground. Let's make it happen."

DANIELLE

Even the tense situation couldn't stop Danielle from admiring her man. Cooper in a tux sent a frisson of excitement through her. His broad shoulders and wide chest filled that tailored jacket to perfection. The anger that fueled him turned his eyes black with fury, but it was the confidence he wore like a second skin that she appreciated the most.

"Let's do a little hunting before dinner," she said. "Can you show me where the crew sleeps?"

"We'll take the elevator."

Hand in hand, they moseyed down the hallway. "Cameras everywhere," he whispered.

"I see them," she replied before they came to a stop at the elevator bank.

Another couple was waiting. "First time here?" asked the man.

"Yes," Cooper said, deepening his voice. "You?"

"Our second," said the woman. "It's a vacation you'll never forget."

The man mimicked his head exploding. "Mind blowing," he said and laughed.

The elevator doors slid open.

"Oops, I forgot something," Danielle said while peering into her evening bag.

"See you at dinner," the woman said before the couple entered the waiting cab and the doors closed. After the cab descended, Danielle tapped the button again.

A different elevator stopped on their floor, the doors opened, and they stepped inside. He tapped the button to the lower level. As they descended, Cooper's intensity rolled off him like a quarterback in the Super Bowl, but this was no game they were playing. This was a mission to save his niece's life.

The elevator doors opened and they stepped into a deserted

hallway. It was identical to the ones upstairs, except the cabin doors were much closer together.

"They're really packing them in down here," Danielle whispered before they sauntered toward the other end.

Midway down, a cabin door opened. The young woman startled, then quickly pulled the door shut behind her. "Hello."

"Good evening," Danielle said.

"No walk here," the woman replied.

Broken English and an accent.

"We got a little lost," Danielle added.

"I take."

She escorted them back to the elevators. "Up." She tapped the button. "Big, open room. You go."

"I love your accent," Danielle said. "Where are you from?"

The woman hesitated. "Russia."

The elevator doors opened and they stepped inside. Danielle turned and eyed her as the doors slid closed.

She and Cooper stood like statues, not uttering a damn word.

Back on the main level, they moseyed through the atrium, continuing on to the formal dining room. As they passed one of the lounges she spotted Lori, dressed in a bright red gown, speaking quietly to a man who stood with his back to them. "Lori's here," Danielle whispered.

"Got it," Cooper replied.

As soon as they entered the formal dining room, they were greeted by a male attendant. "Good evening. Your suite, please?"

"Eighteen," Cooper replied.

En route to a table, Danielle checked out their surroundings. Two, four, and six-person tables filled the expansive space. Dazzling crystal chandeliers hung from a gold-embossed ceiling, bathing the room in an amber glow. Elegant flower arrangements adorned each linen-covered table. Peppered in amongst a sea of tuxedos were the smattering of female guests in evening gowns that popped with color.

While the attendant pulled out Danielle's chair at their two-top, she asked, "Why aren't we sitting with a group?"

"Do you know anyone here?" he asked.

"Not yet," she replied.

The employee offered a polite smile. "When you do, tell your butler, and we'll seat you together." He handed them small menus, made a few suggestions, and left.

Despite not having eaten since breakfast, Danielle was too keyed up to even think about food. "I can't stomach anything."

"Order something so we blend in." Cooper scanned the menu. "What about the salmon?"

"That's fine."

After the server took their order, Cooper laid his hand, palm up, on the table. She placed hers in his. "Relax," he said. "We got this."

"No, we don't. We definitely don't."

She was glancing around the room, hoping to spot Tessa, though her expectations were low.

"Look at me," he said.

When she did, the intensity in his gaze sent a burst of adrenaline buzzing through her. "We do have this," he murmured. "We've got each other's back and we're playing this right. Trust me."

The heaviness in her chest lifted. "I absolutely trust you. Do you trust me?"

"With my life."

That made her smile. "Thank you."

Danielle hated doing nothing while Tessa could be held captive. Their entrees were delivered, their water goblets filled. Cooper sliced into the chicken. Danielle forced herself to take a bite of salmon.

Movement had her glancing over Cooper's shoulder. "Lori's making the rounds," Danielle murmured.

"Can you leave?" he asked.

"Too late. I won't say much."

Lori Shannon stopped at their table and smiled down at them. "Welcome to Fantasea Oasis. How are we doing this evening?"

"Very well," Cooper replied, setting down his fork.

"I'm Shannon, the cruise director." She offered Danielle a pleasant smile, then glanced at her mostly uneaten meal. "Is your salmon unacceptable?"

"It's delicious," Danielle said, hoping her fake accent wasn't coming across that way. "I've always been a slow eater."

Lori nodded. "That's very healthy. I wanted to see if we could get you set up for some activities while you're here. Unless you're just interested in Quiet Time."

There's that Quiet Time, again.

"What do you recommend?" Cooper asked.

"That depends on you," Lori replied. "What's your poison?"

Cooper flicked his gaze to Danielle. "My wife," he replied, then winked at Lori.

Lori offered a polite chortle before dropping her hand onto Cooper's shoulder. "Great answer. Do you need masquerade masks for the party?"

"We have them," Cooper replied.

"The party starts soon. Don't be late." Lori cemented her gaze on Danielle. "I used to know someone who wore tinted glasses, only his were blue."

"Small world," Danielle replied.

When Lori continued on to the next table, Danielle's stomach churned. "Let's head back to the room."

They said nothing on the way back to their suite. Though Danielle had programmed the software to notify them with Tessa's location, Danielle confirmed they were both running. Concern sent a shiver racing through her. It was almost eight at night and the dark waters of the bay were frigid cold.

They slipped their comms into their ears.

"How long until we're past the bay and into the ocean?" she asked.

"A few more hours." He placed his strong hands on her shoulders, kissed her forehead. "Don't go there."

She forced a smile before breaking away to retrieve their black masquerade masks from her luggage. Before putting on the mask, she tucked her tinted glasses away. "I can't wear the glasses with the mask."

"The dark wig and contacts disguise you." After they'd pulled on their masks, he opened the suite door. "We got this."

"Yes, we do," Danielle replied as she breezed past him.

As they made their way to the atrium, she wanted to believe him, but they had absolutely no idea what they were walking into.

28

SAVING TESSA

COOPER

While guests waited in the atrium, smiling crew members offered bubbly champagne in crystal flutes. Jazzy music floated around them while murmurs of conversations filled the air. The energy in the air had shifted, the feeling of anticipation floating through the crowd.

Even the employees wore black masquerade masks, but some of the guests stood out with ornate face coverings that included a gold roman mask with feathers, a few metal masks, and a handful of devil masks.

"Here they come," someone blurted.

Cooper swept his gaze up the winding marble staircase, and across the upper level as far as he could see. That's when he spotted Lori, in her bright red dress, leading what appeared to be an army of women toward the stairs. They followed in pairs, all wearing evening gowns and masquerade masks.

"Here we go," he said.

Danielle followed his gaze and gasped. "What. Is. That?"

Lori, wearing an ornate mask with a plume of feathers,

stopped midway down. A dutiful attendant hurried up and handed her a mic.

With an exuberant smile, she regarded the audience. "Welcome, welcome, to the place where all your dreams really do come true."

While she bowed, the guests applauded. Cooper glanced around, not fully comprehending what the hell was happening.

"We have a stunning variety for you this week, so use the next couple of hours to meet and mingle. It's your time to—as I like to say—fill your dance card."

A polite laugh cascaded through the space.

Lori addressed the line of women behind her. "Ladies, please, join me."

In what looked to be a choreographed performance, an orchestral selection of music floated through the atrium while masked women of all shapes, sizes, and colors paraded down the stairs. With hair styled to perfection and lips glistening with gloss, their plastic smiles stretched their lips wide as they formed a horseshoe around Lori. The music grew to a crescendo that ended when the last woman stepped into place.

The silence hung for an extra beat while Cooper scanned for Tessa. He didn't see her. A sinking feeling filled him with dread. If his niece wasn't there, then where was she?

"At long last, your wait is over," Lori announced. "I present your entertainment for the week."

Entertainment?

He and Danielle exchanged glances as the audience broke into enthusiastic applause.

As the bizarre scene unfolded, Cooper absorbed the full weight of the situation. These women were here to sexually entertain the guests. His expression didn't change, neither did his pulse, but the anger that bubbled just below the surface escaped in a dark, menacing growl.

"Are these women lovely or what?" Lori asked.

Another round of applause erupted as Danielle slid her hand around his forearm and squeezed. Then, she leaned up and whispered, "I don't see Tessa. Do you?"

He peered into her eyes. "She's not here."

"Is Lori running a brothel?" Danielle whispered.

"This. Is. Fucked. Up."

"Friends," Lori said, crashing in on their hushed conversation, "it's my extreme pleasure to introduce you to the mastermind behind Fantasea Oasis. My friend, mentor, and partner in crime…" With a dramatic sweep of her arm, she gestured across the atrium. "Please welcome, G.E.!"

Everyone turned as the glass elevator slowly descended from the top floor. The man stood with his back to the glass, dressed in a black cape and black dress pants.

What the fucking fuck?

The elevator doors opened and the sole occupant backed out, then swirled around, arms extended so his cape expanded like the wings of an eagle.

Cooper's muscles turned to steel. Even in the black mask, there was ho hiding the fact that the man was his mentor and godfather, Geoffrey Edelman.

No fucking way.

Cooper stilled while the weight of the situation pressed heavily on his shoulders. He'd stepped into a nightmare he wasn't prepared for.

Loud cheering and heavy applause smacked Cooper out of his daze.

Geoffrey stepped onto a small makeshift stage and an employee handed him a mic.

"Hello, dear friends," Geoffrey began. "Welcome back to our regulars and welcome aboard to our *virgin* cruisers." He grinned while laughter floated through the atrium. "Kink is my true passion and my joy is sharing it with you. I love that you're escaping reality with us to explore your own carnal lusts for one unforgettable week. But… I would be remiss if I didn't show my profound gratitude to Shannon." He peered across the room. "Join me, my dear."

The crowd parted like the Red Sea as an affected Lori Shannon half walked, half waltzed across the room with a dramatic flourish. She stepped onto the small stage and the two hugged.

Cooper swallowed down the bitter bile.

"Shannon works tirelessly to find the perfect mix of lovely ladies to join us on our cruises. We can boast ninety-eight of the most beautiful, sexiest, and talented women that we've ever had. Yes, we've got our reliable regulars, but there is a plethora of new additions to make all your wildest dreams come true." His smile fell away as he gazed out. "Before we move on to the meet-and-greet—which I know you're very excited about—I'd like to take a moment to mention the passing of one of my dearest friends. He was such a big part of Fantasea Oasis, and his shoes will never be filled. Over the years, he introduced us to so many Russian beauties. Let's share a moment of silence to pay our respects to a great man, Ivan Salimov."

Cooper's blood turned to ice.

This cannot be happening.

But it was happening. And it was a fucking nightmare.

"Thank you." Geoffrey fastened on a grin. "Now, on to the fun. The women are wearing name tags. The crew will pass out good old-fashioned paper and pen so you can make notes. There's no limit to the number of women you can enjoy during your stay. As I like to say, it's an all-you-can-eat buffet, so let's chow down!" He threw back his head and cackled. "We've got some additional activities this year, like the strip poker challenge and the small group parties. Shannon and I take your feedback to heart. We want you to explore your kink and do whatever the hell you want. On the open waters, anything goes. As we know from past cruises, Quiet Time is anything but."

More laughter floated through the open space.

"Ladies, it's time to mingle." Geoffrey set down the mic before he and Lori stepped off the stage and launched into the crowd.

Fighting against the urge to wrap his hands around Geoffrey's neck and choke the fucking last breath out of him, Cooper needed to ensure Geoffrey didn't see him and Danielle. When he turned to her, a jolt of electricity charged through him. Danielle wasn't there. He looked around. No Danielle. She'd been clutching his arm one minute, the next she was gone. What the hell was happening?

He covered his mouth. "Danielle, where are you?"

DANIELLE

Danielle had gotten an alert that the IDware had located Tessa, so she slipped away to find her.

When Cooper's godfather had revealed himself, Cooper's entire body had tensed. A growl so deep had rumbled out of him that the man in front of them had turned around, but Cooper was too locked on Geoffrey to notice.

Despite her whispering in his ear, "Tessa's here," she wasn't able to snap him out of his trance. She hoped her abrupt departure went unnoticed by their perverted hosts.

Are Geoffrey and Lori running a brothel or are the women being trafficked? A chill skirted through her. Either way, the situation was bad.

On the way to their suite, she covered her mouth to ensure the surveillance cameras wouldn't pick up her voice. "Cooper, are you there?"

Silence.

"Cooper, IDware found Tessa."

She hurried into an elevator and up to their floor. To her relief, the hallway was deserted. Inside their cabin, she bolted the door and unearthed both their laptops from their locked luggage.

Everything felt like it was happening all at once and in slow motion. Despite her desire to hurry, she couldn't rush the next steps or she'd blow their chance at rescuing Tessa.

First, Danielle jumped onto Cooper's laptop, opened the IDware software, and keyed in on the flashing blip. After enlarging it, she could see that Tessa was in cabin twenty-seven, at the end of the hall on the lower level. Then, she reprogrammed her keypad, giving her access to that room.

Next, using her laptop, she needed to hack into the ship's surveillance system, deactivate it, then insert the loop she'd recorded from earlier. Her fingers were flying over the keyboard as she worked to get it done.

Then, she stilled and sat up straight. Rushing would guarantee a careless mistake. If the security team realized they weren't watching live feed, they'd find her in seconds.

I got this.

Refocusing her efforts, she reviewed what she'd done, added in the code to include the old footage, and watched as the system went dark for a millisecond, then came back online.

After returning their laptops back to their suitcases, she grabbed her keycard and left the suite.

As she walked with purpose down the hallway, she opted to take the stairs to avoid running into anyone in the elevator.

"Cooper, are you there?" she whispered.

"Where are you?" he asked, his voice urgent.

"We got a hit on Tessa."

She pushed open the fire door at the end of the hallway and flew down the stairs, passing one level after the next. Before exiting on the lower level, she said, "Cooper?"

Silence.

She tapped the comm. "Power, ninety percent."

She opened the door to the lower level and peered down the

hallway. The dim lighting, paired with the silence, sent a shiver through her.

"Cooper, are you there?"

No response.

As she headed down the hall, she didn't know if the comm wasn't working because she was below deck, they were too far away from each other, or because someone had rendered him unconscious.

A wave of fear hit her in the chest, but she had to push forward. Their goal was to find Tessa and she was so close to doing that. Glancing at cabin numbers, she stopped in front of twenty-seven. She swiped her keycard, the light turned green, and she slowly opened the door.

Tessa was gagged and strapped to the bed, her wrists and ankles bound together. Her skin was sallow, her hair mussed, but the fear in her eyes ripped through Danielle. She hurried over, and knelt.

"Tessa, it's Danielle," she whispered as she removed the gag.

"Oh, thank God," Tessa murmured.

"Are you hurt?"

"I'm scared, but okay."

"I got you, and Cooper's here, too." Danielle started untying Tessa's wrists, bound together with black cloth rope.

"BDSM rope," Tessa whispered.

Danielle struggled to untie the first knot. Once it loosened, she hurried to free her wrists, then moved to her ankles.

"Did Lori do this to you?" Danielle asked.

"Yes," Tessa replied. "She's so evil."

Danielle untied her ankles, then reached under the bed to unhook the strap that held Tessa in place. "Hang in there, Tessa. I'm gonna get you out of here."

"Like hell you are," said a voice behind her.

As Danielle turned, she was struck in the side. "Aiiieeeeeee!" Pain shot through her like an explosive wildfire and she fell back onto the floor while pangs of electric heat incapacitated her.

COOPER

Cooper heard Danielle say she'd located Tessa, then the comm cut out. His battery was at full capacity, so he concluded that she'd gone to the lower level where the signal was weaker. He didn't want to run from the atrium, so as the masked ladies moved in to mingle, he started walking in the opposite direction.

Nothing like a six-foot-two man *leaving* a room filled with women to draw attention to himself.

His mind was still spinning from what he'd learned, but he'd deal with his asshole godfather later. He was on the fringe of the group when a hand clamped down on his shoulder.

Turning, he stared into Geoffrey's soulless eyes. As Geoffrey pulled him in for a bear hug, Cooper wanted to vomit. After a brief slap on Geoffrey's back, he separated. To his complete disgust, Geoffrey had tears in his eyes.

"This is such a wonderful surprise," Geoffrey said. "I had no idea you were into the Lifestyle."

Cooper forced a smile through gritted teeth. "Likewise, G.E."

"Are you here, alone?"

Cooper leaned close and whispered, "I brought a kink companion."

Geoffrey beamed. "Wonderful. Is it that stunning blonde, Danielle, from Thanksgiving?"

"No, and I'd appreciate you keeping this our little secret. What she doesn't know won't hurt her. My kink partner is a brunette with a wild streak."

Geoffrey slapped Cooper on the back. "I couldn't be happier. This is like a dream come true for me."

And an absolute fucking nightmare for me.

Cooper needed to leave, but he had to play this chill. "Why is that?"

"We have even more in common than I ever realized."

I've been hunting monsters like you my entire career.

"Let me find you our best lady," Geoffrey continued.

"That's going to be impossible," Cooper forced himself to say. "They're all so lovely."

"It's definitely our best crop yet."

What the hell? He called these women crops. "Where are they harvested?" Cooper asked with a chuckle.

When Geoffrey stopped laughing, he said, "America, Russia, South America. Who the hell knows, anymore? Shannon manages the women. Let me introduce you to her."

"Unfortunately, I have to excuse myself for a quick minute. My partner had a little motion sickness and is resting in our suite—which, by the way, is absolutely phenomenal—and I want to check on her."

Geoffrey's proud smile fell away. "Let me come with and we can call for a nurse if she's not well."

"Discretion is what you do best. She would be humiliated if you came to our room."

Geoffrey nodded. "I understand." He placed his hand on Cooper's back. "Ask for me when you return and I'll set you up for the entire cruise. Nothing but the best for my son."

Cooper pulled him in for a hug while hatred filled his heart. "I appreciate that."

He broke away and took off toward the elevator, his long strides eating up the shiny marble flooring.

"Danielle, you there?"

She didn't reply.

Not wanting to wait for the elevator, he took the stairs, three at a time, then strode down the hallway and into his suite.

No Danielle. He opened his laptop and logged in to the

program. The blip was coming from cabin twenty-seven, lower level. He shoved his burner into his pocket and took off down the hallway.

Though he assumed she'd turned off the surveillance system, he covered his mouth with his hand. "Danielle, can you hear me? I'm on my way."

DANIELLE

Danielle was sitting on the floor of the cabin, staring up the barrel of a gun, while Lori Shannon glowered over her. She should never have taken off without Cooper, but she had tunnel vision when it came to Tessa. Now, they were both going to die.

Except… she wasn't tied up. If she could somehow distract Lori, she could disarm her and take her to the floor.

Lori ripped off her own masquerade mask and threw it down. "My security team told me cabin twenty-seven had been breached. Who the fuck are you and how did you get into this room?"

Danielle remained silent.

"You're gonna answer me or I'll beat it out of you. You think being tased was a bitch, that's nothing compared to my right hook."

Danielle should have been scared, but she wasn't. She was laser focused on getting that gun out of Lori's hand.

Lori yanked Danielle's mask off, pulling the wig halfway off with it. Realization flashed in her eyes as she tore off the wig, exposing Danielle's blonde hair, tied in a ponytail and pinned down.

"I cannot fucking believe it!" Lori blurted. "What the hell are you doing here?"

Isn't it obvious, bitch?

Refusing to answer, Danielle said nothing.

"I'll ask you one last time. What are you doing on my ship?"

"Bringing Tessa home," Danielle replied matter-of-factly.

Lori laughed. "I don't think so. I'm the one holding the gun."

"For now," Danielle replied.

"You and your nosy little friend, here—" she pointed the gun at Tessa— "are up in my business and you have got to go. My guests paid a fortune for a perfect fantasy cruise and you won't stop me from giving it to them."

"It's over, Lori," Danielle said. "Your floating brothel is finished, and so are you."

"It's not a brothel," Tessa interjected. "She and Geoffrey are trafficking these women."

Lori's sinister smile sickened Danielle. "The shelters provide the perfect way to lure unsuspecting women—women down on their luck, women who need a fresh start. The majority of them get that, but a few choice ones get a whole lot more. They get to live here, in the lap of luxury, and create the perfect fantasy week for our guests. I never had anyone question where some of the women went... until Tessa." Lori glared at Tessa. "You asked so many fucking questions about Val, I wanted to slit your goddamn throat."

"You're insane," Danielle growled.

"No one will ever know about Washington's best-kept secret because you two are about to get tossed overboard. You won't last ten minutes in the frigid water."

Danielle glared at Lori. "You. Won't. Win."

Lori knelt down and narrowed her eyes. "Yes, I wi—"

Danielle leapt at her, grabbed the gun, and pushed to her feet, taking Lori with her.

"Noooo!" Lori screamed, yanking on the weapon.

Danielle struggled to keep a firm grasp on the gun. Lori pulled her in and bit her hand. Danielle spun away and delivered a kick that knocked Lori backward against the wall.

BANG!
Lori had pulled the trigger.
"*Aaiiiiiieeeee!*" screamed Tessa.

COOPER

Hearing the gunshot and the scream, Cooper broke into a full-on sprint and flew into the cabin. Lori was pointing a gun at Danielle and Tessa was tied to the bed. All three whipped their heads in his direction.

"Drop it!" he roared.

Lori didn't.

BANG! BANG! BANG!

Lori stared at him for a split-second before she collapsed, blood pouring from her chest. He'd hit her in the forehead and twice in the chest.

Danielle hurried over to Tessa. "Were you hit?"

"No," Tessa replied.

"Danielle, were you hit?" Cooper asked.

"No," Danielle replied as she unstrapped Tessa from the bed.

Tessa threw her arms around Danielle. "Thank you for rescuing me. I knew if I called Uncle Cooper, he'd find me."

Cooper unearthed his phone, made the call.

"Go," Stryker answered.

"We've got Tessa," Cooper said. "Ship appears to be a floating brothel."

"It's way worse," Danielle said. "Lori and Geoffrey are trafficking these women."

"Sex trafficking," Cooper said to Stryker. "We need to take command of the vessel. How far out are you?"

"Two minutes," Stryker replied. "Where's the helipad?"

"On the bow. I'll meet you on deck and bring you in." Cooper shoved the phone into his pocket and flicked his gaze to Danielle. "We gotta go. Watch for security."

"Tessa, can you walk?" Cooper asked.

"Yes," she replied.

"Danielle, you've got Tessa," Cooper said. "Here's the plan."

Within a minute, they were ready to move out.

Danielle pulled her weapon from her thigh holster. Cooper cleared the hallway, then led them up the stairs. The fastest way to the bow was through the atrium, but he couldn't risk Geoffrey seeing them.

As he led them around the atrium on the upper level, they passed a masked male passenger making out with one of the women. Cooper wanted to deck the son of a bitch, but he had to stick to their plan.

"Coop, can you hear me?" Stryker said through the comm.

"Loud and clear," Cooper replied.

"We just touched down. Get us the hell inside."

29

WHERE'S GEOFFREY?

COOPER

Cooper shoved open the fire door and was hit with a blast of freezing air. His team rushed inside, dressed in SWAT gear, weapons in hand.

"Damn, it's good to see you guys," Cooper said.

Emerson handed him and Danielle Kevlar vests.

"The captain and his crew saw us," Jericho said. "Kinda hard to miss a chopper landing on the bow's helipad."

"Stryker and Hawk, you're with me," Cooper said. "Danielle will take Jericho, Emerson, Herrera, and Slash to the atrium. When the captain makes his announcement, separate the guests, the women, and the crew into three separate groups. Questions?"

"What's our cover?" Slash asked.

"FBI, undercover," Cooper replied. "We good?"

They were.

"Let's move out," he commanded.

Danielle clasped Tessa's hand before taking off toward the atrium, her team in close pursuit. Cooper headed toward the upper level with Stryker and Hawk, stopping in front of the security office. As Cooper expected, the door was locked.

BAM-BAM-BAM. "FBI, open up!" Cooper yelled as they aimed their weapons.

The door opened.

"On the floor, face down," Cooper hollered.

Stryker and Hawk secured both men with zip ties while Cooper stood guard outside.

"What's going on?" asked one of the security officers.

"I think you know," Cooper replied.

"Ah, shit," said the other.

"I got this," Stryker said, sitting behind the console.

Cooper and Hawk took off for the bridge. Another locked door.

BAM-BAM-BAM. "FBI, open up!" Cooper yelled.

The co-captain opened the door. "Good grief, what's going on?"

Hawk flashed his FBI badge as they entered the spacious room, lit by the massive console spanning the entire front of the bridge.

"Stop the ship," Cooper barked.

"I can't do that without Mr. Edelman's approval," said the captain.

Cooper got in his face. "Are you in the business of human trafficking, Captain?"

"What? Of course not."

"Then, stop the vessel," Cooper bit out.

The captain's shoulders sank. "Understood."

"Good choice," Cooper said. "This ship is returning to port."

"It's gonna take some maneuvering to turn her around," the captain replied.

Cooper glared at him. "Then, you better get started."

After the captain gave his crew their orders, Hawk snatched the marine radio and contacted the Coast Guard.

"Make an announcement," Cooper said to the captain. "Tell the passengers to return to the atrium immediately and to comply with the FBI on board."

The captain picked up a different hand mic off the console. "Good evening, this is the captain speaking. All guests, please return to the atrium. The FBI has boarded our ship. Return to the atrium and comply with law enforcement."

Cooper stepped away from the console. "Danielle, update me."

"Emerson, Jericho, and I are in the atrium," she said. "We're separating the guests, the women, and the crew, and making everyone sit down. Geoffrey's not here, so I showed the team a pic of him. I've got Slash and Herrera checking the cabins."

"How's Tessa?" he asked.

"She found Val and they're sitting on the floor beside me."

"Herrera," Cooper said. "Any sign of Geoffrey?"

"Negative," Herrera replied. "Our search has turned up a few couples in suites. Slash has been escorting them back to the atrium."

"Let me know if you find Geoffrey."

Cooper walked back over to Hawk who was giving the Coast Guard operator the ship's coordinates.

"How long?" Hawk asked.

"Closest cutter is seven to ten minutes away," said the operator.

Cooper unearthed his burner and dialed.

"FBI, what's your emergency?"

"Cooper Grant, Special Agent."

"Yes, sir, what's your emergency?"

"My team and I have taken command of a small ship in the Chesapeake Bay that's trafficking women."

"Has the Coast Guard been called?" asked the operator.

"Yes. They're seven to ten minutes out. We're gonna need—"

"Coop," Stryker said through the comm. "Starboard side. We got a rabbit."

Cooper flicked his gaze outside and spotted a lifeboat moving up the river. *Geoffrey*.

"I've got a runner in a lifeboat," Cooper said to the FBI operator. "The captain is turning the vessel and will be returning to the Port of Baltimore. I need a team waiting when we dock."

"How many on board?" asked the operator.

"Over two hundred."

"Is this the best number to reach you on?" asked the operator.

"Yes, but I'm about to chase down the runner, so if you need to reach us, call agent Emerson Easton." He rattled off Emerson's number and hung up.

"Team," Cooper said after tapping his comm. "Hawk and I are going after Geoffrey. Jericho, I need you on the chopper. Emerson, on the bridge."

"On my way," Emerson replied.

"Copy," Jericho added.

While waiting for Emerson, Cooper and Hawk watched as the twenty-six-foot skiff motored toward land.

A moment later, Emerson said through the comm, "I'm here."

Hawk opened the door and Emerson stepped onto the bridge.

"Coast Guard is six to nine minutes out," Hawk said.

"FBI has been called. If I can't answer, they're calling you," Cooper said. "The captain has halted the ship and is in the process of turning it around. You good?"

With her gun in hand, Emerson eyed the men. "I got this."

He and Hawk exited the warmth of the ship to face the bitter cold bay. The wind smacked Cooper's cheeks as they made their way to the helipad. Hawk jumped into the pilot's seat, Cooper opened the door to the craft and hopped inside. While Hawk fired up the chopper, Cooper pulled on a black knit cap and black gloves, then strapped himself in as Jericho joined them.

Cooper flipped the comm to a closed channel for him, Jericho, and Hawk.

"Yo, bro, this is some fucked up cruise," Jericho said after he closed the chopper door.

"Geoffrey's a monster," Cooper said, the anger coursing through him. "I just wanna kill him."

"Pump him full of bullets and throw him overboard," Jericho said while strapping himself in. "We can add it to all the other secrets we keep."

"He needs to pay for his crimes," Cooper said. "The devil can't have him, yet."

"Here we go, boys," Hawk said as the chopper lifted off the helipad, then headed in the direction of the lifeboat.

"He knows we're coming and he's zig zagging." Hawk chuckled. "He is one scared rabbit."

"If he jumps, you cannot—*cannot*—go after him," Jericho said to Cooper.

"He's right, Coop, no diving into that frigid water," Hawk said.

"No fucking way," Cooper said before sliding open the helicopter door. "I'm not going down with him."

"We're in position," Hawk said. "You got this."

Cooper threw out the rope, grabbed it with both hands and watched as Geoffrey drove the boat toward the right, then toward the left. He rappelled down, but had to hold until he was over the back of the craft.

As the boat zagged by, Cooper dropped into the back of the open skiff and pulled his Glock.

Geoffrey turned toward him, panic flashing in his eyes. "I… I, I can explain."

"Shut the hell up!" Cooper roared. "Throttle down to neutral!" Geoffrey slowed the boat's engines. "Face down, over here." Cooper pointed to the open area at the stern. "You try to pull a fast one, I'll kill you. Do you understand?"

Geoffrey nodded several times before dropping face down onto the floor of the boat.

"Hands behind your back."

Cooper shoved his Glock into his pocket, then zip-tied Geoffrey's wrists together. He expected a full-on, drag-out fight, but Geoffrey didn't resist. Next, Cooper zip-tied his ankles, then patted him down. After finding no weapon, he cut the engine and tapped the comm.

"Secured," he said to his guys before pulling Geoffrey to his feet and shoving him onto a seat.

"Ready for the basket?" Jericho asked.

"I need a minute," Cooper replied.

Cooper glared at Geoffrey. "I thought I knew you."

"You do, but now you know me better," Geoffrey replied. "There are some desires that can't be denied."

"You're no better than Salimov. He raped my sister and you kidnapped my niece."

Geoffrey furrowed his brows, then shook his head. "What are you talking about? Tessa's not here."

"She's been held on the ship for days."

"Oh, God. Lori must've done that. She was in charge of the entertainment."

"You mean, the crops?"

"They were a means to an end."

Cooper glared at him, hatred pouring from the depths of his soul. "You. Disgust. Me."

Geoffrey said nothing.

It took all of Cooper's self-control not to choke the life out of him with his bare hands, then toss him overboard.

"Geoffrey Edelman, you're under arrest for human trafficking."

After Cooper Mirandized him, Geoffrey said, "I thought I knew you too."

"You do. Once a lawman, always a lawman." Cooper tapped the comm. "Let's get this scumbag the hell outta here."

30

SO HAPPY TOGETHER

DANIELLE

It was three in the morning when Fantasea Oasis pulled into port. Over twenty agents rushed into the atrium, but waited until Cooper spoke with the one in charge. When a subdued and zip-tied Geoffrey was handed over, the women sitting on the marble floor erupted in applause.

"Rot in hell, Geoffrey," yelled one of the women.

"Die in prison," yelled another.

Many had tears streaming down their cheeks, while some were hugging each other as he was led away.

It was a powerful moment that had Danielle silently vowing to continue her fight against violence and other atrocities against women.

After Geoffrey was led away, the agents moved into action. They secured the passengers' wrists with zip ties and led them off the ship to another hearty round of applause.

Cooper approached his team. "Geoffrey and the cruise-ship guests were arrested for suspected sex trafficking. When the agents come back, the women and crew will be questioned."

When it was time for Tessa and Val to be questioned, Tessa grasped Danielle's hand. "Please don't leave us."

"I won't," Danielle replied.

As they walked with the female agent to a table in a nearby lounge, the agent asked Danielle her name. "Ursula Jones. I'm sorry, I don't have my badge on me."

"It's okay. I can look you up."

Danielle waited while the agent plugged in her name. A moment later, the agent said, "Gotcha."

The agent turned to Val. "You okay going first?"

Val nodded.

"How did you end up on this ship?"

"I'd been a resident of Shannon's Shelters for two months when Lori Shannon, the Executive Director, told me she had a great job opportunity for me on a luxury cruise ship. The pay was sensational but I couldn't tell any of the other residents because they'd be jealous."

When Val hugged herself, Danielle offered her an encouraging smile.

"She took me to a house in Great Falls and left me in a jail cell for a day," Val continued. "That was terrifying. When she came back, she drove me to this ship, which was docked here. It was dark and I was scared when I came on board. I was brought to a room on the lower level, where she told me I'd be working a cruise that would be out to sea for a week. One of the women told me that I'd be giving the men massages, but later, someone else said I'd have to have sex with them." Val's eyes filled with tears. "I'm so grateful my friend Tessa never gave up looking for me."

"Were you assaulted?" asked the agent.

"No, but I would have been if the agents hadn't shown up," Val said.

After the agent finished questioning Val, she turned to Tessa. "What brought you here?"

"I work at the shelter," Tessa explained, "and when Val left without saying goodbye, I knew something was wrong. I asked Lori Shannon what happened to her and she told me that sometimes people just left, but I knew Val wouldn't do that. I searched the files and learned that other residents had also disappeared. Lori asked me to come in one night, and when I did, she attacked me, gagged me, tied me up, and drove me to the ship. She told me that she couldn't put me to work because I was like family to Geoffrey, so she was going to throw me overboard when we got to the ocean. I was able to steal a phone from one of the crew. I called my uncle, who used to work for the FBI." Tessa smiled. "Except, he never really stopped. I think he's undercover, now."

"Thank you," said the agent. "Were you sexually assaulted?"

"No."

After a few more questions, both women were told they were free to leave.

Once outside the lounge, Tessa threw her arms around Danielle. "Thank you for saving us. You're my heroine. You're the bravest woman I've ever known."

Cooper strode into view and Danielle's heart took off in her chest. After this mission, she admired him even more. He'd stayed in control, led the team through their stressful ordeal, and saved both her and Tessa's life.

She was going to love this man for a long, long time.

COOPER

"There you are," Cooper said. "How's everyone doing?"

"They did a great job with the agent interview," Danielle replied.

"Uncle Cooper, I thought you left the FBI," Tessa said.

"Well, now you know the truth," Cooper said, "but neither of you can tell anyone the names of the agents who were here, including Danielle and me. Is that clear?"

"I'm so grateful," Val said. "You have my solemn promise."

Tessa hugged him. "I love you Uncle Cooper and I'll keep your secret forever."

He kissed her forehead, then broke away. "If either of you need to talk to a professional about what you've been through, we'll find someone you're comfortable talking to, okay?"

They nodded.

"No worries about the money," he said. "Val, where are you staying?"

"I'm moving in with Tessa," she said with a smile.

"That's great," Cooper replied.

"We've got to grab our things from the suite," Danielle said.

"Already taken care of," Cooper replied.

"Thank you. Tessa and Val were cleared to leave."

"Then, let's get the hell off this floating nightmare."

It was six in the morning when he ushered them out to the front of the ship and over to the waiting helicopter. They climbed in to find the team waiting. Tessa sat next to Jericho and smiled up at him.

"I should be surprised to see you, but I'm kinda not," Tessa said with a smile.

"Hey, Tessa. I'd ask if you've been staying out of trouble, but I already know the answer to that," Jericho replied with a wry smile. "Strap yourself in."

Cooper pulled the door closed. After buckling up, he tapped the comm. "We're all here, Hawk," he said. "Take us home."

Hawk fired up the chopper and they lifted into the sky. Cooper glanced out the window as the ship grew smaller and smaller, before he cast his eyes on the horizon and the start of a new day.

Then, his gaze fell on Danielle and his entire future fell into place. They shared a loving smile as the chopper sliced through the early morning sky and back to a life he cherished and loved.

Two hours later, Cooper parked his Jeep in the driveway of his parents' house, and all four traipsed up the walkway. The second he opened the front door, his mom rushed into the foyer and pulled Tessa into her arms.

"We've been so worried about you." She kissed her granddaughter's cheek, then stepped back to study her. "Are you okay? Are you hurt?"

"I was scared, but I'm better now," Tessa said. "Uncle Cooper and Danielle were so, so brave. It was the coolest thing I've ever seen, but I was so freaked when it was happening."

Tessa broke away and hugged her grandfather as Chantal hurried into the foyer.

"I'm so relieved to see you," Chantal said as the two hugged.

"This is my friend, Val," Tessa said, introducing her friend to her family.

"Can I hug you?" Emily asked Val.

"I would love that," Val replied before Emily folded her into a warm embrace.

While Cooper hugged his dad, his dad whispered, "Thank you, son."

Pride filled his heart.

Then, his mom hugged Danielle. "I heard you rescued our girl."

"That was the plan, but it went a little south," Danielle replied. "Fortunately, you've got an amazing son who saved us both."

"We're grateful you both got there in time," Cooper's dad said.

They moved into the kitchen where they ate breakfast together. As Cooper glanced around the table, relief had him biting back the emotion. Things could have gone so differently. They could have lost Tessa, and he could have lost Danielle.

But I didn't lose either one of them. They're here and they're safe.

He did for them what he couldn't do for his brother. For the first time in twenty years, the grief and anger stood down a little. Across the table, Danielle caught his eye. As they shared a smile, he was certain he'd be spending the rest of his life with this amazing, brilliant woman who ran *toward* danger, even if it meant risking her own life.

After stomachs had been filled, and the dishes had been cleared, Cooper had to tell his family about Geoffrey.

"I know you've got a lot of questions," Cooper began. "All I can tell you is that I've gone undercover with the Bureau." Cooper had to say something, and since he couldn't tell them he was an ALPHA Operative, this explanation would satisfy most of their questions.

His dad's expression was a mix of happiness and pride. "Thank you for telling us that. We're very proud of you, and I'm happy you're doing something you love."

"I'm not surprised," his mom added. "I know you loved working there. Your work must be very dangerous."

Silence.

"Well, I'll try not to think about that," his mom said.

"Good idea, Emily," his dad replied, and the family shared a laugh.

"Do you really own the gym?" Chantal asked.

"I do, plus the restaurants with my guys," Cooper replied.

"Can we assume Danielle is also FBI undercover?" his mom asked.

Cooper and Danielle exchanged glances.

"I work with Cooper," Danielle replied.

"You can never tell *anyone*," Cooper added. "Not even Henry or Aisha."

"I called Henry as soon as Tessa called me," his dad said. "I told him Tessa was fine."

"And?" Tessa said.

"He was relieved you're okay," his dad replied.

Tessa's expression fell and Chantal reached over and clasped

Tessa's hand. "You're safe and you're with us. We love you sooo much."

"Thank you," Tessa replied with a smile, though her eyes had misted. "I love you guys so much, too."

Cooper's heart broke for his niece. He loved his brother, but it seemed like he never made his daughter his top priority.

Cooper pushed away from the table. The news he had to share would be difficult for his parents to hear, but they needed to know the truth. He topped off everyone's coffee and brought the carton of orange juice to the table. But the beverages weren't going to do a damn thing to ease the blow of reality.

"I have some hard news to share," Cooper began. "Tessa and Val had been taken to a ship that was being used for sex trafficking. Many of the women were Russian immigrants, but some were from the shelters where Tessa works."

"No!" his mom blurted.

"Ohgod, that's terrifying," Chantal murmured.

"Fortunately, Cooper and Danielle got to me before anything really bad happened," Val said before regarding them. "I will always be so grateful for what you did, you have no idea."

Danielle put her arm around Val and gave her a little hug. "I'm a phone call away if you ever want to talk."

"Thank you," Val said.

"What about you, Tessa?" his mom asked, her voice a whisper.

"I was taken hostage by my boss for asking too many questions when Val disappeared," Tessa explained.

Cooper smiled at his niece. She could have told them she was going to be killed, but she knew to hold that back.

"This is unbelievable," said his dad.

"Even more shocking is the person running the sex trafficking ring was Geoffrey Edelman."

Their mouths dropped open. The atmosphere darkened with angry energy.

His father pushed away from the table. "I'm going to kill that son of a bitch."

"He was arrested and the woman running the shelters is dead," Cooper explained. "I know it's a lot to digest. I'm sure you have questions and I'll answer what I can. For the moment, I don't want to waste another second on that sorry excuse of a human, but I did have an idea I do want to talk about."

"Tell us," Danielle urged.

"I need a lawyer so I can take ownership of the shelters," Cooper explained. "Someone needs to provide a safe place for those women and we're going to make that happen."

There was not a dry eye in that room.

"What?" Cooper asked as he stared at the emotion surrounding him. "What's wrong?"

Danielle hurried around the table to hug him. "You are the best man I have ever known or will ever know."

Cooper grinned, then kissed Danielle's cheek. "Looks like I found myself a keeper."

"Well, I know the first thing we're going to do," Tessa said as Danielle sat back down in her chair.

"What?" Chantal asked.

"Change the name," Tessa replied.

"I know," Chantal said. "We can call it A Safe Haven."

"I love that," Tessa said.

"What about A Safe Harbor?" Val asked.

"Ooooo, I love that, too!" Tessa exclaimed as she pushed away from the table. "Let's brainstorm in the family room."

As Tessa, Chantal, and Val moved as a pod into the adjoining room, Cooper regarded the love of his life. "I love you," he mouthed.

"I love you," she mouthed back.

DANIELLE

Three weeks later, Danielle walked into Fly the Coop, Chantal by her side. After stopping at the front desk to introduce Cooper's sister to Naomi, they continued on to the back of the gym and into the kickboxing space.

"I'm going to stay in the back," Chantal said.

"I come around and work with everyone," Danielle explained, "so you'll still get my personal attention."

Chantal smiled. "I'm just happy to be here."

"Me, too," Danielle replied.

Danielle was relieved her class had three less students than usual. That allowed her to spend a little extra time with everyone. She was so thrilled that Chantal had continued with the sport, and even more bowled over when Chantal told her she wanted to try a class at the gym.

It was what she and Chantal were doing *after* class ended that had Danielle's stomach tied in knots. But if Chantal could be brave enough to leave the house, Danielle would keep up her end of the deal.

After class, Chantal couldn't stop smiling. "I did it," she said to Danielle once the other students left. "I came here and I did a kickboxing class."

Danielle grinned at her. "It's a big moment. You did a great job, too."

"And I had fun, a lot of fun."

Danielle loved seeing the transformation in Chantal.

When they entered the rock-climbing area, Danielle was hoping Cooper would be scaling the wall or helping a newbie attach their harness. To her disappointment, no Cooper.

After she showed Chantal how to use the harness, she attached hers, then ensured Chantal's was secure.

"My heart is pounding so hard, right now," Danielle whispered.

Chantal placed a comforting hand on Danielle's shoulder. "We're going to do it one step at a time, together."

"Right, together."

One small step at a time, they climbed. When they got a third of the way up, Chantal looked down. "Oh, boy."

"I'm right here," Danielle said a few feet away.

After a moment, Chantal continued. They got halfway up and Danielle looked around. She'd never climbed this high and took a moment to acknowledge the win.

Then, to her surprise, Chantal pushed on a few more steps, turned and said, "Three more steps and then, we'll climb back down."

Danielle couldn't resist the challenge and pushed herself to take those few remaining steps. The climb back down was met with a high-five from Chantal.

"This is such a huge accomplishment for me," Chantal murmured. "I never would have imagined this for myself. Thank you for being here for me."

"Right back atcha," Danielle said. "I've never climbed that high before. Thank you, Chantal."

Chantal beamed at her. "I'm happy I could make a difference for you."

She drove Chantal home, went inside to say hi to Emily and Eric, then continued on to Cooper's. Over the past few weeks, they'd moved all her things into his place. In the new year, they were putting her home on the rental market.

His house still felt new to her, but being with Cooper felt like home.

She had to pack for their flight to Atlanta, the next day, where she and Cooper would be spending the Christmas holiday with her family. She'd missed them so much and couldn't wait to see them *and* introduce them to her man.

After a quick shower, she got to packing. She heard the garage door open and hurried downstairs to greet him.

Cooper walked in through the kitchen, swept her into his arms, and kissed her hello like he hadn't seen her in weeks.

"Whew," she said, pausing to catch her breath. "That was one sexy kiss."

"I've got a lot more of those to hand out, if you're interested."

"I'm *always* interested," she replied.

"Whatcha doin'?" he asked.

"Packing."

He gave her the once-over. She'd thrown on tattered jeans and a black sweater. "Can you come out with me for a little while?"

"Now?" It was almost ten o'clock.

"One hour."

She gave his backside an affectionate squeeze. "I'll get my boots. Where are we headed?"

"Jericho Road."

As they drove out of the neighborhood, she asked about his day.

"The FBI is getting full credit for taking down one of the biggest sex trafficking rings in the region," he said.

"We know the *real* story. I'm not doing it for the accolades. I'm doing it because it's what I'm meant to do."

"What else are you meant to do?" he asked.

"Be with you." She clasped his hand. "I like riding, a lot. How 'bout you? You borrowed Stryker's bike a few times so we could ride together. You seemed to like it."

"It was fun. I loved that we did it together."

She leaned over and kissed him. "I love that you're a romantic."

After parking in the empty lot at Jericho Road, he stood in front of the scanner to unlock the front door.

"Why is it closed so early?"

"Jericho said something about a private party." Cooper brought her inside, locked the door behind them, clasped her hand, and headed toward the back of the quiet restaurant.

"Don't you want a drink?" she asked as he led her past the bar.

He stopped, pulled her close and kissed her. "I don't, but we can make you one."

"I'm okay. Why are we here?"

"To line dance. Will you dance with me?"

She smiled up at him. "Of course."

He brought her into the large dance room, walked over to the DJ's table, hit a button, and a country song filled her ears. They started line dancing to the beat, and in sync with each other, which is exactly how she felt with him... in complete synchronicity.

Whether it was at work, or at home, even at the gym, she felt this invisible thread connecting her to him. Life was ever-changing, but she knew they would always be a constant for each other.

He'd come into her life, refused to let her push him away, and loved her fiercely. As they did another quarter turn, she admired his backside. While he was physically her type, Cooper did it for her in so many other ways. He was smart and loyal, hardworking and determined. He adored his family and friends, and always made time for them. No matter how busy he was, he always put her first. She felt totally loved and completely adored.

Her heart was happy for the first time since her sister's death, and it overflowed with love for this amazing, one-of-a-kind man.

When the song ended, and a slow song came on, they met halfway, holding each other close while swaying to the ballad. He dipped her, then pulled her close and kissed her.

"This was just another restaurant I had a financial interest in... until you came here."

She smiled at him.

"We had our first kiss in the parking lot."

"And you taught me to line dance," she replied as she ran her fingers through his soft hair.

"We had our first date here."

"The Halloween party."

After a moment, he said, "You're the love of my life, Danielle."

When she gazed up at him, so much love stared back. "You're mine. You know that, right?"

He kissed her. "I do. And I'm never going to stop loving you."

"Never?"

"No. You're the one." As he got down on one knee, he pulled a small box from his pocket and opened it.

As she stared down at him, her heart took off in her chest.

Oh, wow.

"Danielle Rebecca Fox, I adore you. Life is so much better with you. You make me want to be a better man, every single day. You are my *everything* and I want to spend the rest of my life showing you how much you mean to me. Will you marry me?"

She placed her hands on his scruffy cheeks, leaned down, and kissed him. "You are *my* everything and I would *love* to be your wife. There's nothing I want more, Cooper Casey Grant, than to spend the rest of my life by your side. Yes! I will marry you!"

He slid the engagement ring onto her finger, kissed her hand, then stood. "Forever," he said.

She jumped into his arms, wrapped herself around him, and gazed into his eyes.

"For starters," she replied with a smile.

She kissed him as the love and passion swirled around them. When the kiss ended, he set her down. That's when she regarded the engagement ring.

"Cooper, this is crazy. It's absolutely stunning! This is the exact ring I've always dreamed about. I can't believe it. How did you—" She laughed. "You had a helper, didn't you?"

"Guilty," he said. "There's no way I could have pulled this ring off without Emerson."

The cushion-cut, diamond engagement ring was surrounded by a halo of bright, round diamonds and another trail of small cushion-cut diamonds that rolled onto the platinum band.

She gazed into his eyes. "It's beyond beautiful. Thank you. I love it." Then, she pushed onto her toes and kissed him. "Thank you for bringing me here to ask me. This makes it extra special. Maybe we'll have our reception here."

He chuffed out a laugh. "I kinda imagined you'd want something a little more upscale."

She shrugged. "We've got plenty of time to work out the details."

"You ready to head out?"

"Do you mind if we make a stop on the way home?" she asked.

"Of course not." He set the restaurant alarm and they left.

Before pulling onto the road, he asked, "Where are we headed?"

"My townhouse."

"I thought we got all your things."

"There's one more thing I need to pick up over there."

When they pulled into the driveway, she brought him to the garage door. "Close your eyes for me."

He hitched a brow. "Are twenty people going to jump out and scare the hell out of me?"

She laughed. "No, it's just us."

He closed his eyes and she punched in the garage door code. After leading him inside, she said, "Okay, you can open them."

He stared at the motorcycle, then flicked his gaze to her. "Whoa, babe, you bought yourself a new bike."

"Merry Christmas. It's for you, my love."

"Seriously, you bought me a motorcycle?"

"It's a BMW, K 1600 GT in black storm metallic," she explained. "And no worries, because it can be returned, exchanged, upgraded, or customized to your liking. Stryker helped me. I swear, I don't know what we'd do without those two."

He folded her in his arms and kissed her so good. "Thank you, babe. This is the most amazing gift I've ever received." After straddling his new toy, he said, "Unbelievable."

"I'm so glad you like it. It was a risky gift."

"I can't believe you bought me this. You are too good to me."

She retrieved a box from the corner and offered it to him, bow side up. "It's an oversized stocking stuffer."

"Shouldn't we open it with your family on Christmas morning?"

On a chuckle, she said, "Definitely not."

He removed the lid, peeled back the red and green tissue paper, and lifted out the bright red corset with white faux fur hugging the hemline. The sexy lingerie was held together with laces tied loosely over the bustline with a zipper that made for easy on… and easy off.

She waggled her eyebrows. "I'm Santa's little helper. Are you Santa?"

"I'm anybody you want me to be, baby. Wow, you are gonna look so hot in this." He kissed her. "Christmas is coming early this year."

She laughed. "How did I manage to snag the man of my dreams?"

"Because you deserve the absolute best… and I'm it."

Sidling close, she wrapped her arms around his neck and kissed his cheek. "You *are* it."

"You're my dream girl, and I knew the minute I saw you."

"Thanks for being there when I was spinning out of control, and for helping me find my way back."

"Same." He pushed off his bike, captured her face in his hands, and kissed her. "I will spend the rest of my life fighting for you and always being there to support you."

"Always?"

"Always," he replied with a smile that melted her heart.

EPILOGUE

Five months later, May

COOPER

Cooper and Danielle admired the new signage on the front of the building.

A SAFE HAVEN

"It looks fantastic," Danielle said.

"Sure does," Cooper replied.

The front door was locked, so Danielle fished her key out of her handbag and they walked into the newly designed lobby.

The ink was barely dry on the paperwork, but all three women's shelters were in the Grant family's name, and they would do right by *every* resident who walked through their doors.

The spring day the perfect backdrop for the grand re-opening of the Virginia shelter. The press had been called and the guest list was a who's who of luminaries in the DC area.

But none of that mattered to Cooper. He cared that his family and his closest friends would be there to celebrate this milestone with him and Danielle.

While Geoffrey had attempted, through his attorney, to contact Cooper and Cooper's dad, they'd decided, as a family, that they would simply move on. Cooper was grateful for the financial help that he'd received under Geoffrey's tutelage, but he couldn't bring himself to look Geoffrey in the eyes without wanting to kill him.

Tessa and Chantal appeared in the lobby from down the hallway and hurried over.

Cooper had asked Tessa if she was interested in being the Executive Director for all three shelters. Without hesitation, she'd said yes, under one condition. She wanted her Aunt Chantal working alongside her.

To everyone's overwhelming joy, Chantal had agreed.

"We're so excited," Tessa said.

"This is such a big day," Chantal added.

"What can we do to help?" Danielle asked.

"The caterers are setting everything up in the gathering room," Chantal explained. "Val is supervising."

"What's the schedule for the other two shelters?" Cooper asked.

"A Safe Harbor in Maryland and A Safe Port in DC open next week," Chantal replied. "Are you coming to those?"

"We'll be in town until Thursday," Danielle replied.

Cooper and Danielle were headed to Miami with six other ALPHA Operatives to take out a notorious drug gang.

Stryker and Emerson entered the building, a vibrant spring bouquet in Emerson's hand. "Congratulations!" She held out the flowers. "I'm not sure who gets these since this was a total team effort."

"Thank you so much," Tessa said, taking them. "They're beautiful. I'll put them in water."

A photographer walked in and Chantal went to greet her.

Danielle and Emerson hugged. "You guys must be so excited," Emerson said.

"We're excited for the residents," Danielle replied. "They deserve a safe place to rebuild their lives."

Thirty minutes later, the gathering room was filled to capacity with family, friends, invited guests, the press, and the residents. Cooper walked to the front of the room, picked up the mic, and smiled at the group.

"Good afternoon. My name is Cooper Grant. On behalf of my business partner and fiancée, Danielle Fox, and the entire Grant family, we're thrilled to be celebrating the grand re-opening of A Safe Haven. Thank you for joining us today."

He paused for applause.

"Our team has worked hard these past five months to make sure residents don't just *feel* safe, they *are* safe. We've created a number of programs designed to ensure that no one is alone, no one is left behind, and every voice is heard." He paused to smile out at the crowd. "We're proud to offer shelter throughout the DMV. In addition to this residence, we have A Safe Port in DC and A Safe Harbor in Maryland. Homelessness is *everyone's* problem. At least, that's how we see it. We believe that everyone should have a place to call home and the help they need to get back on their feet. To talk more about our programs is Executive Director, Tessa Grant."

Both Tessa and Jericho joined him at the front of the room.

"Looks like we've got two Tessa Grants today," Cooper said, and the crowd cracked up.

"Hey, everyone, I'm Jericho Savage. Me, Stryker, Hawk, and Prescott wanna show our support." He handed Cooper a check.

It was for five million dollars.

Cooper pulled him in for a bro-hug. "Thank you. Seriously, this is awesome." He tapped his fist to his chest while he regarded his closest friends in the world. "I love you guys."

"We love you, Coop," Hawk called out from the first row.

Cooper addressed the crowd. "We're all about transparency, here." He held up the check. "Five mil from my four closest friends."

As the crowd hooted and hollered, both men took their seats. When the group grew quiet, Tessa launched into her prepared speech.

Cooper clasped Danielle's hand and she smiled over at him. The look of love in her eyes was something he'd never take for granted. Loving Danielle was the easiest thing he'd ever done, and he was grateful for every day he got to show her how much she meant to him.

"Forever," he murmured.

"For starters," she replied with a smile.

A NOTE FROM STONI

Thank you for reading VENGEANCE! For some time now, I've wanted to write a story where my heroine is a vigilante, so when Danielle's sister was killed in DAMAGED, and sweet, chandelier-obsessed Danielle Fox fell apart, I knew I'd found that character. The fun started when my law-enforcement hero, Cooper Grant, was assigned to find the killer… and the game of cat and mouse began.

The longer there's conflict on the page, the happier my muse is.

Some of my characters from previous stories are hard to let go of, so they find their way onto the pages of my current project. Since my world of ALPHA is always growing and expanding, there's room for new characters and plenty of opportunity to include some of my favorites, too.

I love hearing from my readers. Getting to know them isn't just fun, it can also spark my imagination. I never know when someone is going to say something that feeds my curious muse. If you want to say hello, drop me a note at Contact@StoniAlexander.com.

And if you haven't joined my Inner Circle newsletter, sign up at StoniAlexander.com to claim your free, steamy short story, METRO MAN. It's a contemporary romance about finding love—that starts with a heaping dose of lust—on a commuter train in the DC region.

All my books are available exclusively on Amazon and you can read them free with Kindle Unlimited!

Thanks for joining me on my writing journey. I hope getting lost in VENGEANCE was a wonderful escape for you!

Cheers to Romance,

Stoni Alexander

Next in The Vigilantes Series
SAVAGE
The Vigilantes, Book Three

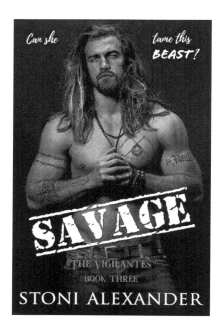

REVENGE SERVED HARD

My friends call me Jericho. My enemies know me as Reaper.

Ain't nothin' more important than family. So, when my baby bro is gunned down in front of me, I go on the hunt to settle the score. Fury drives me forward. Sleep becomes my enemy. I'm out for blood.

I work alone. No spotter. No backup. I get you in my sniperscope, you're already dead.

But someone hidin' in the shadows sees what I'm up to. Not good.

Then, she inserts herself into my life. Even worse. She's the last person I want up in my business.

The. Last. Person.

I send her away. Not interested. Wouldn'cha know, she's got a stubborn streak that's worse than mine.

Way. Worse.

She makes me a deal I can't refuse, so I got a partner I never asked for and can't escape from. We're together twenty-four seven, takin' out the scum who shredded my family. Doesn't help that she's smokin' hot, brilliant, and all grown up with a body that does not quit.

I. Am. So. F*cked.

There's no way this'll end well… for either one of us. Turns out, I'd rather die with her than live without her.

NOVELS BY STONI ALEXANDER

THE TOUCH SERIES

The Mitus Touch

The Wilde Touch

The Loving Touch

The Hott Touch

In Walked Sin

Dakota Luck

THE VIGILANTES SERIES

Damaged

Vengeance

Savage

Wrecked

Broken

Rebel

BEAUTIFUL MEN COLLECTION

Beautiful Stepbrother

Beautiful Disaster

Available on Amazon or Read FREE with Kindle Unlimited

ACKNOWLEDGMENTS

Each writing project is filled with wonderfully supportive people who help me kick it off, move it along, or assist me in getting it out the door. This time, these terrific people did just that!

Johnny, Johnny, Johnny. Better Together. Every. Single. Day.

Son, thank you for your constant love and support while you're taking your career to new heights. Dad and I love you so much and are so incredibly proud of you.

Terry McM, thank you for being so willing to talk to me about life in a wheelchair. While we've been friends for years, it's not something that's ever come up because your life has always been limitless. You roll toward every new adventure, never allowing your physical challenge to stop you… or even slow you down. I admire your courage and strength, for conquering every obstacle placed in your path, especially the ones you place there yourself. I write about heroes, but you are a real one, living your very best life.

Cara, I always love hearing from readers, but your offer to crochet me a blanket touched my heart. Thank you for making me one filled with bright colors *and* for donating it to the children's hospital in my name. More than your generous, thoughtful gift, I loved getting to know you! When you shared your passion for kickboxing, I knew that was the *perfect* sport for my kick-ass vigilante heroine, Danielle Fox. Thank you! Our creativity and kindness fed off each other's. If only everyone in the world was like that. What a different world it would be…

Thank you to my ARC Team. I love how some of you have been with me since book one, and I'm excited to welcome new ones who've also fallen in love with my stories. I appreciate your being a part of the Stoni Alexander team!

Readers, I appreciate your loyalty so much! You have millions of choices and I'm always so grateful when you choose my love stories. When you reach out to introduce yourself, or tell me how much you've enjoyed my novels, it's the best break from writing that I wasn't even expecting. Your kindness fuels me! Thank you.

Muse, you ready to have some fun with Jericho Savage? I know you are because you brought him into BEAUTIFUL DISASTER way before it was even his turn. Then, you brought him back again for this story. Well, now, let's put him front and center, throw some major problems at him, and then, get the hell out of his way. I'm confident he'll be able to handle them all… and get the girl in the end.

ABOUT THE AUTHOR

Stoni Alexander writes sexy romantic suspense and contemporary romance about tortured alpha males and independent, strong-willed females. Her passion is creating love stories where the hero and heroine help each other through a crisis so that, in the end, they're equal partners in more ways than love alone. The heat level is high, the romance is forever, and the suspense keeps readers guessing until the very end.

Visit Stoni's website:
StoniAlexander.com

Sign up for Stoni's newsletter on her website and she'll gift you a free steamy short story, only available to her Inner Circle.

Here's where you can follow Stoni online. She looks forward to connecting with you!

- amazon.com/author/stonialexander
- bookbub.com/authors/stoni-alexander
- facebook.com/StoniBooks
- goodreads.com/stonialexander
- instagram.com/stonialexander

Made in the USA
Columbia, SC
19 April 2025